The DICKTIONARY Club

Sophie Gravia is a Scottish author, nurse and podcast host known for her humorous and candid novels about modern dating. Her debut novel, *A Glasgow Kiss*, shot straight to number one in the erotic charts and has been a word-of-mouth sensation ever since, leading to a series of bestselling sequels, including *What Happens in Dubai*, *Meet Me in Milan* and *Hot Girl Summer*. Her books have collectively sold hundreds of thousands of copies, with *Meet Me in Milan* becoming a *Sunday Times* bestseller. Her success has also led to a collaboration with BBC Studios to adapt *A Glasgow Kiss* into a television series.

Alongside her writing, Sophie continues to work as a nurse in Lanarkshire while raising her two children.

The DICKTIONARY *Club*

Sophie Gravia

ZAFFRE

First published in the UK in 2025 by
ZAFFRE
An imprint of Bonnier Books UK
A Bonnier Books UK Company
5th Floor, HYLO, 105 Bunhill Row,
London, EC1Y 8LZ

A CIP catalogue record for this book is
available from the British Library.

ISBN: 978-1-78512-757-1

Also available as an ebook and an audiobook

3 5 7 9 10 8 6 4 2

Typeset by IDSUK (Data Connection) Ltd
Printed and bound in Great Britain by Clays Ltd, Elcograf S.p.A.

The authorised representative in the EEA is Bonnier Books
UK (Ireland) Limited.
Registered office address: Floor 3, Block 3, Miesian Plaza,
Dublin 2, D02 Y754, Ireland
compliance@bonnierbooks.ie
www.bonnierbooks.co.uk

This book is dedicated to all the girls who have been hurt or deceived on dating apps. I promise, we are not the problem! Hang in there, trust your gut and your boundaries.

We got this,

Sophie x

Chapter One

Ella

'Where is Katy?' Andrea snapped at the bullpen of our office floor. Her face was red with anger as she stormed through the desks, squinting, trying to locate my friend. She flew past me, then paused, slowly turning back to shoot me a death stare. 'Ella?' she asked.

I gulped. 'Oh, she was here a second ago. But she is completely raring to go, Andrea,' I lied, fist-punching the air with faux excitement.

Andrea's face remained thunderous, only her jet-black bob quivering as she spoke. 'She's pitching to a prospective client in ten minutes. They're waiting in the lobby as we speak. If she's not here, and someone has to wing it with no prep, then she's out!' Andrea slowly ran one finger across her throat, then smirked. I knew it was a threat aimed for Katy but I couldn't help but wonder if she meant it for me too.

I nodded back, trying my best to appear calm, but I could feel cold sweat travel from my forehead to my arse crack. *What a psycho!*

Andrea turned and headed back to her office. As soon as she slammed the door shut, I swivelled on my chair towards Zola. 'Zo! Where the fuck is she?'

My friend already had her phone out and was dialling Katy's number, motioning me to come closer.

'Hello.' I heard the familiar sobbing drone of my friend down the line. *Not to-fucking-day, Katy*, I thought. I rested my head against Zola's as we listened together.

'Where the fuck are you? Your nine o'clock client is here and Andrea is screaming for you!' I kept my voice low, in case one of our boss's arse-licking spies on the floor overheard and reported back to her.

'I'm . . . I know . . . I'm . . . I'm sorry!' Katy wailed.

Zola rolled her eyes at me and attempted a more sympathetic approach. 'Babe, don't cry! Look, where are you? We'll get you. Are you OK?'

'HE DUMPED ME!' she shrieked by way of reply, heaving loud sobs on the other end of the phone.

Zola and I automatically reared back from the intense screams coming at us from the phone.

'*Oh, no!* Not another one, babe!' Zola managed.

I darted a glare at Zola and her shitty attempt to be supportive. She shrugged back, looking confused.

'What happened?' I asked.

'He said . . . he said . . . we needed time apart. He said I was a nice girl, but didn't give him that *oomph*!' She broke into sobs again. 'I thought he was the one. I thought he really liked me. He literally told me that last week!'

I shook my head, wondering if that was before or after he had gotten into her knickers. It always seemed to be the same routine with Katy and the dickhead guys she'd grown accustomed to. Yip, she was madly in love for a week or two, planning the wedding with us, changing all her likes and dislikes to suit the guy, swapping girls nights for date nights at any given chance. But then all of a sudden, and completely out of the blue for Katy, she was dumped and it was down to us to pick up the traumatised pieces.

'*Oh, no!* Katy, it's his loss! You know you can do much better than him anyway. It always feels awful breaking up! Come on, where are you?'

She sniffled. 'I'm in the bathroom at reception. But I can't come out. I mean it. I'm not coming out, Ella. I can't face it.'

Zola hung up the phone, and we scurried across the office floor together. I noticed some of my colleagues stare up from their computers. Wondering if they had overheard the commotion, I found myself overcompensating with a massive grin.

'Morning!' I chirped.

We headed through to reception, and I glanced at the clock above the desk: *08.55.* As we approached the smartly dressed couple in the waiting area, I could feel my pulse race. *Only five minutes to sort this shit storm out!* Zola forced a grin onto her face and pointed to the company sign.

'Good morning from all of us at Smart Reputations. Someone will be with you in just a tick.'

She winked at the pair, who nodded back in bemusement at her strange introduction. I was already heading into the bathroom, with Zola quickly behind me. The stalls were quiet. All I could hear was a drip from one of the taps echoing through the space.

'Hello, Katy,' I called out. 'Are you in here?'

There was a slight sniffle from the middle cubicle. Zola motioned her head at the locked door. I sighed.

Here we go again, another Monday morning pep talk.

I popped into the stand next to Katy's, while Zola headed to the one on the other side. I yanked down the toilet lid and stood on top of it, hanging my head over the cubicle wall, looking down at my friend. Zola did the same on the opposite side; her long braids hanging down as she hovered high in the air.

'Hey, babe,' I said.

Katy peeked up at me, then Zola; her face was blotchy and red, and her eyes looked irritated from hours of crying. I hadn't seen them so swollen since the summer when she'd had a severe case of pink eye.

'Why is it always me?!' she moaned dramatically, shouting up to the pair of us.

Zola propped her elbows on top of the stand. 'I know, girl. You've had such a hard time lately, but hey, at least you're putting yourself out there!'

'Oh, come on, it's not you, Katy!' I said. 'It's the awful dickhead guys on dating apps! Look at you! You're bloody amazing!'

She heaved as I continued, running her hands through her mousy brown hair.

'You are smart, absolutely gorgeous, funny and . . .'

'And – and somewhat of a legend around here, you know,' Zola added.

Katy's whimpers simmered a little. 'A legend?' she repeated, curiously.

'Oh, yeah!' Zola nodded. 'Everyone says so.'

Katy turned to me, and so I joined in the nodding.

4

'You land the biggest marketing deals on our floor. You are a genius at your job,' I said.

'And you are about to get another landmark company on board! Babe, you've planned this Blaze Boost pitch for ages. And the reps are sitting in the hallway, waiting for you to impress them.'

Katy's eyes looked heavy. She was mentally swaying. 'It's just . . . I don't think I can, not after . . .'

'Oh God.' Zola scrunched her face at me. 'Her legend status is dwindling, isn't it?'

'*Hmm*, yeah. Maybe Andrea was right?' I gasped. 'Is the legendary Katy losing her touch?'

'*What?* What do you mean?' Katy was darting a look between both of us.

'When I moved here from London, I had heard rumours of the badass PR and marketing girls in the Glasgow branch. They all said you guys were a different breed up here, you know, totally career-focused and always able to deliver. And everyone said Katy McIntyre was one of the baddest of the badasses.'

Katy sighed. 'I know what you guys are doing!'

A smile washed up on my face. 'Babe, just go get the client. Land the deal. You deserve this bonus.' I grinned, full beam at her. 'And I promise Martin will have messaged you by the end of the meeting!'

'Mark!' she sobbed back, throwing herself back on the pan.

'Well, I can promise you, Katy, either way, he will be sliding into your DMs apologising when we post the shit out of you landing one of the biggest upcoming energy drink suppliers in the country!'

My friend remained motionless.

I glanced towards Zola, who shrugged slightly, not knowing what way this could swing. Not knowing if our efforts had worked this time around.

'I suppose I do know the presentation inside out,' Katy eventually whimpered.

A sigh of relief washed through me. *Thank fuck for that.*

'You see!' Zola laughed. 'Come on out, girl! Let's have a look at ya!'

I hopped off the toilet and walked out of the cubicle where my two friends were standing. I glanced at my watch – *one minute left.*

'You ready for this?' I asked Katy, flattening the collar of her blazer.

Her eyes were still heavy, but she nodded, giving a gentle sigh.

'Come here, girl.' Katy turned, as Zola wrapped her arms around her. 'I have some lippy. You want some?'

Katy shrugged. 'I don't care,' she whined pathetically, but pursing out her lips anyway.

I leaned my hand against my head frustratedly and, once a fresh layer of Velvet Teddy was on, I turned her body towards me. 'OK, enough. Do you think you'll get this deal with that attitude, Katy? Like, seriously? You've gone on and on about this client for three fuck-ing months! Countless emails back and forth, and now today is the day you give them the best pitch of your career, OK?'

She bobbed her head, looking a tad more inspired by my speech.

'We will sort the Mark or fucking Martin situation out when you come out of that meeting, but I promise you, he will come back. They always fucking do! Eh?'

'Mmmhmm,' Zola agreed. 'Men are like boomerangs with balls.'

Katy gulped, finally agreeing. 'OK,' she breathed, and I watched her shoulders drop. 'I got this! Yeah. I can do this.'

'Yes, you fucking can!' I hyped back. 'Come on, get out there.'

I pulled open the toilet door, allowing Katy to walk out in front. She turned to the clients sitting at reception and smiled.

'Oh, you must be Patricia and Alan. It's so lovely to meet you both in person,' she said in her best professional manner, welcoming them.

They stood up and each shook her hand.

'Thank fuck I'm engaged,' I heard Zola mumble. Then I felt a nudge from her, noticing the palm of her hand down low, waiting for a discreet high-five. I quickly slapped my hand off hers. We watched Katy lead the Blaze Boost clients into the boardroom and both breathed a massive sigh of relief.

'*Pssst.*' I turned back and noticed Katy's head pop out of the door. 'Do you really think he'll call, Ella? Like today?'

'*Erm* ... duh ... yes, of course he fucking will!' I flapped my hands, motioning her to go back in.

Katy beamed brightly and retreated to the boardroom, closing the door.

I watched her through the glass window as she strolled over to the laptop, finally looking confident and inspired to pitch.

I turned to Zola, who was totally puffed from the stressful morning routine we had unfortunately gotten so used to.

'Do you really think he'll call?' she asked, also gazing through the window towards Katy.

'Honestly?' I paused, biting my bottom lip, thinking of all the men Katy had recently been pumped then dumped by. 'Not a fucking chance.'

*

Zola and I retreated to our desks and began working on our own projects. I had been running PR for an artist's pop-up gallery that was passing through Glasgow in a few weeks. The artist was huge throughout Europe, famous for painting brightly coloured, luxury oil portraits of celebrities and the wealthy, but quite honestly I had been finding it difficult to glamorise the exhibition to the Scottish crowds. Normally I was an expert on the beauty market and high street. I'd been working this pitch for over a month now with no real breakthroughs or any idea where I'd even hold the exhibition. I swivelled around on my chair to face Zola.

'Help!' I pleaded.

Zola laughed. 'Still no luck with the gallery?'

I shook my head.

'I can help with the social content and invites, but you need to come up with the plan, babe! And let's face it, the clock is ticking!'

Zola was Smart Reputations' creative IT director. She transferred up from the London office to help boost our social media presence and support clients when revamping their websites. She's basically a whizz-kid for content creation and graphic design, and was an instant hit with Katy and me from the moment she showed up on her first day with her long colourful braids, a belly top and ripped jeans. Andrea almost spat out her morning coffee at the team meeting when she spotted her office attire, but I loved how quirky, cool and loveable she was. So much so that we welcomed her into our little friendship bubble with open arms shortly after.

'What you working on, Zo?' I asked my friend.

'*Ummm* . . .' She swivelled in her chair. 'Revamping the website for Luxe Lengths hair extensions. It's a fun one to do. Have you got any further forward on the art exhibition?'

'Oh no. I've sent out emails to old clients who might be interested in coming and I've received two replies. Two! Remind me why I asked for this campaign?' I mumbled.

'I don't know. Because you like a challenge? Look, don't stress yourself. You always pull through, Ella.' Zola smiled brightly, giving me a little nudge.

'No one in Glasgow seems to care about buying a ridiculously overpriced portrait, though.'

She laughed. 'And do you blame them? It's not fucking *Bridgerton*, babes. It's the Barras! People nowadays seem to prefer the *Live, laugh, love* B&M shit hanging on their walls, not some fancy portrait.' She laughed. 'You'll need to think outside the box with this one.'

I felt my eyes rolling at the suggestion, having wasted countless hours testing new ideas to funk the exhibition up a little. But truthfully, I had never felt so stuck at work. I was always the one coming up with new and innovative ideas for my clients, but this campaign was way out of my league, not to mention Andrea seemed to be on the war path recently and I knew she was looking for an opportunity for me or one of my friends to fuck up.

'How do you think Katy's getting on?' Zola asked.

I flopped back on my chair. 'Well, she's still in there. That's a good sign.'

Zola hummed a little. 'I think she'll land them.'

'Even after one of her wobbles? I don't think she's ever had an early-morning pitch straight after a dumping before.'

'True! But girls, especially after breakups, are unstoppable. That's when we deliver. I remember my high-school boyfriend dumped me for some skinny blonde white girl with no ass . . . no offence.'

I pulled a face, briefly flicking my creamy blonde hair away from my shoulder and her firing line.

'And the very next day, I applied to university and landed a badass scholarship. Yip, I didn't allow myself to get stressed or beg for *him* back. I even booked up to travel to Bali that entire summer. Bitches be getting PhDs after breaking up while the boys sit around playing video games and chasing the latest girl on Instagram.' She tittered.

I laughed. 'Well, firstly, I don't think your high school boyfriend is the same as Katy's, what, three-, four-week Tinder situationship, and secondly, I have got a fucking arse!' I reached over to slap her arm while she dodged out of the way.

'*Ummm* . . . you think so?' she teased, glancing down towards my arse. 'Like, really?'

We turned as we heard the door closing across the office floor and saw Katy trekking through. I sat up apprehensively as she approached us.

'Well, how did it go?' I asked, clutching my hands together.

Her straight brown hair was bopping up and down as she nodded. 'Yeah, I think they liked my ideas. They're going to talk to the CEO and let me know.'

'Katy?' Andrea called her name from her office. She leaned against the doorframe, swinging one leg of her glasses as she summoned her over.

Katy's shoulders tensed again as she steered herself towards our boss. I averted my gaze back to my desktop.

'What is she saying?' I whispered to Zola. 'Can you hear?'

'Can't hear, but she's not shouting.'

The pair chatted briefly before Katy was dismissed back to her desk. On the way, she pulled out her phone.

'He's not texted me. Ella, you said he'd text.' She plonked her arse down on the chair and turned to me, frustrated and unhappy.

'I assumed he would.' I raised an eyebrow. 'But never mind him, tell us about your pitch. And what did Cruella want?'

Katy shrugged. 'It was fine, honestly. I spoke a lot about promoting the product in gyms – I made out I was one of the gym girls, like you. And Andrea was surprisingly fine; she said she knew I'd do well. That's why she chose me to pitch and all that stuff.'

I huffed, knowing an hour earlier she was threatening to sack my friend.

'So, babe, what happened with Mark? I thought you had planned a nice romantic meal?' Zola asked, keeping her voice low to spare the half-dozen in the marketing team working beside us.

I watched Katy's eyes fill once more.

'*Jesus*, Katy, don't cry! Come here,' I said, shuffling my chair towards her.

'Honestly, Ella, if you hug me right now, I'll go full-on *Notebook* tears.'

I paused immediately, reminding myself that the first time we watched that movie, she could not talk or breathe appropriately for two days solid.

'Well, I invited him over. He had been working all day out in the rain, so I ran him a lovely bath with my good Lush bath bomb set, you know, the one you got me for Christmas?' She scowled at the thought of sharing her sweet Snowfairy scent now.

I nodded.

'Oh yeah, well, I certainly remember it. And the two Canesten pessaries I had to buy after using mine. Those scents seriously threw my pH balance off the charts.' Zola squirmed.

'Well, hopefully, it's done the same to his dick!' Katy added with venom behind her eyes. She paused, regaining her train of thought, then continued, 'So, we had a take-away from LaVita. Everything was going great.'

'Until?' Zola questioned impatiently.

'Until we were having sex. So, he was thrusting away on top of me when all of a sudden, his watch buzzed a notification from Tinder, and I saw it. He told me only *last week* he was off all dating apps because we'd connected so well. So, he sort of ignored it and continued the shagging, but the notification was really annoying me, so I said, "Mark, why did you have a Tinder notification on your watch there? I thought you said you deleted it?"'

I leaned in, engrossed in her latest drama like I was watching an episode of *MAFS* on catchup.

'And he said,' she lowered her voice, trying her best to imitate his deep twang, '"*I'm a serial swiper, Katy, it's an addiction,*" then laughed it off!'

I gasped and turned to Zola, who was shaking one finger in the air at the downright disrespect.

'So, I said, "*Oh right, but you told me you came off Tinder and didn't want to speak to anyone else?*"'

I nodded, fully agreeing with her line of questioning. 'Yep, and what did he say to that?'

She teared up, slightly tilting her head. 'He said, "*The thing is, Katy, I like you, I do, but I don't get that pure overwhelming oomph feeling with you, and I don't want to settle for anything other than that. My standards are set pretty high, and I'm not . . ."*' Her bottom lip trembled. '"*I'm not going to settle for you just because you're a nice girl!*"'

My face fell in disbelief.

In shock, Zola slammed her hand off her lap. 'No, no, no! Tell me he did not say that to you, Kates!' She stood up dramatically, her chair shooting back behind her. 'Someone pass me a gun. I swear, pass me a mother-fucking gun!'

Katy nodded back, looking embarrassed. She glimpsed around the office as some of our colleagues were beginning to stare. I tugged on Zola's jumper for her to sit back down.

'But the worst part was he was still inside me,' Katy whispered, on the verge of tears again, 'so he sort of pulled out, shaking his head because I'd ruined his shag and then he got dressed without saying another word.'

'Katy, what the actual *fuck*?!' I leaned over and held her hand, disgusted at how someone could be so cruel towards my friend.

'I'm fed up being the nice girl, Ella. I'm always someone's back-up just to pass the time. I want to be someone's true love. I want to give someone that over-whelming *oomph* feeling. Why can't it ever be me?'

I stood up quickly and wrapped my arms around Katy's head; I kissed her hair, smelling the fresh coconut scent of her shampoo.

'Hey, maybe you're looking in the wrong places? Why don't you come off Tinder for a bit, meet someone normal, at the pub or something?' I murmured into the top of her head. 'The guys you meet seem really nice at the start, Katy, but they always end up exactly the same – thinking they have better options out there. It's far too easy to swipe for the next girl. Maybe if you met someone normally, and not online, it would be different?'

She pulled away from my grasp with something between a sob and a giggle. 'Yeah, like we ever go anywhere apart from the office. I can't do this anymore, honestly. I'm so angry and so fucking hurt. I hate them all. I'm never going to meet anyone who actually wants *me*. I'm going to die all alone.'

Zola gently shook her head at the drama. 'Look, why don't we head to Wunderbar tonight? Get a couple of after-work drinks? Talk about how much we hate men together?'

I smiled. 'I'm up for it. It beats hot yoga! What do you say, Katy?'

'I don't know. I just don't think I'd be much company tonight.'

I sat back on my chair. 'Babe, you're never much company. You only get invited to make us look pretty,' I teased and watched as a genuine smile appeared on her face.

'Oh fine, but only a couple of drinks. No men,' she demanded.

I laughed a sigh of relief. 'Absolutely no fuckin' men.'

Chapter Two

Ella

We set off towards Wunderbar through the dull Glaswegian streets that evening after work. It was approaching summertime in the city, but the roads were still damp from the usual downpour we received most days. Katy had been pretty quiet the rest of the day, hardly touching her chicken wrap for lunch, just in case her perfect size-twelve figure was the real reason she got ditched. I knew it wasn't. I knew how wonderful, caring, gorgeous and kind she was, but I also knew how dating apps – and the men who used them – wore you down. After all, I'd been there too. I split from my ex, Joshua, just over three years ago, and he'd been everything to me. We were inseparable; sometimes, I genuinely thought the cunt could read my mind. But he wanted kids, and I didn't. I suppose the older we got and the closer to thirty I became, he thought I'd change my mind and, well, I believed I'd be enough for him. We broke up just after my twenty-seventh birthday when I reiterated to him after a pregnancy scare that me being a mum was never going to happen. He insisted he couldn't imagine his life without children and, honestly, I couldn't imagine anything worse, so he left. I was devastated. Completely heartbroken, unhappy and traumatised for years. I felt like my heart had been ripped out and stabbed a million times over. And I suppose I always thought he'd come back. Until he didn't.

After Joshua and I eventually stopped communicating, I joined Tinder, and my confidence took somewhat of a beating when it came to returning to the single life. Every fucking guy I met was great at the start – funny, charming, handsome – then, slowly but surely they'd start waving their red flags. From narcissistic dickheads to downright fuckboys, from compulsive liars to scores of secretly married men. No man in Glasgow seemed to be left who genuinely wanted a monogamous relationship. And after six months of swiping, I eventually had to delete all of my apps and accept that a life without a man was one I'd happily accept if it meant my mental health stayed intact. Even when my vagina starts wailing pitifully from my knickers when a gorgeous guy smiles in my direction, I'll tamp her down and put those longings to the side, because I know life is so much easier without all of that. Now I spend my time at the gym, going out jogging, or socialising with my friends. Honestly, I've never worked harder or been more career focused. I'm finally excelling at life, without constantly trying to maintain another person's happiness. My life is less complicated, more effortless, better structured and simple now I'm single. I just wish Katy recognised that her life could be the same.

*

It was just after six when we entered Wunderbar; our favourite place in the city, it had live musicians singing the best pop classics every night and a great lively atmosphere any time of the day. A group of rowdy students was screaming along to the ultimate Swiftie compilation, so we sat together in the undercover outside seating area to chat properly as it felt a bit less chaotic. Zola headed to the bar for the first round of drinks, while I squeezed up beside Katy.

'You OK?' I asked, noticing Katy check her phone.

She forced a smile. 'Yeah, I'll be fine. Another one bites the dust, eh?' she replied softly, her eyes glazed over in defeat.

'It's so shit, Katy. How men think they can treat us so badly and get away with it. You realise what Mark did to you was so cruel, right? He's fucking out of order.'

'Yeah, maybe.' She hesitated. 'But what if he was just being honest, Ella?'

'Then be honest, but just after a few dates or whatever. If he felt like the connection wasn't strong enough for him, then he should have broken it off long before now. Not go round to your house, have a fucking bath run for him, a dinner bought, tell you he's focusing on you, then dump you while you're having actual sex because you've caught him messaging other women!' I could feel myself getting riled up on my friend's behalf. 'Was he going to keep you as an option on the back burner if you hadn't seen that notification?'

'I know.' She was in a daze, staring into space. 'It wasn't nice at all, Ella. Honestly, I curled up crying the whole night.'

I shook my head. 'I wish you would have called me.'

Katy shrugged. 'And say what – guess what's happened *again*! It's pathetic!'

'He's the pathetic one, Katy. Not you!' I insisted.

'Do you know the really sad thing? I even texted him once he left and apologised for causing the argument. Who does that?!'

'But you didn't do anything wrong, Katy.'

'But our night would have been perfect if I hadn't seen that notification or just kept my big mouth shut.'

That's *so* not true. 'And he'd have strung you along for months,' I protested, 'waiting till your feelings were even stronger and then dropped you. You did the right thing.'

I watched her head drop, still comprehending it all.

Zola returned to the table holding a large tray with an infectious grin on her face. 'Three vodka Red Bulls, and . . .' Her eyes darted from side to side. '*Jägerbombs!*'

I started laughing loudly at the thought of shots on a school night while Katy plunged for the tray, more than ready for the alcohol buzz to dull her emotions.

Zola and I lifted our Jägers into the air.

'To Katy,' I said, 'the baddest bitch in marketing.'

'Hell, yes!' Zola replied, smashing her shot into mine.

Katy shook her head, giggling, and together we downed our first shot of the night.

*

Inside the bar, the musicians began playing some old-school classics, as we sipped away at our drinks. It felt nice to be out again; I could feel the mild, fresh Scottish air breeze around us and started to feel excited about the warm summer nights approaching.

'So, how are we planning on getting revenge on this Mark punk?' Zola asked.

I laughed and nudged Katy, urging her to plot against him in a bid to lift her spirits. 'We could key his car? Or start an ugly syphilis rumour?' I joked.

'What's the point?' she sulked. 'Let's face it, he'll already have moved on to his next victim.'

'God help her!' I said, raising my glass in an ironic toast.

'I just wish there was a way we could warn other women about him. I wish there was like a review segment on Tinder or something.'

Zola chuckled loudly. 'Could you imagine, though? Decent job, shit dick. Two stars!'

'But at least you'd know what you were getting.' I backed up Katy's suggestion. 'It makes sense. I wouldn't invest in something – not even a new pair of leggings – without reading reviews first. Why don't we do the same for people?'

'That's because you're an over-organised control freak.' Zola giggled. 'I can never be bothered to read the reviews.'

'I think she has a point, Zo. This could be a thing we could pitch to dating apps,' Katy said, her tone deadly serious, like we were in a work meeting. 'We could call it "the no more arseholes campaign"?'

'Babe, it would be overrun by scorned women! It would never work. I'm not saying it would be a bad idea in theory. I get it, I do. But apps like that make too much money idealising the dream of finding the perfect part-ner. They ain't gonna be promoting a bunch of one-star players with dicks they don't know how to use – no one would be swiping for them!' Zola declared and sat back, sipping on her drink some more.

I knew she was right – who wants to admit their prod-uct is a sham? But surely we weren't the only women to be affected by two-timing, love-bombing, self-obsessed men who thought they could get away with sleeping with half the town? I turned to Katy and watched her glare into the bottom of her glass, all the bright and bubbly personality sucked out of her by Mark the Munter.

Suddenly I had a thought.

'Girls, maybe we should make our own website.'

Katy looked baffled. 'A dating website? We've just agreed that we hate all men, Ella!'

I jerked my head as the light bulbs sparked in my mind. 'No, more like a *rate my date* kind of thing. We upload all the men we've dated or slept with over the years and give honest reviews.'

'Well, I'm excluded, obviously.' Zola flashed her stun-ning Tiffany & Co. engagement ring in our faces and beamed.

'Well, yeah, of course you are! But let's face it, you'd be the brains behind the tech side of things. We could create a website and upload the usual Tinder suspects, who are always on the bloody prowl. We would basi-cally date as many men as possible, then review our experiences – good *and* bad, obviously – to help other women out there.'

'So, we date them, then write a review?' Katy asked, wrapping her head around it all.

'Exactly! Think about it! We could get other girls to do the same, make it an online community. That way, if they've started speaking to a guy and thinking of meeting up, all they do is punch their name into a search bar and *voilà*, honest reviews on that guy. A wee bit of a heads-up before they turn psycho, fuckboy or ghost mode.'

Zola let out a scream of laughter. 'You are not serious, though, Ella?'

'I am deadly serious. Look what they're doing to our friend, Zo. It's our public duty to expose them, separate the cunts from the cuties!'

I could tell that Katy was swaying, utterly unsure of my master plan.

'But what's stopping the men from going on and reviewing themselves? Bigging up the size of their cocks, bragging about their bedroom techniques, making false promises about their commitment to monogamy?' Zola countered now. 'And not to mention the law – wouldn't it leave you open to so much legal action? I mean, would it not be defamation of character?'

Katy shook her head. 'But if it was honest? Just brutally honest feedback?'

'It would be your word against theirs, babe. You have to be proper careful in this day 'n' age!'

I sighed – all my dreams of doing a good deed for my fellow Glaswegian women well and truly shat on.

'But . . .' Zola eventually said. 'There might be another option . . .'

I sat up and turned to Katy, who now looked equally as excited at the re-ignited prospect of revenge.

'I suppose you could make it a secret club,' Zola started, gathering her thoughts. 'I could set up a facial recognition feature or something on the webpage, or get some form of ID clearance that only allows access to women.' She was thinking out loud now. 'Yes, we'd set up an admin that only allows verified users to access the site. *Oh, girl*, I got it! We could make people pay a sub-scription for the information; that way, it cuts a lot of the drama out. No timewasters or women who just want a nosey.'

'Yes!' I agreed, almost bouncing out of my seat.

'You two would have to date A LOT too. We would have to set up a forum section for the women to share their experiences about the men they've dated. But we would take no part in slandering the men. We'd encour-age everyone to write openly and honestly about their dating stories, just objective facts, no personal opinions.'

Katy was engrossed, nodding her little head like the Churchill dog.

'And I suppose we'd have to set clear rules,' Zola continued, 'to ensure we weren't acting like a secret kind of *Gossip Girl*. We don't want this to be bitchy, it's got to go for a more informative vibe.'

'Rules? Like what?' Katy asked.

'We could set membership rules, ones that our sub-scribers have to fully agree to before we allow them access to the page. They can't include or hint at the men's last names, or where they work – none of that type of thing. And no slandering their physical appearance, that would be far too immature and cruel. I suppose we'd have to market this page as a way of safeguarding women – it aims to highlight toxic, unsafe men – and can be used as a way of identifying and promoting the good ones.'

'Well, it would do all of those things. Think of the situations you've been in, Katy!' I said as a shiver ran down my spine.

'God, I know. Remember the guy who followed me home, begging me to let him inside?'

'Yeah, and I also remember we couldn't report him because you threatened him with an illegal pepper spray you bought off the fucking internet!' Zola giggled.

I chuckled at the thought of Katy almost getting lifted for possession of a dangerous weapon. 'Well, it's just as well she did! Who knows what that creepy cunt would have done?!'

'To illegal pepper spray!' Katy raised her half-empty glass in the air, and we followed suit, clinking them together.

'I know you said no slagging off of physical attributes, but could we mention the size of their cock?' I asked. 'I mean, it's a great thing to know. There's nothing worse than disappointing dick after slogging your way through a third date!'

'We could maybe add that to a premium package?' Zola suggested, easily persuaded to backtrack a little. 'Package being the operative word, ladies.'

I clasped my hands together, excitement bubbling through me. 'Jesus, this is the first business plan I've felt excited about in a long time!'

'It sure beats oil portraits!' Zola winked.

I laughed, agreeing with my friend. 'No, but I genuinely think this could take off, girls, I honestly do.
Imagine we could finally break away from Andrea and
her dictatorship.'

Katy giggled. 'Now that is the dream!'

'Cheers to that!' Zola added.

Katy drank then smiled with a knowing look at me.
'If we do this, you realise it will involve dating again,
Ella Banks?'

I felt clammy at the thought. I couldn't stomach half
of the men I'd dated before, and my tolerance for their
shabby behaviour since I'd gotten older and listened to
my friends' experiences had seriously taken a dive. I suppose I'd always had a knack for calling out their bullshit,
but still, I hated the dishonesty of dating in general. The
vulnerability of putting myself out there again, especially
when my life was good. I was settled, in the best possible
way. I didn't need a man to fulfil me.

I paused, letting the idea sink in. 'But it's not *me* dating
them, is it? I'd be dating the men on behalf of the website.
No strings attached. No emotions involved.'

'Too right.' Zola laughed loudly. 'So, girls, are we up
for some serious revenge on the fuckboys of Glasgow?'

'HELL YES!' I shrieked.

'I'm in,' Katy said, then reached over and grabbed a
shot of Jäger.

'Let's fucking get them!' Zola cackled.

Chapter Three

Ella

The following morning, I was heading towards the office with a hefty hangover dulling its cloudy weight over me, but I had taken some paracetamol and drunk my usual milk thistle, praying for a quick fix. I left my flat in Hillhead and travelled on the subway from the West End towards the city centre, still unsure if I was safe to drive after last night's alcohol consumption.

As I entered the small open-plan office space, I spotted Zola and Katy slumped over their desks, hardly speaking. I laughed as I approached them.

'Morning!' I called out.

Both of them screwed up their faces and covered their ears immediately.

'*Sssshhhh*, keep it down,' Katy moaned.

I pulled my leather jacket off and placed it over my seat before gladly taking a seat.

'Why do you look like that?' Katy pointed at my sheer white blouse and pencil skirt.

'Yeah, it's very annoying. Just come in looking like shit for one day, hun. We'd respect you more,' Zola said, resting her head on her hands.

'No, I am rough. This is just a disguise. But I drank lots of water when I got home. I texted you both and reminded you to do the same!' I laughed, examining my friends in their creased clothes, both looking like they had spent the night sleeping in a hedge.

At that moment, Andrea's precision bob bolted through the office. 'OK, so listen up, people! Could we all gather round?'

I stood up and turned to my friends, who were dragging themselves to their feet. We joined our colleagues in a familiar circle-time meeting.

'Let's make this one short and snappy. I want everyone to tell me what they're working on this week and where you expect to be by the end of the week.' Andrea's sharp eyes narrowed as they scanned the group, and I watched them pause on me.

I stood up poker straight, readjusting myself.

'Let's start with you, Ella Banks,' she said, one brow raised to the sky.

'OK, yes, sure. Morning, everyone . . .'

'Short and sharp.' Andrea clapped her hands.

In my peripheral vision, I could see Zola shake her head disapprovingly at Andrea's lack of manners. The London office was a lot more zen than Glasgow. That lot would take their shoes off at meetings and stretch back on bean bags to brainstorm. They could work from home if they pleased and were always encouraged to bounce ideas off their boss without fear of being struck down by a lightning bolt of criticism. Fuck, they could even bring their pets to work on a Friday. The Glasgow approach was much more formal, businesslike – and utterly shambolic for Zola, but she'd moved here for a promotion. And although she detested Andrea and her culture-of-fear methods, there was no denying it – we always achieved the best results.

'So, this week, I'm continuing to prioritise Alexander Cambi's art exhibition. I'm sussing out venues and emailing art world clients RSVPs to get an idea of how big the venue will need to be to host it.'

'Weren't you,' Andrea cleared her throat, then mimicked my voice at an obscenely higher pitch than her own, 'prioritising that last week?'

I gulped. I had been prioritising this project for a fucking month with no idea how I'd pull it off.

'Yes,' I admitted. 'It has been quite tricky. The art world in Glasgow isn't as . . . keen for his style of traditional portraits as elsewhere, it seems.'

'You have one more week to prioritise it. Book a venue, establish a guest list, sell the paintings. Cambri wants to launch this collection in three weeks, Ella.'

I nodded, feeling clammy and out-of-sorts, unsure whether it was from last night's binge or the uncomfortable sudden pressure.

But Andrea was already done with me, shifting her gaze sharply to my right. 'Zola?'

'I'm creating the website and revamping the social media for Luxe Lengths hair extensions. The owner, Lisa, is renowned in her field and has a lot of celebrity clients, so I've created a website showcasing her talent. It should be done by the end of the day.'

Andrea's head tilted, which was as close to appreciation as any of us were going to get today. She shifted her gaze along once more.

'And Katy, Katy, Katy . . . Will I tell you what you will be doing?' Andrea asked, folding her arms with a smirk.

Katy's eyes darted between Zola and me and then back to Andrea, not knowing how this would turn out.

'The Tunnock's campaign?'

'No. Tina, that's now your pitch.'

Tina straightened in an instant, immediately scribbling into her notebook.

My stomach twisted. Was Katy about to get fired? *Or a warning?* I could hear my heart pound in my eardrums. Andrea had fired two senior PR girls last month alone for having low engagements on a post for one of their client's social media accounts. She sent them to HR stating they were unable to carry out their job description and we never saw them again. *Why do I even try to do this job under this wannabe fucking mini-Putin?!*

'You will be working on your new client, Blaze Boost. Congratulations!'

A wave of relief washed through my body. *Thank fuck!*

I turned to Katy, whose mouth was gaping wide. 'Wait. I . . . I . . . got it?'

Andrea attempted to smile, but her face always looked like it was in pain when she showed her teeth. 'You did. And this week you'll be hitting the gyms, selling their products. See which ones work, then we can pitch an idea to them at the end of the month.'

Katy nodded, gulping down hard. 'OK, thanks, Andrea, thanks so—'

'Short and sharp now, Katy.' She pointed towards her, giving her a brief warning.

Thankfully, Andrea then moved on to the rest of the group. After she advised and dictated her views on their workloads, we returned to our desks to get started.

I put one arm around Katy and smiled. 'I knew you had this. Well done!'

She breathed out a long sigh, seemingly relieved. 'Thanks, although I wouldn't have gone in there without you guys.'

'True. Very true!' Zola said, laughing as we all sat down.

'How am I going to smash this campaign?' I asked softly, glancing over the hundreds of RSVP emails I'd sent out without even a glimpse of success. I felt like an absolute failure. I wasn't used to struggling with anything, let alone work. I wondered what Andrea would do to me if I couldn't pull this off. Would I get a warning? Or just sent out the door with my P60 in hand?

'*Oh my God!* Guys! Guys! Look! He's . . . he's back with his ex.' Katy stood up, her face furious. She brandished her phone at us, displaying Mark's Instagram, where he'd posted the perfect stack of pancakes at Bramble and tagged his ex.

I watched my friend's face glow scarlet with rage.

'Katy, sit down. Babe?' Zola tugged on her arm, and she flopped to her chair.

'Is he serious? He had sex with me two days ago. Two fucking days ago, Zo!' Her eyes filled up with tears.

I shuffled my chair over towards her and rubbed her shoulder. 'Hey, he doesn't deserve you, Katy. You know that.'

'He never tagged *me*. He never took *me* for brunch. Why am I never the girl they want to show off on Instagram or buy fucking pancakes for?' Her bottom lip was quivering.

'Do you honestly think he will treat her well?' I insisted. 'Babe, you just said he was shagging you two days ago. Do you think he'll be able to keep this going with her? He's incapable of a long-term relationship, Katy. Just like most of his generation out there.'

Katy covered her face with her hands.

'Look, I know it's hurtful, and it's not what you want to see, but you are free now. No more questioning his intent, overthinking his short-ass messages, constantly wondering if he's being dry, if you said something wrong, or if he's just too busy. You know now. Let's move on,' Zola said gently but firmly, and I agreed. 'Plus, stop following him on Instagram, yeah?'

'Move on?' Katy laughed. 'Move on *again*. I'm thirty-three, Zola; my ovaries have fucking dust mites on them. Honest to God!' She sighed heavily. 'I'm not even mad at Mark. I'm mad at myself for allowing myself to get hurt *over* and *over* again by these fucking men. No, these *boys*! I've had enough of it.'

There was a silence between us as the truth of Katy's words struck home for us all. Then, suddenly, I remembered our conversation from last night.

I turned to them and laughed a little, suddenly nervous about speaking about the website in a more sober circumstance. 'You're not thinking what I'm thinking, are you?' I asked the others.

Katy wiped down her face quickly and looked up with a resigned expression. I could tell she was considering the ultimate revenge she could take. 'Do it. Make the page, Zo.'

Zola glanced towards me. 'You're one hundred per cent in, Ella?'

I looked at Katy, and I saw how much she wanted this. She needed this distraction.

'Yeah, yeah. Do it, I'm in.'

'OK. Payback commencing, bitches!' Zola laughed wickedly, turned to her computer and began typing furiously. She was like that the whole day. Occasionally, Katy and I would try to sneak a peek, but she batted us away. I wasn't sure if she wasn't wanting to draw attention to the fact she was creating it on the clock, or if she just wanted to show us the end result only when she was finished.

I continued researching the best places for Alexander's art exhibition, but I needed more motivation. I knew very little about the art world, never mind how to promote it. I made some *Coming Soon* posters for Instagram detailing the artist's visit to Glasgow and sent them to my contacts in the press. I wasn't convincing even myself that it would be enough to make a difference.

Around six, Zola turned to us.

'It's almost done!' she whispered. 'I mean, I have to add the special features and the security and things but I have the home page and tabs ready.'

I scanned the empty office. I'd been too engrossed in my own project to notice that everyone else had left.

'Let's see then,' Katy said, barging over to Zola's desktop.

'Oooh, yeah, show us what you've got, Zo,' I enthused, sliding my chair over.

'Welcome to . . . drum roll, ladies . . .' She tapped her hands off the desk as I giggled beside her. '*The Dicktionary Club!*' Zola announced as she let out an evil laugh.

'Oh my God,' I squealed.

'We can change the name,' she suggested. 'I just thought it was fitting.'

'No, I love it,' I admitted.

'Yup, works for me,' Katy said.

We both looked on, eagerly awaiting the virtual tour.

'So, this is the home page,' Zola said.

I glanced down at the cute girly-pink background with red edging. *The Dicktionary Club* was written in an elegant font, like an invitation to a Gatsby party, but she had replaced the 'i' in 'dick' with a golden aubergine. 'I'll add a brief introduction explaining what the page is about, blah blah blah, but the coolest part is here: I've managed to sync every guy from every dating app in Glasgow to our search engine. And it's age specific.'

'Every dating app?' Katy gasped at Zola's skills.

'Yep, well, the most popular ones. I haven't delved into the niche apps yet, but I can do that in time. So, basically, you can search a guy's first name here, then select the age range, and if he has a dating profile on Tinder, Bumble, Plenty of Fish or Hinge he will appear. There is nowhere these fuckboys can run now, girls.'

'Can we click and review one now?' Katy asked.

Zola smiled mischievously as her finger hovered over the search button, scanning through the thumbnails of photographs.

'We could look up anyone. Poor Toby, what about him? Or Andrew there?' She was picking out pictures of random men on the screen.

'Do Mark, Zola. Search for Mark. He's thirty!' Katy interrupted impatiently from behind us. She was bopping up and down like a toddler.

'OK, let's have a look, then,' Zola said. She typed his name into the search engine and scrolled down the surprisingly large amount of Marks in the city until, lo and behold, his Tinder profile popped up.

I turned to my friend and grinned. 'You are a fucking genius, Zola! What the fuck?!'

Zola nodded. 'Totally, right? Oh wait, this is my favourite part – I've added a feature which means we can rate them in flags. Green for nice, amber for *hmmm* . . . he's all right, pink for a bit of a dick or crimson red for watch out, girls, this one's a *massive* cunt.'

'CRIMSON RED! Massive cunt, please!'

We all burst out laughing.

Zola clicked on the red flag, and a small question-naire dropped down.

Date of meet-up, how it went, the man's interests, any warning signals to look out for, a brief description of the date and, lastly – for top-tier members only – penis size (an estimate was fine).

'Zola, this is insane!' I gasped. 'How did you do all of this in one day?'

34

She sat back, proud of her work. 'I had all this spy software left over from another project in London, but I sync'd it to Glasgow and downloaded the codes.'

'Ermm . . . *OK*, that means nothing to me, but it's class! Like seriously, this could be a massive hit.'

'Yeah, I agree, but you two will have to date A LOT before we make it public and you also need to go back and rate all your previous dates. We need some content! We can obviously get our users to provide their experiences too, but we will have to have a fair few rated before it goes live. There's no point in advertising the website if there's no juice on any of the men, you get me?'

I gulped down nervously at the thought of dating – even if it was only fake dating.

'Just think of how many women could catch their partners cheating too!' Katy stated.

'I know, it's as easy as a search bar,' I said. 'No more second-guessing. No more wasting your life on idiot detective work.'

'And think how many crazy men it will help avoid. You know, I think that's the most important point here. I've added a full tab on the dangers of internet dating and put a link to Clare's Law in case anyone wants to ask the police for information on their partner for domestic violence or abuse reasons. Just some general guidelines and advice.'

I beamed, squeezing Zola's shoulders, unbelievably impressed with her work.

'So, will we be charging for access? Did we decide?' I asked. My brain was still alcohol-foggy from the night before.

'We should, but not a lot. A fee will help to avoid any trolls writing information on someone that's not true. We have to be careful of that. Maybe something small, like a fiver? It will cost us to keep the website active and moderated, and I honestly think we should patent the idea so no one can steal our genius site.'

'Yeah, that's fine. How much will we have to pay to start it up?'

Zola hummed 'Roughly, I reckon, like three, four hundred each?'

I recoiled a little. Jesus, I really had to nail my campaign or being out a job and four hundred quid down in the space of a month would put me out of my home and on to my arse.

'I'll transfer you now,' I agreed.

'Me too,' Katy said, pulling out her phone.

'I've also downloaded an entry form to gain access. I've ensured that no men can just decide to hop on and write positively about themselves. So, women have to apply to be a member and we vet them first. This has to be a strictly women-only. The Dicktionary Club is a cock-free zone.'

'Jesus, we've created a secret society here!' I turned to my pals excitedly.

'No, we've created the ultimate prick list,' Zola confirmed.

Together we hugged, laughing and screaming in delight. I could feel my heart bounce off my chest in anticipation.

'Well, the hard part is done on my end, ladies,' Zola said. 'Now it's time for you two to start dating! And

I can tune up the other features over the next few days,' she added.

My nerves returned in an instant, and I glanced towards Katy with a pleading look. 'You're going to have to show me the ropes.'

'Pass me your phone, Ella Banks,' she said. 'You've got some serious swiping to do!'

Chapter Four

Ella

I entered my flat just after eight and slipped my shoes off in the hallway before bending down and angling them perfectly onto my shoe rail. I breathed a sigh of relief at returning home, hoping that by tomorrow my hangover would have shifted completely. I headed into the open-plan living room and kitchen area and slumped down on the soft, cream corner sofa.

I'd always loved my flat, my safe place to chill out and relax. I loved the high ceilings, the terrific central location, the granite worktops, and the pristine condition of every room. It combined the Victorian character of the building with my own modern twist. But I hadn't always loved living alone. I bought the flat almost on a whim after seeing it listed on an auction site shortly after my breakup with Joshua and used my entire life savings to purchase it. I told myself I needed the distraction, that I needed to rebuild my life, so I focused every ounce of energy and penny I had into making it the dream apartment.

But truthfully, I wanted to impress him, to prove to him he'd made an enormous mistake, to show him what he was missing. Fuck, I even added in features I knew

Joshua would approve of – like an alcove displaying an impressive record collection, knowing fine well the only music I listen to is Taylor Swift or Adele. I added a his-and-hers-style dressing room. Joshua was heavily into fashion and designer labels, and he'd always promised to build a space for us both to get ready together when we finally ditched our rented studio and purchased our dream home. So, yep, I dedicated ten months of non-stop graft, overtime and endless frustrated tears just to be able to plaster the finished result on Instagram in the desperate, needy hope that he'd message me or ask to come round and then my dream flat would ultimately win him back. Yes, I tried to lure my ex-man back to me with a try-too-hard closet and a record collection, for fuck's sake. He never did message, of course, and when I think of it all now, I still feel an achy pain grumbling in my chest, realising how utterly pathetic it was to decorate my entire home for a man who would never even set foot in it, let alone live there with me.

I mean, we had split up over a year before, for God's sake, but still, I would lie in bed at night imagining scenarios of how he'd come back when he'd seen how well I was doing in life. Not that I wasn't doing well before, but I wanted to show him how I'd managed to accomplish all of his expectations in my home all by myself. That I was so organised and had the dreamiest apartment and this great fucking life he could still be a part of. It was some unhinged attempt to prove my point, that my life was amazing and I was achieving everything and it didn't revolve around procreating. Even now, it completely infuriates me that I allowed myself to love someone so deeply that it made me a crazy, chaotic, desperate person, and truthfully, I wasn't prepared ever to let that happen again. Not now. Now that I've finally got my shit back together. I am happy, a happily single woman, and I'm in control. I have my friends, my job and a stunning flat, and I couldn't think of anything worse than a man coming along to ruin my peace.

*

Ping.

I pulled my phone out of my back pocket.

Katy: *The first coffee date is arranged for lunchtime tomorrow! How you getting on? X*

I rolled my eyes, having not yet set up my Tinder profile after Katy downloaded the app for me at work.

Ella: *Not long home. I will set it up just now. What pics should I use? X*

Zola: *YES, girls! I love the one of you in Italy with your tits out, babe x*

I burst out laughing, thinking back to our summer holiday when we all went to a nudist beach, and Zola took a photo of me topless, holding two strawberries at my nipples.

Ella: *That would get the dates in. Haha x*

Katy: *NO! Bad advice, ZO! I know this answer though, I saw on TikTok you should add one candid, one laughing, one businesslike, and one with an animal. Maybe a dog? Little cute vibe? Xx*

Ella: *I don't have a fucking dog!!! Surely people don't make TikToks on this?!*

Katy: *We will find you a dog in the street for a pic, El. haha! Xx*

Katy: *And they make TikToks on everything.*

I couldn't help but smile at her expert take on the online dating scene and, inspired, finally clicked on the Tinder app to set it up.

A series of questions popped up and I began clicking.

OK, I am a woman seeking a man for a short-term relationship.

Name. I paused. Reminding myself of an article I read recently on the rising amount of stalking cases happening in the UK since dating apps and social media. Not to mention all of the Netflix documentaries that highlighted the complete psychopaths out there. I swore to myself after bingeing *I Am Stalker* never to reveal my name or personal details to anyone outside of work or family life from then on. Especially when I lived alone, and let's face it, I would make a great statistic. Fuck, I even told the over-smiley barista at Starbucks my name was Tina last week – just in case.

And I especially didn't want any comeback with these men we were about to expose. I wanted to keep my details private. I mean, this was technically a business venture. I hummed a little, *but what name could I use*? I felt my fingers hover over the keypad of my phone, until I eventually had it.

Name: *Bella*
Age: *30*
Biography: *Hey guys, new to dating and wanting to meet casually for dates. Come say Hi!*

I felt nauseated. What if someone recognised me from my photographs? A distant cousin or a client? Panic set in that I'd do something that would mean my clients would look at me unprofessionally. OK, if I got caught or if Andrea had an issue with it, I could say someone stole my snaps and was catfishing as me. *Yes, I'd go down that route.* I mean, I hadn't given my actual name. *OK, it's OK. This is work, Ella. Don't stress. Think about this from a business perspective.* I breathed deeply, calmed myself down – and saved my details.

My phone quickly flashed up men's profiles, from handsome laddy types to vegan nerds. I reluctantly swiped right to them all. As match after match blew up my phone, I suddenly became more engrossed in swiping than arranging potential dates. I could feel my nerves settle as each match boosted my ego. It felt oddly thrilling, sitting back and judging man after man purely on their physical appearance. I continued the swiping charade for over an hour until I eventually called a halt and clicked on the messages tab. I knew I had to pick the perfect red-flag candidates – the ones who seemed to be serial daters. I felt more set on avenging my friend and the females of Glasgow than trying to find a nice guy to rave about.

Kevin: *Can we agree that we'd both make beautiful babies?*

Bingo! I swiped through Kevin's photographs. The first showed him driving a Ferrari through Vegas, not so subtly flexing. The rest were mostly holiday snaps, such as posing at an infinity pool in Dubai or working out at the gym. There were also some curvy Ikea mirror selfies with him flexing his pecs. He seemed like the ultimate fuckboy. He needed me to vet him. I mean, don't get me wrong; he was handsome and gorgeous, with thick black hair and a beard that was so pristinely shaped it looked like he spent more time at the Turkish barbers than at home. But he undoubtedly loved himself, and I could only imagine the women he had strung along during his years of Tinder bashing.

I took a deep breath and scanned his profile.

Bio: *Lookin' for my baby mama, the wifey to my lifey. Gotta be a gym girly. Come say Hi first, I don't bite . . . unless you want me to!*

Wow. I felt sick scorch the back of my throat. *Do women fall for this shit?* Who talks about children as an opening line? Who mentions biting? Was I so much out of the dating loop that this behaviour was now classed as normal chat? I shook my head, then smiled evilly as I began typing, resisting the urge to explain that some women, like me, never want to be *baby mamas* or *wifeys*, especially with someone as self-obsessed as him. I paused momentarily and thought hard about the task in hand – what would Katy say?

> **Bella:** *Hey! And YES! I think we would definitely would, Kev! Can you imagine the six-pack on the kids? Wow.*

> **Kevin:** *Haha defo! Let's catch up, maybe start practising ya wee beaut* ☺x

A shiver ran through me. Wow, getting your hole on this app was seriously easy. I wanted to immediately block him for his lack of manners and downright audacity, but I played along.

> **Bella:** *Ooooh. That sounds fun! But maybe a coffee first? Ease me in a little? X*

> **Kevin:** *Cool, darling. I'll ease you in no bother* ☺ *Where are you from? Xx*

I continued to message Kevin into the night, arranging to grab a coffee together the following day at the same time and place Katy was meeting her match. After that, I'd only have half an hour on my lunch break to write up his review for the Dicktionary Club, so I prepped possible questions on my notes tab that women might want to know about him. I then began scrolling through the mounds of messages my matches were sending.

**

James: *Wow, you are stunning!*

**

Michael: *Fuck me! Is this what love at first sight feels like??*

**

Shaun: *Hey, cutie x*

**

Ryan: *Hey, nice profile. How is Tuesday evening treating you? It would be great to chat back, as you have a very interesting profile.*

**

Philip: *What's a secret talent you have nobody knows about? Bet it's something naughty?*

**

Gary: *Hey Bella. How are you? Have you got much on this week?*

**

Ewan: *I can tell you have first-class handwriting. Perfect for the Christmas cards we will be sending from 'us'.*

**

Gerard: *Well, that's a face I'd like to wake up to. Do you like big guys?*

**

The screeds of messages blew my mind, and I wondered how we'd possibly date enough of these men to make even the smallest dent in the Glaswegian dating scene. I replied to a few and then retired to my bed, but my mind was buzzing with ideas on how to safely and secretively enhance the Dicktionary Club. This task seemed too big for Katy and me to handle on our own.

Chapter Five

Ella

The following afternoon, Katy and I were rounding up some work before breaking for lunch. Kevin had messaged a couple of times, and I'd replied once to say our coffee date was still on. I felt quieter today, more in my head at the thought of going on a date, even if it was fake. It made me anxious just thinking about creating shitty small talk or listening to God-awful cheesy chat-up lines for the first time in years.

I ran over the possible things Kevin could say or want. What did he expect from this? To see one another again? To pump and dump? Would he promise me the world to get me into bed and then ghost me the following day? I'd seen it happen enough times to Katy, after all, and I wasn't prepared to fall for anyone's bullshit. I knew I had to approach this task with detached coldness and have zero emotions despite the compliments that could flood in.

But the very idea of putting myself out there again, straight back into the lion's den, made me nauseous; I hated the games and ulterior motives. How they all presumed a bit of charm and a well-tamed beard could drop the knickers of any woman in Glasgow. Well, not this fucking one.

I stopped my mind briefly, realising my hands were shaking; I wasn't sure if it was from nerves or from overall, built-up resentment. I breathed deeply and then reminded myself this was not an actual date. This was a project that would ultimately serve the women of Glasgow. Girls who weren't necessarily as strong-minded as me. Girls who perhaps dreamed of having children one day and wanted to enjoy a family life with a decent family man. Girls like Katy. This project would help them stay clear of the arseholes lurking around the Tinder drain. It could save them months, if not years, of wasting their lives on some unable-to-commit prick with a below-average-knowledge of how to use his penis for anyone's pleasure other than his own. I knew deep down I had to do this. Hunting down these players and exposing the truth was basically a long-overdue act of public service.

I turned to Katy, watching her giggle while secretly messaging her new match, Ali, from under her desk. He was, allegedly, five ten, lived in Rutherglen and worked in the city centre at Virgin Media. His photos were the same as most men's when trying to impress online – partying with friends at the Ho Wong, on holiday in Tenerife, or walking up hills on weekends. He dressed well in mostly Zara-type outfits, with the odd designer label thrown in here and there, and he seemed to have a matching hat for each of these outfits. He had a friendly face, though, and from Katy's laughter, I guessed he was pretty flirty. She stressed that he insisted (*like they all do*) that he was completely fed up with trying to conduct a decent love life on the apps. Katy, unlike me, seemed pretty smitten with her new match already.

'How are you feeling about today, Ella?' Zola asked me, leaning back in her chair.

'It's coffee and then I file a report. I can do that.' I shrugged it off.

'And you, Katy?'

Katy was engrossed in her phone. Zola and I looked at one another, and she rolled her eyes.

'Katy!' I hissed.

'Mmmm . . . huh?'

'How are you feeling about your coffee date?' Zola repeated.

'Good. I'm looking forward to it, actually.' She smiled brightly, her dimples showing through, and I watched Zola shake her head.

'Will we sit together, Ella?' Katy asked.

I laughed. 'Maybe it's best not to. It might give the game away, plus I think you'd distract me,' I said, giggling at the double-date situation these men were about to unknowingly find themselves in.

'I am going to love this! It's going to be so much fun!' Zola clapped her hands, laughing hard.

'You?' I questioned.

'Uh-huh. You don't think I'm letting you girls go on the Dicktionary Club's first mission without me observing the entire thing, do you? Besides, this poor man probably needs protection from Ella; he has no idea how much of a hater she is! I'll grab a table with my iced latte. Hopefully, they'll have a bucket of popcorn for me, too.'

I reached over to slap her arm jokingly.

'I'll be fine, he'll be fine. I'm just writing up a basic report at the end of the date! No strings.' I glanced across to Katy, 'You should be keeping it professional too, Katy! You're giggling away there, entertaining this guy. Keep it causal! It's a one-time coffee date.'

'Oh, excuse me if I have a little fun along the way. I could meet the man of my dreams on this project, I'll have you know.'

Both Zola and I let out an exaggerated sigh and slumped back in our chairs.

There was a slight shuffle of movement around us as people got up from their desks, and I turned to the clock: *1 p.m.* I glanced back to Katy, who was adding a layer of gloss to her lips.

'It's time for our date, biatch! Get your bag!'

*

As Zola, Katy and I headed to Costa, I glanced at my Tinder profile again, studying Kevin's photographs and ensuring I knew exactly who I was meeting. *OK, he is handsome*, I thought. Nerves swarmed my stomach, and my breathing had changed to shorter, shallower breaths. *Why am I nervous?* I didn't want to impress him in the slightest. Maybe it was because I hadn't had a coffee with a stranger I wasn't trying to pitch to in years. Katy, on the other hand, seemed ecstatic. She was buzzing with energy at the potential of Ali, her latest dream man.

'OK, I'll walk in first, place my order, then sit where I have both of you in my eyeline,' Zola said with a smirk, putting her head down and stepping into the coffee shop.

'Walk in together?' Katy asked. I wondered if she could sense my nerves.

'Sure.' I smiled, squeezing her waist as she pulled the heavy glass door open.

The coffee shop was bustling with businesspeople and Gen Z crowds snapping photos of their drinks for social media. Katy and I huddled together, observing the lunch-rush crowd.

'Can you see them?' I asked, squinting around.

'I can't see Ali. He texted to say he was here, though.'

We continued scanning the busy room.

I felt a buzz from my pocket and saw a Tinder notification from Kevin.

Just getting parked will be one minute toots x

'Kevin's parking. I should probably grab a seat?' I shrugged.

'Wait. Just wait, I can't see mine,' she said, her voice quivery with panic. I watched Katy's pale complexion turn red with stress at the idea she had been ghosted already.

'Ah, Katy?' a voice called out. We both turned around to see a small man with an extra-large, extra-glossy bald head smiling cheerfully.

Katy looked at me and back to him. 'Yeah?'

'Ali?' He seemed confused, pointing to his chest. I did a second take as Katy's mouth fell open.

His head was fucking huge, like monumentally notice-able even in the crowded coffee shop. It was massive, and to make it worse the sun seemed to catch and reflect its glare like a mirror. *Jesus Christ, I wish I'd brought my Ray-Bans*, I thought, adjusting to the brightness. Poor Ali must have photoshopped his bonce smaller for his photographs or stood ten foot behind his pals in every picture. Katy stood in absolute disbelief with her mouth wide open, gaping in horror at the gradual realisation that this man was the same person from the photos. I mean, if you shrunk the noggin or put an extra-large hat on him, I suppose he would be kind of similar – but today, she most definitely got the Temu version.

'I think you better go,' I murmured, nudging her.

She nodded, eyes still spanning over Ali's vast dome. 'Have fun.'

As Katy followed Ali, I immediately felt more unsettled about the person who would show up for me. I could hear deep cackles from the corner of the room and, as I turned, I watched Zola with tears streaming down her face, clapping the air in hysterics at Katy's situation. I automatically burst out laughing myself.

'You seem happy?' a male voice said close by.

I turned to see a handsome, tall man with a beard so sharp it could cut glass.

'Sorry, yeah, I just saw a friend. How are you?' I asked.

He leaned in and kissed my cheek.

'I'm good now, darling.' He paused, and I watched his dark green eyes scan up and down my body. 'Well, you are stunning, aren't you?' He bit his lip ever so subtly and then let out the smallest purr of delight as he finished ogling my body.

My cheeks blushed, knowing my friends were almost certainly watching and judging our initial interaction.

'Shall we take a seat?' He pointed to an empty table directly across from Katy and her date.

'Sure,' I replied confidently, briefly making eye contact with a flustered Katy, whose date was rummaging around awkwardly in his wallet, pointing to the large-screen coffee menu.

'What's your order? I'll go grab it,' Kevin said much more smoothly as I sat down at the table.

'Oat milk latte, please,' I said, smiling back as he turned towards the counter.

When both men were away, I giggled at Katy, who held her hands up, still in disbelief at Ali. My phone buzzed.

A new notification from the group chat.

Zola: *Hahahahah, this is amazing!*

I smirked at my phone, noticing Katy typing furiously across the aisle.

Katy: *Oh yep, it's amazing! Ella is practically on a date with Prince fucking Charming while I am sitting here with Shrek!*

Zola: *Even Shrek's head ain't that big, sweetie xx*

I burst out laughing and then looked up cautiously, ensuring my date wasn't watching me or getting suspicious that anything weird was happening.

Ella: *She's right, babe. Don't diss Shrek!! Xx*

Ella: *Mine is handsome but has player written all over him. The way he checked out my body, EWWW! Xx*

'One oat milk latte for the *insanely* gorgeous Bella,' Kevin declared, eventually returning to his seat.

'Thanks,' I replied, watching Katy's man clumsily make his way back to their table, banging into chairs along the way.

'I'm glad I was in front of that guy at the counter, by the way.' He tilted his shoulder towards Ali. 'Did you see the size of that heid? No one is clocking the menu from behind that.'

I nodded, suddenly feeling weirdly defensive about Ali. It felt OK when my friends slagged him off, but it somehow irritated me when Kevin did.

'Stop it, that's a wee shame!' I warned him, raising an eyebrow. 'So, tell me, Kevin, when was the last time you had a date?' I asked, getting straight to business.

I watched Kevin shuffle slightly in his chair. 'Oh God, do you know I can't quite remember, Bella, probably three or maybe four months ago now?' I watched him blink a few times as he avoided eye contact, glancing at his coffee and then back to me. *Yip . . . I watch too much CSI to know the classic body language of a liar, Kev!*

'Cool.' I smiled, clocking his every move. 'So, what brings you to the dating apps now? You're obviously an attractive man. Why not go out there and meet someone the old-fashioned way?'

Kevin gave me a look. I admit, he seemed genuinely surprised. 'I could ask you the same question. I mean, you are beautiful.'

With his attempt at flattery, I felt my eyes roll to the back of my head without warning.

'You don't think you're good-looking?' he asked, catching my eye roll. 'Because, babe, trust me, you have a great body, smooth long legs. I mean, I can tell you work out with that arse.'

My jaw dropped open.

'Oh *yes*, don't act like you weren't adding a little wiggle for Big Kev when you strutted over here.' Kevin tapped his fingers on the table and smirked.

Indeed, I was not! *And Big Kev, Big Kev? Who even refers to themselves in the third person like that after high school?*

My fuckboy senses were tingling, alarm bells ringing in my brain. This was precisely the type of man we women should avoid. I just had to dig a bit more to prove it.

'Oh damn, looks like you caught me.' I laughed loudly, struggling to hide my disgust. 'So, you liked what you saw?' I leaned in as sexily as possible, allowing him to inhale my favourite Chanel scent.

'Jesus Christ.' His eyes popped open like a cartoon character's at the prospect of chatting about my arse after the first five minutes. 'I did, darling, and I'd like to see a lot more of it.' He matched my body language, leaning over the table.

'Play your cards right, and you might . . . at some point. I'm a lady.' I smirked and sat back in my chair.

God, this was too easy, I thought.

'So, you're up for meeting up again? Maybe a bottle of wine at mine?' he asked ever so casually.

'At yours?' I repeated, trying not to choke on my latte.

'I mean, we could get to know each other better, with no distractions, just me, you and that sexy strut of yours. I like a lady – outside of the house. And I like a naughty little girl inside.' His voice was deeper now; he was trying sooo hard to be sexy, seductive.

I felt my face twist. What a creepy cunt. But I took a breath and hid it well. '*Mmmm* . . . I'll think about it,' I replied, taking a large gulp of my drink.

'OK, fair enough,' Kevin said, sliding back into his chair, his smooth, bulging arms resting effortlessly on the table. 'It's better than a no, I suppose.'

'Tell me more about you, Kevin. I don't like jumping straight into things here, be gentle with me. Let's chat about our lives.' I took another sip of my drink, grateful for it hiding me a little, as my face reddened with the chat. I was keen to gather as much background information for a fully detailed report.

His eyebrows lifted. 'Be gentle with you? Cheeky girl.' He smirked as if I'd intended the phrase sexily. 'I can be gentle with you all right!'

I stared back, unimpressed.

Kevin huffed. 'Right. Well, what you wanna know? My star sign? Like every other girl.' He laughed and took a swig of his coffee.

What a prick, I thought, *but he's definitely a Scorpio!*

'No, about your work, your goals, your last serious relationship, anything and everything,' I replied.

'Oh, well, I work at the bank; I think I told you that,' he began.

Yes, you did, Kevin, but you're obviously chatting with so many other women you can't remember who you've told what.

'And my goal is to work hard, play harder.' He winked cheekily, which made my oat milk curdle in my stomach. 'And you do not want to hear about my ex.' He shook his head wildly. 'When I say psycho, I mean off the charts. *Baby Reindeer* Martha style!'

The alarm bells in my head rang louder as I nodded innocently, pretending to be shocked. I couldn't imagine any girl wanting to stalk this fanny.

'Why, what made her so bad?' I asked.

'She installed a tracker device in my fucking car! And would log into my Ring doorbell to see who was coming around my place.'

Genius move, I thought.

'And who was coming around your house?' I asked curiously, still sipping my drink, intrigued by his slip-up.

'You know, my mates and that.' He seemed flustered. 'She's a fucking loony!'

I hummed and nodded quietly.

'She still texts me now, you know. All this stuff about how she can't eat because she's so depressed. I just reply and say a few pounds off won't do you any harm, love. Know what I mean?' He laughed, thinking I'd join in, but I could feel my blood boil. 'She's not got a body like yours, if you get me.'

I was stunned, appalled and furious. I didn't know whether to call him out, make a scene, or just bide my time, not wanting to blow my cover. I needed to get all the revenge I could for this poor girl via the Dicktionary Club.

I zoned out as Kevin continued waffling on about his ex and focused in on Katy's conversation. She seemed to be nodding away at everything her man was saying, and I couldn't help but wonder if Ali was as much of a narcissistic cunt as so-called Big Kev. Fuck it, I'd much rather be dealing with someone with a head like an elephant's arse than this prick.

*

'So, what do you again?' Katy asked Ali, while pulling a face towards me, summoning me for help.

'Well, I'm *head* of recruitment, so you know how that is. Busy, busy workload. And yourself?'

I noticed Katy's eyes expand widely at the word 'head' and I covered my mouth to hide my amusement while Kevin continued to talk at me.

'Erm . . . marketing and advertising. It's stressful, but good. I enjoy it.'

'Great! You have to work hard to get *ahead* in that industry.'

Katy started gulping down her drink, trying to distract herself so as not to laugh.

'Mmmm . . .' she eventually managed to say. 'Yeah, absolutely! My boss can be hard work though, she honestly bit my *head* off last wee . . . *Oh God, I'm . . .*' She was sweating profusely staring at the shiny wall of skin facing her.

'Carry on?' he said, seemingly completely unaware.

*

'Do you get me, Bella?' Kevin followed up, and I forced myself to snap back to him.

'Yeah, God. Sounds mad!' I replied, scanning my watch for the time.

'You need to go back to work, don't you?' I looked at his self-important face and realised that he seemed genuinely sad.

I pretended to pout. 'I do, and so do you! This was fun, though.'

'Aye, definitely. You're my cup of tea, sweetheart. And once I got past that arse, we found out all about each other. We're practically best mates now, eh?'

I laughed too hard for it to be believable, realising that he hadn't asked me one question about myself this whole time. I stood up, and he joined me.

'Well, thanks for the latte.' I smiled, putting my hand out.

'Er . . . you're welcome, Bella.' He reluctantly shook my hand, as if confused by my formalities.

We both went to walk out together, but then I paused.

'Actually, I'm gonna nip to the bathroom first. I'll speak to you soon,' I said and cut in front of him, so I didn't have to spend more time than necessary in his company.

I entered the bathroom and stood at the sink, staring at my reflection for a few minutes. *Well, you're not missing out on the dating life, Ella*, I told myself.

Zola: *The coast is clear. I'm outside x*

I headed back through the café, noticing Katy standing up and politely hugging her date, then I stepped outside into the fresh air to meet Zola.

'Well . . . how was it? He was fit!' she said, impressed at my pick of suitors.

'It was awful. He was a complete narcissist, slagging off his ex and saying how she needed to lose weight! He was even making comments about my arse.'

'*Your* arse!' She seemed totally shocked at that.

'Yes, my arse!' I slapped her arm. 'I told you guys love my arse.'

'Wow, imagine if he saw mine!' She bent over and gave a little twerk, and we both burst out laughing. 'Oh, here she comes.'

Katy suddenly emerged from the coffee shop and started sprinting towards us like Usain Bolt gunning for gold. We linked arms with her and began walking away as quickly as we could so as not to get spotted by any of our dates.

'I was catfished!' Katy panted. 'Totally fucking catfished!' She brought out her phone, clicked on her Tinder app and began scrolling through pictures of Ali. 'I was one hundred per cent catfished, look!'

'No, Katy, you were hat-fished!' I started chuckling at my own smart-arse joke and pointed out every picture in which her date conveniently concealed his head or cropped its true size from the photographs.

'Yeah, you have been totally hat-fished, love! How the fuck is he fitting into those hats, though?' Zola grabbed her phone, examining the images, still in disbelief.

'Custom-made, I'm guessing! Maybe he was prescribed them on the NHS,' I added.

'I feel violated!' Katy cried. 'I had to sit there staring at his glossy, sweaty head. I was staring at him, taking it all in, when I realised . . . he's the real-life Humpty Dumpty!'

Zola and I burst out laughing. I felt tears stream from my eyes at my friend's bad dating luck.

'I thought I liked him, too,' she said more quietly.

I tutted in disapproval. 'I know you did. But this is work, Katy. It's our business venture, remember? There can be no feelings involved. Detach yourself, like I do!'

'Like I do.' Zola mimicked my voice. 'Yeah, OK, babe. There's no need to get *big-headed* about it!'

We both erupted into laughter again as Katy walked beside us, looking sombre.

'Oh, come on, babe, that was good!' Zola shoved her shoulder playfully.

'I thought he was my dream man, Zo,' Katy whimpered sadly.

'He's a sniper's dream man, more like!' Zola almost spat at her own joke as I wrapped my arm around Katy, trying to comfort her.

'Well, if it makes you feel any better, my date was an utter prick. I probably . . . *no*, I most definitely hate him.'

Chapter Six

Ella

We returned to the office and, between actual work and meetings, I managed to write up a full, in-depth review of my first date with Kevin. He was everything I hated in a man: utterly full of himself, basic-level flirty, and a fucking sex pest. I added my review to the Dicktionary Club and rated our date a measly one star. I watched Katy type angrily, slamming the keys as she reviewed her fuck-up of a date with Ali, carefully explaining how his physical appearance wasn't as his photos would lead you to believe.

'OK, the first two dates are now officially reviewed! And there are hundreds more to follow before we even get up and running!' I pushed my chair back, feeling overwhelmed as I finished off my day's work.

'Once we launch the website, though, the girls subscribing can upload their own reviews, too,' Zola added. 'Before we know it, a chain will happen.'

'In theory,' I replied.

'Come on.' Zola shoved me. 'We can do this! Look, if we start something here with enough subscribers, what's not to say we'll make enough to leave this shit hole? Start up Dicktionary Clubs all over the place?'

Katy's face suddenly turned from slapped arse to beaming with possibilities. 'Oh my!' She grinned. 'The Spanish Dicktionary Club?'

'Le Club Dicktionnaire Français!' I gasped, impressing myself with my language skills. 'Il Club del Dickzionario Italiano!'

'Jesus Christ, can you imagine? Mamma Mia!' Zola put on her best Italian accent and we laughed. 'But the point is, we need to stick in there.'

'It's all right for you, Zo; you're not getting ogled by narcissists on your lunchbreak!' I countered.

Zola tutted, shaking her head sarcastically. 'Yeah, God love you, Ella. It's such hard work being so attractive and getting taken out for nice meals. Fucking hell, girl!'

'Well, tonight I have a date with Harry.' Katy smiled. 'He looks stunning, plays rugby, and I've cross-matched his Instagram photos, so *I know* he looks like his dating pics, at least.'

Zola seemed impressed. 'This is what I'm talking about, yes! And what about you, Ella?'

I scrunched up my face. 'Seriously? Two in one day? I'm exhausted.'

'Get swiping! We need to launch this app at the end of the month at the latest. We are four hundred quid down here and I can't afford that out of my wage. That gives us like three weeks to get a *head* start!'

Even Katy giggled at Zola's head-themed joke this time.

'Me neither,' I admitted. 'Right, fine! I'll start swiping, but I'll arrange dates tomorrow night or something.

I'll try my hardest to get a few scheduled for the next week, but I really need to sort a venue for this art exhibition first, or Andrea's going to fire me and I'll have zero income.'

'Yeah, you do,' Katy agreed. 'I need to hit the gyms tomorrow, too, to get some feedback and snaps for the Blaze Boost campaign.'

'I can help with that,' I offered. 'If you can help me find a venue for this exhibition?'

Katy smiled. 'Deal!'

'And what about me?' Zola pursed her lips.

'You can arrange my dates?' I suggested. 'I'll give you my Tinder password.'

Her face lit up in delight.

'But no munters, please, Zo. I'm begging you!'

'Would I ever?' She let out an evil cackle, and I instantly regretted my proposal.

Chapter Seven

Katy

That evening, Katy headed to Bluedog in the city centre. It was a small, charming cocktail bar with live jazz. Her date, Harry, had suggested it, and she felt encouraged by its classy vibe. Katy wore her brown hair in a sleek ponytail, as she didn't have time to wash it after work, and she'd picked out a short, pale pink chiffon dress with matching heels. The city was relatively quiet as it was a weekday, the weather was clammy but dry, and despite her earlier disastrous date, Katy felt optimistic about meeting Harry.

Katy favoured the fact her date was arranged so quickly, giving her lots of topics of conversation still ahead of them for the night. In fact, she hadn't asked Harry much about himself at all. Still, from a casual stalk of his social media, combined with a snoop of his mother's, gran's and sister's too, she knew Harry fiercely supported Celtic, and had travelled Australia for a year with his ex, Tammy, before coming home alone. Tammy had remained in Oz, married an Australian and had been granted citizenship last year. *No worrying about bumping into the ex then*, Katy thought. She also learned that in 2005, Harry had met *his idol* Rod Stewart at Glasgow airport and liked to share the memory on his Facebook page every year.

Katy walked confidently into Bluedog and was greeted by the friendly staff.

'Hi, I'm just waiting on someone,' she said, glancing at her watch. It was 8 p.m.; she was right on time.

'There's a guy up the back. Could it be him?' one of the servers replied.

'I'll have a look, thanks,' she said, walking up several stairs to the booths at the back of the bar. The deeper Katy stepped into the bar, the darker it became, and it took a few seconds for her eyes to adjust.

A man was sitting studying the menu. He looked smart in a navy shirt and jeans.

'Harry?' Katy called out, walking towards the table.

The man glanced up from the menu, but she didn't recognise his face from his pictures. If this was another catfish, he was a lot fucking better-looking in real life, she thought.

'Sean.' He tilted his head to the side curiously, his Irish accent catching her off guard.

Katy blushed, cringing for herself.

'Shit. I'm sorry. I'm meeting someone and I thought you might be him,' she said. She turned back, squeezing her eyes shut in pure mortification at her blunder, as she headed towards the front of the bar.

'Ahhh, first date is it?' the stranger called out.

Katy felt as if her face was twisting even more as she swivelled to face him and nodded in reply.

'Well now.' Sean's gaze skimmed her up and down. 'He's a very fortunate man. Good luck!'

Her teeth glimmered at his approval, and she stared back for a few intense seconds.

'Thank you,' she replied eventually, then headed back to the front of the bar.

As she walked towards the front she spotted Harry hovering at the door. Katy waved briefly, and he walked straight up and hugged her.

'Hey, how are you? I wasn't sure if you were here already.'

Katy smiled, enjoying how warm he seemed. 'I'm good, thanks. Yeah, I toddled up the back in case you were up there.'

'Aghh, I see. Nope, just late as always!' he admitted, seeming a little nervous now. 'Will we take a seat? You look lovely, by the way.'

Katy glowed at the compliment. 'Thank you, yeah, sure.'

'There's an empty booth just here,' Harry suggested, 'or there might be some further back.'

Katy shook her head and pointed to a booth near the front door. 'Here is great!' As she sat down, her eyes crossed to Sean. Even through the darkness of the bar, she couldn't help but notice that he was grinning widely at her.

'So, what are we drinking, then?' Harry asked, opening the menu. 'This place is great. Have you been before?'

'Erm, I have, yeah. It's nice. The musicians are insane! I just hope they play a bit of Rod tonight.'

Harry's face dropped in surprise. 'Rod Stewart?'

Katy blushed, hoping her stalking skills weren't too obvious. 'Yeah, I mean what other Rod is there? I know he's old school, but I just . . .'

'Katy, I LOVE him!' Harry clapped his hands in excitement. 'He's like . . . he's my idol!'

Katy gasped as if she couldn't believe the chances. *I've got him eating out the palm of my hand already*, she thought.

'What's your favourite song of his then?' Harry asked.

Oh, shit, shit, shit, shit, shit, shit! In all her pre-date research about Harry, she hadn't thought to fire up big Rod on Spotify. Katy hummed as if she was thinking, but her mind was blank. *Surely to fuck I must know one, just one, of Rod Stewart's fucking songs? Did he sing 'Maggie May'? Or 'We Are the Champions'? Wait, was that Freddie? Fuck.*

'In fact, let's get a drink first, then you can tell me, eh?' Harry said.

Saved by the fucking bell. She puffed a slight sigh of relief.

'Sure, I think I'll have a Pornstar Martini.'

'Good choice! I'll have the same. I'll be back in a second.'

As Harry went to the bar, Katy quickly examined him. He was a little smaller than she'd hoped, probably around five feet eight inches. She had noticed his height was missing from his profile, so she wasn't overly surprised. But he was very handsome, with gorgeous blue eyes and short blond hair. He wore a plain white T-shirt with a checked jacket over the top and a pair of Nike trainers, looking casual but cute. As he ordered from the bar, Katy brought out her phone and quickly googled Rod Stewart songs.

A few minutes later, Harry returned with the cocktails and sat beside Katy.

'Thanks for this,' she said, sipping at the drink. 'And "Maggie May" *and* "I Don't Want to Talk About It" are my favourite Rod tunes.'

Harry looked warmly into her eyes. 'I've got a great feeling about you already, Katy.' He smiled. 'So, tell me, are you working tomorrow?'

'Yip, up bright and early! What about you? What do you do?'

He slurped at his own cocktail. 'Yeah, I was in Australia for a while there travelling . . .'

Katy pretended to be surprised. 'Wow, amazing!'

'Yeah, it was good fun, but I decided to come home and get a proper job, so I've started working with my old man. We fit new boilers, nothing interesting, but it pays well.' He shrugged. 'What about you? It says on your Instagram that you work for a marketing company. How is that?'

Katy giggled. 'Oh, did someone have a little stalk, Harry?' she teased, knowing full well that his passing glance wouldn't have been a patch on the deep dive background check she'd undertaken. 'But yeah, it's fine, I suppose. I'm promoting a new energy drink at a gym tomorrow. Every day is different, depending on the project, I guess.'

'In that case, I won't have you out too late, I promise.' He smiled, the look in his icy blue eyes instantly sending vibrations between her legs.

*

As the night continued, Katy and Harry seemed to get along just great. She disclosed her *love* for Celtic, having actually never been to a football match, or cared about any sport at all, but again, she knew it was exactly what he wanted to hear, and it prompted Harry to show her his multiple tattoos dedicated to his team. After their fifth drink, she decided it best to call it a night and reluctantly head back to her flat.

'I can walk you down to your place if you'd like?' Harry offered, as they stepped outside.

Katy found herself swaying, knowing the date had gone well and feeling the undeniable starvation, the longing to pump him, but also knowing that if she did, she would probably never see him again.

'Thanks, but it's probably best not to. I've had an excellent night, though,' she replied, consciously taming her vaginal urges.

'Me too.' He grinned, staring into her eyes for a few seconds.

'Well, see you, Harry.'

Katy lifted her hand to wave, and he pushed his fingers through hers, then pulled her to him. She was so close she could feel his fruity cocktail breath hit her face; he leaned in and kissed her hard. His mouth opened and Katy felt his soft tongue wrap around hers. She moaned slightly as his hands grazed over her waist and pulled her in even closer. She was aware of his groin skimming her dress, only a tiny piece of material keeping them apart.

A few seconds later, Katy pulled away, wiping her mouth and laughing. 'OK then! Wow.' She giggled, 'Goodnight, Harry.'

He laughed too, flustered. 'Best date ever, Katy!' he said. He walked a few steps, blew her a kiss, then crossed over the road.

Katy's mind was racing. *This is it*, she thought. *Dun, dun, da dun, could this be the man I marry?* He was cute, kind, funny and respectful. She jumped a little in excitement and started the walk back to her flat.

Her phone beeped.

Harry: *How good was that date? X*

Katy grinned widely and began typing. Then she noticed a car pull up at the side of the road. The window slowly lowered and she saw Sean, the stranger from the bar, smile towards her.

'I take it your date didn't go too well?' he asked.

Katy looked back, confused. 'What? Why? It went really well, actually.'

Sean's dark shaved head bopped, and he hummed back. 'Mmmmm?'

'Why did you think it didn't go well?' she asked, wondering if he had observed something she hadn't.

'You see, if it were me, I would never have let you go home alone.' His deep Irish accent combined with his overconfidence was making her heart pound. 'Especially in that dress.' Sean's dark eyes darted up and down her legs.

Katy felt chills travel up her spine. 'I mean, he did try, obviously, but I'm not like that,' she lied, knowing fine well she loved a shag on the first date as much as any man, but she was trying hard to follow her friends' advice.

'Not like what? Not into a bit of fun?' Sean's eyes stared straight into Katy's and he smirked slightly. She felt a wave of hotness flush over her skin.

'Not . . . *no* . . . not, like, not on the first date, anyway,' she stuttered. 'Should you be driving anyway?' She had to change the subject before she couldn't breathe entirely.

Sean laughed. 'I don't drink. I'm only in town for business.'

Katy turned to him, crossing over her arms, 'You were in a bar? Alone.'

'I enjoy the music!'

'OK.' She shrugged. 'Bye then.' And with that, she continued to walk.

'Wait, I have to know, why no sex on a first date? I'm curious.' Sean's dark eyes remained fixed on hers. There was an intensity to him, Katy had never quite felt before.

'Because!' She almost spat the words out. 'I'm a lady!' she added for good measure.

Sean laughed under his breath. 'You know,' he said as he bit his lip and shook his head a little, 'I don't buy it. Get home safe, kiddo.'

As he sped down West George Street in his grey Audi like Dick Dastardly, Katy was left speechless.

Who the fuck was that gorgeous, cheeky bastard of a stranger?

Chapter Eight

Ella

I had sent Zola my Tinder password and a copy of my calendar, hoping and praying she would be kind when scheduling my upcoming dates for the Dicktionary Club. I then headed to David Lloyd gym in the city's south side. It was a pretty average morning, with the sun intermittently escaping through the dark grey clouds. Still, being a true Glaswegian meant that even with the slightest hint of sun, I'd left my jacket at home and entered the gym wearing only my pale blue Gymshark leggings and matching crop top. I was meeting Katy to instigate a buzz around Blaze Boost, the new energy drink she was marketing. David Lloyd's had its own Blaze fitness class for high-intensity workouts, so it made sense to start marketing the product here, even if the match with the name of the drink was coincidental.

As I entered the gym, I spotted Katy waving me over from behind a table at reception. She had already set up mini cups and laid out cans of Blaze Boost for passersby to try.

'Ella, just come through,' she said excitedly, and I wondered how many cans of the product she had already swigged.

I approached the turnstile, where the receptionist scanned me through.

'Thanks.' I smiled as I approached my friend.

'Looks good, eh?' Katy said proudly.

I examined the table, turning some of the cans slightly to ensure they all faced the exact same direction. 'Yeah, it looks fab! Have you handed any out yet?' I asked.

'Yup!'

'And . . . ?' I gazed at Katy, who looked confused at my questioning.

'And . . . I've handed out samples.'

'Katy, you need to ask them for reactions so we can film it for the client's socials.'

'But most of them are hurrying past to get to a gym class or something,' she replied, quickly defending herself.

'OK. Watch this.' I grabbed a can of Blaze Boost and approached a group of girls striding through the reception in clouds of chatter. 'Hey, would you girls like to try out the best new organic energy drink on the market?'

They paused, hovering slightly.

'Come on, it's free!' I beamed.

'Can we try after class? We're running late,' one eventually answered for them all.

'Sure!' I replied cheerily. 'Have a great workout!' As soon as they were gone, I turned and headed back to a smug-looking Katy.

'Told ya!' she crowed. 'Maybe we could catch them on their way out?'

'Why would they want the energy drink *after* the workout? That's literally the full point of the product.' I budged her shoulder and knocked her off balance slightly. We both giggled. 'We just need to think of how they can't say no.'

'Oh my God! Don't look. Don't look, Ella!' Katy blushed hard, and I immediately turned to see what I shouldn't be looking at.

A tall, handsome man in a suit was striding into the gym. The girl at reception almost flew off her chair to scan him through the turnstile, yet he only acknowledged her with the slightest tilt of his head. Still she seemed to instantly cream her knicks.

'Excuse me. Excuse me, sir – would you like to try Blaze Boost, the best new energy drink on the market?' Katy slobbered the words so quickly that it took me a second to make sense of what she'd actually said.

'No. No, thank you,' he replied, his voice deep, dark and husky-ish. Although he spoke to Katy, his eyes remained fixed on me.

'It will take one second to try, sir. We are only looking for honest reviews,' I added.

A group of glamorous women passed us, whispering and giggling in his direction. He turned when he noticed the crowd and without another word, he lowered his head and walked towards the changing rooms. Katy finally exhaled when he was out of sight.

'Oh my God! Did you see him? Did you see the way he stared at you? Can you believe he stared at you like that?'

I nodded. 'I know, disgusting, right? Like I'm some piece of meat.'

'Piece of meat! Do you realise how lucky you are, Ella? Do you even know who that was?'

'The manager?' I shrugged back, having never seen the man before in my life.

'He's Philip Khan!' she almost screeched, and I noticed people glance over at her bubble of excitement. 'The owner of the biggest hotel and nightclub chain in the UK. He owns that posh place in Edinburgh, the one we went to at Christmas and we got chucked out because Zola snuck in a bottle of Glen's! Don't you remember?'

I burst out laughing at the memory of us all, half cut, getting thrown out on the streets of Edinburgh in the snow.

'And I heard the Beckhams spent the week partying with him on his yacht last year in Cannes. I didn't realise he trained here! Wait till I tell Zo. Mate, fucking Phil Khan, aaaaagh!' She brought out her phone and began typing.

I reached over and pulled it out of her hands. 'We still have our own CAN to FILL because that cunt wouldn't drink any of our product, Katy! We need to concentrate.'

'Ella, it's Philip Khan,' she persisted.

'Who cares, babe? He looks like another womanising prick if you ask me,' I snapped back, reminding myself of his dark eyes scanning my body.

'Oh, he is! He dated Miss Scotland for two years, but I heard he dumped her on her twenty-fifth birthday.' Katy's eyes expanded, like she would explode if she didn't get out everything she had on this man.

'Are you sure that wasn't Leo?' I asked, vaguely familiar with the famous actor's preference for younger women.

Katy tilted her head to one side. 'Hmmm . . . maybe actually. But he definitely dumped a girl on her birthday. Like a supermodel or influencer or something.'

I let out a sigh, unimpressed. 'Yep, just as I thought, he sounds like another prick.' I was beginning to feel deflated by the number of arseholes I'd encountered over the past few days of the Dicktionary Club being set in motion, and I'd still only been on the one real date.

But Katy was obsessing, craning her neck to see further into the gym. 'Where do you think he went?' she asked.

I rolled my eyes. We had all of the Blaze Boost to shift and not one piece of footage to share to socials. I knew how important it was to gather good content for the client and Andrea, or our boss would definitely kill both of us.

'Katy.' I popped my hands on my friend's shoulders. 'We need to focus on Blaze Boost right now, OK? If you pull it off, this will be big time,' I said, trying to ground her.

'Yeah . . . OK.'

I sighed. 'Thank you!'

'So, do you think he trains here or has a meeting in the coffee shop?' she asked, having retained nothing of what I'd just said.

'Yeah, he trains in his shirt and trousers,' I snapped. 'He's obviously in the changing rooms or . . .' I felt a smile appear on my face. 'Wait. That's it! Grab your phone. I'll take the cans.'

Katy looked confused as I crammed as many cans as possible into my arms and headed towards the David Lloyd changing rooms. I pushed open the women's door with my shoulder and Katy followed me inside.

Immediately, we saw a bunch of around ten girls crowded around one woman who was visibly upset. They were in their late twenties I'd say, and they all seemed to have had some work done, and I wasn't sure if it had made them look younger or older, but they were certainly all beautiful in their own glamorous way.

As soon as the door shut over behind us, the girl began sobbing loudly.

'Wow. Tough crowd already,' Katy whispered.

I bit my lip, trying not to laugh. Katy approached the group.

'Hey! We're so sorry to interrupt.'

The girls turned around to us, looking surprised.

'So, I'm Katy, and this is Ella, and we work for . . .'

Shuddering heaves were coming from the girl who was crying, and one of the other women had wrapped her arm around her.

'Oh. We're so sorry, this is obviously a bad time,' Katy said.

'It's . . . it's fine. What's up?' the upset girl managed between sniffles.

I glanced at Katy, who was swaying between full pitch mode or wanting to join in on bitch mode. 'Are you sure? Are you OK? Hey, what's happened?'

Bitch mode it was.

'I'm fine . . . honestly. I'm fine, angel.' But the girl had barely got the words out when she burst into tears again, holding her face in her impeccably manicured hands.

'Look, she's just going through something at the moment. An incredibly tough, emotional breakup,' one of the other women piped up in the poshest Glasgow uni accent I'd ever heard.

'Oh my God,' Katy puffed, her shoulders finally relaxing. 'I know how that feels, trust me.'

'She sure does,' I clarified.

'And the guy who broke her heart and basically is the LOHL just ignored her! We were planning on going to a spin class and he just stormed past her without saying a word!' one of the other girls added.

'LOHL?' I whispered to Katy.

'Love of her life,' she interpreted quietly.

'I just feel like such a fool!' The crying girl began sobbing loudly, comforted by the surrounding group of women.

Katy and I tutted in disgust.

'What a dick!' I said. 'Were you together long?'

She nodded through sobs. 'We only had two official dates, but they were incredible. You know that way when you meet someone, and you just know it's going to be forever?'

'YES!' Katy agreed instantly.

And there lies the problem, I thought.

'Then he walks past me like I'm a piece of shit on his shoe!'

'He was wearing Prada shoes. Did you notice that?' one of younger girls asked another.

'I've phoned and messaged him so many times, but he's totally ghosted me! I knew he was going on a work trip, and I even checked the flight scanner just in case his plane was hijacked or bombed or something. I was scared. I mean, I almost Facebooked his mother, for

God sake! It's like, you meet someone, have this instant connection, plan your entire life out in your mind with them, just so they can stroll right past you a week later like you're a complete stranger!'

An older woman, who must have been overhearing the conversation while towelling herself dry, shook her head in disgust. 'It's so triggering.'

'Awful,' another added. 'To be blanked like that. Traumatic, much?'

'Wow! Hey! Look, you girls need to stop,' I panted, feeling overwhelmed.

They turned to me, their eyes all wide in surprise.

'I know this man has hurt you. It's bad, and I'm so sorry you built this up in your head, but God, if he can just ghost you without an explanation, then aren't you glad to be rid of him? What would happen if you actually did something wrong? Trust me, you're better off finding out now what sort of person he is rather than a year down the line.'

'Ella!' Katy warned, giving me a sharp elbow to the ribs.

'No, I'm sorry, but men are dicks, end of. Especially this generation. Let's face it, they think we are so easily accessible and expendable. If they get bored or the chase is over, they can easily swipe right for the next poor girl!'

A silence fell on the group.

'OK, look, what's your name?' I asked the teary-eyed girl.

'Natasha,' she mumbled.

'Natasha, did you sleep with this man?' I asked.

She began to nod, and the wailing recommenced. 'We made *love*, yes!'

'OK, and did he instantly go cold afterwards?'

I watched the cogs slowly turn in her head, trying hard to admit the truth to herself. 'Well . . . *yes*. But honestly, the night was so romantic, beautiful and perfect. It was like a movie!' She paused momentarily. 'Well, I thought it was.' Natasha glanced up to me in a panic. 'What did I do wrong?'

I shook my head, put down the cans of Blaze Boost and squeezed my arse onto the bench beside her. 'You didn't do one thing wrong, OK? I bet he had the best night too! BUT after that, the chase was over for him. He got what he wanted and moved on to the next silly blonde!' I paused. 'No offence, girls,' I added, noticing the amount of peroxide hair surrounding me.

'So, what should we do? Never have sex again?' one of the girls asked, laughing at my pep talk.

'Not an acceptable option, right?' Katy said, then smirked towards me. 'So instead . . . you could get payback!'

I nodded at my friend, who had finally caught up with my idea. 'How would you girls like to work for us, getting revenge on ALL the men in Glasgow who have mistreated you, simply at the click of a button?' I asked, observing their curious faces.

When I saw that they were receptive, I went on with my pitch. 'We have created a club, exclusively for women who have been through similar experiences to Natasha and my friend Katy here.'

Katy held her hand up. 'Yip, I was fed up of constant heartbreak and getting abandoned to feel like it was all my fault. But my best friends reminded me that it wasn't actually me at all. It was the horrible dickhead men who are out there on dating apps.' She took a breath and continued, 'So, we have thought of the ultimate way to expose them! How would you girls like to be part of a community of women who leave honest and vital feed-back on the scumbags they've dated?'

'We,' I butted in, pointing to Katy, 'are currently trying to date as many men as possible to create the foundations of our database of pricks, but if we have a team of girls like you dating as many men as you can, the website will go live to subscribers even quicker!'

I looked around; these women were entranced! I knew they wanted to hear more, so on I went.

'So, if you start talking to a guy, for instance, and you think, *hmm, he seems nice, I might meet up with him*. Right? Rather than wonder how genuine he is from the get-go, you can cut all the crap and simply log in to the website and read previous reviews from women who have dated him in the past. You'll get a sneak peek on how he really treats us!'

'So, it's like a Trust Pilot for men?' one of the women asked.

'Precisely!' I smiled back.

'And you just need us to go on dates?' a smaller red-headed girl asked, raising her shoulders.

Katy smiled. 'Go on dates, have fun. We'll give you a list of questions, and you can submit them onto the webpage after the date.'

'Like, how good were his manners?' the posh girl piped up.

'Like a general review, yes. *Did he pay? How was his chat? Did he make his intentions clear? Was he a catfish?*' I smothered a laugh, reminding myself of Katy's big-headed beast date from yesterday.

'And, if things go well, how big his dick is!' Katy added. The girls burst out laughing.

'Help us give the women of Glasgow their power back in the dating world!' I said, feeling inspired. *This was the best off-the-cuff pitch I'd done in ages.*

'I'll do it,' one said.

'Me too,' another added.

'I will as well!'

'Natasha?' Katy held out her hand, and Natasha grabbed it.

'Sign me up! Yes!'

I wrapped my arm around Natasha and hugged her tightly.

'Wait. What is the website called?' she asked.

Katy caught my eye and we both smiled widely. 'The Dicktionary Club!' we cried in unison.

Over the next half-hour, we collected the girls' phone numbers and added them to a WhatsApp chat called *the Dicktionary Divas*. We also filled in Zola, who promised to create logins so they could start uploading reviews immediately. Then, not forgetting what we were there for, we filmed some great content for Katy's Blaze Boost campaign in the changing room.

As Katy and I headed out, I felt empowered and lifted up by the women we'd just met. They were just as excited at the prospect of the Dicktionary Club as us, and I started to think of the opportunities it could bring. Like, maybe we could create merchandise? Or a podcast channel? With mine and Katy's marketing background and Zola's tech genius skills, the possibilities were endless.

Katy was scrolling through her phone at the videos of our new friends with a giant infectious grin. Her brown hair was scraped back from her face with a little claw clip holding it together, and I was struck again by how she had the smallest, most delicate features. Sometimes she would moan about them and say she wanted her lips done, but I loved her mouth. She had perfectly defined little lips and straight, white teeth. Katy was beautiful in the most natural way.

'What do you think?' I asked her, heading back to reception.

'It's great! I think Andrea will be buzzing with this,' she said as she scrolled. 'But. Wait . . .' Katy paused and grabbed my arm.

'Oh, what? What now?' I moaned.

'It's all women! We need men!' She jolted her head towards the male changing rooms, and I laughed.

'No! No way! We'll get lifted,' I insisted.

'We need men, Ella. We can't look like we're advertising a drink for women only!'

'Why not? Yorkie did it, remember?' I cleared my throat and imitated the annoying advert that used to piss me off as a child: '*Yorkie – it's not for girls!*'

Katy stared, not amused. 'We really need to get a few men before we head back. Come on!'

Reluctantly, I agreed, knowing I had work for Alexander Cambi's exhibition to deal with when we got back to the office.

'OK, we'll head to the gym then, not the men's changing rooms, for fuck's sake! Come on.'

We turned and steered towards the gym. I had trained at this one before and was familiar with the layout of the machines. Immediately I walked towards the weights section, noticing a few men darting around the machines as Katy followed sheepishly behind.

'Are you pitching?' I said quietly.

'No,' she whispered back.

I swung around to face my friend. 'It's your pitch!'

'I have gym anxiety, Ella! It's a real thing.' It was true; Katy seemed incredibly uncomfortable all of a sudden.

'Fine!' I hissed back.

We walked a few more steps and then I spotted a ripped bodybuilder posing in the mirror for a selfie.

'Hey.' I smiled, intentionally flicking back my long blonde hair.

As he faced me, I watched his eyes light up. 'You OK, darling? Do you need a hand with a weight?'

I resisted an eye roll and shook my head, knowing I could probably outbench most of the men here. 'I don't, but we do need help. We're here promoting this energy drink for a client, and we need content of really buff guys drinking it for their socials. Would you mind trying it and saying how much you love it? We may get fired if you say no.' I innocently pouted out my bottom lip.

I could see he was lapping up the compliments. 'You needed a buff guy and came straight to me, eh?'

'Well, who else would even catch my eye in here?' I continued, turning my flirtation skills up a notch.

'Of course I'll help, sweetheart. Where do you want me?' he replied, flexing his biceps in the mirror, ensuring they were up for the challenge.

'Katy?'

'Yip, I'm on it.' She stepped forward. 'OK, so if you stand behind that big-looking device thing, maybe you can put the bar up, take a swig of the drink and say, "Blaze Boost. It's why I'm in this shape." Something like that! OK? Flex your arm or something.'

He seemed happy with her instructions. I stepped back to watch him stack up the weight on the bar before Katy began filming.

'Why haven't I seen you here before?' a voice said from behind me, and I turned to see Philip Khan wiping sweat from his handsome face with a crisp white towel. I immediately noticed his initials embroidered on the fabric of his towel and resisted a smirk.

'*Mmm* . . . because I tend to train elsewhere.' I turned my back on him and continued watching Katy film.

'Which gym do you train in?' he asked. *God, his voice is so deep*. I wondered if he had ever considered joining a choir.

I huffed slightly at his interruption, wanting to focus on my friend. 'Why?' I responded, keeping my eyes resolutely in front.

'I'm curious,' he said.

'I train at House of Fitness. Have you heard of it?'

'City centre, yes, I've heard of it,' he replied. 'What are the facilities like there?'

'*Sssshhh*,' Katy hushed, then immediately blushed, giving me major side eye when she noticed who I was speaking to.

I eventually turned my body around to face him. His eyes were so dark that it was hard to distinguish the pupil from the iris, and he had perfectly tanned skin. I wondered if it was from cruising with the Beckhams or hitting Sun Shack at the weekends.

'It's OK, I suppose. The women's changing rooms could do with a spruce up, but apart from that, it's decent. Now, anything else I can help you with? My yoga class timetable, perhaps?' I replied sharply, not wanting to entertain another man and his ego.

'Yoga, *mmmm* . . .' He raised a brow suggestively.

I began turning back to my friend, unimpressed and not wanting to hear a clichéd yoga flexibility joke when Philip grabbed hold of my arm.

'What is your name?'

I felt my jaw drop slightly at his boldness.

'My what?' I repeated, completely off guard.

'Your name,' he repeated again, not shying away from the question or the numerous men walking around us overhearing our conversation.

I could feel my heart beating in my chest. Why was I getting nervous?

'My name is Philip, for instance, and yours is . . .'

I didn't like giving out my name to strangers, especially not when there was no need to. I had no urge to ever see this arrogant, overconfident man ever again. I wondered why he wanted my name. To stalk me? Katy did say he had money; he could hire a private investigator no problem. *Shit*, he already knew where I trained. What was he planning?

My eyes suddenly caught on the glass wall behind him and the class full of stretched-out bodies, and I panicked. 'Pilates.'

'Pilates? Sorry,' he tittered. 'Your name is Pilates?' he repeated, with a proper snigger appearing on his lips.

I gulped down. Why the fuck did I not make up a normal, boring, bog-standard fucking name?

'Yip! Why? What's wrong with that?'

'I wonder what your mum was up to when you were being conceived, eh?'

'And I'm K—'

'Carol!' I interrupted Katy's introduction; her face twisted at the new name I had created.

'Lovely to meet you, Carol.' Philip shook Katy's hand. 'I see you are the bubbly one out of you and Pilates over here.'

Katy immediately giggled hard at his compliment.

'Mr Khan, would you like to try the new energy drink we're marketing today? It's a freebie.' She held out a can of the drink, and he finally accepted it.

'Thanks. I'll hold on to it for later,' he said. 'Well, it was nice meeting you girls, and if you fancy promoting this energy drink at the House of Fitness, then you're more than welcome to.'

'House of Fitness?' I repeated, utterly confused.

'Yes.' Philip took a few steps back, with a slight grin on his annoyingly handsome face. 'I kind of own the place. Phone reception and ask for Patricia. She'll arrange it for you.'

I felt my own face redden with utter cringe. 'Oh . . .'

'And Pilates?'

'Uh huh?'

'I'll be sure to sort out the women's changing facilities, too.' He laughed, shaking his head and walked off.

We watched Philip Khan disappear into the changing rooms, both of us standing in stunned silence. Eventually, Katy turned to me, slapping me gently on the arm.

'Pilates, *Carol*? What the fuck, Ella?' she whispered.

'I panicked, OK? I thought he was a stalker. He was very intense, asking me loads of questions. Who does that?'

'So, I get landed with my fucking great-gran's name, and you go all exotic with Pilates?' She huffed, indignant.

I burst out laughing and linked my arm through hers. 'Come on, Carol, let's get fucking out of here!'

Chapter Nine

Ella

When Katy and I stepped back into the office, Andrea had the rest of the team lined up for a catch-up meeting. As soon as we clocked the firing squad, our chatty giggles subsided and we wedged ourselves in beside Zola.

'Nice of you to finally join us, ladies.' Andrea darted us a sharp glance with her beady eyes, and I felt my insides curl. *Why does this woman make me so nervous?* 'Continue where you were, Catherine, please, prior to the interruption,' she added, just to make us even more uncomfortable. I knew I'd emailed her a copy of my morning schedule at the gym with Katy. Why was she pretending I went rogue? If she had an issue she could have replied and said she'd rather I stayed in the office.

Catherine, who worked on PR crisis control, continued, bright and bubbly as always. 'Yes, as I was saying – I managed to get them in most of the press doing some charity work, and I even got them trending on TikTok. So, the story of the unsolicited pictures he sent has been totally forgotten about!' Catherine smiled widely for a job well done. She seemed to be waiting for a *way to go!*, which I knew would never come from Andrea.

'Not forgotten by his wife,' Zola mumbled.

'Zola?' Andrea said, raising an eyebrow.

Zola didn't miss a beat. 'Yes, so, I created the three new websites sent over last week, linked all their social media accounts, and they've all received way more interactions already.'

Andrea nodded. 'And Katy?'

Katy immediately straightened next to me. 'Yes, today I was at David Lloyd's, and we handed out samples of Blaze Boost to fitness freaks or *erm* . . . gym goers. We also shot lots of content. I'll put it together today and pop a teaser on the Blaze Boost socials.'

'Uh-huh.' Andrea sighed. 'And finally, Ella? Who is looking very casual today, isn't she, everyone?'

I watched the line of my colleagues nodding back, agreeing with Andrea judgementally. *Jesus, last time I checked, there was no uniform policy here. Bastards. And what about Katy?* She was in bobbly leggings and a hoodie, yet a pristine matching combo gets called out.

'Yes, well, I helped out Katy this morning with her Blaze Boost campaign and—'

'Sorry. Sorry. I have to stop you there. I must have misheard you.' Andrea stepped closer to me. 'You . . . what?' She turned her right ear round to face me, but I wasn't sure if she genuinely wanted me to speak up or if it was another intimidation method she was practising.

'I helped Katy this—'

'You helped out?' Andrea interrupted again, sounding sterner this time. Her eyes were bulging and fixed on me now.

The room turned completely silent, and my legs felt like lead. *Say something*, I thought. *Apologise for helping or stick your ground.* I could make up a story of how Katy was struggling, but I didn't want to get her in trouble. *Shit, speak, speak!* But nothing. I said nothing. Instead, I opted to have a staring contest with my boss. I could almost feel the heat radiating off her face with the anger that was no doubt bubbling inside her.

Eventually she said, 'That was a question, Ella.'

'Erm . . . yeah, I helped out.' I tried to act confidently, but my hands were trembling. 'I emailed you a copy of my schedule,' I added.

'Wow. How kind of you. She is so kind, isn't she?'

Andrea motioned to my colleagues, and again, everyone agreed. I wondered how far these clones would actually back her up. The way they were going, if she asked them to take a shit in their mothers' mouths, they'd all probably drop their drawers and start squeezing. Besides, apart from Zola and Katy, I had never really socialised with any other of the Smart Reputations crew. I would of course help them on campaigns or with general work chat, but outside of the office they seemed a lot more reserved than our little group.

'Well, I take it your Alexander Cambi art exhibition is finalised? If you have all this time to help Katy, that is. We can't wait to hear where you're hosting it, can we?' She spoke in her usual dull, dragged-out way, then darted a glance at the others for a reaction.

'Can't wait!' and 'So exciting!' came from my colleagues.

Cunts! They all knew I still needed to secure a venue.

I could feel my palms sticky with sweat. Until now, I was usually on the ball with my work; I am organised, great at time management, and genuinely fantastic at marketing. I really thought I could pull off the coolest, most elaborate art exhibition Scotland had ever seen, but I had well and truly fucked up. No one seemed to care, not even the press. Not to mention all the fancier venues were completely out of budget and, realistically, even if I managed to secure a top-notch place, I had no idea who the target market would be. I'd promised Andrea I would be the right woman for this campaign as I fancied a new challenge in the office. All of my previous marketing experience was in the beauty or fashion division, and I really wanted to expand into various sectors. I'd pitched myself to Alexander when I heard he needed a Glasgow lead to handle his event north of the border, following one of our monthly zoom meetings we shared with the London office. Some posh twat from down there had pitched to him for the London exhibition and Alexander was a huge fan of his *exquisite* art knowledge, so much so that he had put his trust in Smart Reputations as a whole and I'd got the job. Although, ever since, I have seriously been missing the beauty industry.

'Well . . . is it finalised?' she repeated.

'I mean . . .' I paused, taking a breath for bravery. 'Not exactly . . .'

Andrea's sharp bob swung back around to face me. Fuck. Was I about to get sacked? In front of my friends and these people I'd worked with for years?

'Sorry? I don't quite understand.' She held her thick black designer glasses in her hand, the tip of one leg resting on her lip. 'But you were galivanting with Katy this morning, working on another project, yes? That wasn't your assigned project. Correct?'

I lowered my head. *Why the fuck did I say I'd help Katy when I knew how much work I still had to do?*

'Yes,' I responded quietly.

'But,' Katy interjected, 'Ella killed two birds with one stone – didn't you, Ella?' She was nodding her head towards me, encouraging me to join in. 'Ella only came along this morning because she had already arranged a meeting with Philip Khan at the same gym. She spoke to him about the exhibition, and he's really interested in hosting it in one of his hotels. Tell them, Ella.' Katy nudged me forward as I tried desperately to hide the look of confusion on my face.

'Yeah, uh-huh, he seemed pretty enthusiastic, I guess,' I added.

'Philip Khan?' Andrea sounded more positive, more inquisitive all of a sudden. 'And you met with him personally?'

'I sure did,' I said, forcing some energy into my voice.

'And? What was the outcome?'

'Well, I have to . . .' My mind was going blank. *Speak, Ella, fucking speak!!*

'She has to arrange a follow-up meeting, to get more in-depth details pinned down about the proposal. But he seemed *very* keen,' Katy lied through her teeth.

Andrea began pacing the floor again. 'I like the idea. We've never worked with Khan before; he normally has his own PR team.' She began speaking more quietly, almost as if to herself. 'But if we could get Philip on board with

94

this, then maybe he'll hire us in future.' Andrea snapped out of her demonic world-domination trance. 'Have the deal wrapped up by the end of the week. Alexander's team needs dates and times for tickets to be released. I'm fed up with that little Italian man filling my inbox.'

I smiled enthusiastically. 'Sure, I was planning on it.'

'OK, back to work, everyone.' Andrea began strutting back to her office but stopped, turning to me. 'And Ella?'

I felt my neck stiffen. 'Yeah?'

'Arrange the meeting with Philip here. I would love to meet him.' She smirked, then retreated.

I turned to Katy, feeling clammy.

'How do we fix this?' I hissed under my breath. 'Fix this!'

She looked as terrified as me, holding her hand to her mouth in shock. 'Honestly, I have no idea.'

I felt dizzy and agitated, like my life was spiralling. How had I gotten into this mess? I stumbled over to my seat and flopped down.

'Good work, Ella. You never told me you had a meeting today as well.' Zola looked up at me, impressed, as she sat at her desk.

'I fucking didn't,' I murmured.

'What?' She grunted, holding her hand to her face; I wasn't sure if she was genuinely shocked or hiding a nervous laugh.

'I'm sorry, Ella,' Katy said, looking really worried now. 'I had to do damage control. I was trying to save you from being sacked!'

'Wait, what?' Zola flung her hands up in the air, utterly confused.

I allowed Katy to divulge the entire story of my chance encounter with Scotland's biggest entrepreneur of the past ten fucking years, Mr Philip Khan. She started from the beginning and then explained everything from the new Dicktionary Club members to the content we captured in the gym to our brief discussion with Khan. Zola sank back in her chair, flabbergasted.

'OK, so . . .' Zola finally said after being stuck in thought for a few minutes. 'I think the only way out of this is to contact Philip Khan directly?'

I rolled my eyes. 'Yeah, he's only one of the busiest men in the country, apparently. I'll just call him now, eh? Oh, wait, I don't have a phone number!' I spat back.

Katy hummed. 'Wait, wait! What did he say again?' She sat up excitedly. 'The woman at House of Fitness, he said you should contact her. Can we start there?'

I threw my head back; my whole body felt pained with dread. 'Well, I suppose it's something,' I said, clicking on my computer and googling the number, then dialling the gym without really thinking what I was doing.

As the phone rang in my ear, I could feel the handset shake.

This was a long shot, and even I knew it.

'Hello, House of Fitness gym and spa, Patricia speaking,' a posh older woman's voice said on the other end of the line.

I cleared my throat. 'Oh! Good morning, Patricia. You're the very lady I was hoping to track down.'

'Ah, lovely. And how so, dear?'

'Well, the thing is, I just bumped into Mr Khan and he was telling me you were his right-hand woman,' I said with an awkward titter.

Katy scrunched up her face, knowing those words did not come out of that man's mouth, but I wasn't opposed to a bit of flattery considering my career was on the line.

'You see,' I went on, gathering my confidence, 'I was just discussing possible plans for my marketing firm with Philip and I have a few follow-up questions to ask. But I seem to have completely misplaced his business card. I don't suppose you could remind me of his personal number just now, and I'll give him a call?'

A polite chuckle followed. 'I'm sorry, miss. I couldn't possibly pass on that information.'

I sighed, noticing my two friends crowding around me to hear the call.

'I do realise it's unusual, but he does know me; I was speaking to him only an hour ago at David Lloyd's and . . .'

'I'm sorry. I could never share any private information, but if you leave your name and telephone number, I'll be sure to pass it on to Mr Khan when I see him.'

'And will that be soon?' I questioned, feeling a sudden wave of desperation.

'I'm not sure, he is a very busy gentleman, you see.'

I could feel my heart rate begin to pick up again. 'I totally understand that. But . . . eh . . . roughly, on average, if you had to give an estimate, how often do you see Mr Khan?'

A sigh echoed through the line. I could tell poor Patricia was losing patience. 'Mr Khan doesn't personally frequent the premises very often at all, miss. If I had to give an average it would be once a month.'

I felt my body slump on the chair in defeat.

'Now, what is your name?'

I glanced between my two friends and lowered my voice. 'It's Pilates.'

Grunts of muffled laughter came from either side of me, and I shooed them both away, covering the handset, urging them to be quiet.

'Pilates?' Patricia questioned delicately.

'Yip. He'll know who I am. And can I pass on my personal telephone number? He can call day or night, whichever suits him best.'

Patricia cleared her throat. 'Of course.'

I finished up the call as graciously as I could.

'I'm screwed,' I sighed as soon as I'd hung up. 'Totally fucking screwed!'

Chapter Ten

Zola

Later that night, Zola was sprawled out in bed, swiping through Ella's Tinder matches and having fun answering each of them back as sexily as she could as the messages poured in. She lay there chuckling, wholly fascinated with her phone, having never experienced the Tinder life first-hand before.

> **Angus:** *You don't often see girls like you on here, Bella! What's the catch??*

> **Bella:** *No catch, just new to the dating game, Angus. Wanna help?*

> **Angus:** *I can help a wee beauty like you out anytime, darlin. Name the place and time??*

Curtis, Zola's fiancé, strolled into the bedroom and smiled. 'And what are you up to?' he asked, his deep Cockney voice tapering off as he wandered around the room. 'Babe?' he repeated when Zola didn't immediately answer.

99

Zola peeked up from her phone. 'Huh? Sorry, babe. How was work?'

Curtis groaned, sounding exhausted. 'Same old! How was yours?' He paused watching Zola type and laugh, not listening to him at all as he jumped into bed beside her. 'Babe, what are you giggling at? Wait. Let me guess . . . TikTok?'

'No, actually! I'm messaging Ella's Tinder dates back for the website,' she said.

Curtis's brown eyes widened. 'Right now?'

Zola laughed. 'Yeah! You should hear some of this chat, babe. Do you wanna help me? I'm scheduling her dates for tomorrow. First, she has Ian in the afternoon. Then I'm deciding if she should meet Angus or,' she attempted a Spanish accent, '*Alvaro* at night.'

'And what are they like? Are they decent men?'

Zola grinned. 'Well, Ian is the director of an engineering company, he travels the world for business. He's had articles and everything written about his success, plus he's clearly got plenty of cash! Angus . . .' She paused. 'I'm still getting to know Angus but he is a PT who seems a bit of a flirt and Alvaro is a Spanish law student. Now, he reads poetry in his spare time and seems like he really has his head screwed on.'

'Well, I don't know, set her up with Ian and Alvaro then. Angus sounds like a dick.'

She laughed, still glaring at the screen. 'OK, OK!'

Curtis kneeled up in the bed. He was in his boxer shorts. His dark, muscular chest was ripped from the gym. He was watching Zola, waiting on her to pay him some attention.

'Zola, why are *you* messaging these boys right now? You know you have a man and he's home from a hard day's work.' He patted his chest in a check-me-out gesture.

Zola's eyes locked with his, and she grinned widely.

'Awww, babe! Come on, don't be jealous. This isn't for me. Ella's just far too uptight. She says she'll organise dates, but she doesn't really want to, so this way, I can tell her where to go and who to go with, and she can't say no.'

Curtis hissed under his breath, looking disappointed in Zola's continued focus on the Tinder app.

'I've told you all about this project, baby. It could change our lives, you know,' Zola insisted. She couldn't help but overthink what would happen for her finances if the Dicktionary Club took off. Since moving to Glasgow, she'd been the main breadwinner and felt pressure each month to hit targets and secure bonuses to help fund both of their lifestyles. They rented a small flat in Cowcaddens, just outside of the city, but she never felt happy there. She dreamed big and wanted more for herself and, up until now, she'd had no clear idea how she'd get there.

But Curtis shook his head. 'I just don't like you sitting in the bedroom messaging other men, giggling like a naughty schoolgirl at some cheesy chat-up lines. I'm right here, you know.'

Zola stared back at Curtis, acknowledging his worries. They had been together since their early twenties, having come from the same East London neighbourhood. When Zola was offered the job at Smart Reputations, she accepted without giving it a second thought, and

Curtis had proposed the very next day, moving up here, too. At the time, Curtis was studying business at a university in London but he'd dropped out of the course to relocate with Zola. He did initially apply to universities in Glasgow, and was even accepted onto a course, but ultimately, he decided to work as a part-time carer in the community instead. He found he had a real aptitude for the role, and he enjoyed the shift pattern, meaning he had more days off throughout the week to himself. Their relationship seemed to work as Zola was direct, career focused and driven, while Curtis was more laidback and enjoyed being there for Zola, supporting all of her decisions.

Zola eventually plopped her phone down on the mattress and kneeled up beside him. 'I know I have a man, but this is just business, baby.'

He simply huffed in response, so she placed her hands on each of his shoulders, then began gently running her long fingernails down his arms.

'I don't like the idea of my girl talking to other men,' he said more delicately, appreciating her hands' soft touch.

'But you know I'm all yours.' She leaned forward, whispering into his ear. 'Don't you?' Zola's fingers continued to travel down Curtis's abdomen. She felt the goosebumps prickle on his skin as she trekked towards his boxers. She wrapped her hand around the bulge of his dick, which was brick hard from her contact, and smiled. 'I think it might turn you on, you know.'

He pressed his forehead against hers. 'What turns me on?' he questioned.

Zola pulled the elastic on his boxer shorts and pushed her hand inside, tugging gently up and down on his foreskin. 'I think you secretly like the idea of me chatting to other men,' she whispered. 'Of knowing how much they want me . . .' She stared into his dark brown eyes.

Curtis let out a slight moan, goosebumps travelling down his spine.

'You like that they can't have me, don't you?' Zola ran her tongue round his earlobe.

'I'm not sure,' he replied, panting while biting on his lip as she expertly wanked him off.

'I think you like how these men want to fuck me?'

'But they can't,' he sighed.

'*Mmmm* . . . they can't, because I'm all yours, baby,' she whispered softly.

Zola pulled her hand out of his boxers and shuffled to the end of the bed, then stood up to face Curtis. She began dragging her pyjama shorts down slowly, feeling unbelievably sexy and desired as Curtis gazed back at the private strip show. She lifted her top over her head, then lowered her thong and slipped it off, watching Curtis stroke the length of his dick while he observed her every move. Naked, Zola lay back on the bed, still holding his gaze.

'Fuck me and show me why I'm only yours then,' she said. With complete confidence, she opened her legs wide, licked her finger and began rubbing her clit. Curtis watched intently, a fire now blazing behind his eyes.

'Jesus, fucking Christ, Zo,' he moaned. She felt herself glisten as she watched his thick dick come closer, already shiny at the top. Then, with one hard thrust, she felt full as he plunged deep inside her.

Chapter Eleven

Ella

I spent the evening trawling through the businesses owned by Philip Khan while tucking into my HelloFresh ready-prepped meal of salmon and asparagus. The registered establishments of this man were unreal, from high-end restaurants in Dubai, London and Manchester to hotels in Scotland, Barcelona and Madrid. My mind kept reverting to our encounter and how blunt I had been – when he asked me where I trained and I replied simply: *why?* Or when he asked my name and I couldn't even give him a convincing fake. *Fuck, why would this man help me after my rude behaviour?* And what if I'd completely fucked the last chance I had at pulling off this art exhibition event? I could feel the tension and worry knotting itself throughout my body. Panicky flashbacks of both Philip and Andrea filled my mind.

In a flurry of desperation, I began googling advertising jobs in Glasgow to see what was up for grabs if everything came crashing down. *Social media manager wanted, 12–15 hours per week.* Great. One part-time post in this entire city. Even then, it didn't pay the way Smart Reputations did, and quite honestly, I didn't want to leave. Yes,

Andrea was a complete bitch, but I had worked my way up in the company, and my best friends worked there too. I couldn't imagine not seeing Katy and Zola every day. Truthfully, they were the only friends I had right now.

When I was with Joshua, he was my world, as slowly but surely all of my teenage college friends dwindled. I couldn't lose Zola or Katy; despite him, they were the only people on the planet I really connected with. I sighed anxiously, thinking of all the possible scenarios in which Andrea would fire me. *Maybe quietly in her office? Not her style*, I thought, knowing how much she loved to stamp down her authority in public so as to prove a point. It would be at my desk or during a pitch, the better to humiliate me in front of everyone else.

I felt my stomach twist and took out my phone to FaceTime Zola and Katy, but there was no answer.

Katy: *I can't talk! At the pics with Harry! He's so bloody cute, man xxx*

I rolled my eyes – so much for not getting attached. Then I shook off the thought. *Concentrate, Ella. Come on. You can do this. You can pull this off.* I searched for Philip on social media but with no luck – *who doesn't have socials these days?* I wondered. Then, I headed to LinkedIn. Bingo.

Philip John Khan.
Entrepreneur.
Director of Khan International Health & Wellbeing
   Group.
Greater Glasgow and Clyde.

I began sliding through his posts, from him in a tuxedo winning some fancy award, to him cutting the ribbon at various swanky charity events. I couldn't help but notice a different woman in each picture standing decoratively beside him. This man clearly got around. I continued scrolling. Jesus, he'd even switched on the Christmas lights at George Square one year! *Where were Cassi and George when we needed them?* I was on a deep, dark delve into his company list, but he hadn't posted recently. Fuck it. I opened a new message and began typing, then stopped. *Shit, I'd have to change my name.* I clicked back on my bare minimum profile, which only stated my stint at university and my current position at Smart Reputations, then edited my name to Pilates. Phew – it let me do it. But really. Cringe! Then I hopped back onto his page and began typing.

> *Dear Mr Khan,*
> *It was great to meet you earlier in the gym! Would you be able to contact me regarding a business proposal? (Time is unfortunately of the essence and, if possible, I would love to catch up with you asap.)*
> *Kind regards,*
> *Pilates.*

Send.

I paused a few moments, glowering at the screen. *Please answer, fucking answer.*

Nothing.

Great.

He's probably spending the night sipping champagne in a suite in Edinburgh, while I'll be enjoying the stench of my asparagus piss for the next twenty-four hours.

I lifted my plate and carried it through to the kitchen, scraped the leftovers into the bin, then washed up. My phone pinged from the sofa and I leaped over – *one new email from Groupon*. I dragged my feet back to the kitchen, wiped down my already immaculate worktops and finally headed through to the bedroom. After brushing my teeth, flossing and hanging tomorrow's outfit neatly on a hanger, I crawled into bed. What a fuck-up of a day! My phone lit up the room, making me jump. I could feel my heart beating loudly in my chest. *Please, please, please!*

> **Zola:** *Sorry missed your call! I got you a date tomorrow afternoon and tomorrow evening, haha! No buts, gal! See you in the morning! Xx*

My stomach sank. Dating anyone, especially when my job was on the line, was the last thing I wanted to do.

Chapter Twelve

Ella

I arrived at the office the next morning to find Katy slumped over her desk, doing her best to disguise the fact she was texting, while Zola sat beside her, gabbing away, totally oblivious that Katy wasn't listening to a word she was saying. I sat down at my desk and began going through my emails. I noticed a notification almost immediately from Banca Di Roma, a popular, trendy restaurant in Glasgow. I had contacted them about a function room to host the art show.

> Hi Ella,
> We'd love to help, but unfortunately, the dates requested are already booked for other functions.
> If there is anything else we can do, please let us know!
> Carlo.

I sank into my chair. Great start to the day.

'How was your night, Ella? Did you get any further with the art exhibition?' Zola asked.

I shook my head, took out my Tupperware box of raspberries and granola, and placed it on my desk.

'Babe, why did you bring food? I've set you up, remember?' Zola scooted her chair closer to me.

'Zo, I'm honestly not in the mood. I need to sort this mess. The Dicktionary Club will have to wait,' I said, feeling exhausted from an entire night of tossing and turning, fretting about my job.

'You can't be serious, Ella. This could be our way out. We could absolutely get our own thing started. I know you're stressed, babe, but you're . . .' She thought about her next statement, huffed, then said it anyway. 'I'm sorry, but you are overthinking it all. I know you like to be organised, right? And you have taken a bit of a risk with this exhibition, and *yes*, it's taking a little longer for you to smash than normal, but you will. You always do, babe!' She grinned at me, and I attempted a smile back, but it was fleeting. 'This website on the other hand is going to be huge. I honestly have butterflies whenever I think about it! Have you seen the update since the girls you recruited at the gym started reviewing guys? They have uploaded loads more dates already. Those bitches are smashing it.'

I turned my head in surprise, having muted the WhatsApp chat from the recruits almost immediately after it was created to stop the constant notifications.

'I haven't seen anything,' I said.

Zola flicked back her braids and leaned over my desktop to log onto the Dicktionary Club. 'So, I sent them over a questionnaire, things they had to answer on each date. Important questions. I've changed it around a little just to ensure every profile on each guy looks the same, and of course they can add anything else on the review tab down at the bottom. Look, they've reviewed all their old dates too!'

I gazed at the screen, watching as Zola clicked through some of the dates that had been uploaded.

'Check this one.' She laughed, clicking on a guy called Sam's profile.

My eyes skimmed the mandatory questionnaire.

The date: *Ice skating, then Nando's East Kilbride (his idea).*

Initial attraction: *Sam was handsome, very similar to his profile pictures. Although not as ripped as his holiday ones suggest.*

Manners: *Friendly and bubbly. Excellent manners, but insisted on splitting the bill – even for hiring skates.*

I felt my face twist, knowing my friends would offer different opinions on the matter, but I always thought that if a man asked you out, he should pay the first date.

What he is looking for: *He says he is looking for a relationship and probably is.*

Red flags: *Very attention-seeking, loud. He seemed to know EVERYONE at the ice rink.*

Green flags: *Good communication. We arranged a second date while on the first.*

Penis size: *3/5 stars. It has a decent length but is thin.*

'Ooooh.' I winced.

'Yeah, no one loves a cheese string, babe.' Zola shook her head.

Review: *Sam was friendly but very over-the-top, showing off. He liked to brag, especially about his dance, skating and physical abilities. I know dating is about putting yourself out there, but Sam was off the charts – I had to persuade him NOT to show me a backflip when leaving the shopping centre. I hadn't ice skated since I was a kid, and warned him I may need help on the rink. But within a few seconds, he was off speeding around the rink like Torvill and Dean, pirouetting and performing tricks. At one point, spectators were clapping, YES, CLAPPING! Like he was some circus act that had come to EK. I half expected an autograph line when we were leaving. Oh, and while this was going on, I was left pushing a penguin created to help 'less experienced skaters' . . . basically kids! My back was broken, my legs were like jelly, and my arse was soaked from many, many falls. He was friendly, though, Nando's was enjoyable, and he opened up about what he'd like in a relationship. I did see him again, and we had pretty standard sex. Overall, not for me. He was a bit too much but was genuine. I think you'd get along nicely if you're really outgoing and are into extreme sports.*

I was laughing hard at the girl from the gym's chaotic date.

'He doesn't seem too bad, like not a player just . . .'

'Just a fucking show-off,' Zola said, 'and no one likes a show-off. So, the questionnaire is easier, yeah? You could go on your dates today and easily fill that out afterwards.' Her bright smile spread and, I admit, it was infectious.

'Who is it with, and where? Tell me it's not fucking ice skating!'

She shook her head. 'No, no. So, lunch is with Ian. You can even meet up for a drink if you don't fancy eating. He is a little older . . .' She lowered her voice and covered her mouth as if she was telling me a classified secret. 'And he is a bit of a DILF if you ask me! He'll meet you at The Social at one.'

I huffed at the thought, although The Social was only around the corner from the office. 'And tonight?'

Zola petted out her bottom lip. 'Tonight is with Alvaro, and he is my favourite out of everyone. He's so adorable, Spanish, and he's studying law. Now this man is a complete sweetheart!'

'And where am I meeting him?' I asked, knowing I'd make my own mind up about his sweetheart qualities.

'Drinks at Ashton Lane, so not too far for you.' Zola turned her head towards Katy, who was still wholly engrossed in her phone. 'Katy, who are you meeting with tonight? Any dates?'

Katy turned, a little flushed. '*Erm* . . . well, I think I'm going to see Harry again.'

Zola tutted. 'Again! We need a one-page review, Katy, not a fucking PhD dissertation on the man.'

Katy giggled and put her phone on her desk. 'Guys.' She paused dramatically. 'I think I might be falling for him.'

Zola and I glanced at one another, then back to Katy, who was beaming.

'Katy . . .' I began.

'Babe, you're not,' Zola interrupted, cutting to the chase. 'You can't fall in love, Katy. This is work! And you've known the man a matter of days.'

I couldn't help but smile at Katy's naivety around men. 'Katy, we literally started this entire website for you to get your own back on these kinds of men. To raise awareness.'

'And if I fall in love in between, Ella? What a bloody story for the grandkids!' I could tell her mind was floating around the clouds like some love-struck teenager again.

'Please tell me you haven't told him this?' I asked, knowing how this would end for her.

'Well, no. Not yet. But I'm out of the Dicktionary Club when it comes to dating. I'd feel bad. We haven't spoken about seeing other people, but I feel committed. He's the one, guys. I can feel it. He's funny, kind, has a good job, he's well-travelled . . .'

'You've only met him – what? – a couple of times, Katy,' I said softly. I wasn't trying to burst her bubble completely, but I wanted her to be more cautious, knowing how many times we'd been in this situation before.

'When you know, you know, Ella!' she snapped back. 'Besides, the recruits from the gym are uploading like mad. I just checked and we have over forty reviews handed in overnight already. Like Zola said, they must be filling out old dates and things.'

'Forty reviews.' I could see Zola's breathing change, like she was trying her hardest not to go completely tonto. 'Katy, do you know how many people live in Glasgow?'

I could feel the tension rise between my friends.

Katy shrugged, looking unbothered. 'Like twenty, thirty thousand?'

'Try seven hundred thousand, and that's in Glasgow alone! A high proportion of that seven *hundred* thousand, in relationships or not, use Tinder or other dating apps! We have SO many more men to review before we launch this site to users and expect them to pay.'

Katy lowered her head. 'Look, I know. I'm sorry. I really am. I just haven't felt like this for a long time.'

I bit my lip, trying not to giggle, knowing how often she fell in and out of love.

'Look, it's fine. Katy, date Harry. I have a couple of dates today, so we'll see how they go,' I said diplomatically, trying to ease the tension at our station. I turned to Zola, who was still visibly fuming. 'As Katy said, the girls from the gym are uploading dates continuously now too. We can still do this! And, Katy, you should also upload all your previous dates from before Harry. That way, the content will still be building.'

'Yeah, yeah, no problem. I can do that,' Katy replied happily, picking up her phone and returning to the screen with a smile.

Zola gestured to Katy. 'And we've lost her again.'

*

Despite the awkward start, the rest of the morning went well, and for the first time I received a few interesting emails from the press requesting more information about Alexander Cambi coming to Scotland. But I couldn't get back to them until I'd secured a venue. I had no new leads, and I still hadn't heard back from Philip Khan. It was looking more and more likely that I'd be packing a shitty bowling club in Possil full of my friends and family posing as art collectors.

Before I finished up for lunch and my first date of the day, Zola showed me a picture of Ian. He looked in his mid-forties, tall with salt-and-pepper hair and a nicely trimmed beard. He was certainly attractive in his photographs, but I wondered why a successful man in his forties had yet to settle down. Or maybe this was his second rodeo after a divorce? Then again, I was about to find out. I wasn't sure whether it was his suggestion or Zola's to meet at The Social, but it did seem a little bit of a younger vibe for a well-to-do businessman. However, I liked it, and with its excellent city centre location and fruity cocktails, I was looking forward to getting the questionnaire filled out and reporting back to the Dicktionary Club.

As I entered the bar, I was approached by a server, who smiled at me.

'Let me guess, Bella?' she said, arching a gorgeously sculpted brow.

I had almost forgotten my profile's fake name till she reminded me, and I nodded back gratefully.

'There is a man waiting for you in the second booth to the left. Would you like a menu?'

'No thanks, it's just a quick drink,' I replied, walking towards the table.

I suddenly felt nervous. With everything happening in the office, I hadn't had much time to overthink and feel apprehensive about another date, but now my stomach twisted.

'Bella!' Ian said, standing up to greet me. OK, nice, I thought. Ian was dressed in a crew-neck jumper and jeans, looking smart but casual. He did look older but was in good shape, with a perfect smile.

'Hey, Ian. Nice to meet you,' I replied, sticking my hand out for a more formal welcome.

'Please, take a seat. What would you like to drink?' He had an accent, definitely from the East Coast, Edinburgh most likely.

I suddenly wondered how much Zola had told him about me and if it would be evident that I was repeating myself by asking questions she could've already covered through the Tinder messages. *Damn*, I should've at least glanced at them. Rookie error.

'You look like you need a cocktail.' He smiled, suavely. 'Shall I order for you? See how well I know you?' he added.

I already felt slightly overwhelmed by his over-familiarity. 'Erm . . . No, thank you. A Cosmo would be great, though. I can't stay long, you see. I have to get back to the office.'

'Spoilsport.' He flashed his teeth at me jokingly. Yeah, they were too perfect, I thought, definitely Turkey specials. Then Ian flagged down a waiter. 'Excuse me, could we order some drinks?'

The waiter took out his pad. 'Sure, what can I get you?'

'Cosmopolitan for the lovely lady and a vodka martini for me,' he replied.

'Shaken not stirred?' I joked, and he arched his brow. 'Precisely!'

'So,' I began. 'Let's get straight to it, eh? What are you looking for when it comes to dating?'

Ian smiled once again, this time looking taken aback. 'For a good-looking lady at my side, I guess. To do fun things with, get up to a little mischief along the way, you know how it is.' He leaned back casually.

God, not another shagaholic!

'And what about yourself?'

'I suppose to meet a best friend,' I replied, know-ing that was exactly the kind of sentimental shit most women would say. Well, what Katy would say, anyway.

He darted his head upwards, only just acknowledg-ing my cute statement. I wondered if he was expecting a sexier reply.

'And would you say you have anything I need to know about?' I asked him. 'You know, like, red flags?'

Our drinks arrived, but as the waiter placed them down, Ian whispered, 'I'll have another, mate.'

Wow, was I that bad? I thought. *It's early afternoon!*

He turned back to me. '*Hmmm* . . . sorry, red flags. Very woke! What age are you again?' He burst out laughing. 'I'm sorry, Bella, couldn't resist.'

I screwed my face into a smile.

'I suppose some women's red flags will be others' green flags,' Ian admitted, gulping his martini more quickly than was perhaps wise. 'This feels like a job interview, by the way. You seem different in person.'

I blushed. *Yep, because you were chatting with my best friend, Ian.*

'I'm sorry. I just don't like beating around the bush. We're both adults,' I said. 'And my job is pretty intense; I'm sure yours is too. So, I like to be clear I'm not wasting my time from the beginning, you know?'

'Yes, of course. I like it. It's very refreshing for a woman to be so direct,' he said, and a strange fleeting sense of happiness seemed to radiate from him. 'Tell me about you, Bella. When was your last date?'

'*Me* . . . OK.' I sipped at my Cosmopolitan, taking a breath. 'I had a date a few days ago, but it didn't go to plan.'

'Ohh.' Ian leaned forward onto the table, crossing over his arms. 'Tell me more! What happened?'

I sighed, not knowing how vague to keep it. 'Well . . . The guy was being pretty . . . sexual, and it was all too much for me. Especially on a first date.'

Ian sat back in his chair and rubbed his chin. 'Oh, I'm sorry to hear that.' He seemed lost in thought for a few seconds. 'But, what made him *overly* sexual? If you don't mind me asking.'

I thought back to my previous date and the continuous comments about my arse and meeting up at his place. 'I suppose he just hinted about sex a lot and commented on my body too.' I took another sip of my drink, then continued. 'I didn't feel comfortable because I hardly knew him, that sort of thing.'

'Yes, that's understandable, to a certain degree.' Ian downed the rest of his martini, just as the next one arrived. I had barely touched mine.

'To a certain degree?' I questioned his wording.

'Well, I suppose it's good to know how sexual someone is at the initial stages, isn't it?'

I didn't know what to respond. I tilted my head slightly, waiting on an explanation.

'Everyone has different sexual expectations, Bella. People are into various things nowadays. They have different views or preferences, fantasies or arousals. It makes sense to know what each person is into from the get-go, yes? Well, I think so anyway. As you said before, you like to be direct and speaking about these things ensures you aren't wasting any time.'

'I guess romance isn't dead, eh?' I lifted my drink, trying to comprehend his point. *But surely dating isn't all about sex?*

Ian laughed. 'Do you disagree? I wouldn't normally talk so openly about this on the first date, by the way.'

I nodded, still trying to understand if I was the one who'd instigated this entire topic of sex. Or if we were merely participating in a healthy debate.

'OK, Bella, here it is. I personally have an extremely high sex drive, and when I say high, I mean off the freaking charts.' He sat back proudly, took another hefty sip of his martini. 'For instance, on a normal day, I ejaculate around seven times.'

Suddenly, my Cosmo went down the wrong way, and I began coughing uncontrollably, the alcohol burning my nostrils and throat.

But Ian continued, unfazed. 'I just couldn't settle down with someone who was, you know, vanilla in the bedroom. I need a partner to satisfy my sex drive. I'd expect a fulfilling relationship to be sex on tap, if that makes sense.'

And I'd expect your partner to need a new fanny by the second week of knowing you, Ian, I thought. I was still flabbergasted. Completely speechless, bar the odd cough which was luckily subsiding. God, I hadn't had sex in three years, and this cunt came seven times a day.

Eventually, I managed to speak. 'Wow.'

He smirked, looking pleased with himself as if he had impressed me with his ejaculation prowess.

'Can I ask why you . . . do *it* so often?' To be honest, I was wondering if that amount of chugging would be classed as an addiction.

Ian's eyes darted briefly to the ceiling as he pondered the question. 'I like to think that it's ultimately the key to success! Have you heard of post-nut clarity?'

'Huh?'

'Post-nut clarity! If you have a problem you can't solve, I can promise you, it will be a much easier fix after an orgasm.' He raised his brows suggestively and I wondered if a cum alarm clock was about to go off to indicate it was time for him to excuse himself for a wank break. 'What do you like in the sack, Bella?'

'I'm sorry?' I replied, snapping out of my astonishment.

'You heard.' Ian winked. 'Be open with me. Come on, miss, straight to the point! What turns you on in the bedroom? What's your kink, your favourite position, what does it for you?'

I was suddenly very aware I was sitting in The Social in the middle of the afternoon getting grilled about my sex life by a complete stranger.

'I er . . . I don't know,' I stuttered, feeling my neck turn red and blotchy with nerves.

'C'mon, everyone knows what position hits the spot.' Ian's hips gyrated, causing the table to tilt off balance, and I steadied my glass from toppling at his alarmingly vigorous hip thrust. I started to wonder how many martinis he'd downed before the date.

'I honestly don't know. I've never thought about it,' I replied, not even remembering the last time my spot was hit.

'Me, for instance. I'm into,' he came closer and whispered, 'Shibari ropes.' There was a glint in his eyes, like he was excited to be speaking so openly about his kink in public in the middle of the day. 'Do you know what that is?' He swigged his drink confidently, looking at me like I was a young virgin and he was the Jedi of the Kama Sutra.

'Well, no. Not particularly. But I could make a pretty good guess from the rope part,' I said, unimpressed.

'I was introduced to the practice when I was around your age in fact, and I've never looked back. You should look it up; it's a lot of fun.' He raised an eyebrow suggestively.

Aye, I bet it is for you, *ya twisted cunt.*

'Well, I honestly don't think I'd be into that, Ian. And frankly, this conversation is all a bit much for me. I don't like speaking about things like this on a first date.'

Ian raised one shoulder casually, then signalled to the waiter for another drink.

'Another one?' I laughed, making sure he knew I was judging him at this point.

'I need it, trust me.' A droning sigh filled the space between us. 'You know, I had high hopes for you, Bella. But you're pretty uptight, aren't you? Come on, babe, loosen up.' Ian shimmied his shoulders as if he was doing the twist at the table.

My jaw dropped. *Was this man serious?!* 'Uptight?' I repeated.

'Look, I hope I don't come across as rude but . . .'

You hope! God, my blood was boiling. Aye, if I wanted to spend my afternoon listening to an arsehole, I'd have just farted. I had to get away from this man and his kinky fucking *ropes*.

'No, not rude, Ian,' I interrupted, 'but this chat simply proves we want different things.'

He nodded. 'I'll say! We certainly do.' He giggled, clearly more than tipsy. 'Another drink, though? One for the road?'

'You know, Ian, I'd better not.' I held his gaze now. 'I don't want to take up too much of your day. After all, I know you've got those seven wanks to get ticked off,' I replied sternly, opening my purse and placing a tenner on the table. 'That's for my Cosmo.' I stood up out of the booth.

To my surprise, Ian laughed not unpleasantly, semi-agreeing with me. 'Great to meet you, Bella. And hey, good luck finding someone a little less adventurous. I truly believe there is someone out there for all of us – we just have to find them!'

I attempted a smile, struggling to hide how insulted I was at his condescending tone. At least I knew from one quick date the real reason this forty-something man had never settled: because the only fanny that could take the amount of pounding that he *expected* in a *fulfilling* relationship was a blow-up doll.

'See you, Ian,' I said.

And I left The Social, strolling back to the office with my Google search now full of Shibari.

Chapter Thirteen

Ella

Zola and Katy were sat munching Pot Noodles when I returned to the office, jumping up excitedly when they saw me. I shook my head and returned to my workstation, pulling off my classic-style trench and hanging it over my seat.

'Well . . .' Katy asked.

'That was quick,' Zola added.

'That was a fucking disaster!' I said and turned to her. She simply rolled her eyes back in despair at me.

'I don't think you'll ever write a good review, you know that? You're too much of a man-hater!' Zola tutted, shoving another forkful of noodles into her mouth. 'We can't fill this website with nothing but negative guys – we do need some good ones too. We need women to have hope!'

'Oh, yeah, well I'm sorry, Zo. I suppose I'll look past the fact the man *you* set me up with casually likes to announce that he cums seven times a day!'

My friends' faces dropped in shock. A second later, they burst out laughing, noodle juice flying down Zola's chin.

'And he is into Shibari, which Google tells me is Japanese rope bondage to restrain your partner. Sexy times!'

I glared at Zola, who held her hands up in defence.

'I swear to God, he never mentioned that on his profile.' She paused, taking it all in. 'But seven times a day, seven days a week? Ouch!'

Katy scoffed. 'I've managed eight before, and it gave me the worst cystitis of my life. I couldn't pee for like a week!'

I giggled at Katy's face, grimacing at the memory.

'It's unrealistic – how would you have time to do anything else? Seven times a day every single day,' I said. I couldn't take it in. When you factor in sleep too, he must bang one out every couple of hours.

'His dick must be throbbing!' Zola shook her head in disgust. 'Although . . . I can't wait to see his review. Pass me the popcorn!'

'Oh, I can't wait to write it,' I said. 'But the worst part was he seemed disappointed in me because I wouldn't tell him my favourite position or anything. It was all too much.'

'Reverse cowgirl!' Katy held up her hand and performed a perfect yee-hah lassoing motion.

Zola tilted her head to the side, looking thoroughly impressed. 'Katy, how do you struggle to keep a boyfriend when you enjoy reverse cowgirl?' She laughed. 'That's a hell no for me, too much asshole in someone's face, you know! I'm a lady like that. It's on top or a casual spoon sesh for me.'

We tried to keep the laughter down as a few people glanced up from their desks, seeming distracted by our chat.

'What's your favourite, Ella?' Katy asked, swirling around in her chair to face me.

My cheeks felt warm again. I've never felt prudish in front of my friends, but when it came to sex, I did feel inexperienced. I'd dated the same man for years, and if I was being brutally honest, the sex between us became a boring, roll-over, wham-bam type of thing. Joshua wasn't adventurous; he was quiet, kind and a little bit cautious. He was more than happy with our bang-average sex life. Truthfully, so was I.

'I honestly can't remember. It's been so long,' I admitted.

Zola gasped and pointed at me. 'You know, she never talks about it,' she said to Katy as if I weren't in the room at all.

'She doesn't!' Katy agreed.

'Babe, have you actually had sex since Joshua?'

I made a squirming face, knowing how much I was about to be judged.

It was Katy's turn to gasp. 'Fucking hell, Ella! That was like,' she looked up to the ceiling, working out the math, 'like, three years ago, at least.'

'It's not a big deal! I don't need it,' I protested, needing to defend myself. 'I can't be arsed with the shit that goes along with it. The emotions, the changing plans, the constant wondering what someone else is thinking about you. The weird jealousies. It's not worth it. I'm honestly happy without it,' I said. I turned to my computer, hoping the subject of my non-existent sex life would be dropped. One new email from Alexander with the subject line: *updates please*. I felt my stomach twist.

'So, how much do you spend on batteries then, Ella?' Zola said, and Katy erupted into pure-filth laughter again.

'Or do you have a plug-in? They're meant to have so much more power. Nothing worse when your batteries are dying, and it takes half an hour to actually get you going,' Katy continued.

I sighed and swivelled back towards them, feeling increasingly stressed and miserable. 'I don't.'

Katy's jaw almost hit the floor. 'You don't own a vibrator?' she announced for the entire office to hear. 'No wand? No rabbit?'

I put my finger to my lips, urging her to be quiet. 'Fucking hell, Katy. But *no*, I don't! I just don't like the idea of it. Its unsanitary; going inside you then sitting in a drawer, eww!' A shudder ran through me.

'So is a toothbrush, unsanitary I mean!' Zola stated. 'But you use that . . .'

'Wait, Ella, how *do* you orgasm then?' Katy continued.

'I cannot believe you guys are more interested in this than the fact that I just went on a date with Glasgow's biggest cum lord.'

My phone began ringing, and relief washed through me as an excuse to exit this uncomfortable conversation was presented to me. I pointed to my phone and picked it up, though there was no caller ID.

'She goes old school – and we thought she got them guns from the gym!' Zola reached over and squeezed my biceps, and both my friends continued to giggle like a pair of immature schoolgirls in sex ed.

I swatted her off me and answered the call. 'Hello?'

'Pilates?'

My heart instantly dropped to the floor, and I ushered my friends to gather around me, putting my phone on speaker.

'Mr Khan?' I replied, trying my best to sound confident.

'How did you know it was me? Recognise my voice already?'

Because you're the only one who calls me Pilates, ya dafty, I thought.

'Exactly that,' I murmured, choosing to humour him instead.

'So, Patricia passed on your message, and my PR team sent over your LinkedIn email request. I thought I better give you a ring before you track down my mother's Vinted account and message her too.' He laughed. I felt my insides curl with mortification.

'Yeah, I'm sorry about that,' I admitted, but at the same time wondering what goodies a millionaire's mother would sell on Vinted. I would seriously have to check that out. 'What it was, well . . . actually . . .' I could feel myself hesitating, and I had no idea why. I was usually so decisive when it came to work.

Zola nudged me and whispered, 'Go on.'

'Well, I need a favour, Mr Khan. You see, I work for Smart Reputations, a PR and marketing firm, and I'd love to speak to you about hiring one of your venues for an upcoming show for the world-renowned artist Alexander . . .'

He laughed under his breath. 'Is that it? I have a team that deals with that sort of thing. I can email you their contact information, Pilates.'

'Yes, thank you. But the problem is, I promised my boss I could get you in the office personally. She so wants to meet you,' I said, wanting *personally* nothing more than to curl up under my desk.

'She wants to meet me?' he replied in a sarcastic tone, as if I was creating an elaborate plan to lure him into my office and promptly shag him against the filing cabinet.

I nodded, then received an elbow in the rib from Zola. 'Be persistent!' she whispered. 'Keep going.'

'She does. And the thing is, if you don't – and I don't mean to put this pressure onto you – but if you don't, I will probably get fired.' I glanced up at my friends. Katy had her fingers crossed in some sort of ritual and Zola was on the edge of her seat.

'And it does need to be by tomorrow. Sorry,' I muffled quickly.

There was a long pause.

'Well . . .' he said eventually, 'we wouldn't want you to be unemployed, would we, Pilates? I could be there at six tonight. Is that satisfactory?'

I jumped out of my chair in celebration. 'Yes! Six is perfect! Thank you, I appreciate it. Will I send you the address?' As I said it, I felt my body cringe yet again, realising I didn't have his phone number. The cunt probably withheld it because of how much I'd already stalked him this week. 'I could send it to your LinkedIn, or something?'

He laughed at my overenthusiastic naivety. 'It's fine, my driver will know where he's going!'

'Thank you so much, Mr Khan. I'll see you soon,' I said, raising my hand to receive high-fives from my friends.

Without another word, the line went dead.

'We did it!' I screeched.

Zola hugged me. 'You did it! Yes, girl!'

'I'm so buzzing! You need to nail this pitch to him now,' Katy said, and I felt the panic set in – for real this time.

'I think he thinks I fancy him!' I said.

Zola nodded. 'Most powerful men think every woman from sixteen to sixty fancies them, sweetie!'

I screwed my face up, knowing he was the type of man I couldn't stand – overly confident, a womaniser, brandishing a huge ego.

'No! Wait, remember you have Alvaro tonight too.' Zola seemed disproportionately cut up about the Spanish hunk I'd have to stand up.

I held my hands up. 'Alvaro will need to wait, Zo. I've got to nail this pitch.'

She agreed, huffing slightly. 'He's so nice, though. Aghhhh. You could fit both of them in, couldn't you?'

'Zola, I really can't. Cancel the Spanish guy or rearrange. Jesus Christ, I need to keep my job!'

Zola blew a raspberry from her mouth in frustration. 'Fine!'

Katy smiled; she was nearly as hyped as me. 'Do you need any help, Ella?'

I was already emailing Andrea with details of my meeting with Philip. 'No, no, I think I got this. Thanks, though.'

Chapter Fourteen

Ella

It was approaching six, and most of the staff had left, but Zola and Katy stayed behind, helping me set up the conference room. Andrea was still lurking around her office while I prepped my pitch, hoping to secure a venue for the exhibition in one of Philip's grand hotels. All of the while praying that Andrea would leave me to take the lead and stay far away; the idea of her coming through and calling me *Ella* or asking too many questions about how we met, or just her intimidating, strident presence gave me crippling anxiety. I was completely caught up in a web of lies, but I had no way out, other than continuing to roll with it all. The only thing I cared about right now was keeping my job, which meant landing a venue – and, realistically, Philip Khan was my only solution.

*

Katy rearranged the plate of salted caramel cookies for the fourth time while Zola loaded up my PowerPoint, ensuring no technical issues – like my recent Japanese bondage search – would appear on the screen. I didn't have time to change, so I remained in my black pencil skirt with a white shirt. My hair was waving loosely down my back, and I opted to wear my black-framed glasses, even though I only require them for long distances and driving, but I thought they added a more professional sophisticated element to my appearance.

A few minutes before six, the elevator door pinged open, and my friends stood up straight.

'That'll be him.' Zola grinned widely, showing all her teeth, then grabbed her coat and bag from one of the chairs. 'Message us as soon as you get out, yeah?' she whispered, although unless he had ears like Isa, there was no need to speak so quietly.

'I will,' I said, gulping down my nerves.

Katy waved excitedly. 'Good luck, Ella! Will we go greet him and send him in?' she asked, swerving towards the door.

'Yes, please. Thanks. Try to be quiet, though. I don't want Andrea storming in mid-pitch.'

'OK, we will!' Katy whispered back.

My two friends left the conference room to greet Philip and bring him to me. I repositioned my laptop, making sure it was completely symmetrical, then inhaled a long, deep breath. *I've got this.*

Suddenly I could hear the high-pitched hyena laughter of both my friends coming closer as they approached the conference room, followed by a deep familiar voice.

So much for keeping the noise down, girls!

I stood up and straightened my skirt as Philip entered the room. He was wearing a light grey suit with a black shirt underneath, open at the collar. His dark eyes fell on mine, and a smile appeared on his face.

'Good evening,' he said brightly.

'Hi, Mr Khan.' I reached out to greet him. 'Or do you prefer Philip?'

He turned to Katy and winked. 'I do like it when you call me Mr Khan, but Carol here can address me as Philip.'

Wow, his ego was even bigger than I remembered. I watched Katy's face contort as she quickly remembered our little espionage game.

'Very well. Please, take a seat,' I replied, keeping my tone as professional as possible. There was no way I was contemplating being taken in by the easy flattery of this man.

'We should go, was so great to meet you, Philip!' Zola said, raising a brow to me.

'Yes, totally. It was lovely seeing you again, Philip.' Katy blushed hard as she headed out the door, mouthing *OMG* to me as she shut it.

'You too, Carol! See you, Zola,' he said, oh so smoothly.

The boardroom felt small, with a large-screen projector on one wall and a huge table taking up the majority of the space. Philip walked past a few seats, then plonked himself down in the middle chair of the row, ensuring he was sitting right next to me.

'OK then.' I cleared my throat, feeling extremely claustrophobic at how close he was all of a sudden. 'So, I'll get right to it,' I began. 'Firstly, thank you for taking the time, Mr Khan, especially at such short notice. I am one of the senior marketing and PR associates here at Smart Reputations. We're one of the fastest growing companies in the UK. My job is to primarily—'

'I know what a marketing company does,' Philip interrupted, crossing his arms. 'Oh, please tell me you haven't prepared a huge speech about how I should do something and partner up – a *la-di-da* type thing. Can we cut to the chase?' His voice was so relaxed and matter-of-fact that I was taken aback.

'Right.' I paused. 'So . . .' The prick had taken me completely off guard. I'd memorised my whole pitch, and now I could feel my head scrambling, trying to get back on track. My fingers hovered over the mouse on my laptop. 'Erm . . . just to clarify. You don't want the PowerPoint then?' I asked.

Philip shook his head, now resting his elbows on the table as he continued to stare at me with his deep, dark eyes. 'God, I've had a long day, please no fucking PowerPoint.'

I cleared my throat. His eye contact was so intense that I struggled to look back without feeling nervous. 'OK, I'll get to the point then. I have a client, an artist. He creates the most wonderful portraits of celebrities and royalty and he is gracing Glasgow for one evening only in a few weeks' time. I have been tasked with planning an art exhibition to showcase his talent across the city, and I was hoping you would allow the use of one of your venues for it.'

Philip tilted his head. 'What about the Gallery of Modern Art? Too Banksy?'

I tittered a little: *too fucking expensive, more like*. 'Well, we have to notify the council beforehand for that venue, I'm afraid; it involves permits.' I turned to him, feeling a rush of excitement at my vison for Alexander. 'I'm thinking this show will be more like a party, not like a regular exhibition, but fun and lively as well as elegant. Consider it a function even.'

'A function?' Philip repeated, not appearing to get behind my vision.

'Exhibitions feel very passive, to me,' I said, lifting the energy of my voice. 'They're all about observation, walking around and looking, am I right?'

Philip agreed, raising his shoulders slightly.

'But I want to really engage and draw people into conversations about the art. I don't want to only cater to the art community either, but I want to break his work through to the everyday person. Alexander is honestly the most amazing artist.' I sighed. 'I have paintings of his on the PowerPoint.' I felt my hand drifting back towards the laptop, but Philip's eyes gave me a warning stare.

'Well, I can email you them across. Look, the point is, I want to create a completely unique experience here, not a regular exhibition. I want people to talk about him, to make TikToks and reels on how amazing the night will be. I am going to further publicise not only his name, but his brand, and of course the venue by extension.'

'And Smart Reputations, of course,' Philip added with a smirk.

I smiled. 'Well, of course.' There was a slight, brief silence in the room.

'Hotels host these kinds of things all the time, right?'

Philip sat up in thought, crossing one leg over the other.

'Yes. We host parties, but I'm thinking from a marketing perspective.' He paused briefly. 'If I were an artist holding some wanky art show in a new city, I'd want it to be lavish and in a grand, distinctive building. My hotels are grand, by the way, but they aren't quite Glaswegian landmarks.'

I felt all hope wash out of me. *He doesn't want to do it. I am going to be fired.*

'Wouldn't you?' he asked.

'Well . . . if I wanted a normal boring exhibition, yes. But I want to create something more here, Philip.'

He leaned back in his seat as if he disagreed. There was nothing more to say, I'd lost him. He didn't get it.

'Can I be frank with you, Philip? Apologies.' I cleared my throat. 'Mr Khan.'

'Apology accepted.' He smirked cheekily.

'The main obstacle I'm facing is getting people up here excited about this exhibition. Alexander Cambi is HUGE in Italy and central Europe, and he's making waves in London, but the people of Glasgow don't know him or his work. If I could secure a smaller, more intimate venue, like one of your hotels, then . . . it would be more appealing to the everyday person. It would be a less intimidating way to visit an art show, wouldn't it? It could bridge the gap between the art world and "real life" and create a bougie boutique experience. And of course, I'm hoping that would also help keep costs within Alexander's tight budget. This partnership would generate great press for your hotel, it's honestly a win-win scenario.'

He hummed, sounding unsure of my proposal.

Jesus, what was there to question? I wondered.

'Well . . . Honestly, I think you can do better.'

I felt like I had been punched in the gut.

'Oh.' I pulled back my shoulders. I'd really believed I had pitched well.

Philip leaned closer to me, his deep voice sounding somewhat softer. 'I think you're doing yourself a disservice by not believing you can spin this and make it huge. Forget a hotel venue; what you need to do is get the people of Glasgow excited about some fancy schmancy artist coming to town.'

I nodded politely, hoping to end this meeting and go home to cry under the covers. *He thinks I can't do my job, and the worst part is, I know he's right.*

Then the door burst open into the room, and Andrea strolled in. I was slightly taken aback by the sheer thickness of makeup she had plastered on her face – presumably a special glow-up in honour of Philip's arrival.

'When I heard Philip Khan was in the building, I just had to come and introduce myself!' she announced. 'I didn't know your pitch had already begun?' She side-eyed me and I felt my spine straighten up in an instant.

I managed to force a smile onto my face. 'Oh sorry! I didn't realise you wanted to sit in, my apologies, Andrea. Mr Khan, this is my boss, Andrea.'

Philip stood and leaned over the table, shaking her hand. 'I've heard many good things.'

Andrea blushed, combing her long, thin fingers through her bob. 'So, how are we getting on here?'

The room turned silent, and I paused, not quite knowing what to say.

'Well . . .' I began.

'Pilates has done a fantastic pitch!'

Shit, shit, the name. I could feel my heart pound as I clocked the look of confusion on Andrea's face.

'I'm very impressed.' Philip turned his head. He seemed to be thinking on the spot, and it was as if I could see the cogs turning in his head – yes, he was thinking that Andrea *really* was a dick, and I *really* could lose my job over this.

'And?' Andrea pressed.

He laughed. 'Deals aren't done overnight, as you well know, Andrea,' he warned, sinking back into his chair. 'We were just discussing potential options.'

Her lips pursed. She wasn't used to people not being terrified of her.

'Well, I do prefer when they are done overnight, don't I, *Ella*?'

Fuck, fuck, she's picked up on the name. I tried desperately to keep my face in some kind of order while Andrea raised her eyebrow at me as if alerting me to the fact that I better get this wrapped up or else.

'Oh, yes! You certainly do, Andrea.' I attempted a fake laugh, nerves bubbling under my skin at her calling out my name.

'Well, we should get back to it then,' Philip announced, staring at Andrea as if to politely say *fuck off*.

'Right, yes,' she murmured, turning to the door. 'And can you remember to switch off the lights when you leave this time? The electricity bill will be deducted from you and your little friends' salaries next time. Honestly,' she laughed hard to Philip, 'you have no idea how many times I have to warn them!'

I tittered a little; but honestly, how bloody embarrassing? Sweetly, I smiled back. 'Sure will, Andrea, goodnight.'

She left the room, and I breathed a sigh of relief as subtly as I could.

The room turned deadly silent again as we both listened to the clip-clopping of my boss's heels echo down the corridor.

I was humiliated twice over. I'd never understand why that woman spoke to me like such a child, especially in front of a client.

Philip eventually burst out laughing. 'Wow. She is a lot. God!' He shook his head in disbelief. 'Now I understand the lengths you went to just to get me here, *Ella*.' He raised a brow, awaiting an explanation.

I could do nothing but gaze at the floor, still far too on edge from Andrea's outburst to laugh it off or come up with a convincing enough excuse. 'Yeah, I'm sorry about the name change, and about Andrea, actually.' I replied quietly, feeling my toes curl in response to my lie having been unravelled.

'Why give me a fake name?' he asked calmly.

I eventually looked at him. 'I didn't know you, and I wasn't interested in getting to know you, so I . . .'

Philip smiled in pure amusement. 'So you created the worst fake name on the planet?'

'I suppose I did. Yes.' I pushed my shoulders back, owning my blunder. 'But you did fall for it,' I added, smirking at the situation.

'Trust me, I really didn't, but I was curious.' Philip paused, weighing up his options. 'Look. Maybe . . . *maybe* something can be done here. I just think you could do so much more with this artist. I mean, you clearly love his work. A hotel venue just . . . *to me* . . . just doesn't cut the mustard.' His voice was deep, gravelly, a little bit cheeky, yet polite. 'Let me think on it.'

Jesus Christ, put me out of my misery here!

'Would you like me to show you my plan for the function or a timeline of the night I've got in mind?' I reached for the laptop again, hoping to persuade him.

He leaned over me, snapping the laptop shut. 'No.'

For a brief moment, I could feel Philip's warm, strong body press into mine, and almost immediately I tensed up. He simply plopped back down on his seat.

'You know, I'm starving,' he announced.

'We have cookies.' I pointed to the pitiful plate of Sainsbury's finest stacked up like a Christmas tree in front of us.

'No, I mean proper food. Shall we go grab some dinner?' he suggested.

I felt my face twist in confusion. I was finding this man was strange. I couldn't get the measure of him. Was he being rude, arrogant, unprofessional? Was this the kind of behaviour needed to succeed in the business world? I wasn't even sure if he'd taken my pitch, *well*, my attempt at a pitch seriously. Had he gotten the entirely wrong end of the stick here? What did he think this was? *Maybe I'll help you, but only if you suck my dick, Ella?* Jesus, it wasn't the nineties.

'Sorry, no. I don't do that,' I replied firmly, tugging at my blouse. *Yes, I can be strong and put my foot down here. I am a professional woman.*

'You don't eat?' he questioned. 'There's a name for that condition.'

I sighed, unwilling to laugh at this joke. 'I don't go for private dinners with men I don't know. I prefer to keep things professional if we are working together.'

Philip laughed. 'I was inviting you out to discuss your proposition, brainstorm if you like, not jump on your bones. I mean . . . unless . . .' His eyes widened.

I felt my jaw drop and aggressively shook my head. 'Sorry, no. That's not how we do business here at Smart Reputations.'

His face lifted, and he pointed to me as if a bolt of lightning had just struck him with an idea. 'Ahh, Ella, you're gay! That's why you opted for the name change.'

My cheeks reddened in an instant. 'I am not!' I protested a little too forcefully.

Philip tutted. 'It's nothing to be ashamed of. My sister is gay and she's just about my favourite person.'

'I'm not gay, Mr Khan. I am single, but I'm professional and not interested in you like that.'

'Wow.' He leaned forward, looking baffled. He paused for a few seconds, as if allowing my words to sink in. 'Really?'

My heart was thundering in my chest. I could feel every muscle in my body seize and tighten from how uncomfortable I felt.

'Really,' I confirmed.

'OK. Wow. That's good to know.' He paused, chuckling to himself. 'Well, I'm going to grab a bite to eat. Let me think on your idea.'

Philip stood up, and I joined him.

'I'll be in touch tomorrow if I come up with something.' He held out his hand politely. 'I would normally hug. I'm a hugger. But I don't want some sexual harassment case filed. I fear I may have muddied the waters there.'

I shook his hand firmly. 'I'm not a hugger. Thank you for your time. I do appreciate it.'

Philip headed towards the door of the conference room, then just as he was leaving, he turned to me. 'And Ella?'

'Yes?'

'For someone who apparently likes to leave on the electricity, you really need to lighten up.'

He reached out a hand and switched off the light. Suddenly the entire conference room was plunged into darkness, then the door slammed shut. I could hear his mocking laugh travel down the hallway as he left the building.

'Ahhhhhgghh!' I cursed, trying to shuffle my way to the switch, bumping into furniture along the way.

What the hell was that man's problem?!

Chapter Fifteen

Ella

That evening, after locking up, I drove home to the West End and got settled on the sofa. My mind was still racing over Philip's words – mainly how I was doing myself a disservice with the Alexander Cambi campaign. I let out a loud squeal and held my head in my hands. That man was unbelievably annoying, irritating and cocky. But I couldn't help but wonder if he was right. Should I be thinking bigger with this campaign? It was happening in a matter of weeks – was it all too little too late now? I heard my phone ping from my handbag. Reaching over, I scrolled through the endless messages from the group chat.

Katy: *Wow! He was even hotter in a suit!*

Zola: *Insane! It says A LOT that he came to the meeting. I've just googled him, and OMG, he's mega.*

Katy: *Yeah! Like so big!*

Zola: *Have you heard anything from Ella?*

Katy: *Nup! You?*

Zola: *I wouldn't be asking you if I had, haha.*

Katy: *Harry's coming over soon! I want updates before!*

Zola: *ELLA!!!!*

Katy: *It must be going well. She's going to nail it.*

Zola: *What, him or the pitch?*

Katy: *It's Ella. The pitch, haha!*

I felt my mood shift as I read through their banter. I scrolled to the bottom of the chat and began typing.

Ella: *Well, he was arrogant, cheeky, and didn't want a PowerPoint! Andrea outed my fake name – AWKS! He also reckons I should think bigger than his hotels for a great art exhibition. But then he said he'll contact me tomorrow – MAYBE! Oh, and he asked me for dinner, and I said no xxx*

My phone began ringing – a FaceTime from Zola. I accepted the call and smiled as I watched her cosied up on her couch with a cup of tea.

'OK. Information overload! Are you OK, hun?' she asked.

I nodded, feeling my breathing relax from seeing my friend's face. 'Honestly, I'm OK. I'm just worried.

Andrea has it in for me just now, and I'm panicking about this exhibition. What if I get sacked, Zo? I would lose everything.' I could feel the fiery panic build up again at the prospect of signing on at the Jobcentre and being rehoused in a scatter flat in Forgewood.

Zola sat up, seeming more serious. 'Ella, since I joined the Glasgow branch, there is not one event you haven't nailed. OK? You are going to smash the life out of this, because it's what you do.'

I attempted an appreciative smile at her efforts to console me. 'Thanks,' I managed, not quite believing what she was saying but grateful for the encouragement.

'And besides,' she added, 'if you get fired, we have the Dicktionary Club to fall back on! Have you seen the latest reviews?'

She laughed and I lifted my laptop to log in. I spent the rest of the night chatting shit with Zola, uploading my latest review on the serial wanker, and agreeing to *finally* meet up with the sweet Alvaro the following night.

Chapter Sixteen

Katy

Katy spent the evening snuggled up with Harry on the sofa, pretending to enjoy the football. Before him, she'd never cared about sport, but after faking being a huge Celtic fan on her first date, she had to engage in a crash TikTok course, memorising the latest transfer windows and the names of the most important players on the pitch. She'd even YouTubed an explanation of the off-side rule. But she didn't mind. It was their fifth date, and already things were moving fast with feelings – although Harry seemed to be the perfect gentleman with regards to taking their relationship to the next level. Besides kissing, with the occasional lip biting, combined with heavy breathing, the couple had kept it PG. Nevertheless, Katy loved it when he hung out at hers, and suggested they watch the latest game together, surrounded by candlelight and the tangy crunch of Doritos, hoping to finally take things to the next level.

Celtic were currently two nil up against Hearts, and Harry was in his element, shouting at the television and then turning to Katy, who would mirror his reactions.

When the final whistle blew, he relaxed back on the sofa and pulled her over for a kiss.

'I think you're my lucky charm, do you know that?' he said, kissing her forehead lightly.

'I think you're mine, more like! We are smashing the season so far!' she replied confidently, having also spent an overwhelming amount of time analysing the league table and the possible outcomes of upcoming fixtures over the next few months.

'I don't mean with the football, Katy.' He paused, looking more serious, 'I mean with everything. I am so happy with you and how things are going. It's the happiest I've been in God knows how long.'

A warm gush of excitement swept over her, and she beamed back, dying to ask if he was happier now than with his ex-bird when they were travelling in Australia. 'I am, too. I don't think I can remember the last time I felt so connected to someone, Harry,' she admitted.

He agreed enthusiastically. 'You are literally the female version of me. We like all the same things! It's so weird, isn't it?'

Katy smiled back but wondered if she had actually given anything about the real version of herself away. She was so busy moulding herself to fit Harry's lifestyle and perception of the perfect partner that she had no idea if he liked the real Katy McIntyre.

Harry suddenly hauled Katy over him, quickly making her forget any insecurities she had about their relationship, until she was straddling his lap. She kissed his soft lips, and her forehead pressed against him as she stared longingly into his eyes.

'I am in love with you, Katy,' he whispered.

She gasped happily and covered her mouth. 'What?'

Harry chuckled, his face turning a little red at his confession. 'I mean it. I know it's soon, but I love you!' He seemed worried. 'Have I scared you away?'

She leaned over, squeezed him tightly, then kissed his cheek, head and lips so fast it was almost simultaneous. 'I love you too, Harry, I honestly do!'

The pair started kissing and giggling until things turned more passionate, tongues intertwining. Harry ran his fingers through Katy's soft hair, and she moaned at the slight tug, feeling undeniably horny. Then he moved his hands down and began rubbing and squeezing her breasts, tugging them out from her bra.

Katy could feel her vagina begin to pulsate and, keen to egg him on, she whispered, '*Mmmm*, that's nice, keep going.' He moved his mouth down, ran his tongue over her breast, biting and licking, so that goosebumps sprinkled up her spine. 'Should we go through to the bedroom?' Katy asked through pleasurable gasps.

Harry nodded, then stopped, pulling his attention away from her nipples. 'Can I ask you something first?'

What the fuck did he possibly have to ask me at this particular moment? she wondered. *It must be sexual.* Her favourite position? What she likes in the bedroom? If she spits or swallows? I mean, we all know the preferred option, but the guy just told her he loved her. Maybe she could swallow this one time and take one for the team.

'Yeah, of course,' she replied, patting down her messy hair and readjusting her bra.

'I know it sounds cringe, but I want to do this right. I'm crazy about you, Katy,' he said.

Katy's heart began thundering in her chest. *Is this a proposal?* she wondered, feeling nervous but excited at the same time.

'I am, too. I think you know that, baby,' she responded, pulling up her top, noticing her nips were still pointing in his face at what seemed to be a sentimental moment.

'So, don't freak out, but I would feel better if we were official before we start sleeping together. I don't want you to feel disrespected in any way by me.' He seemed nervous and shy as he spoke, and Katy's heart melted at his sweetness. She could feel her bottom lip quiver.

'Oh my God! I'd love to be official with you, Harry,' she said softly, gazing into his sweet blue eyes. 'I have been telling Zola and Ella in the office how I would never speak to anyone else. I'm invested, believe me.'

His face shone with relief. 'So, you're my girlfriend, then?'

'And you're my boyfriend!' she screeched happily, wrapping her arms around him tightly.

The pair hugged lovingly on the sofa for a while, giggling between kisses like teenagers. Katy thought how she had never met any man – especially on a dating app – with so much decency before. Harry seemed to be mature, consistent, and he had tunnel vision only for Katy. She wondered if withholding sex on the first date may have been the answer all along.

'Hey, why don't I come round tomorrow night?' Harry interrupted her thoughts. 'We can do this properly when it's not so late on. We've both got work in the morning, and I don't want to rush the first time we . . . you know. I want to take *all* my time and for my new girlfriend to *really* enjoy herself.' He side-eyed her, and Katy felt her stomach pinch with nerves and anticipated pleasure.

'Yeah, of course.' She nodded, understanding, but also disappointed that her hungry vagina wouldn't be fed tonight. 'I want you to enjoy yourself, too.' Her hand very deliberately grazed past his groin, and Harry grinned widely.

'Hey!' he scolded playfully, pulling her hands to his.

'Oh, I know, I know.' Katy laughed. She straddled his lap again, and they stared into each other's eyes, their fingers interlocked with one another, blissfully content in the moment.

'You have small hands,' she murmured, examining the size of them in comparison to hers.

Harry smirked. 'You think?'

'Yeah, look at them. Mine look bigger, and everyone says I have small hands, too.'

He linked his fingers back with hers. 'It's the only small thing about me, Katy,' he whispered, and shockwaves pinged off her fanny immediately.

'Harry!' she warned. 'You need to stop this, or you won't leave this house with your dignity intact.' She could feel the horniness descend once more, but it felt like something more, something special. Katy had waited years for a connection like this and she desperately wanted to be as close and intimate as she could be with Harry.

'Mine and your dignity will be out the window by tomorrow night, sweetheart, trust me!' he said, letting out a frustrated puff of breath.

They both laughed, and she flopped off his lap and back onto the couch, smiling and chatting away, crunching on the last of the Doritos and feeling completely and utterly in love.

Chapter Seventeen

Ella

As I approached my desk the next day, I spotted a large gift, perfectly wrapped in shiny red paper, waiting for me. I glanced at Zola, then at Katy, and pointed to the parcel on my desk.

Zola, who was crunching on an apple, shrugged. 'It was here when we arrived.'

'Oh! Maybe you have a secret admirer!' Katy gushed, wheeling her seat over to my workspace.

I pulled off my coat, shaking my head. 'I bet I know exactly who this is from.'

'Who?' Katy asked, glancing at Zola, who seemed equally confused.

'Philip Khan! I offended his ego last night and now that prick thinks he can buy me,' I muttered, unimpressed, as I began tearing open the paper.

I lifted the box for my friends to see the grand reveal. *Maybe it would be some expensive dress or luxury scarf he asked one of his assistants to pick out for me.* But as soon as I turned it around, I realised I was holding up an extra-large Rampant Rabbit in the middle of the office. Both my friends erupted into laughter, and I immediately hurled the offending item under the desk.

'Seriously! Guys! Fuck sake, we're at work!' I felt my face turn purple with embarrassment as my friends' eyes acknowledged the outburst of laughter in the room.

'Your face!' Zola snorted. '*Oh, I know who this will be from,*' she declared, in a poor imitation of my Glaswegian accent.

Katy doubled over, gasping for air. 'You honestly thought Big Phil was buying the big dil! When you said you didn't have one, Zola and I bounced straight onto Love Honey.'

I couldn't keep my laughter in any longer, even though I was mortified. I glanced at the box under my desk which featured a photograph of the toy. It was massive: thick, made from rubber and a deep dark purple. There was no way that thing was getting anywhere near my vagina. I pride myself on my pelvic floor workout, and that device would have it in tatters.

'Well, I don't think I'll need my Rabbit anymore, girls,' Katy said proudly.

Zola and I turned to her, thirsty for some gossip; well, I was thirsty for a distraction from my solo sex habits.

'You sealed the deal with Harry?' I asked, excited to hear the details but even more relieved she wasn't in a ball crying on the floor.

'Not yet . . .'

Zola threw her head back and sighed dramatically, disappointed in her.

'But . . .' Katy continued, 'Harry asked me to be his girlfriend last night, and I said yes.'

Zola and I gasped.

'*And* he said he loved me!' she added. Her eyes glazed over with tears.

'He loves you! *Wow*. After what . . . like a week?' Zola questioned, bursting her bubble.

'When you know, you know, Zola. I told you both how I felt the other day and, well, he feels the same!' Katy snapped.

'I'm happy for you, Katy. Honestly, I am.' I leaned over and hugged my friend. She never seemed to have any luck when it came to dating, and from what she'd told us (and what I'd second-hand stalked) about Harry, he did seem like a genuinely decent guy.

'I am too! Of course I am, but you know, it is fast, and we know you have previous with falling hard,' Zola said, crunching down on the last bite of her apple. 'I'm just protecting your feelings, babe. But I'm very happy for you!'

'So, tonight is the night!' Katy's face brightened. 'He's going to shag the living daylights out of me!'

I smiled widely. 'Yes, girl! And, of course, we want all the details.'

Katy scoffed. 'That's if I don't have to take a sick day.' She lowered her voice. 'He's a big boy,' she said and winked.

'Jesus, no wonder you wifed him off! How do you know?' I asked, hoping for at least a sloppy BJ story.

'He warned me.' She raised her eyebrows.

'Ouch!' Zola said.

'I'll tell him to go easy. There's nothing worse than feeling like you've birthed a hedgehog after a long night in the sack.'

'Nothing better, more like!' Zola countered.

They both gazed at me for something back, but I shrugged and said, 'Yeah, can't relate.'

Zola toddled over to my station, snatched my boaby box out from under there, ran back to her station and ripped it open, pulling out and fully exposing the giant cock-shaped vibrator under her desk.

'No! Zola, stop, put it down!' I warned, gazing around the room, desperately hoping no one else was watching her.

She turned the settings to vibrate and threw it over to me, giggling. 'You can relate now, girl. Wooo, woooo!' I grabbed the giant rubber dick in both my hands, fiddling with the buttons under the desk to stop it moving and slammed it into my drawer.

'Enough!' I spat, a shiver running down me at the thought of it. Then I reached for my sanitiser, drenching it over my hands.

'You know, be careful with the settings. Stick to *buzz, buzz, buzz*. The others are like a form of Morse code. I have no idea who that pleases,' she said, dishing out her expert advice then heading back to her desk. 'And you know you might not need it anyway. You have a date with the gorgeous Alvaro tonight, remember? Ashton Lane – *don't be late!*'

'I remember!' I turned my chair to her. 'You're really bigging this one up, you know.'

Zola held her hand on her heart. 'He is adorable, Ella. Honestly, I was messaging him until two this morning. Well, technically, *you* were messaging him.'

Both me and Katy burst out laughing.

'What the fuck was *I* saying?' I giggled, keen to know the background chat before heading out for my date.

'I'll screenshot you the important bits, but overall, it was Alvaro being a complete sweetheart,' she gushed. 'He's kind, caring, warm, funny, and did I mention he's Spanish and gorgeous?'

'YES!' Katy and I said simultaneously.

'Yeah, well, you're going to love this one. I mean, not like after a week kind of love – no offence, Katy. But he will be your first five-star review for the Dicktionary Club, I know it.'

I rolled my eyes, knowing there was no such thing in my book as a perfect man. Well, not since Joshua.

I turned back to my desk after the morning catch-up subsided and switched on my computer to begin working on my Alexander campaign. It was getting closer to the launch date, and his PA had been emailing me for updates and to clarify plans. I noticed Andrea was now copied into the emails too, and the pressure was beginning to build.

My phone pinged from my desk.

Unknown: *Pilates! Are you free? Can you meet me? Philip.*

I turned to my friends, who were wholly engrossed in their workload.

'Guys, Philip Khan wants to meet up,' I announced.

'Da fuck! Well, say yes. Say yes,' Zola encouraged. 'You do want to meet him, right? He could have a proposition on a venue.'

'Or just a proposition.' Katy giggled.

But she was right. I needed to figure out what this man's intentions were.

I paused for a moment, then began typing.

Ella: *Hi Philip. Sure, I'm at work, though. Could we meet back in the conference room?*

Philip: *I'll pick you up outside your building in ten. Almost passing. Philip.*

I turned my phone around to my friends.

'What do I say?' I asked, needing their advice. 'Will I ask what it's regarding?' I turned my phone to begin typing. 'I have to stay professional. I don't want him getting the wrong idea.'

'Why would he?' Katy asked.

'Because he's a man!' I snapped back.

Zola hummed briefly. 'OK, look, you have been professional all through this. It must be regarding a venue. I say, do it! I know he was a bit arrogant . . .'

I pulled a face. 'A bit!'

'But he has great connections,' she added.

Katy smiled. 'And great eyes. Tell me you two have noticed the eyes!'

I couldn't deny it; his eyes were remarkable and mysterious. But I'd never admit it out loud, even to my best friends.

I continued typing.

Ella: *Sure, Mr Khan. I can move a few things around and meet you for a debrief following our meeting last night.*

Ten minutes later, after emailing Andrea my out-of-office plans, I stood outside the building, chittering. I wasn't sure if it was from nerves or the cool wind blowing my hair away from my face. The sun was finally making an appearance through small gaps in the clouds, but still, I threw a black blazer over my cream, fitted dress, keeping a professional look.

A black Bentley SUV drew up and parked outside my office building, and I spotted Philip behind the wheel. He looked much more casual than he had the evening before, dressed in a black polo shirt buttoned to the collar and wearing dark sunglasses. He stepped out of the car and walked over to greet me. As he leaned his body towards me, I tensed up, reminding myself he was a hugger – but he took hold of the passenger-side door handle instead.

'Good morning,' he said brightly and grinned, holding the door open and gesturing for me to sit.

I slid into the car, resting my handbag on the floor.

'Morning, and err . . . thank you,' I said, squirming at his attempt at old-fashioned chivalry.

Philip joined me in the car, and I could smell the musky aroma of his aftershave engulf the small space between us. That definitely wasn't Davidoff's Cool Water.

'Our chat last night got me thinking,' he began, pulling away from Smart Reputations.

'Yeah?' I replied curiously.

'Well, I made a few calls, and I have potentially hired a venue for your big gallery exhibition. It would have to be in a couple of weeks' time, though?' He turned to me, his dark shades covering most of his handsome face, but not enough to hide his smug expression.

158

I screwed my face up, utterly confused.

'This is usually the part where you say thanks,' he said, grinning like the Cheshire Cat.

'Well, where is the venue?' I opted to say instead.

'I'm about to show you. Patience.'

I sighed quietly, unsure if this was all a game to him. This was my career, a job I'd worked hard at for years, and here I was, playing along in some stupid fucking treasure hunt.

We drove through the West End, and I gazed out the window, admiring the familiar streets of my neighbourhood. It was my favourite place in the city: I loved the chilled vibe, its many bars and restaurants, Ashton Lane with its cobblestones and fairy lights, going for runs in Kelvingrove Park – and, of course, the local Paesano Pizza. I was looking forward to sitting in the park with Zola and Katy, guzzling cocktail cans on a picnic blanket, sunbathing and watching the world go by.

Philip continued driving and eventually turned, parking up on Dumbarton Road, alongside Kelvingrove Park.

'Here?' I questioned. 'In the park?'

He scoffed. 'No! In the art gallery of course.'

'*What?*' I gasped, whipping my head around to face one of the most iconic buildings in the city.

'Isn't it perfect?' Philip smiled widely, taking off his shades.

'A room in the museum, right? A small room? Like it would be a cupboard or something, surely?' I was stuttering, trying to find my words, keep my cool.

Kelvingrove Art Gallery was one of my all-time favourite places, with its impressive architecture and grand, ornate design. It stood like a palace in the heart of Glasgow's West End.

'The entire gallery will be yours for the night,' he said, as if this was the most rational and obvious conclusion. 'Come on.'

He unbuckled his seat belt and leaned over to me on the passenger side. I felt his minty fresh breath hit my face. *Fuck, is he about to kiss me?* I wondered, not knowing how I'd react. *I could punch him, or jolt my head away.* Then he pressed to release my seat belt.

'I'll show you around.'

I was dizzy and overwhelmed. How the hell did he manage this?

I took a few seconds to let my heart rate settle, then exited the car. My eyes squinted, taking in the huge silhouette of the museum against the sunlight.

'Philip,' I said.

He was a few steps in front and turned around. 'Yes?'

'I appreciate this, I honestly do, but this will be completely out of budget for me to host here. It's one of the country's most sought-after venues,' I said, having never even attempted to think of it as an option with regards to Alexander's campaign.

'Not at all. It's a favour. There's no fee. Come on, let's take a look,' he continued, casually heading through the park and climbing the mountain of stairs towards the gallery's grand entrance. We passed under the sandstone arch together.

No fee? I couldn't wrap my head around any of it. How had he managed this? Why would he do this? I'd only just met this man, and suddenly he was pulling more favours out of his arsehole than Sticky Vicky during a late-night show in Benidorm. As we entered the building, squeezing and dodging between crowds of tourists, an older man in a suit approached.

'Mr Khan, we were so happy you called. Is this your partner?'

Philip grinned. 'Yes! Good to see you again, Seamus.'

Seamus held his hand out for me to shake, and when I did, I clarified, 'Business partner – well . . . sort of. I'm Ella. Pleased to meet you.'

Seamus winked at me as if to say he didn't believe a word of it and proceeded to walk around the gallery.

'This is of course the main foyer, where we hold events or particularly special occasions for our VIP guests,' Seamus said, leading us through to the grand room. I had been here so many times before, but suddenly I was more aware of its beauty. It was like a cathedral, with ornate yellow and black marble floors, vast sculpted ceilings and sweeping staircases.

'Wow,' I said softly.

'We can display paintings against the walls and have the main space for guests to mingle. What were you thinking, Ella?' Seamus asked.

I looked at him, but my mind was blank. I was so overwhelmed with excitement and fear that I was entirely speechless.

'Pilates?' Philip said, nudging me.

'Ahh. Pilates. Well, we've never had that before. But we once held a silent disco for the kids,' Seamus said.

Philip and I smiled at one another. He was clearly enjoying the funny side of my espionage game.

'No, Seamus, not Pilates. But I love it, honestly. It's stunning. I'll have to regroup and consult with my team before I have an exact plan. The space is unreal, so I want to make the most of it. I need to think up ways to get the people of Glasgow talking about this event; then, if it's OK with you, could I get back to you with the plan?' I asked. My mind was running on overdrive, trying to piece together where everything would go, how I'd make sure we maximised this in terms of attendees, and envisioning how impressed Andrea would be when she found out.

'Certainly, Ella.'

'And, Seamus, do you have the list of dates that the gallery is available?' Philip asked.

'Yes.' Seamus scrambled into his pocket, pulled out a piece of paper, and handed it to me. 'These dates are the ones we have in the next few weeks.'

I grinned, noticing my proposal of 31st July was there. I'd previously mentioned it to Alexander.

'Can we confirm thirty-first of July, please, Seamus?' That would give me just under three weeks to get organised.

'Certainly, Ella. I'll get that added right away.' He held his finger to the sky and walked back across the foyer towards the front entrance.

'I'll be in touch, old man!' Philip called back, and Seamus pointed his finger back as if to say, *you better be!*

Philip wandered over to me, still taking in the space. 'Well?' he asked.

I shook my head. 'I don't know what to say,' I admitted, awestruck.

'This is usually the part where you say thanks,' he repeated, and I smiled.

'Thanks,' I mustered, feeling my cheeks flush, amazed at my good fortune but still hating the fact I was so indebted to this man. 'But I do have to ask, why are you doing this? I'm sorry – and I don't want to sound ungrateful – but you don't know me. I don't understand why.'

Philip gazed up at the impressive ceiling and its massive gold and white lights and then back at me. 'I don't know, I guess. You intrigue me. And I can.'

'I intrigue you?' I repeated, unimpressed.

'Yes, you aren't like most women I meet, put it that way, Ella. And *yes*, it's a compliment.'

I arched my brow suspiciously. 'What are most women you meet like?'

'Well, they seem to fall madly in love with me after only a few minutes of conversation.'

'In love?' I giggled at that. 'With you or your wallet?'

'Ouch!' He laughed, holding his heart jokingly.

I began to walk around the museum, taking in stunning new visons of what the event could look like. I imagined an outrageously grand event, champagne on arrival, a red carpet. I could set up a stage for Alexander to speak at the centre and position his paintings all around him.

'So, what are you thinking?' Philip asked.

I could feel his eyes on me as I wandered.

'Right now?' I paused briefly. 'Honestly: how do I fill this place with so many people who have never heard of the artist? My usual demographic is young women, from like twenty to thirty-five.'

Philip sighed. 'Same!'

I shook my head and shoved his shoulder a little. 'Yes, but I normally PR beauty products to influencers, not hound them like you do!'

He turned to me. 'Believe it or not, I don't normally hound women. I usually have a much better reception to my charm. Plus, let's not forget you practically messaged me on eBay to get me into your office.'

I shot him a stare, not keen on where the conversation was leading, and instead continued my walk through the different rooms of the gallery, admiring the Egyptian relics and vivid old paintings of fashionable ladies and imposing men in kilts.

'So,' Philip said as he caught up to me. 'I'm curious. Why did you take on an art exhibition if your target market is influencers?'

I paused, having repeated the same question in my head over the past few weeks. 'To be taken more seriously, I guess. I'm usually the one for the Instagram market, or the go-to TikTok campaign girl. I guess I wanted to push myself and show I could be more than that, but trust me, I won't be bidding for any more lucrative art projects anytime soon again.'

He laughed. 'Are you into art?'

I shook my head. 'No, but I appreciate it. When I saw Alexander's paintings, I was completely taken aback. They are so captivating. The expressions on the faces, the bright colours, everything is just wow. And I'm not trying to pitch him here, but you never see paintings like his. It's as if he was born to paint modern-day royalty or something.'

Philip tilted his head and looked into my eyes. 'Well, fuck.'

'What?' I dropped my shoulders, waiting for a sarcastic comment to follow.

'Nothing. But, for what it's worth, it sounds like Alexander picked the right woman for his exhibition.'

I felt my cheeks turn warm at the compliment. 'Yeah, well, I hope so.' I gulped down, feeling suddenly crushed by the timescale I had to put this together. 'Are you into art?' I asked to distract myself.

'Well, yes and no. I have some pieces around my home. I can show you if you'd like.' Philip's tone was teasing and I shot him a withering stare. 'I was joking, unless . . . you did want to come to my home of course . . . I would be more than happy to oblige.'

'I don't,' I confirmed.

'Well then, I am very much like you, art wise. If something catches my eye, I appreciate it. I actually enjoy reading about art history. I was watching a documentary series on Michaelangelo the other evening, in fact.'

Wow, I was surprised. I knew more about the teenage mutant ninja turtle than the painter. I didn't picture Philip as having much substance or culture. He seemed flashier, and egotistical with his high-class hotel chains, cocky attitude and mountain of wealth. It was hard to imagine him watching anything except his reflection in the mirror.

'I didn't have you down as an art guy. Do you have a favourite artist then?'

Philip's phone began ringing. He scooped it out of his pocket, signalling to me that he'd just be a couple of minutes, and began chattering as he walked a few steps away. I could faintly hear a posh female voice on the other end. 'I can't talk just now, Amelia, I'm in a meeting,' he said quietly, and then, 'I'll be there soon.'

I continued to wander around, not wanting to appear like I was eavesdropping, but also wondering who Amelia was. I guessed he probably had a million women at his disposal.

A few minutes later, he ended his call and joined me at an ancient Egyptian sarcophagus.

'Has this guy helped with any great ideas yet?' Philip asked, motioning to the massive stone coffin.

'Nah, he looks smart, but he was useless.' I laughed. 'I should head back to the office now, I suppose, and get brainstorming.'

Philip sighed. 'Yes, me too. Let's head out.'

*

We travelled back to the city centre while Philip took a work call over his hands-free about a new hotel he was renovating in Berlin. He was still on the call when we pulled up outside Smart Reputations, but he raised his hand for me to wait and quickly hung up.

'Sorry about that. It never stops.'

His phone began ringing again, and I couldn't help but spot Amelia's name pop up on the screen of his car, along with a small pink heart emoji beside it.

'That's OK. I'll let you get that. Well, thanks again. Seriously, you have saved my life with that venue.' I unbuckled my seat belt and opened the car door. 'I owe you one.'

As I stood on the pavement, about to close the car door, Philip leaned over to the passenger side, sticking his head out. 'You really do owe me one, eh?'

I rolled my eyes and shook my head at his cheeky reply.

'I'll pick you up around seven.'

My face dropped. 'Sorry, what?'

'Send me your address, and I'll pick you up. You owe me one dinner at least,' he replied confidently.

'At least?' I repeated, wondering what 'at most' would mean.

'Oh, come on, Ella. I'll help you brainstorm for the exhibition. I'm invested now,' he said and smirked. 'You can show me some of his paintings and I'll give you my artistic opinion.'

His phone rang again, and my eyes automatically glanced at the screen. This time, Sienna was calling. 'You better get that.'

I shut the Bentley's door and headed into the building.

Chapter Eighteen

Ella

I scurried through the office to my desk to spill the news to my friends. Zola nudged Katy when she saw me, and they both spun their chairs around, eager to get the lowdown.

'Well . . .' I could see nervousness behind their eyes, and I immediately wondered if Andrea had been making threats behind my back that they weren't telling me about.

'Yes, well?' a voice said behind me, and I turned, managing a welcoming smile at my boss, who had a face like a slapped arse once again.

'Oh, good! You're here, Andrea,' I began. 'So, I have secured the venue for the Alexander Cambri exhibition, which will take place on the thirty-first of July.' I beamed proudly, and I noticed the wave of relief pass over my friends' faces.

'Where?' Andrea asked immediately.

I stood up straight as I delivered my killer blow. 'Kelvingrove Art Gallery.'

I noticed the shocked look descend onto her pinched face.

'We have the entire building for the evening, at no cost. This will allow me to spend the entire budget on delivering the very best décor and beverages.'

'No cost?' she questioned, still hovering above my desk as if it was a trick.

'Nope.' I smiled. 'Philip pulled some favours. Great news, eh?'

'*Hmm* . . . Well, yes,' she was forced to admit. 'Great news indeed, Ella. You certainly excel at networking, eh?'

A wave of pure relief washed through me.

'But tell me, what does a man like Philip Khan expect in return?' she asked.

I paused, glancing around me.

'Nothing,' I said. 'We're friends; well, more business acquaintances really.'

Andrea cackled a high-pitched laugh. 'I'd say best friends with your little nicknames.' She sneered. 'Huh, Yoga!'

'Pilates,' Katy piped in, correcting her.

'Sure.' I screwed a face up to Katy. I totally wasn't in the mood to divulge the full fake-name scenario, especially not to a woman who hated me.

'Pilates, whatever. At least it's done. It took you long enough,' she muttered under her breath, then turned around and strode towards her office. 'And *I'll* let Alexander know,' she added, as she slammed the door behind her.

My two friends began squealing and hugging me.

No! No! How the fuck did you manage that one, Ella?' Zola asked.

I sighed, slumping onto my chair and leaning back, feeling completely exhausted after a day with Mr Khan. 'Honestly, I didn't. He did.' I rolled my eyes.

'You do realise Andrea is in that office right now, speaking to Alexander and taking full credit for the venue, right?' Katy shook her head, annoyed at the thought, but I was perfectly aware. 'You've smashed it, though! I'm proud of you, Ella.'

I reached over and grabbed both of their hands. 'Thanks, guys. I'm so happy. But I now have to find enough people to come. As in A LOT of people. The venue isn't exactly intimate. It's huge.'

'If we have to hand out flyers to every Tom, Dick, Harry and Fanny in the city, we will,' Katy said, giggling. 'Though we can already count on at least one Harry.'

'Yes, we fucking will all right! But wait, tell us about Big Phil. Was he polite or pervy?' Zola asked, sipping on a bottle of Starbucks Frappuccino.

I made a face. 'He is always kind of pervy.' I paused. 'Though maybe more flirty, I'd say. But I did notice a lot of women phoning him, like the entire time we were there.'

'Ohhh,' Zola tilted her head and let out a tut in disapproval.

'And he told them he was in a meeting.' I laughed. 'Anyway, I'm obviously very grateful to him. But at the same time, I just don't get it. Why is he helping me?'

'Maybe he is just really kind?' Katy suggested innocently.

Both Zola and I erupted into laughter.

'Wait, what?' she said, looking confused.

'No man is that kind, babe. I can't even imagine the favours he's pulled to get one of the country's most expensive, prestigious venues to hire . . . and for free!'

'But he could be a nice man? There are genuinely nice people out there,' Katy exclaimed.

'And this attitude is precisely why you get yourself into the situations you do. You believe the best in people.' Zola turned to me. 'Mr Khan wants into your knickers, darling. That's it, plain and simple. It's the law of the jungle.' She shrugged.

'He did ask me to go for dinner tonight too. He said he would pick me up at seven,' I confessed.

Both of them gasped.

'Sorry. *What?* Wait. Are you going?' Katy asked, bouncing up and down on her seat excitedly.

'Of course I'm not. He's Glasgow's biggest playboy.'

'Write about it,' Zola said, a light going on in her eyes. 'For the Dicktionary Club! Babe, you have to. Go along, humour him and write up a profile!'

'But does he even have Tinder or Bumble or any regular dating apps?' Katy questioned. 'His photo might not be on the database?'

Zola lifted her phone and began typing ferociously.

'I don't know,' I said. 'And fuck that, even if he does, the man is a zillionaire; he would sue the life out of us for defamation of character.'

'Shit! He doesn't have any of the regular apps,' Zola said with a grunt, placing her phone back on her desk.

'That cunt probably only uses Raya!' I said, reminding myself of the exclusive dating app I would only consider joining to track down Henry Cavill.

'OK, so we should still do a profile on Big Phil, like a feature piece. Once a month, we could write about some B-listers! Some semi-famous or well-known guys around the city. We won't give personal details like the venue of the date or where they were, just in case they track it all back to us. But we could give hard facts on their personality and how they treated their date.'

Katy was swaying. 'But he's treated her nicely so far. He's just saved her job, Zola!'

'Let's face it, Katy, Philip Khan has an ulterior motive. He's a fucking *man*!'

I gulped down, feeling nervous about going full-on spy mode. 'He did make a joke about me coming to see the art in his home.'

Zola let out a tut. 'And you know what art is code for, Katy?'

Katy shrugged.

'He wants to show Ella his crown jewels!' Zola winked.

We all began laughing, then kept it down as the stares came our way.

'C'mon! This could be the edge that the Dicktionary Club needs! It's like a little gossip column about someone relatively famous,' Zola persisted.

'I suppose you could do one date,' Katy said, coming round to the idea. 'And if it's a good one, then you write it up as a good one.'

I rolled my eyes, understanding the method in her madness. It was certainly a hook for subscribers, but I couldn't afford to jeopardise the Kelvingrove gig. 'One date?'

'One simple report, and that's it. Look how Andrea's just spoken to you, Ella. This website is our Golden Ticket out of here!' Zola put her hands together as if to pray.

She was right. Andrea's domineering ways and bizarre mood swings were close to unbearable. I turned towards her office and watched as she giggled like a fucking hyena on the phone. I knew she was in there, taking full credit for my work.

'OK. Fine!' I accepted the challenge.

'Thank you. Now, what are you going to wear?' Her eyes brightened.

'It has to be sexy, something to get him interested,' Katy said.

'I'll need to see where we're going first.' I brought out my phone and texted my address to him. 'I can't believe I'm doing this. I have never given a man my home address. If he stalks me now, it's on both of you.'

'He knows where you work, Ell? And where you train? If he wanted to stalk and murder you, he would just follow you home, OK?'

'Oh, thanks, Zola,' I replied. 'That's really put my mind at ease.'

Zola gasped. 'No! Fuck! Wait! Alvaro! You can't let him down again, Ella.'

I felt my shoulders drop. 'Seriously? You've just spent ten minutes convincing me to write up Philip.'

Katy giggled. 'I'm so glad I'm taken for now. You girls are crazy!'

'Right, fuck sake! I'll text Alvaro,' Zola moaned, throwing back her head in dread. 'I suppose it's an excuse for me to message him all night instead.'

Katy gently slapped Zola's arm. 'That's terrible!'

Zola shrugged her off. 'Oh please. He's replying to Ella's pictures, not mine. It's like Andrea said – it's only networking!'

We all laughed together.

Philip: *Perfect. See you at 7. P x*

Ella: *Where are we going?*

Philip: *For dinner x*

I huffed at his secrecy. And at the kiss. Why couldn't this man ever give a straight answer? I liked to know plans. I hated uncertainty. I enjoyed being in control, but Philip seemed to know this and enjoyed torturing me by denying me it. Instead of replying to his childish guessing game, I turned on my laptop and began emailing Alexander, copying in template designs for set-ups he might like for his exhibition, dropping subtle hints that *I* secured the venue at the stunningly perfect Kelvingrove Art Gallery.

Chapter Nineteen

Zola

Zola had messaged Alvaro an hour earlier to apologise that *Bella* could no longer make their date due to an *unscheduled meeting*, but he hadn't responded. She found herself refreshing the Tinder app repeatedly, hoping for an understanding reply from him. But as she travelled towards Cowcaddens on the subway line, she was soon feeling disheartened that she'd let him down one too many times. Alvaro had moved to Glasgow a year ago, leaving his small Spanish hometown to study law. He seemed to enjoy the bustle of a big city but had told 'Bella' he could find it overwhelming at times and in his spare time he loved exploring the stunning Scottish highlands, something Zola had always wanted to do since arriving but had never quite gotten around to.

Zola had spent hours chatting with Alvaro over the past few days, as he poured his heart out about past relationships and values. The pair shared a love of music and travelling; their dreams aligned in so many ways. Alvaro was entirely focused on his career, he wanted to really make something of his life; he was determined, sweet, and a very sincere person. Zola was equally motivated;

she was a go-getter – one of those people who knew exactly what she wanted and how to get there.

Sitting on the subway, Zola tried to refresh Tinder for the fifth time since cancelling the date she'd set up between 'Bella' and Alvaro. No signal. She could feel her frustration and disappointment rise, knowing she might have upset him. Alvaro seemed like the type of guy they hadn't had really the pleasure of writing up on the Dicktionary Club yet. A good, honest man with something special about him. The subway stopped at Cowcaddens, and Zola wandered across the road to her flat.

When she entered, she spotted Curtis sprawled on the sofa, playing the Xbox with his headset on.

'Hey, babe!' Curtis called out, glancing up briefly as he heard her enter.

Before she could reply, she was hit with a horrible odour. 'Jesus Christ! What is that smell?'

Curtis shot her a grin, then his gaze returned to his game.

'Babe?' Zola walked in front of the TV and stared down at him. 'I'm asking you why our flat smells of shit.'

Curtis pointed to his headset to warn her to keep the noise down to ensure his gamer friends didn't hear her. Zola held her hands up to him for a reply, but he ignored her and continued interacting with his mates online. She huffed, scrutinising the state of the living room. Empty energy drink cans and yesterday's washing remained hanging over the clothes horse. She headed to the kitchen, popped her bag on the worktop and opened the fridge.

Suddenly a loud fart echoed through the apartment. Zola paused, turned around and shot Curtis a stare through the doorway.

'So, that's why our flat smells of shit!' she yelled in disgust.

'Babe, come on!' He pointed to the TV again, not wanting anyone to overhear a domestic.

'Seriously! You don't want your mates to hear me, but you're fine with them hearing your arse rattling, yeah?'

She slammed the fridge door shut and stormed through to face him. Even when she was standing right before him, his attention was still darting between her and the TV.

'Babe, come on. I'm sorry,' he eventually managed.

'Look at this fucking place, Curtis. You've been off the entire day!'

'Oh, you need to calm down, woman! It's been my day off.'

'*Woman?*' Zola spat. He knew how much she hated that chat.

There was a silence between them, then he groaned under his breath.

'I do everything, Curtis. I go to work, I do the washing, I make the fucking dinner. I'm tired, Curtis. Just help more,' she said more softly, feeling emotional this time. 'It's not nice to come home to this.'

'I will, Zo. I do my best. I'm sorry, babe.'

Zola felt her shoulders relax, feeling almost guilty for storming in and creating such an atmosphere.

Then another huge fart exploded out of his arse. Curtis erupted into laughter, curling up into a ball, his eyes watering with tears. Zola stood in front of him turning rigid with fury, anger rippling through her veins.

'I can't do this!' she hissed, almost choking on the stench, appalled by his disrespect. She returned to the kitchen, grabbed her bag, then stormed into their bedroom.

'Babe, oh come on!' he called out. 'It's only a fart!'

She opened the door just wide enough to scream, 'It's fucking disgusting. The entire flat smells of shit! You smell of Wotsits and shit!' Then she slammed the door again.

From the living room she heard Curtis's muffled voice say, 'All you do is feed me vegetables. What do you expect?' But she chose to ignore him.

Curtis had never been the tidiest person in the world, but since they moved to Glasgow, he'd had more free time and had chosen to spend it mostly in the gym or playing video games. He wasn't domesticated, but it had never bothered Zola when they lived in London together. He was hardly in the house then, but in Glasgow his social life took a dip, and now that he was working part-time hours and hardly leaving the house, it really bothered Zola. She'd begun to loathe him for it.

Zola began lifting clean clothes from the laundry basket, hanging them on rails and leaving a large pile to be put away on his side of the bed.

'Zola,' she heard him call out, but still she ignored him. 'Babe, come through. Sit with me and watch me play!' Curtis moaned.

She held her head in her hands briefly, opened the door and said coldly, 'I'm not your mother, Curtis. I'm not impressed by video games or how loud you can make your arsehole sound! Get to the fucking toilet.'

She heard the echo of laughter from the men he was playing with over the TV and banged the door shut again.

'She sounds like your mother, bro,' she overheard one of them say.

'Nah, she's all right,' Curtis replied coolly.

Zola sat down on the bed, feeling herself shake with anger and frustration. She brought out her phone.

One new Tinder message.

Her heart bounced in her chest. She felt panicky, wondering if Alvaro had replied or if it was just another potential date she had lined up for Bella.

Alvaro: *I'm sorry you can't make it, Bella. I was thinking of you all day. If you don't like me, then I have to know x*

Zola's heart melted as she imagined the sweet accent behind his words. Immediately she began typing.

Bella: *I do like you, Alvaro! I'm so sorry. I've told all my friends at work about you today and how amazing our chats have been! Please, meet me tomorrow. I promise I won't cancel; if I do, you never have to chat with me again. X*

Zola paused, biting her nails at the three dots as he typed.

Alvaro: *OK. Tomorrow. x*

Alvaro: *Tell me about your day, beautiful x*

Zola lay down in bed and continued to message Alvaro late into the night, telling him all about work, about Andrea, and making up a story about her unexpected meeting and deadlines she had to make. She giggled at his replies as he described his hectic day as an intern at a law firm and his take on Glasgow so far. Zola completely understood what it was like coming to Scotland as an outsider: a new city, new people with rough-sounding accents. She empathised with his struggles and how he was missing home.

Chapter Twenty

Ella

Meanwhile, in the West End, I was sitting anxiously on the edge of my sofa, watching the clock count the minutes down to 7 p.m. I hadn't really wanted to tell him where I live, but in the end I'd messaged my address to Philip earlier. Then I'd spent ages choosing my outfit carefully, but as I glanced at myself in the mirror now, I wondered if I'd made the right choice. I'd picked out a navy, one-shouldered, knee-length dress, but now observing my look, I wondered if it was too fancy *or* not fancy enough. Philip hadn't told me where we were going, which was playing havoc with my anxiety. Before any engagement, especially dinner, I liked to know every detail, to ensure I was correctly dressed and could download and study the menu. Philip's insistence on spontaneity didn't sit well with me, but I imagined his idea of dinner wasn't going to be a cheeky Nando's, so I opted for a classy dress, and glammed it up with a pair of cream heels and a matching bag. My hair fell neatly down past my shoulders in a classic Hollywood wave. I was always grateful for my hair; it was thick and shiny, and it sat pretty much any way I attempted.

By five minutes to seven, I could feel my legs shaking with anxiety – *what was I doing?* I stood up and glanced down at the busy street, lined with parked cars below me. I sighed heavily. *It's not a date. It's work*, I reminded myself. *All you have to do is write one article about this man, Ella, and that's it.*

The sound of my phone made me jump.

Philip: *Which buzzer?*

My heart dropped to my arse. Fuck. There was no way I was telling him which flat it was.

Ella: *No need to come up. On my way down.*

I picked up my bag and locked the door behind me, then checked it again, just in case. I took a deep breath in the hallway, straightened my shoulders and headed down the stairs. I could see a black shirt through the entrance glass; it must be Philip, standing with his back to me. I closed my eyes briefly, taking one last breath of courage – but when I opened them again, he was staring back at me through the glass, watching me walk down the stairs. I felt my cheeks redden, and finally pulled open the door when I reached the landing. Instantly, I could smell his musky, deep scent, which was becoming familiar now.

'Hi,' I said, meeting his gaze.

'Good evening. Wait – are you nervous?'

I pulled a face of confusion. 'Why would I be nervous? It's just dinner.' I watched him smile at my confident reply. 'Are you?'

He shrugged casually. 'A little.'

'Hmm . . .' was all I could say, probably because I didn't believe him. I couldn't imagine this man getting nervous over anything. *Did he think I'd find that cute? Oh, the renowned millionaire is soooo into me that he's nervous about taking me to dinner?* Well, I didn't fucking buy it.

I followed him down the stone steps to a black Audi parked up against the kerb. *How many cars did this guy own?* As he approached it, he pressed the fob key, and opened the door for me.

'After you,' he said, leaning on the door and watching me bend to sit down. He closed the door, and my heart pounded in my ears. *Why did he make me feel like this?* I wondered. *Why was I so nervous and we'd barely even said hello?* I decided it must be a red flag, my body's own nervous system's way of telling me this cunt was terrible news.

I pulled it together by the time Philip opened his door and sat down, slipping on his seat belt.

'So, how did your boss take the news of the gallery?' he asked as he pulled smoothly away from the kerb and into the flow of traffic.

I smiled, thinking of Andrea's stunned face earlier that day. 'She was surprised and happy. Not that she'd ever say well done or anything. But yeah, the entire office is buzzing about it.'

'I'm glad.' Philip glanced across at me, and I felt my eyes drop to my knees, too awkward to hold eye contact. 'Now, let's celebrate, eh?'

As we drove through the city, I kept my eyes mostly out of the window, occasionally glancing over and observing Philip. He was well groomed, with biceps that bulged through the outline of his tailored shirt. But the most compelling thing about him was his eyes. I had never seen more mysteriously dark eyes. They made him incredibly difficult to read, and I hated that. He oozed confidence and charm. I could see why this man would make vulnerable girls like Katy out there fall so hard, so easily for him.

'So, what's next on the gallery project?' Philip asked.

'Well, I have to make sure enough people come. I sent out press invites today, as soon as we secured the venue. Everyone from the office will be there, of course.'

'The thirty-first you agreed, wasn't it?'

I nodded.

'I thought so. I've realised I'll be in Berlin, unfortunately,' Philip replied, sounding disappointed.

'I'll forward you the photos. I could even make you a sponsor on the press release?' I replied, still feeling distracted by my workload. 'I need to start creating some social media hype around it, too.'

'There is no need for including me as a sponsor, it's a favour. But yes, it's all about socials these days,' he agreed.

'I do have a good influencer network, but I'll have to see which brand Alexander would fit best with. Maybe some of the home accounts,' I said, thinking out loud.

'Like Mrs Hinch?'

I tilted my head and laughed. 'Yeah, exactly like Mrs Hinch!'

'Why are you giggling at that?' he asked, showing his perfectly white straight teeth.

'I don't know. I suppose I didn't think you'd know who Mrs Hinch was. I didn't think you'd be following those types of socials,' I admitted.

'Not at all! She introduced me to the Minky Cloth. Well . . .' He paused. 'She introduced my cleaner, and I bought a job lot of them for her to use at my place.' Philip laughed at himself, and I joined in, shaking my head. 'Plus, Mrs Hinch is extremely attractive!'

He was right, of course, so I agreed, still smiling at the thought of this man and a box of Minky Cloths.

'Alexander's focus will be on showcasing and selling his paintings,' I continued, 'but one lucky guest can bid to win a unique commission. When that happens, they'll book in with him to paint a loved one or have a self-portrait done. So, I'm going to build the advertising campaign around that.'

'Wow! So, someone wants to buy a giant portrait of themselves? I didn't think anyone would do that these days!' He sounded shocked. 'To what? Hang above their fireplace?'

'Yeah, I guess. But it doesn't have to be of themselves, maybe people want one of their kids or something. Their dog even. Basically, the auction winner will email him the image they would like painted, and he'll recreate it with his style. It's an unbelievable prize, Philip. His paintings sell for two hundred grand a pop.'

'I suppose if it's good enough for King Charlie!' Philip laughed.

'Exactly!'

'Surely your usual influencer market would enjoy that type of thing? You're creating a unique experience and girls love these big royal events nowadays, don't they? To plaster all over TikTok and Instagram, that type of thing.'

I gasped as an idea struck me.

'Ella?'

I was silent as the idea expanded and clarified in my head. This could be brilliant.

'Is everything all right?' Philip asked.

'Please *ssssh* just now,' I said and closed my eyes to concentrate. Finally, after weeks of stalling and uncertainty, my brain had clicked into action.

When I opened my eyes again, I noticed Philip had stopped the car at a bus stop near the city centre and was gazing over at me curiously.

'Fuck. I'm so sorry, Philip. But I think I have to go!'

'What?' he said.

'I know I sound crazy, but I've just had a great idea for this exhibition, which I have to work on straight away.' I felt my jaw tense. I didn't care what he thought of me right now, I just knew that I had to work.

'Like, right now?' He seemed a little confused, but also entertained at my impulsiveness.

My legs were bouncing up and down, full of the thrill of this new idea. I nodded back at him, eager to get started.

'Well, yes, of course you can go. You're not a hostage. I can drop you. *Errr* . . . Will I take you home?' he asked, starting up the engine again.

'Erm . . . no. Back to the office, please,' I replied, feeling the adrenaline pulse through my body. This was it – I was finally ready to nail this project.

Philip swung around and began driving towards Smart Reputations. I sat back with my eyes tightly closed again, holding my head in my hands, piecing everything together in my mind. A few minutes later, I felt a tap on my shoulder.

'You have arrived at your destination, Ella.'

I immediately pressed down on my seat belt and smiled gratefully. 'I'm so sorry about this. I honestly am. But if I don't work on this right now, I might simply lose it all from my brain. I've been waiting a month for this moment to happen.'

He let out a chuckle, baffled and delighted at the same time. 'Go! Seriously. Can I help?'

I shook my head. 'You've helped, trust me.' I opened the car door and swung my legs out, saying, 'Thanks for this. I promise I owe you big time!'

'Yep, certainly the most intriguing girl I've ever met,' Philip mumbled under his breath.

I smiled at him and shut the door, then watched as he drove off.

I unlocked the door of the office, entered the dark building, switching on all of the lights and heading to my station. The Smart Reputations floor felt strange at night. I had only been in a few times before when I had forgotten my purse or bank card, but I'd never come back to actually work. It felt eerily quiet, without my friends chipping in or slipping me their sarcastic comments and gossipy updates. I sat at my desk and pulled off my shoes to get comfortable, then grabbed some paper and pens from my drawer. I loaded up my desktop, desperate to get cracking, my mind and body still thrilled by what I'd come up with.

I started by researching Alexander's most famous art pieces and studied them intently. His primary focus was on traditional portraits, which were so realistically done that they almost looked like photographs, with the exception of the bright primary colours he liked to use. Alexander changed the skin colours and features of his portrait sitters with a unique, hyper-real brightness, making his work completely distinctive and sought after. In his earlier days, he'd painted landscapes and briefly had a spell as a street artist, doing fancy murals and public commissions. But his portraits seemed to be the most recognised and celebrated of his works. Most of Alexander's collectors were wealthy international businesspeople, but he had painted a duke and duchess before, and I knew that one of his most recent pieces was hung at Balmoral.

I began creating a mood board, focusing on reds and golds. I sat for hours scribbling, making detailed notes on exactly how I wanted everything to be at the exhibition, from the décor to the floral arrangements to the music. I even thought about what canapés and drinks we could serve to match the vibe. I could work wonders with Alexander's ten grand budget now that, miraculously, I didn't have to pay for a venue. Not only that, I actually had the most gorgeous art venue in the country. I then opened my laptop and created template invitations for the guest list beyond the press people I'd already alerted. I was sure Zola could probably do a better job, but the adrenaline was still pushing through my veins and I wanted to map it all out while my creative streak was alive.

It was 2 a.m. when I finally I sat back, with a solid plan mapped out. I, Ella Banks, was about to throw the best art exhibition this city had ever seen.

Chapter Twenty-One

Ella

The following day, I woke up on my sofa to the sound of my alarm ringing out from my bedroom, still wearing the navy dress from my extremely short date with Philip. I rubbed my eyes, dragged myself up and headed through to switch it off. What a night, I thought. But then I felt a smile appear on my face, remembering my breakthrough with the campaign. I couldn't wait to continue what I'd started, to tell the girls my ideas and watch the emotions play out on Andrea's smug face when I finally had the results this project deserved. I brushed my teeth, combed through my hair, and got myself ready before heading to the office.

When I arrived just before nine, most of the staff were standing in line for our usual debrief, so I scurried across the floor to my desk, lifted the mood board I had spent hours creating last night, then squeezed myself back into the firing line. There was no sign of Katy, but Zola stood casually slouched as Andrea began.

'Good morning to everyone who made it here in time,' she began.

Zola and I shared a look. It wasn't like Katy to miss the debrief. I pulled my phone out to check for any messages – *no new notifications*.

'I'm not interrupting you, am I, Ella?' Andrea scowled at me.

Shit, caught. I tossed the phone behind me onto my desk. 'Not at all!' I smiled back.

'Let's start with you, shall we? What has Miss Banks been doing all week?' Her tone was so condescending. She was setting me up for a fail, but not-to-fucking-day, you arsehole!

I cleared my throat. 'Well, as you know, Andrea, yesterday *I* secured Kelvingrove Art Gallery for Alexander's exhibition.' I paused for gasps of praise from my peers, but none came. *OK, tough crowd.* 'And I've put together a plan for this event that I think could attract a lot of attention.' I turned over my mood board, revealing it first to Andrea and then slowly turning it to ensure everyone else could see.

'What's this?' There was a smirk forming on Andrea's small-lipped face.

'It's my mood board,' I answered.

'Oh.' She pulled her glasses down slightly, glimpsing my work momentarily before pacing her line of minions. 'Is that what you call it?'

'Yes, and I have chosen *The Royal Painter* as a theme. I'm throwing a royal ball celebration in honour of this exhibition. Here.' I pointed to the cutouts of dainty canapés I'd found online on Gordon Ramsay's latest restaurant's site, then stuck to the board. 'I want expensive, themed canapés and champagne *or* prosecco if I have to watch the budget.

You can see I've gone with the classic military red and gold décor to represent royalty. I'm also planning to have violinists playing throughout the night, but their tunes will be poppy rather than classical to give that contemporary crossover vibe. We'll use our in-house photographer and videographer to create some really exciting content for all of Alexander's social media accounts.'

'This all sounds riveting, Ella. But who is going to come? It's a very large venue, after all. Have you thought about the guest list and how many people it will take to fill a venue of that calibre?'

I tried not to bristle. Andrea seemed almost keen on the idea of me failing.

'Yes, of course. I've sent invites out to a whole bunch of people already, from artsy home account DIY vloggers to Glasgow School of Art professors, from major news outlets to small boutiques and art shop owners. But I will also focus on *my* regular client demographic as well.' I watched everyone's smiles fade into confusion.

'Your usual demographic is young influencers in the beauty and fashion markets,' Andrea said with an unmistakable snigger. 'This isn't their vibe, Ella.'

'My plan is to pack the venue with TikTokers and influencers, who will, in turn, promote Alexander's artwork to a much broader audience. These girls have the largest followings in the city, and they love an event. Especially a royal ball in the grandeur of Kelvingrove – think of the content!'

Andrea's head tilted as if she was at last beginning to take my proposal seriously.

'We'll also be holding a competition,' I continued. 'We'll get the guests to post Alexander's artwork on social media, make a bid and the person with the highest bid will receive a personalised painted portrait of their choice. The media and press invite templates are already made up, and of course I would love it if each of you could send them out to all of your contacts.'

I finished and gazed around at my colleagues; I had to admit, they seemed impressed. Zola was nodding her head encouragingly.

'Well . . .' Andrea sighed.

The room was quiet. My palms were sweaty with anxiety.

'Finally, you have devised a half-decent pitch for this, Ella. Next time, I don't expect it to take a month.'

I felt my face turn blotchy as she moved swiftly to the rest of the team. That was it? After all my stressing and planning and staying up till two in the morning – after connecting with Philip Khan and landing the most insane venue, for free? Why could she never just say 'well done'? Why did she always have to criticise? Why *was I staying* in this shitty fucking job run by a woman who was surely fucking Kim Jong Un's favourite mini dictator? I was running over and over in my head all of the crazy, hurtful things Andrea had done in the past, shaking with anger inside until I felt a nudge from Zola.

'Are you OK?' she asked. 'That was blinding, y'know.'

I glanced up. Around us, everyone was dispersing. The meeting was over and I hadn't even noticed.

I could feel myself quivering. 'I'm fine,' I lied, not wanting to risk getting upset in front of the whole office.

'Babe, you smashed it! This royal ball thing you got going on. *Like what?* You will be the talk of the place! It sounds amazing.'

I nodded, knowing it would be great, but all the enthusiasm I'd felt for it had just been shat on from Andrea's fucking arsehole.

'Where's Katy?' I asked, realising she was still MIA.

Zola shrugged. 'She was getting ready for her night of passion, remember? Hopefully, she's not slipped a disc, yeah?'

I managed to laugh, even though I was still livid. 'She can't miss the meetings, though. Andrea's already gunning for us.'

Zola scoffed. 'She guns for everyone. I'll call Katy now. But seriously, great work, babe!'

I leaned into her warm shoulder, grateful for the compliments she gave so easily and genuinely, and we returned to our stations.

Just as Zola took out her phone to contact our missing friend, the office door swung open and Katy marched up to us. She was without makeup, puffy-eyed, and looked like she had been in a fight with a pit bull.

'Wow, late-night gal!' Zola exclaimed as she approached us.

Katy's face turned red and her eyes began watering.

'Oh no. What has he done?' I huffed, just knowing Harry must have been another lying, deceitful dick playing her.

'What has he done? What has he *not* done, more like.' Katy began blubbing, and I noticed a few stares from around the room.

'Hey, babe, let's go into the conference room, people are watching,' Zola replied, ushering her out of harm's way, gripping her shoulders tightly while I followed behind.

As soon as I closed the door, Katy burst into tears.

'He lied to me!' she cried.

I was already shaking my head, waiting for an adultery scandal to drop.

'Why? What happened? Katy, calm down. We got you.' Zola tried to soothe the situation, but Katy continued to blub like a baby.

'He told me he loved me!' she moaned.

'I know, I know. But what did he do?' I asked again.

Katy took in a deep breath and began. 'It was supposed to be the first night we, you know . . .'

'Fucked?' Zola challenged.

'Made LOVE!' Katy snapped back at her, with blood-shot eyes. 'And I was so excited. I had shaved, loofah-d, fake tanned and stretched! I was ready for the time of my life. The night of passion he'd promised me!'

Both Zola and I nodded in anticipation.

'So, he came round, everything started heating up, I got down on my knees ready to . . . you know . . .'

'Suck him off?' Zola interrupted, blunt as always.

'And I pulled down his boxers . . .'

'And?' I was beginning to feel deeply uneasy.

'And the lying bastard has a fucking micro penis!' She screwed up her face in disgust, slightly hitting the boke at the memory.

I bit my lip, trying not to laugh at how dramatically my friend had explained the situation.

'Babe, no!' Zola burst out laughing. 'But wait, how small is micro?' She held up her pinkie, trying to gauge the size.

'How small? *How small?* It's non-existent. He's all balls down there. There's more meat on a butcher's apron – put it that way. His dick is a fucking innie!' Katy cried.

Zola covered her mouth to smother her laughter.

'I thought that only happened with belly buttons?' I asked, genuinely confused as I tried to visualise what she was describing.

'Apparently not. His dick goes inside of him. It was like so small. I felt like I was sucking a thumb!'

I started to giggle. 'So, you did give him a blow job? You went through with it?'

Looking traumatised, still in a haze, Katy sighed and said, 'I mean, if you could call it that, Ella. I thought *maybe he's a grower?* You know. Some of the hottest guys are. I gave him the benefit of the doubt and tried.' It was at this point she retched, and Zola and I jumped back. 'But I could have sucked that . . . *chipolata* and eaten a Big Mac at the same time. I didn't even know it was in my mouth.'

Zola was pacing. 'But wasn't he giving it—' She put on her best manly Glaswegian voice. '*Oh, you're going to be sore tomorrow*, and all this chat?'

Katy nodded. 'Yip! I thought my cervix would be sore, not my fucking pride!' Then she burst into tears again.

'OK, there's no need to cry, Katy!' I tutted. 'He can't help the size of tadger he's got.'

196

She looked at me through teary eyes, seeming angry all of a sudden. 'He tricked me, Ella. He made me fall in love with him first and made out it was because he had morals. But no, he just wanted me to get emotionally attached so I would attach my mouth to his tiny prawn dick!'

Zola and I started giggling again, but she shot us down with a deadly stare.

'I'm sorry, Katy. It's not funny. I know you liked him, but maybe he has a tongue like a fucking lizard, or fat fingers like the king. There's more ways than one way to orgasm,' I protested, trying to seek some silver linings to this cloud.

Katy looked up, seeming heartbroken and empty. 'It's done. I'm concentrating on the Dicktionary Club now. These men are not getting away with this anymore!'

'He did lie to you,' Zola agreed.

I shrugged. 'I suppose he did. But maybe he doesn't know how small he is? Maybe he's not aware how small is small?'

'Men watch porn, Ella. Don't kid yourself. Just get back on the dating train, Katy, write about his pecker and get it out there!' Zola urged her. 'No more women should suffer like this.'

'How are the gym girls' entries coming along for the website?' I asked Zola, wanting to get away from the subject of Harry.

'Great! They've added hundreds more dates from their friends' experiences, too.' She smiled. 'I told them about our new feature piece every month and said this month's would be on Philip Khan. They LOVE the idea!

A lot of the girls have heard all about his womanising! Wait, how did that go last night?'

'*Erm* . . . it sort of didn't go last night.' I scrunched my face up, knowing exactly how my friends would react. 'Look, I got in his car, had my breakthrough about the exhibition just as he began driving, so I asked him to drop me back at the office,' I explained.

Katy turned to Zola and then back to me. 'So, no dinner? You used him as an Uber? And what breakthrough?'

'No. Wait. No write-up for the website?' Zola pushed me slightly, making me step back. 'This is important, Ella. Jesus, look how Andrea is treating us! This Dicktionary Club could be our escape plan here.'

I knew Zola was right, but I really wanted to avoid being fired before we got the Dicktionary Club up and running.

'I know. I'm sorry. I'll contact him tomorrow once I've tied everything up with the exhibition. I need one more late night, then I promise my head will be completely on the website. I'll explain my idea when you're calm, Katy, but I've sorted the whole thing. I need one more night to finalise everything while it's fresh in my head.'

'One more late night? Ella! You have Alvaro tonight. I rescheduled again,' Zola moaned, throwing her hands up in the air in despair.

'Zo, I can't. Not tonight, there is no way!'

Zola tutted. 'You can't cancel this. I won't let you!'

'Look, fuck Alvaro, he's just another giu! I can't do anything tonight. I have to work, Zo.' She was still glaring at me, looking baffled. 'Ghost him! If you're that bothered and want to save face – my face, by the way – rather than sending an awkward message. Just let me wrap up Alexander's campaign tonight, and then I'll go on a date with Philip and do our feature piece as planned.'

'We all need to focus on the Dicktionary Club!' Zola warned us.

I thought back to Andrea and how she spoke to me. I felt my stomach twist with resentment towards her.

'I know. I agree. I'm all in. Let me sort this campaign tonight and we can speak about the launch date afterwards.'

Zola huffed, finally accepting that I needed to pass on Alvaro. 'I think we should launch it on the first of August. That gives us another fortnight of dating, before we get it out into the world.'

I agreed, realising that meant scheduling to launch it the day after Alexander's event at Kelvingrove.

Katy sniffled. 'Well, I'm certainly back to dating. And I'll be reviewing Harry and his chipolata! There's no more holding off to catch the feels for Katy McIntyre! I want verified dick pics for approval before I start saying the L word ever again!'

Zola laughed. 'Wow. She's back!' She held up her hand for a high-five, and Katy slapped it hard.

'Oh, I'm back all right and ready to review those bastards!'

Chapter Twenty-Two

Ella

That evening, Zola and Katy left the office while I stayed behind. I was on a roll with Alexander's campaign and wanted to tick off as much of the organising as possible now that my plan was fresh in my head. I had just spent an hour speaking on FaceTime to Alexander and his PA about my plans and the itinerary of what to expect on the night, and I could tell the pair were finally impressed with my efforts.

I couldn't help but dream up possible opportunities for the Dicktionary Club, too. I found my mind wandering throughout the day, thinking up new and refreshing online marketing strategies we could create to finally allow the women of Glasgow to take back some control of the dating world. I knew this concept would be unique and, with all of our backgrounds, I really believed we could build a unique business and an escape plan that could potentially free us from Andrea's hell hole. I wanted to create a better life for myself. I was holding onto the idea of not living in constant fear anymore, that if I made the wrong move on a pitch or a concept, or even left the fucking lights on again, I'd get fired.

I was all in and couldn't wait to smash this campaign, then launch our website.

It was approaching 8 p.m., and I had just emailed over the last of the PR invites to my list of influencers. I'd also created an RSVP document for the guest list, and added a link to Alexander's and Andrea's email accounts so they were able to keep tabs on the people attending too. Suddenly everyone seemed to be buzzing. There was certainly a hype around this Royal Ball idea, as the art scene and influencers' replies filled my inbox in a flurry. The younger millennials and Gen Z crowd seemed especially excited about a promised night of great social media content for their channels.

I was finishing up my late night by sending over the deposit to the funky, classically trained violinists I'd got lined up when I heard footsteps from the hallway.

I froze.

Oh no. This was exactly how young – *OK, middle-aged* – women got murdered in the movies. The footsteps were getting closer and I stood up from my desk, praying it was just the cleaner doing an extra-thorough job.

What could I grab as a weapon? I turned quickly, looking for anything to pick up. Nothing. Absolutely nothing. Then I looked at my heels. At lightning speed, I kicked them off and picked one up.

'Hello!' I called out, slowly walking towards the office door, wielding my high heel over my head. 'Who is it?' I could feel my breath quicken. 'I'm phoning the police as we speak. This is private property!' I warned.

The door suddenly swung open onto the office bull pen, and I leaped towards the figure with my shoe high in the air.

'JESUS CHRIST!' a man's deep voice yelled out.

Standing there with a carrier bag in one hand and a huge bouquet of black roses in the other was Philip Khan. My jaw almost hit the floor with a thud.

'Philip?' I managed, entirely out of breath from being ready to defend my life. Slowly, I lowered my arm, the shoe dangling by my side.

'You scared the crap out of me!' He was shaken up, the veins on his forehead popping out.

'I'm sorry, I thought you were . . . I don't know, breaking in or something?'

'So, you attacked me with a Jimmy Choo?' He was beginning to chuckle as the situation simmered down a little.

I fucking wish it was a Jimmy Choo, I thought, analysing my Zara classic heel.

'I called out, you didn't answer!' I said defensively, before shakily making my way back towards my desk. Philip followed behind me, and I was aware that I could still feel my pulse pump through me. 'What are you doing here?'

He approached my station and set down the carrier bag. I could immediately smell the aroma of delicious spices heating the air. 'Well, apart from being attacked, you mean?' He smirked. 'You cancelled dinner, so I brought dinner to you! I thought you might appreciate someone to bounce ideas off too?'

'Oh . . . right. I've sort of pitched my idea. It's all done, and both Alexander and Andrea seem really happy with it.'

Philip stood for a second, thinking up his next move. 'Well, maybe you'd appreciate some company, perhaps?'

I examined him. It was strange. I wasn't sure if I felt sorry for him, or if he was a huge player shooting his shot. If a man turned up to the office unannounced for Katy, I knew she'd be humping him in the conference room within fifteen minutes, overcome with gratitude at the *sweet* gesture. Is that what he expects?

My eyes fell to his hands. 'Are you attending a funeral after dinner?' I glanced at the black roses, curious about his choice of flower.

'No! These are for you. Black roses represent new beginnings.' He sighed. 'And, well, death it seems. I thought in regard to your project, it's a new beginning after all? I wasn't thinking of the mourning aspect of them.' He paused. 'Shit.' He looked at the ground briefly, overthinking his gift, then his dark eyes glared up at mine. 'Did I fuck up?'

I started to laugh, enjoying watching his usual confidence take a wobble. 'That depends on what food you have going on in there.'

Philip grinned widely. 'Agh, I nipped to the Ho Wong and got us some curry and ribs!'

'Right. OK, well, I'll *err* . . . grab us some plates?' I said, walking over to the tea cupboard across the room and gathering plates and cutlery.

Why was he here? Why would he just stop by unannounced? I was grateful for the munch, but I could never work out this man's intentions. What was he playing at?

On my way back I couldn't help but notice how out of place Philip seemed in my small, empty office. Smart

Reputations only had two men who worked there and both were gay. Philip was buttoned into a full suit, shirt and tie, looking unbelievably smart yet tired, as if he had been stuck in meetings the entire day.

I passed him a plate, gesturing for him to take my chair while I wheeled Zola's over to join him at my desk. It all felt quiet and awkward. I had no idea why he would come to my work unannounced. Fuck, I even texted and phoned my mum before stopping by the family home. *Who turns up without warning?*

'So, this is where the magic happens?' he asked, dishing out the rice and curry. I watched him, looking so unusually domesticated. He passed my plate over to me.

'Thanks. And, yeah, I suppose it is. The offices are not as flashy as you might first think, eh?' I glanced around the room with its cheap carpet and Ikea furniture, and imagined what Philip's offices looked like. Probably glass-topped tables and polished marble flooring.

'As long as everyone is happy at work, that's all that matters. Oh, here.' He rummaged into his trouser pockets and pulled out two cans of Irn Bru. 'No more hands, with the flowers and food.' He smiled brightly.

'Oh, right! That's what that was!' I teased, reaching over for a can. 'Thanks.'

'Cheers!' He held up his own can and we banged them together, then began tucking into the food.

A few seconds later, with my mouth full of delicious curry, I was still trying to make sense of the situation. 'Sorry to ask again, but why did you come here? Were you passing by?' I asked, feeling out of sorts.

'No. I wanted to see you. To help you.' His dark eyes glanced up at me as he lifted a rib to his mouth. He winked.

I rolled my eyes, unwilling to fall for his charm.

He sat back in his chair. 'What?'

'I don't know.' I shook my head. 'I suppose I just don't buy it. It feels weird.'

'Ohhhh. OK. So, you're not used to men being spontaneous and doing nice things for you?'

I hummed a little, knowing he was trying to play the misunderstood martyr card. 'I'm the one who does nice things for myself, Philip. I don't need anything from a man or from anyone, I guess. And I don't mean to sound rude, but it feels strange that you'd come here. We were practically strangers a week ago, and suddenly you've saved my job *and* now you're bringing me Chinese food, plus a bunch of morbid roses?'

'Yes. You're welcome, by the way.' He tucked into his food again, and I could feel my blood boil. *Do women actually fall for this shit? The Mr Nice Guy act?* I could see right through him. We ate in silence for a while; the food was good and I wasn't going to let it go to waste.

'How long have you been single, Ella?' Philip asked.

'A while,' I replied bluntly.

'Yes, I can tell.' He gave a cheeky grin, pushing his plate over to the side of the desk, having had enough.

'What's that supposed to mean?' I sat back in my chair, wondering if my shoe was ready to come off again.

He looked me up and down. 'It was just an observation.'

I didn't want to give in to his schoolboy tactics, so I took a few more spoonfuls of curry.

'How long have you been single?' I eventually returned the question, remembering the unanswered calls from different women showing up on his phone.

Philip laughed loudly. I could tell he felt uncomfortable with the roles reversed. Then he let out a huge groan and rubbed his head.

'*Ahhh*. It's not long then – that's if you're even single now!' I tutted. I stood up to clear the plates, but as I reached for Philip's, I knocked over his can. 'Oh, shit!' I panicked as the sticky orange liquid spread quickly all over my desk.

Philip jumped up to save his expensive suit. 'Are there any tissues or a cloth?' he asked.

'Yeah! Erm . . . In the drawer,' I said, flustered, picking up my keyboard to avoid it being flooded. 'Fuck, hurry!' I said, hating the idea of working in a sticky mess.

'I am trying!' Philip rummaged through my desk drawers, eventually finding the tissues. As he lifted them out, he gasped. My eyes darted down to my drawer, where the giant Rampant Rabbit sat proudly.

'Oh my God!' I said.

'Jesus Christ! Look at the size of that bad boy!' Philip burst out laughing, and I felt my insides curl.

I slammed shut the drawer behind him, pulled tissues from the box in his hand and began mopping my desk. My face was radiating enough warmth to heat the entire city.

'Well, Ella! You keep surprising me, don't you?' He really was laughing loudly.

I ignored him, not knowing what to say. His guffawing continued. Eventually, when my desk had been saved from the orange tsunami, I turned to him.

'It's not mine!' I spat.

Philip pouted and arched a brow as if he didn't believe me. I could feel the anger build up inside. I vaulted the soaking wet tissues right at him.

'It's not mine, I said!' I could hear the thunder behind my voice.

Eyes wide, Philip grabbed the soggy tissues, then threw them directly back at me. I dodged out of the way.

I paused, noticing the large orange stain on his pristine white shirt, and held my hand over my mouth, trying not to laugh.

Philip glanced down.

'And now you owe me a shirt!' he hummed, dabbing at the stain, but smiling under his pretence at anger. 'It's Armani, in case you were wondering!'

We paused for a few more seconds, then I began to giggle. He joined in, shaking his head.

'I don't suppose you want me to take it off?' he said, his voice much lower now. 'You could give it a quick clean for me?'

I shook my head, reaching for the dirty dishes as originally planned. 'I don't suppose you want to be hit by a shoe again?' I replied, smirking before taking the plates through to the little office kitchen.

I was scraping the leftover Chinese into the bin when I heard him enter. 'I can help you with that,' he said and I sensed him walk up behind me. Next, I could feel his warm body press against my back. His hand lowered to mine clutching the dish.

I felt my breathing change, as I clung on to it. Short, shallow breath took over me, and I stood rigid, completely unable to move.

'Ella?' Philip said softly.

I turned slightly towards him; his face hung over my shoulder, his dark eyes stared back to mine, and I felt goosebumps travel down my body.

'No. It's fine. I got this, thanks. I have a certain way I like to wash them anyway.'

He pulled a face of amusement. 'OK.' Then he headed back out the kitchen.

I stood there for a few more seconds, catching my breath. *Why does he make me feel like this?* But I allowed the feeling to pass, before eventually returning to the sink, where I began double washing, rinsing and drying off the plates.

*

When I walked back to my desk, Philip was resting his arms on top of it.

'You opened the drawer again, didn't you?' I crossed my arms suspiciously, feeling my red neck return.

'I didn't!' He held his hands up, then shrugged. 'OK, I had a little peek. But can you blame me? I'm just trying to understand when you have the time at work.'

I sighed loudly, unwilling to engage in a discussion about sex toys with Scotland's biggest playboy.

'Oh, come on, tell me!' Philip pressed. 'Do you take it to the bathroom? *Oh*, wait. I get it!' he announced as if he had just solved the identity of Jack the Ripper. 'That beast is why you have so many late nights "in the office", isn't it?'

I shook my head, unimpressed. 'Yeah, that's it. I hang out in my office when everyone's gone home for the day, hoping the cleaner catches me with a huge purple dildo inside me.'

'Rarrrr . . . Risqué! I like it.'

My eyes bounced to his.

'It was a gift, OK? I don't want it; I don't plan on using it. That's why I stuffed it in a drawer.' I held my hands up, embarrassed.

'Oh, a gift, that makes sense then,' he agreed. 'It's funny because I was actually swaying between the roses or a butt plug for some time.'

'It was from my friends, not a man. It was more of an inside joke gift.' I blushed at my inadvertent double entendre. 'And I don't want to talk about it.'

He grinned, staring at me from a few metres away.

'Look, I should go. I've had a long day,' I said. 'Thanks for the takeaway, I appreciated it.'

'Sure. Let's head. I'll walk you down,' he replied.

I lifted my jacket, my bag and the flowers, and we steered towards the lift.

'So, when are you free?' he asked as the doors pinged open and we stepped inside.

I felt tension between us as the doors closed over. It was such a small space.

'Philip . . . I . . .'

'Ella,' he replied cheekily, making me sigh.

'Look, I don't know why you're pushing this. I'm not the girl who will fall at your feet or find your sense of humour witty or charming. I'm not into dating right now, and even if I was, guys like you aren't what I'm after.'

'Wow. Thanks for clarifying.' He smiled. 'And what type of guy am I?'

I stared at him.

'C'mon, I'm curious.' Philip crossed his hands over his body, awaiting my reply.

'OK,' I said, slowly. 'Well, you're a rich, successful man.'

'Such a red flag, I know,' he interrupted, tutting sarcastically.

'Women call your phone all the time. You don't seem to do serious relationships and . . .' I paused, feeling my breathing quicken again as he glared down at me with his stunningly beautiful eyes. 'Look, if you think this is some sort of chase, and that's the reason you keep coming back or doing nice things for me, I promise I'm not interested. I'm one hundred per cent never going to date you or have sex with you.' I paused, then looked up at him. 'Like ever!'

Philip burst out laughing and slapped his chest hard. 'Ouch!'

'I'm sorry, I know it's harsh, but I don't want to lead you on.'

But as the elevator door opened, I remembered my promise to Zola and Katy for the Dicktionary Club profile. *Shit!*

'I mean,' I sighed, turning to him. 'I suppose we can have one proper sit-down dinner or something, if you like. But it will be my treat, as a thank you for securing the exhibition. My friendship is all I can offer you.'

I stepped out into the lobby, but he didn't follow me. I turned back to see him leaning against the back wall of the lift, his arms crossed in thought.

'Friendship?' he repeated.

I nodded back. 'Yip.'

'Like best friends?' He smirked.

This man was infuriating. I gazed back, unimpressed. 'Seriously, please don't push it!'

Chapter Twenty-Three

Zola

Zola headed back to Cowcaddens that evening with an unsettled feeling lingering over her. She understood that Ella had to finish the Alexander campaign and how important it was to the firm, but at the same time, she couldn't help but feel guilty for another cancelled date with Alvaro. As she tried to shake off the feeling, she found her fingers hovering over his unopened messages on Tinder. He was due to be meeting 'Bella' in half an hour and Zola still hadn't cancelled. But she felt worse at the thought of Alvaro getting dressed up and heading to Ashton Lane only to be stood up. Zola knew she would likely never cross paths with him and even reasoned that people ghosted dates on a regular basis, right? But, at the same time, she felt sick about letting him down.

Zola spotted Curtis lying on the sofa as she crossed the road from the subway station to her flat. She felt a large sigh come out of her when she saw him lying there, with a headset on, looking like an oversized child, gaming his life away. Zola knew he'd want to spend another evening glued to the TV, while she'd be tidying up the mess he'd created in the flat throughout the day. She put out her hand to open the door, then paused. She couldn't.

Instead, Zola took a deep breath of bravery. She quickly sprinted away from the door, glancing over her shoulder to check that Curtis hadn't seen her, but of course he was too fixated on the screen. Before she knew it, she'd hopped in a taxi and asked the driver to take her to Ashton Lane.

From the back seat of the taxi, Zola took out her phone and messaged Curtis.

I'm going out with the girls tonight. Don't wait up x

Then, she opened Alvaro's last message.

Hi, Bella. I am here? I will wait for you. X

Nausea struck Zola in an instant, and she lowered the cab window. *What am I doing?* she wondered. But still, a spark of excitement ignited in her. She wanted to meet Alvaro, apologise in person that Bella couldn't make it, and do the right thing by him. He was one of the good guys, after all. Surely he deserved an explanation and not to be left ghosted in a town he hardly knew?

Curtis: *Sweet. Have fun x*

Zola read his message and instantly closed it, feeling another pang of guilt. *I'm not doing anything wrong,* she told herself. *This is the right thing to do.*

The taxi pulled up at Byres Road, and Zola clicked on the ApplePay option to pay the cab driver. She stepped out onto the street and skimmed over her clothes. She was still wearing the mini skater skirt and V-neck jumper she had worn to work all day, along with a pair of Doc Martens. She pulled down her jumper, pushed back her shoulders, then headed down to Ashton Lane.

Zola walked along the cobbles and under the picturesque twinkling fairy lights of Ashton Lane, glancing around the small groups of people enjoying the Scottish sunshine, until she clocked Alvaro. He was also scanning the crowds, waiting hopefully for blonde Bella to join him for casual drinks. Alvaro was wearing a pair of jeans, brown trainers and a cute cord blazer. Zola approached him from behind, gently tapping on his shoulder.

'Alvaro?' she said.

The handsome Spaniard turned and smiled welcomingly at Zola, trying to figure out who she was. 'Yes?'

Zola immediately blushed; she had imagined his voice so many times and it sounded even sweeter in person. He was gorgeous too, exactly as his photos suggested. With sun-kissed skin, dark brown hair and large eyes that looked just like Bambi's.

'My name is Zola. I'm friends with Bella,' she began.

A look of confusion instantly washed over his face. His head tilted as she continued.

'I work at the same marketing company as Bella, and she's unable to make it tonight. I'm really sorry!'

Zola watched his welcoming smile fade. 'Oh, I see. No Bella?'

Zola nodded. 'No, Bella, I'm sorry.'

'And she sent you? No message or anything?' he asked, bringing out his phone to check up on Tinder.

'She erm . . . she asked me to come and cancel in person. She was caught up, and she honestly felt too awful to cancel you again.' Zola paused. 'Look, I know she's let you down several times, and she didn't want you to think—'

'That it was me?' he interrupted.

Zola smiled widely at his innocently sensitive nature. 'Well, yeah. Exactly.'

'Ahh, I see.' Alvaro eventually shrugged. 'Well, thank you for coming to tell me . . .'

'Zola,' she clarified her name once more.

'Zola,' Alvaro repeated.

They gazed at one another for a few seconds until Zola was forced to look away.

'Well, look, I better head then, Alvaro. It was really nice to meet you,' she said, turning and taking a few steps.

'Wait. *Erm . . . Zola!*' Alvaro called softly. 'You don't fancy having a drink, do you? I mean, you could always tell Bella how great it was afterwards and make her eyes turn green?'

Zola started to giggle. His accent was so undeniably charming, and she felt herself swaying. Well, she had told Curtis she was out with the girls, she thought. And he'd ask too many questions if she came home early. *But was it wrong to have a drink with another man? Even if it was just to be polite?*

After a slight delay, Zola finally answered, 'I suppose I could have one drink?'

'Agh. Perfecto.' His face lit up. 'Will we go here?' Alvaro pointed to the Gardener bar, a pretty cocktail bar draped in ivy, which seemed lively. Zola watched groups of young students cackle outside on the terrace enjoying their cocktails together.

'Yeah,' she said. 'Sure!'

Alvaro headed inside for a table and Zola followed, as he held the door open politely. She glanced around, ensuring no one at the office was around. *You're not doing anything wrong*, she reminded herself. Alvaro pointed to a small empty booth snug in the corner of the room, and together they weaved their way towards it. 'What would you like to drink, Zola?' he asked.

'Erm . . . A vodka and diet Coke, please.'

As Alvaro went to the bar, Zola sat on the grey leather seat and felt her hands turn sweaty against it. She thought about Curtis alone at home and wondered how he'd feel if he knew where she was. A stab of anxiety pierced her heart and suddenly she stood up.

'Hey! Hey! Where are you going?' Alvaro asked, returning with the drinks.

'Look, I'm sorry! It's just . . . I have a fiancé, Alvaro. I probably shouldn't be doing this,' Zola admitted, completely panicking. It all came out before she could stop it.

Alvaro seemed deflated, yet sat down regardless. 'Probably.'

'It's just that Ella told me all about you, and she showed me some of your messages. I suppose I thought you seemed genuine and like one of the last remaining good guys out there. I was curious. But now I'm here, this all seems wrong.'

216

'Zola. You can't have me getting abandoned twice in one night, eh? Look, it's just a drink. Tell me about yourself.'

Zola hovered, hesitating.

Alvaro pushed her glass towards her. She glanced at his innocent face. She knew if she left now, it would ruin his night completely, plus Curtis would definitely think something was off. Eventually taking a seat again, Zola swigged some of the alcohol.

'Well, what do you want to know?'

Alvaro shrugged. 'Everything, I guess.'

*

Two hours later, Zola was laughing hard with Alvaro, feeling tipsily drunk. They were enjoying a fantastic night, sharing one another's dreams and ambitions for the future, even if she had to act at least slightly surprised when Alvaro repeated a lot of his from the messages he'd sent 'Bella'. Alvaro planned on graduating in Scotland and working here for a few more years before travelling the world, particularly Asia. Zola shared that she wanted to launch her own online marketing and social media business, which would allow her to travel, read more, plus spend time with her loved ones back home in London.

She felt alive speaking so openly with someone equally as passionate about success and making something of their life. With Curtis, Zola felt like she always had to dampen down her dreams or ambitions around him, as he seemed to lack any sort of drive himself. Zola snorted with laughter at Alvaro's encounters on the 240 bus, when he first arrived in Scotland; he told her how he'd been completely baffled at the accents and how he'd been witness to a knife fight following an old firm bust-up. Zola also shared her thoughts about the people she'd encountered since relocating north of the border; ultimately, she said, she did love it here, but it did take a bit of readjusting. As time passed far too quickly, Zola became aware of how much quieter the bar was becoming, and although it seemed inevitable that the night would have to end, she wasn't ready to leave him just yet and so the pair carried on drinking.

But, eventually, the bell on the wall rang for last orders.

'I've had so much fun tonight, you know,' she admitted.

'I did, also, Zola,' Alvaro agreed. He opened his mouth to speak again, then stopped himself and shook his head.

'What?' Zola giggled. 'Come on! What were you going to say?'

Alvaro laughed, looking flustered. 'I was just going to say I'm glad Bella decided not to show. I know it sounds unkind, but I can't imagine having this much fun with anyone else.'

Zola nodded. 'I'm glad she didn't show, too. Hey, it's her loss!'

'Drink up, people!' the barmen called out loudly once more.

Alvaro groaned, stood up and put on his cord blazer. 'Where to now?' he asked.

Zola shook her head as she stood. 'Well, I suppose I need to go home.'

Alvaro lightly brushed her hand. 'And you have a boyfriend at home?'

Zola felt another gut punch. She nodded back, feeling slightly ashamed.

'I understand why. You are the most beautiful woman in the whole of Glasgow that I have seen! It makes sense to me you have a boyfriend.'

Zola couldn't help but smile, lapping up the compliment. Something about how he spoke English, with a few tiny idiosyncrasies, was even sweeter in person.

'Well, there aren't many Glaswegians who look like you either, sunshine.' She winked playfully, returning the compliment, and they headed outside.

Ashton Lane was much quieter now, with only a couple of people staggering in the distance. Zola smiled at the twinkling strip of fairy lights above them, which seemed so much brighter now against the dark night sky, and together they strolled down the old, cobbled street.

'I'll flag down a taxi on the main street,' Zola said.

'Me too.'

They continued chatting before turning down the quiet alleyway between Ashton Lane and Byres Road. Suddenly, she felt Alvaro pull on her hand. Zola shut her eyes briefly, then opened them again. His hand felt soft, warm, gentle.

'Zola,' he said calmly.

She turned.

'We have to see each other again, no?' Alvaro's hazel eyes were heavy and honest. There was no denying the sparks that flew between them.

Zola lowered her gaze to the ground. She knew she wanted to, but she also knew she couldn't.

'Alvaro, I can't. I'm afraid that if we did, then . . .'

Alvaro pulled her closer to him, resting his forehead against hers. She could feel the warmth of his body incredibly close. He felt safe, good – and right. Zola's eyes fell on his. She felt his hand carefully touch her face, his eyes remaining locked on hers as he leaned forward, kissing her gently. Zola froze. She couldn't move. His soft lips broke away from hers, and she could feel adrenaline surge through her body, making her shake.

'I'm sorry.' He pulled away.

Zola wasn't. She grabbed hold of his arm and dragged him back to her, kissing him more deeply. She opened her mouth wider, allowing his tongue to caress hers. It was the most passion she'd felt in years – the most excitement and lust. Alvaro's hands skimmed down her body, brushing past her breasts in a way she found almost unbearably exciting. She panted through the kissing, trembling at every touch he offered. Zola pushed herself against him, urging him to continue as his bulge pressed between her legs. Then she felt his fingers slowly travel up her thigh, beneath her skirt. She parted her legs a fraction, wanting him to continue exploring her body. With his other hand, Alvaro pushed Zola against the wall, pinning her into place. Zola could feel every nerve in her clitoris pulse. He tugged her underwear to the side, gently rubbing her clit.

'Fuck, yes!' she panted as he continued working her up, pushing his fingers in and out of her at the same time. He was kissing her in between moans, enjoying the moment just as much as her.

220

Zola briefly opened her eyes, examining the quiet lane; she could see people passing by on the main street, but never giving them a second glance. There was something so thrilling about the risqué situation. Alvaro licked and bit her neck, continuing to caress between her thighs. *More!* she urged, not knowing if she spoke out loud. She felt herself build up; warmth travelled all over her body, and with a groan of delight, Alvaro brought her to orgasm.

Panting and tingling, Zola momentarily rested her head on Alvaro's shoulder, her whole body pulsating. It was amazing, exciting, like nothing she had ever done before. She almost wanted to laugh.

When she finally opened her eyes, he smiled back. But then a sudden rush of fear took over. *What the fuck am I doing?* Zola wondered. Alvaro removed his hand gently from her underwear and pressed his forehead against hers.

'Good?' he asked.

Zola could feel her heart quicken and stood up straight. She pushed past Alvaro and shook her head.

'I shouldn't have done that,' she said, feeling her bottom lip quiver with a rush of regret.

'What? Zola? Are you OK?' he asked, looking confused while readjusting his erection in his tight jeans.

Zola just shook her head, almost imperceptibly, then kept walking quickly down the lane onto the main road.

'Zola.' Behind her, he picked up the pace.

'Don't fucking follow me, OK?' Zola called back. She took out her phone and searched for a nearby Uber – *two minutes away.*

'Zola!' Alvaro said. 'You can't go? Not like this.' His sweet voice sounded upset and entirely in disbelief at what she was doing.

But Zola ignored him and rushed to the next corner of the road. She crouched down on the kerbside, running her hands down her braids.

Why did I do that? she asked herself over and over. *What the fuck?*

The Uber driver pulled up, and Zola jumped in, speeding to Cowcaddens without a backwards glance.

Chapter Twenty-Four

Ella

The following Monday, I was feeling refreshed and ready for work after a quiet weekend of yoga, fresh fruit and tidying the flat till it looked perfect. I felt fired up with enthusiasm about my plans for Alexander's exhibition. I hadn't heard from Philip since he turned up at the office and, quite frankly, I was glad. I didn't even feel a proper date was necessary to write his review for the website. I already felt like I had enough on him to speak about his cheesy chat-up lines, his flashy show-off style and annoying over-familiarity. The Dicktionary Club was shaping up nicely. The gym girls had added even more reviews, and I finally felt like we were making a dent in the Glaswegian dating scene. Which was why we were preparing to launch in just over a week's time.

I entered the office to the sight of my friends hard at work at their desks.

'Morning!' I said, passing by them and taking a seat.

'Hey!' Katy beamed.

'Hey,' Zola replied, looking distracted with her workload.

'Good weekend?' I asked out of habit, but I knew exactly what they had been up to. The WhatsApp chats were pinging nonstop with photos of our food, potential dates for Katy, and double-chinned selfies of Zola lying in bed feeling under the weather most of the weekend.

'Yep, I met three guys,' Katy bragged.

'Three? It was only two last night?' Zola swivelled in her chair.

Katy pursed her lips and flicked back her hair. 'Yep, Alfie came round last night!'

I burst out laughing.

'And?' Zola pressed her.

'You can read all about him on the page, his review is already up.'

'And did you?' I leaned in, conscious that maybe not everyone wanted to tune into my Monday morning smut. 'You know. Rate his eggplant?' I mumbled.

Katy smirked. 'Uh-huh! And well . . . it was bang average.' She blew out a disappointed sigh.

I sat back on my chair, gutted not to have gotten some juicy sex story first thing in the morning. 'That's annoying. And how are you feeling now, Zo?'

'I'm . . . fine, I guess,' she said, her tone completely flat.

Katy turned. 'What was up with you anyway?'

'I'm not sure to be honest.' She paused, some thought seeming to linger. 'Hey, do you girls fancy taking a walk at lunch? I feel like I've been cooped up all weekend.'

'Yeah! Duh! Of course!' I beamed back. I loved a lunchtime workout, especially in the summer months.

Katy moaned and reluctantly nodded, tending to hate any form of exercise. We returned to our computers and continued chatting the morning away while I designed the backdrop for the exhibition.

*

That afternoon, the three of us strolled through Glasgow city centre, sipping iced lattes from Starbucks and enjoying the rare Scottish sun beaming down on our faces.

'So, what are you girls working on today?'

'I'm doing a pitch for Blaze Boost to sponsor the hospitality awards this year. It's in August – a big fancy do in the Hilton – but it will be great coverage for them if we land it,' Katy explained.

'That would be great if you got it,' I agreed, knowing how worthwhile sponsorship could be, especially in a room full of company directors.

'I'm revamping social media for Individualise Aesthetics Clinic. Maybe I'll get free botox for doing it,' Zola said, crossing her fingers to the gods. 'How's it with the art thing?'

'Good! I have everything booked, and the guest list is continuously growing. I'm not only going to pull this off – I'm going to smash it! Alexander's PA is buzzing,' I said.

'And so they should be!' Katy hugged my arm. 'I knew it would work out.'

I turned to Zola for some positive reassuring speech on how well I had turned around the campaign, but her eyes were solely focused on the ground.

'How crazy was it of Philip turning up to the office like that, by the way?' I gasped, wanting to dive into a bitch session with my friends.

'Oh my God! I know, Ella. But why do I sort of love it, too?' Katy seemed smitten by his attempt at flattery.

'You would! Wouldn't she, Zo?' I asked, turning to my friend, who was zoned out once again.

'What?' Zola replied, not having listened to a word I was saying.

'Are you OK, babe? Are you still feeling shit or something?' Katy asked, noticing Zola's quietness.

'I'm fine.' Zola shrugged back defensively.

I turned to Katy, who pulled a face at our friend, looking too terrified to press the subject, and I paused.

'Wait, Zola, is this because I cancelled Alvaro? Are you annoyed at me or something?' I knew there was something going on with her, she seemed irritated or upset with me, and it was the only explanation I could fathom.

'What? No! Of course not. What are you talking about?'

'Well . . . What's wrong?' I asked. 'Something is bothering you, Zola.'

Zola paused and turned to face both Katy and me. She suddenly looked worried, and I glanced behind me, half expecting to be ambushed by the hyper-religious speakers who liked to hang out on Buchanan Street.

'Zola, what is it?' Katy stomped her feet like a toddler demanding an answer.

'OK,' she sighed at last. 'I do have something to tell you both, but you can't tell a soul. I have done something awful, and I suppose . . . I don't know how to fix it. Please don't judge me.' Zola's brown eyes began to well up.

I turned to Katy, who looked as concerned as I felt.

'Hey, stop!' I hugged her. 'We got you! You can tell us anything, Zo. I mean it.'

'Anything!' Katy confirmed. 'Where's the body? We'll help you bury it, babe.'

Zola smiled, but only for the tiniest second. 'The other night, I sort of . . .' She paused, inhaling for courage. 'I cheated on Curtis.' And then she burst into tears in the middle of the high street.

I was suddenly aware that my jaw was hanging open and immediately closed it.

'Zola, I'm sorry. What? When?' I eventually managed.

'With who?' Katy added, also clearly pretty shocked.

My mind couldn't think of anyone Zola met up with or was friends with in Glasgow other than us. I'd never known her to talk about any other man that she liked or fancied and I'd always assumed she was genuinely happy. I knew she moaned about Curtis on occasion, but it was for housework, or his laziness. No big deal. I felt completely baffled.

Zola's head lowered. She looked ashamed, like she'd been carrying this huge secret all weekend, terrified we'd judge her the instant we found out. 'Alvaro,' she admitted softly.

I gasped. 'No!'

'I met up with him to tell him you wouldn't make the date in person. I felt bad we'd cancelled on him so many times. Then we had a few drinks and a laugh together. The next thing I knew, we were kissing down a fucking alleyway.'

She covered her face as the tears streamed. I put my arm around her, guided her over to a bench, and we took a seat, the metal cold on our arses.

'A kiss is soft cheating, right?' Katy said. 'It's not like you shagged him.'

Zola hesitated.

'Oh God, you didn't shag him, did you?' I asked.

Zola shook her head immediately. 'We didn't have sex, but he did . . .'

'Licked your ditch?' Katy bellowed, rapidly absorbing the information.

I nudged her to hush her voice as a couple of passersby glanced our way.

'No . . . he sort of . . .' Zola sighed loudly, then looked at us. 'Rang the devil's doorbell.'

Katy's face screwed up. 'He what?'

'He poked her off,' I interpreted.

'And I came! He made me cum in a fucking piss-stinking lane.'

I was in shock, completely in disbelief. In all the years I'd known Zola, she had only ever spoken about Curtis. We'd laughed about her messaging Alvaro, but it hadn't even crossed my mind that she was truly interested in him. I wondered how much influence the Dicktionary Club had played in this. She would never have been speaking to someone else if it weren't for our project.

Eventually, I found my words. 'And I take it you're questioning what to do? As in, do you want to see Alvaro again? Do you like him, Zo?'

'No, of course I fucking don't!' Zola insisted with a grunt. 'It was a stupid thing, it was weird, and as soon as I came, I knew instantly that I had made a massive mistake.'

'Post-nut clarity,' I announced.

'What?' Katy asked, looking from me to Zola and back again.

'The serial wanker told me that's why he cums so much. Orgasms allow you to see things more clearly. It's what helped make him so successful, apparently.'

'I am ashamed, and I feel fucking awful for Curtis,' Zola mumbled. 'I know I moan about him, but we're engaged, for Christ's sake.' Her bottom lip quivered. 'He moved up here to be with me, and now I've done this to him! I don't know what to do.'

'I mean, does he need to know, Zo? You've made a mistake. You've learned your lesson. Is there any point in upsetting him?' Katy asked, shrugging.

Although Katy made valid points, part of me did think Curtis had a right to know. I mean, I know I would want to be told. I'd have to know every fact and detail to work out how to deal with it.

Zola hunched forward, hugging her legs. 'But it's the guilt! That man gave up his spot at university to move to Scotland with me. He gave up his career, his friends, his entire life.'

'And that was his decision, Zo.' I gently rubbed her back. 'You can't hold the weight of your entire relationship on your shoulders because he gave up a university place years ago.'

'Well, what would you do, Ella? Be real with me right now.'

'Honestly?' I sighed. 'Personally, I would have to be honest. Look at how the guilt is making you feel right now. If not for Curtis, do it for yourself, Zo.'

She glanced up at me, then to Katy, and nodded her head.

'Can you cover for me this afternoon? Say I'm working from Individualise or something?'

'Wait. Are you telling Curtis right now?' I asked, hoping she hadn't made a life-altering decision on a whim.

'I have to. I know I'll never get past it if I don't. He'll be finished work in an hour,' Zola said. She stood up from the bench, seeming strangely relieved. 'Hey, can I stay round one of yours for a few nights? Just in case things get bad?'

I felt my insides crunch up. I loved my friends more than anything, but the idea of their toiletries or clothes and clutter taking over my perfect sanctuary gave me severe anxiety.

'Of course you can!' Katy piped up.

Thank fuck for that, I thought.

'Yeah, of course,' I added, knowing that I sounded somewhat less enthusiastic.

Zola reached out and hugged us both.

'I don't know what I'd do without you,' she whimpered, then turned. 'I'll message you later.'

*

That afternoon, Katy and I walked on eggshells. We explained to Andrea that Zola was researching ideas with a client, and although our boss didn't bat an eye-lid, I felt sick. Everything was racing through my mind. *Why did she do that? Should I have met Alvaro instead? What would Curtis say? What if he hurt her?* I didn't think for one second that he would be capable of that, he was always such a chilled-out guy, but I'd watched far too many true-crime series to know it was always the ones you least suspected. I felt like the clock was ticking slowly, and I'd occasionally catch Katy's eye. She looked equally worried.

Eventually, just after four, our phones beeped simultaneously.

One new message from Zola:

That's it done. Katy, can I come round to yours after work? X

I breathed a sigh of relief. My friend was still alive, but I knew it hadn't gone well if she now needed to stay away from her flat.

Katy: *Of course! Are you OK? Xxx*

Ella: *I'll come too. I'm proud you did the right thing. x*

Zola: *Thanks. See you soon x*

Chapter Twenty-Five

Ella

Katy and I sat nervously on her small green chesterfield sofa that evening after work. I'd always liked Katy's flat; it was bright and homey, just like her. She had pink tiles in her kitchen, with smiley-faced emoji artwork hanging on the walls, and apart from the odd bit of clutter darted around, like hairbrushes on the coffee table or kirbies that seemed to pile up in a half-burned candle, she kept it clean and tidy. It wasn't my pristine aesthetic vibe, but it suited my friend to a tee. Around six, Katy's door knocked, and we both looked at one another cautiously. Katy stood and went to answer it.

'Hey, are you OK?' I heard her ask.

There was a quiet, muffled exchange from the hallway. Zola came towards me with a small suitcase wheeling behind her.

'Hey,' I said.

'Hey,' she responded.

'Oh, I can take this,' Katy offered, taking the case and wheeling it into her bedroom. 'You can sleep in with me, it'll be fun!' she called out, sounding excited at the prospect, like this was a childhood sleepover and not the end of our friend's life as she knew it.

Zola slumped down on the sofa, closing her eyes.

'Can I get you anything, Zo?' Katy asked, returning to the living room.

'Have you got any paracetamol? My head is pounding.'

'Erm . . .' Katy popped into the kitchen, and I could hear her rummaging through her drawers. She returned a few moments later. 'I haven't got paracetamol, but I have wine!' She smiled widely and revealed a bottle of Chardonnay from behind her back. 'Ta-dah!'

I laughed at how cute she was. 'You're the perfect host, Katy McIntyre.'

Katy grinned and squeezed onto the sofa beside us, forcing Zola into the middle.

'Well, how'd it go?' I asked as Katy jumped back up, fetching the glasses from the kitchen.

'Terrible. Well . . . you can imagine. He asked me to repeat the story over and over and over again.' Zola rubbed her eyes, which were swollen and irritated with tears and the trauma of the awful situation. 'He said he couldn't be with me after that. He said he might move back to London, that nothing was keeping him here.'

Katy gasped loudly, returning and pouring the alcohol.

I pulled a face for her to be quiet, trying my best to soothe our friend. 'He's probably in shock, though, Zo. Let him cool down for a few days, then talk about things. No one cheats for no good reason,' I said, trying my hardest to offer some sort of support.

Zola was zoning out, lost in a daze as whatever she'd been through that afternoon played out in her head again.

'Have you been happy, Zo?' Katy asked, sounding nervous at probing her.

'I'm not sure,' she said softly, taking a long pause as her mind worked overtime to assess her situation. 'Curtis can be hard work at times. He plays those stupid games twenty-four-seven if he's not at work, he is unmotivated and quite happy to lie around all day every day. Sometimes I feel like he's my child and not in a nice way; it's not exciting or romantic or anything like that anymore. But it did feel different when I spoke to Alvaro. He was different. But I suppose that's just the chase, the thrill of the unknown, isn't it?'

'*Hmm* . . . Maybe. And have you heard from the Spanish guy?' Katy asked.

That seemed to startle Zola. 'No! I blocked him immediately. Fucking hell, I don't want to think about him ever again! Look at the drama it's caused.'

'OK. Fair enough.' Katy retreated, sinking back on the sofa and slurping her wine.

'God! I just don't know why I'd be so stupid.' Zola sighed deeply. 'I suppose I felt like I connected with Alvaro. He liked the same things as me. He had dreams, ambition, integrity – plus he was fucking gorgeous!'

'It always helps.' I raised an eyebrow and smiled warmly towards my friend.

'But I didn't want to hurt anyone, let alone my fiancé.'

The room fell quiet for a few sombre seconds.

'And when I told Curtis he just kept saying, "Look at me, look into my eyes!"' she said, expertly mimicking his manly tone.

A shudder ran through me, thinking of how uncomfortable Zola must have felt.

'And what did you do?' Katy asked.

Zola hummed. 'I tried to look at him but I couldn't. Fuck, I'd rather look into a solar eclipse without any sunglasses than see the pain I've caused that man.'

I squeezed her hand. 'You're human, Zo. You made a mistake, but it does sound like you've been unhappy.'

Zola's face squirmed. 'Relationships are difficult, you know.'

Katy nodded, encouraging her to go on.

'He's not a bad person,' she said sadly. 'He just doesn't do anything with his life. Curtis has zero drive to better himself. I make most of the money, and sometimes I begrudge him for it. He works one or two days a week, and I'm out working hard every day for what? To let him scratch his arse on a sofa? We should be saving for a wedding! Going on holidays! Planning our future!'

'I get it, I do!' I agreed. 'Did you tell him that?'

Zola huffed. 'Yeah. He said he's found it hard up here, and he's lost his purpose.'

The room felt silent, as a pang of guilt rippled through me for Curtis.

'How was Andrea when I was out?' Zola eventually asked.

Katy took another swig of Chardonnay. '*Mmm* . . . Totally fine. She didn't even question anything.'

Zola's shoulders seemed to drop slightly, looking a tiny bit relieved that she hadn't lost her man and her job on the same day.

My phone pinged on the table, and I reached forward to grab it. I felt the colour drain from my face instantly.

'Please tell me Curtis hasn't messaged you, Ella. Is he asking where I am?' Zola panicked, sounding as if another drama would send her over the edge.

'No, it's Philip Khan,' I announced, reading his name on my screen.

'Saying?' Katy asked, bolting towards me.

I pushed her off, opened the message and began reading aloud:

'How are you? I'm opening a new bar in Edinburgh on Friday. I'll pick you up at seven.'

'Wow!' Zola managed a giggle.

'The sheer confidence!' Katy picked up a magazine from her coffee table and began fanning her face, then opened her legs widely, fanning her vagina.

We all laughed together, the first proper laugh we'd had in hours.

'It's the sheer arrogance, more like!' I shook my head.

'What are you going to say?' Zola asked, finally taking a sip of her wine.

'I think I'll turn him down. What's the point? He's only going to be . . .'

'Ella!' Zola snapped. 'For fuck's sake! You made a deal. The Dicktionary Club profile! He's the secret weapon, remember?'

I huffed. 'I know, but—'

'No buts! I have just been booted out of my home because you refused to meet the last guy you were supposed to, Ella. You are going to write a review on Philip Khan. End of.'

God, I almost flinched I felt so under pressure. It wasn't my fault Zola met up with Alvaro. I mean, I didn't make him itch her ditch and then tell her to run away. Yet somehow, I felt guilty because of it all. Reluctantly, I agreed that I'd meet with Philip, and began typing back to him.

I'm good, thanks. OK. See you Friday.

'Done!' I announced. 'But for what it's worth, I could probably open my laptop right now and write up a complete review of his red flags with no date needed.'

Zola shrugged. 'Well, fucking do it! Make a start. What's stopping you?'

I grinned, reaching over to my bag and pulling out my laptop. 'Fine!'

I logged into the site and began typing.

Name: *Philip Khan.*

Red Flags: *Cocky, arrogant, flashy, big-time show-off. Philip thinks he can buy affection with flowers and dinners. He is a complete womaniser . . .*

'OK, and, guys, when we're done with Daddy Warbucks, I need you both to tell me what you think of this guy,' Katy said. 'I'm meeting him tomorrow night at Blue Dog.'

'Jesus, Blue Dog again?' I said, beginning to notice a trend in Katy's dating preferences. 'Are you still hoping to bump into the Irish guy you met on your first date with Harry?'

I watched her blush. 'What? No. Sean? No!'

'*Hmmm* . . . Sean,' I teased. 'Such a seductive name, eh?'

'It's the music! It's class. The musicians are *so* talented. We should all go one night.'

Zola hummed suspiciously. 'OK, calm down, Simon Cowell! Are you sure you haven't sorted out a sponsorship deal for the Dicktionary Club with all the visits to the venue being mentioned that you're just not telling us about?'

Katy looked surprised. 'No! But kind of a genius idea, Zo.'

'God, even depressed Zola is kicking our arses with marketing ideas,' I grunted from behind my laptop, still typing away.

Zola chuckled and tossed a pillow towards me.

Together we laughed into the night, typing and plotting and ogling our next targets.

Chapter Twenty-Six

Katy

The following evening, Katy was dolled up to the nines for her date at Blue Dog. She arrived a few minutes early and was scanning the booths of the small bar. No Irish guy again. Katy scoffed. She was beginning to wonder if the man she met a few weeks back was real at all.

'Katy!' one of the bar staff called out to her. 'Back again?'

Katy felt her cheeks begin to burn. 'I know. I promise I don't have an alcohol issue,' she said, but she was questioning if she would develop one with the amount of dates she'd been racking up in the past few weeks.

'Who's the lucky guy tonight?' the young woman at the bar asked.

Katy leaned in. 'His name is Dom Black. He's thirty-five and a car mechanic.'

'And I think he's behind you.' The girl's eyes darted above Katy's head. As she turned, she spotted a tall, bearded man in a leather jacket and jeans scanning the room.

'Yip, that's him.' Katy turned away from the bar. 'Dom!' she said, as if she'd just spotted him.

A bold, cold smirk broke onto his face when he clocked her.

'How are you, sweetheart?' Dom leaned over and kissed her cheek. 'Nice place this, isn't it?'

Katy bounced her head, still glancing her date up and down. 'Yeah, I'm good, thanks. It is nice. I've only been here a couple of times,' she lied, not wanting to admit to her serial dating escapades.

'I'll get the drinks in then. You'll find us a seat, yeah? What are you having?'

Katy immediately liked how direct Dom was, how he took control of the date already.

'I'll have a classic mojito, please.'

Dom walked up to the bar and placed the order while Katy sat in her usual seat by the door. She watched him casually, leaning against the bar, chatting to the barmaid, oozing confidence and style. His beard was a bit bushier than in his photographs on Tinder, but Katy found it weirdly attractive, as if he were a giant lumberjack who could fetch them wood in their imaginary cosy cottage of the future.

Dom returned with Katy's cocktail and a pint of lager for himself.

'Cheers,' Katy said happily, tilting her glass towards his.

'Aye, cheers!'

'So, how are you finding the whole dating experience?' she asked, keen to complete her questionnaire before the cocktail buzz began.

'Aye, well. Not too bad. I have dates, you know. But I don't know. It's difficult, eh? I don't have a standard type either, which makes nailing down the perfect partner a bit more difficult.'

Katy agreed, feeling a tad more insecure all of a sudden.

'So, you don't have a type at all?' she asked quietly.

'Hmmm . . . No. Not physically, anyway.'

'I take it you go off connection then?' she asked, trying to gauge her date.

'Connection, good morals, that type of thing. Looks are influential, don't get me wrong, but shared values are the sexiest thing on the planet for me.'

Katy enthusiastically agreed. 'Yeah. God. Totally!' But at the same time she was wondering exactly what his values were. Was he religious or spiritual? Did he not believe in sex before marriage? What could he possibly feel so passionately about? Katy then wondered about her own morals – or if she even had any? Were there specific things she looked for in a man other than a big dick and a handsome face? It had never crossed her mind before. She had always moulded herself to fit her dates' expectations, and now this stranger's words were making her wonder what type of person she actually wanted in life.

'So, tell me about your work then, Katy?' Dom asked, sipping his pint.

Katy sat back, feeling much less vulnerable when chatting about her career. 'Well, I work at a marketing firm.'

'OK.' He continued sipping.

'I pretty much get a client or company assigned to me, and it's my job to find ways to boost their brand. It can be pretty fun when you have a cool thing to pitch. So, if you ever think of opening your own garage, I'll bring the broken-down cars of Glasgow straight to you,' Katy said, giggling. 'I'm pitching an energy drink brand at the moment to gyms; it helps prolong workouts with natural ingredients. Do you work out?'

Dom chuckled. 'Does it look like I work out?'

Katy scanned his broad shoulders and overall look. She couldn't see much beyond his leather jacket. 'I think you do,' she replied curiously.

'I do a lot of heavy lifting as part of my job, but I play football on weekends.' He sipped again at his pint. 'I've never been a huge lover of the gym, but I wouldn't say no to a workout with a girl like you.'

Katy blushed, enjoying the compliment and letting his innuendo go straight over her head. 'So, do you play for a football team or five-a-sides?'

'A team; it's pretty minor leagues just now. We play for fun.' He sat back. 'We have a great team of guys there.'

'Cool. That sounds fun,' Katy replied. They both took another drink. 'And have you been single long then?'

Dom let out a sigh. 'Yes and no. I've dated a few people here and there but haven't become official with anyone for about five years. What about yourself?'

Jesus, she thought. *Officially, I had a boyfriend last week!*

'Yeah, pretty similar to yourself. A couple of years, but I have dated on the odd occasion.'

'And what do you look for in a man, Katy? If you don't mind me asking,' Dom said.

Katy gazed at him, still summing him up. He was certainly attractive, with that whole macho vibe going on.

'I suppose someone who likes similar things as me, who I get along with, someone I can have a cuddle with and who is up for a laugh. You wouldn't think that'd be so hard to find in this dating world, would you? Trust me, it is!' she insisted, slurping another drink of her minty mojito.

'What about a man who looks after you? Who wants to protect you at all costs?' he asked. 'Is that important to you?'

Immediately, shockwaves travelled between her legs. Jesus, why is there something so manly about a man who wants to protect you? *I mean, I know Glasgow gets a bad rep, but it's hardly the Bronx.*

'Yeah, I think I'd like that,' she admitted, feeling flustered by arousal. 'It's very attractive.'

'Good. Because I like to care for people, but it's an old-fashioned value. I get how women like to be independent these days, but I like to protect and keep whoever I'm with safe.'

'Aw, that's nice of you. It's really kind actually,' Katy said, knowing she had well and truly ducked at the first hint of a red flag.

A couple of hours later, the bar was quietening down. Katy had already received a text from Zola saying she was heading to bed, but no matter how much she knew the countdown for work in the morning was looming, the cocktail buzz was well and truly flowing.

'I've had such a great time tonight,' she admitted to Dom, feeling unbelievably tipsy.

Dom grinned. 'Me too. You are adorable.'

He pressed on her nose cutely, and their eyes locked across the table. As Dom came closer, leaning in, Katy felt her breathing change. She shut her eyes in anticipation of a sloppy snog but felt a soft peck on the cheek instead.

What the fuck? she wondered. She opened her eyes to see Dom looking around, slightly shy at his gesture. But Katy managed a smile.

'I better walk you home, Miss McIntyre,' Dom declared. 'Before it gets too late.'

Katy agreed, only a little reluctantly.

Together, they finished off the rest of their drinks and staggered out of the bar.

'Which way?' Dom asked.

'No, no, don't be silly. I can make my own way home. I only stay on Argyle Street. Don't worry about me!' she chirped.

'Absolutely not! I invited you out with me tonight, so I'd like to ensure you return home safely, Katy.'

She blushed at his overprotective chivalry. 'OK, right.'

They turned, and she began leading the way to her flat.

'I would love to see you again,' Dom said while they strolled, hand in hand.

Katy nodded. 'Of course! Me too.'

'Maybe dinner next time?' he suggested.

'That would be lovely.'

'It lets me observe your cooking skills, too,' he added.

Katy laughed loudly, but Dom frowned at her. *Fuck, that wasn't a joke*, she thought.

'You can cook, can't you?' Dom questioned.

Katy gasped. '*Erm* . . . Of course, I can,' she said, knowing full well that she lived off Koka noodles and takeout.

'Good. I want my partner to cook for me. Especially after a hard day's work in the garage.'

Wow, now he's taking these old-fashioned values a little too far, she thought.

As she guided Dom to cross over the road, he put his arm around her until she crossed safely. She couldn't help but feel turned on by this amount of care. Katy couldn't remember the last time she felt someone actually wanted to look out for her. There was something that felt sweet and warm about having someone there in your corner.

'So, cooking is noted. But is there anything else you *expect* from your partner, Dom?' she asked, trying to sound as sultry as possible.

Dom's eyes expanded. 'You mean in the bedroom?'

Katy smirked, encouraging him to carry on.

'Well . . .' He cleared his throat. 'I do like to be dominating. Dominic by name, dominating by nature, you see . . .'

'OK . . .' Katy was intrigued.

I suppose a dominating guy means less time on top – result!

'I also want my partner to be pleased sexually. I take great pride in how much pleasure I can provide. I enjoy bringing them to orgasm. Whether it's with a man or woman, I want to satisfy them.'

Katy could feel her underwear begin to moisten with his words, then her head tilted, catching up with his last sentence.

'Oh . . . sorry. You're bi? You're bisexual?'

Dominic laughed. 'I'm not anything, Katy. I told you I go off connection. I suppose if you *really* had to categorise me . . . you'd say I was . . . demi-pansexual.'

And I'd say you were a greedy bastard, Dominic! she thought.

'But right now,' he continued, 'I feel very connected to you. Your bubbly personality is such a turn-on for me. I feel the need to look after you, and to, well . . . pleasure you.'

'Oh . . . God . . . right.' All Dom's red flags were dissolving into the night air as Katy felt her fanny twitch. 'That sounds positive!' she blurted.

'Look, Katy. Here it is. I want to fuck your brains out, but only if you follow everything I say. Every word. Every command. I'd start with basic orders the first couple of times, but over time, I'd get stricter with you.'

Her mouth gaped open, strangely turned on. On the one hand, she knew this sounded wrong. But on the other hand, she had never been with someone so sexily confident before.

'I have to ask: are you a squirter?' he said, his face completely serious as if he had simply asked her the time of day.

Katy coughed in complete shock.

'I'm . . . *I mean* . . . I haven't before, but . . .'

Dominic stopped walking. She turned to face him.

'I can make you squirt, Katy,' he announced bluntly.

Katy's brows rose to her hairline. *How can he be so sure?* she wondered. And if he couldn't, how could she possibly fake a squirt?

'Tonight?' she replied simply, feeling too curious, and too horny, to pass on a night with the Glaswegian Christian Grey.

'Anytime, anyplace. I can make you squirt.'

'I mean, I have always wanted to,' Katy admitted. 'It's sort of been on my bucket list.'

The darkness cast a shadow over the couple, standing staring at one another beneath the night sky.

'Consider it done,' Dominic replied.

And with that one statement, she was gone. Katy leaped towards him and the pair began kissing passionately in the street, walking a few steps, jogging, then stopping and kissing some more. She could feel his bushy beard tickle her face and couldn't help but wonder how it would feel between her legs. His tongue pushed slowly around her mouth as they connected.

'My flat is just up here,' Katy eventually panted between kisses, unlocking the close door and leading Dominic upstairs.

The living room was in darkness.

'Oh, my friend is staying over tonight,' Katy whispered, taking care to make her footsteps quiet. 'But she's in the bedroom.'

Dominic pulled off his leather jacket and nodded, not breaking his carnivorous stare from Katy.

'Lie down flat with your legs parted right now, and make sure you're naked,' Dom demanded.

Holy fuck, who shat in his granola? she wondered.

Katy giggled. 'Sorry? What?'

'Don't fucking answer me back! You want to squirt for me, don't you?'

OK, a little bit of role play, I got this.

Katy slowly kicked off her shoes, then pulled her dress off and threw it onto the floor. Next, she lowered her underwear to the floor. She lay naked on her sofa, feeling somewhat vulnerable and overexposed.

Please, God, don't let Zola walk in, she thought.

Slowly, Dominic strolled towards her. The darkness cast shadows throughout the room of his tall, manly physique.

He kneeled on the floor, slowly running his fingers up and down Katy's naked body. She observed him enjoy the control he had over her and began to feel more relaxed as she watched him getting turned on.

'Now, ask me to make you squirt.' His voice sounded profound, as if he was ready to perform some miracle on Katy that she had begged for.

Katy cleared her throat. 'Please,' she whispered.

'Please, what?' His voice was strict and authoritative. Katy immediately thought of Andrea and then shook that image from her mind.

'Please, please make me squirt, Daddy!'

Dom's head tilted.

Oh, shit. Did I go too far with the Daddy patter? she wondered.

But all of a sudden Dom's hands began ravishing her and he pulled Katy's legs wide apart.

God, please bury that beard deep into my pussy! she thought, having wondered the entire night what it would feel like rubbing against her clit. She could feel herself vibrate between her legs, longing so hard to be touched, stroked or licked.

Dom slowly ran his fingers up her legs instead, eventually pushing his finger inside her.

'You're wet!' he declared, tutting a little.

Katy panted, nodding, agreeing with him. 'Sorry,' she shrugged. *Was that what he wanted her to say?*

'But not quite wet enough for my liking.'

With that, he began moving his middle finger furiously inside of her. Katy's entire body was being pushed further up the sofa.

'Oh, oh, oh God!' she whimpered. She did not quite understand the feeling. Her mind wandered, wondering how awkward this would be if he failed in the mission he was so adamant he'd pass. God, it felt strange, definitely not like any orgasm she'd had before – only a semi-pleasurable feeling, more uncomfortable than anything.

Dom's hand was still twitching furiously inside of her, moving his fingers around as if he was playing a rendition of 'Bohemian Rhapsody' on her cervix.

She could feel something build inside, a pressure in her stomach, but she wasn't sure what the feeling was. It definitely didn't feel like a regular orgasm.

'Oh,' she squirmed. 'God, wait, hold on,' she implored.

Dom smirked. 'This is it.'

He continued his vigorous movements, completely fixated on the cause until—

'Jesus!' Katy cried, and a sudden gush of warm water catapulted out of her vagina, drenching her green chesterfield.

Dom continued moving his hand until Katy was jerking around the sofa, trying to push his hand away until eventually he extracted his hand proudly, splash marks from the aftermath making his torso soggy.

Katy was panting, overcome and almost beside herself. 'Oh my God! I . . . I did it. You did it! I'm a squirter!' she proclaimed happily.

Dom leaned forward. 'I told you, didn't I?' He pecked her lips. 'You did as you were told. Good girl.'

Katy repositioned herself away from the enormous wet patch, now taking up much of the sofa. She sat up. 'What the fuck, though! That was insane! Did you see it blast out of me?'

Dom sucked his teeth, relishing the fact he was the king of squirting.

She pulled him closer to her, running her hands over his bulging erection.

'Katy! Is that you?' Zola's voice called out from the bedroom.

Shit! She could feel herself panic. 'Yeah, yeah, just me, Zo. Go back to sleep.'

Dominic breathed a disgruntled sigh. 'We shouldn't finish this when your friend is here. It would be rude, and I have tricks up my sleeve that no friend should have to listen to.'

Wow! OK, Paul Daniels, Katy thought. She was more than up for a quick bend over the couch to finish him off. It was the least she could do after him welcoming her so warmly into the squirting community.

'Katy?' Zola's sleepy voice called out once more.

Jesus, what a cockblock, Katy thought.

'Let's finish this off another time, OK?' Dom said, pecking her forehead.

Katy looked up and smiled.

'I mean, if you're really sure! I feel bad that I've, you know . . . exploded.' She shrugged, still feeling fluid run down her legs. 'And you haven't?'

'Katy? Are you alone?' Zola's voice echoed throughout the flat again.

She threw her head back in despair as Dom reached over and grabbed his leather jacket.

'It gives me enough pleasure knowing that I've done that to you, and no one else can. I'll head. I'll drop you a message.' He winked and turned to the door. 'Get to bed now. You have work in the morning. And that's an order,' he instructed.

Katy nodded, fully agreeing with her new master.

As soon as the flat door closed, a bright smile appeared on Katy's face and she ran towards her bedroom.

'Zo, Zola.' She shook her friend, who was half in and half out of consciousness.

Zola jumped. 'What? What is it?' she moaned, trying to wake up.

'I'm a fucking squirter! Ahh! I've just squirted! Like seriously, I was like a waterfall. I'm the fucking Niagara Falls of Glasgow, Zola. I'm here!'

Zola's eyes eventually opened, and she took in Katy hovering above her in the darkness.

'Please tell me that isn't your minge in my face right now?'

Katy glanced down, realising she was still bollock naked. 'It is, and I'm sorry. But I am a motherfucking squirter!' she squealed happily. 'AKA, I am the dirtiest bitch around town!' She was humping the air.

Zola leaned up on one elbow, shaking her head. 'You will be a dead dirty bitch in a minute if you don't get to bed! We are working in the morning.' She flopped back down again.

Katy started laughing and jumped into bed, unable to stop smiling.

'Zo?' she whispered.

'*Mmm?*'

'I think I *really* like this one!'

Chapter Twenty-Seven

Zola

The following morning, Zola woke to the sound of her alarm going off. She turned in the bed, still half asleep, and smiled, stretching out one arm and wrapping it around the warm body beside her.

'Ugh! Tell me it's not time to get up?' Katy's croaky voice moaned back, and Zola's eyes opened wide. For a second, she'd forgotten where she was. She sat up in bed and rubbed her eyes.

'You OK?' Katy asked, noticing that her friend seemed startled.

'Yeah, yeah, I'm good. I just . . . It took me a second to remember I wasn't in my own bed with . . .' Zola stopped herself, not wanting to begin her morning feeling upset again.

Suddenly, two arms lunged for her and pulled her back into the mattress. They both laughed.

'But how are you feeling? Are you hungover?' Zola asked Katy between giggles.

Katy let go of her and sat up, looking dishevelled. 'You know, I'm not. I feel great. Last night was so weird. That date with Dominic was fucking intense!'

Zola tittered and swung her legs out of the bed.

'Zola, did I tell you, I squirted? I squirted like a hose! Like a fucking fire hydrant in the middle of New York City! I was scooshing about like a water pistol.' Zola was laughing hard as Katy described her transformative experience. 'Honestly, Zo. It is fucking mental how your body can do that with the right person. I kind of feel invigorated, you know.' Clearly, Katy was still on cloud nine after her night with the king of squirt, Dominic.

'Babe, I know. You woke me up to fucking tell me,' Zola chuckled, shoving her feet into her slippers and heading towards the door.

A bright Katy jumped up, wrapped her silky house coat around her and followed behind.

'Have you ever done it, Zo? It was strange. I imagined this out-of-body experience where I'd levitate above my body, but it was actually pretty normal. Like he was just poking me off, but in the right place . . .'

'Ew, babe! Too early.' Zola loved juicy sex chat, but right now she felt a bit disgusted by her friend's over-sharing. Katy continued regardless.

'And then I suddenly felt a pressure build inside. I didn't know what it was. It didn't feel like unreal good, but then gush! I was wetter than a whale in a bubble bath drinking a bottle of sparkling water! And that felt so amazing, like I had to get rid of it.'

As the two friends continued into the living room, Zola stopped in her tracks and faced Katy. Both of their faces had screwed up at an overwhelming stench.

'Babe, what the fuck is that smell?' Zola asked, covering her mouth and nose.

Katy shrugged, rushing to the windows and opening them widely.

'What is that?' Zola asked again, sniffing.

'Oh God,' Katy gasped. 'The heat from the sun is making it worse!'

Zola continued sniffing around like a police dog until she reached the sofa. Hesitantly, she kneeled on the floor. She glanced behind her at Katy, who stood nervously, looking on.

'I think it's coming from here,' she said.

'Lift the cushion! Maybe there's rotting food fell down the side?' Katy suggested.

'A rotten corpse, more like.' Zola lifted the sofa cushion, but there was nothing suspicious apart from some crumbs, a chocolate wrapper and a few sad hair bobbles.

'It's like a kipper! I feel like I can taste kipper,' Katy said, becoming more and more revolted by the smell.

As Zola held up the cushion in the air, searching the sofa, she reared back like a frightened pony. 'It's the cushion. It's coming from the cushion!'

'What?! Why? Are you sure?' Katy gasped, stamping her feet like a child. 'Oh, I hate this!'

Zola gulped, bravely leaned in and inhaled a whiff: 'Oh, Jesus Christ, Katy!'

'What! What is it?'

Zola stood up with tears in her eyes. 'Squirted? You think you squirted?'

Katy looked confused. 'What? I did! I honestly did.'

'No, Katy! I'm sorry to say you pissed yourself. That is urine. And very fucking strong, concentrated urine at that, girl,' Zola's face was twisted in horror. 'What the fuck were you drinking?'

'Cocktails,' Katy insisted, suddenly questioning every part of the night with Dominic. 'But honestly, I squirted, Zo. I did. It was. He said . . . he said he could make anyone do it.'

'Yeah, well, the dirty bastard's made you empty your bladder, Katy. And you now have a roommate, so it's fucked us for watching *Love Island* tonight. That's one hundred per cent piss, girl!' Zola pointed at the sofa. 'C'mon, we need to get ready for work.'

*

Later that morning, the pair sat at their desks in complete silence. Zola checked her phone, but there were no new messages from Curtis. She searched his Instagram, but he hadn't uploaded any new pictures or stories. Ella walked in and sat at her desk, looking cheerful.

'Hey.' She smiled.

'Hey,' Zola replied.

'Hi,' Katy said quietly.

Ella nudged her head towards Katy and turned to Zola. 'What's up with her?'

Zola swivelled around in her chair. 'She's just upset she pissed her sofa last night.'

'Wait, what?' Ella burst out laughing as Katy turned red with pure mortification.

'Ella, I squirted,' Katy said, as quietly as she could. 'I swear it was an orgasmic squirt.'

It took a minute for Ella's laughter to subside, but when it finally did, she said, 'There has been research that shows squirting during sex is actually just pee, you know!' She was trying hard not to laugh too much at Katy's expense.

'Well, we can confirm that study from Katy's own research last night, can't we?' Zola replied, turning back to her desk.

'I'm so angry,' Katy fumed. 'I honestly thought I'd joined this elite category of women and now I know it's all a lie,' she mumbled.

'Oh, babe! It's not a lie. Did it feel good, though?' Ella asked.

Katy was thinking back. 'It felt weird, I guess. I'm not sure if it was good.'

'Will you see him again?' Zola asked, typing away.

'I think so, but maybe not this week. I have a few more dates planned with other people. He did also say he dated men, which, before you say anything, I think is pretty cool. He is obviously very woke and stuff,' Katy said, seemingly impressed with Dominic's varied tastes.

'Katy, babe,' Ella began. 'You have a hard enough time coping if a hot girl walks into the bar around your man. Imagine how you'd feel with hot men *and* women!'

'I am more secure now, Ella,' Katy waffled back.

Zola was laughing hard. '*Mmmm* . . . OK, well, let me know if he's making another appearance and we'll get some plastic sheeting down. But, you have certainly enough to review him, so there's not really any point in revisiting. Besides, there's only so much Febreze we can afford here!'

Ella and Zola laughed wickedly. Katy rolled her eyes, but there was a slight smirk on her face.

'How are you feeling about your date with Philip, Ella?'

Ella's neck immediately turned blotchy. 'Fine, it's only one date. Then I can say I've done it. Finish the review, and my part is complete for the launch.'

'And do you have an outfit planned?' Zola asked.

'I'm thinking of this black silk off-the-shoulder maxi-dress I have, something like that.' She seemed distracted by her workload, but even still, Zola sensed she was uncomfortable talking about her upcoming date.

'Sexy choice,' Zola replied, pursing her lips.

'It's a fancy venue. I don't want to go underdressed,' Ella explained.

'No, I like it! You would look good in anything,' Katy chirped in.

Ella smiled warmly at Katy for the kind compliment.

'And who knows, you might actually enjoy the date,' she added.

Ella laughed under her breath at that.

'And have you heard from Curtis?' she asked Zola.

Zola felt her chest turn heavy at the mention of her fiancé's name. She hadn't heard a thing, and in all honesty she had expected him to reach out. Zola had no idea what Curtis was going to do. She wondered if he'd actually want to return to London. And if he did, what that would mean for her. As the silence continued she felt more nauseated by the fact she could have lost the person she was supposed to marry.

'Radio silence,' Zola managed. 'He's probably too busy on his Xbox!'

'So . . .' Ella pressed.

'So, I'll give him some space. Let him figure out what he wants to do. I don't blame him either way. I've done a horrible thing, and I deserve this.' Zola's eyes seemed sorrowful as she spoke about her fiancé. 'I just have to let him make up his mind, and we can take it from there, I guess.'

'Well, you can stay with me for as long as you like, Zo,' Katy reassured her.

Zola nodded hesitantly. 'Yeah, thanks, babe.'

Chapter Twenty-Eight

Ella

Friday evening had come around incredibly quickly, and I found myself pacing my living-room floor, waiting for Philip Khan to pick me up. I had already FaceTimed Zola and Katy three times, questioning my night, my outfit, and my entire existence on this earth. Truth be told, I wasn't up for an evening of cheesy chat-up lines and his suave efforts to wine, dine and sixty-nine me. Nevertheless, as planned, I wore my silky black dress and tonged a loose wave into my long blonde hair. I added dark eyeliner and subtle makeup to my face. Despite my trepidation, I felt good. It was the first time I had been dressed up this way for a long time, and although I didn't want to give Philip the wrong impression – *that I had made all of this effort for him* – at the same time, I wanted an excellent write-up for the Dicktionary Club to go live. Our launch date was fast approaching, now just a week away. And while the girls racked up the reviews, I knew Philip would be the perfect candidate for our standout feature. Most women would be intrigued by what a night with the multi-millionaire was like, and I also accepted that, from a marketing perspective, this would help sell the hell out of subscriptions to the website. So, cautiously, I flicked back my hair and waited for him to arrive.

I'm here. P x

Instantly, my heart began beating fast in my chest. I lifted my bag, phone and keys, applied another layer of gloss to my lips, then headed out into the hallway. I fastened up my bag, and as I headed down the old stone tenement staircase I watched Philip's eyes gawp at me through the glass pane once more. I pulled open the door and smiled.

'Hey,' I said.

Philip looked unbelievably smart in a black tuxedo, so I was immediately glad about my dress choice.

'Hey, yourself.' His eyes darted down my body and eventually returned to my face. 'You look incredible,' he said, edging forward in an attempt to kiss my cheek.

I dodged the kiss by taking a small step towards the outside stairs and turned back to him. He was smirking.

'Not a hugger or a kisser? Noted.'

I faced the road, feeling somewhat in control.

'Yeah, I'm not much of either,' I said, trying to hide my amusement. 'Where's the car?' I asked.

Philip caught up with me and pointed to a black Range Rover. A man was sitting in the driver's side.

'You're not driving?' I asked.

'No. I thought I'd join you in the back. I got us a nice bottle of champagne,' he said, heading towards the vehicle and opening the door for me.

There was no denying it: this man had exceptional manners. I slipped into the back and watched the twinkling lights on the ceiling give a starry-night effect. My Fiat 500 was lucky if it had half a tank of fuel in it.

Philip wandered to the other side and joined me.

'Thanks, Pat. That'll be us now,' he said in his deep voice to the driver.

Pat pulled out and we headed towards the motorway.

Philip poured me a glass of champagne and handed it over; I waited for him to pour his own, then held my glass up.

'To your new bar. I wish you all the luck in the world with it,' I said.

Philip's dark eyes hung on mine for a second, then he grinned. 'Thank you. And to your exhibition! It's getting closer.'

'Yep, next week.' I grinned.

We clinked our glasses together, and I sipped at the bubbles.

'Which door do you actually live at, by the way?' Philip asked as he took a swig.

'What do you mean?' I laughed. 'You were just at my house.'

'No, I was outside your home. But normally, people let me up. It is courteous, you know, rather than leaving someone outside in the cold.'

I shook my head. 'I don't let strange men into my home. Plus, it's like twenty degrees, Philip.'

'Strange men? Wow.' He sank back into his seat.

'You know what I mean.' I laughed it off. 'I just like my space to myself, I guess.'

'I bet you're a secret hoarder or something. Do you have pets? Maybe you have a zoo up there and don't want me seeing how you really live,' he suggested playfully.

I paused, wondering if this was some reverse psychology trick to get back to my apartment later. 'Yeah, I'm a secret hoarder. How did you know?'

Philip smirked, knowing I wasn't falling for his tricks. 'Have you always lived alone, Pilates?'

Fuck, every time he said that name, it gave me the fear. I rolled my eyes at him for teasing me for it.

'No, not always.'

Philip hummed. 'It's going to be a long night if you don't engage in conversation.'

I simpered. 'Well, nosy, I lived with my ex, Joshua, for a while. It was another flat, though. I've always lived alone in this one,' I told him.

'And why is Joshua an ex?'

I suddenly felt uncomfortable. I didn't want this man's pity or to look like a damsel requiring rescue, so I mimicked his earlier hum.

'We were young, and I wanted different things. I was really passionate about my career, he was passionate about other things, so ultimately, we were incompatible.'

'Ahh. I see.' Philip pondered. I could tell he was thinking up his next question, but I didn't fancy chatting about Joshua again.

'Have you ever lived with anyone?' I asked.

Philip sighed. 'Oh yes!'

I started to laugh, unsurprised.

'I was married,' he said.

I felt my brows rise to my hairline. Jesus, my Google searches hadn't told me that!

'But we divorced after a few months. I like to think of it as an expensive mistake.' He laughed, but we both knew it wasn't funny. 'And after that, I suppose I was never interested in settling down.'

My ears pricked up a little, knowing this could be the moment I needed for the website.

'Do you date a lot now then?' I tried to ask him as casually as possible, taking another drink.

'I wouldn't say date.' He adjusted his bow tie.

Permanent fuck boy status, I thought.

'More like, have fun.' He shrugged.

My mind searched for a reply that wouldn't make me sound like I was judging him. I wanted him to expand, but at the same time, I felt the need to stand up for the women he'd undoubtedly hurt along the way.

'Do the women you have fun with realise they are just playthings?'

Philip seemed surprised. He turned to properly face me. 'Well, I do try to make it clear. Let's say, I wouldn't invite them to a bar opening or anything with substance like that.'

If this was his attempt at flattery, a way to say I was different from the rest, then he was doing a terrible job of it.

'So, you would just turn up at their workplace with flowers and Chinese takeaway?'

Philip laughed uncomfortably. 'Most women would be happy with that gesture, you know.'

I rolled my eyes and turned to face out the window. Suddenly, I felt Philip's warm hand touch my chin, turning my head back to his.

'I don't look at you like a plaything. I guess that's what I'm trying to say here.'

I gazed at his perfect bone structure. For a moment I understood exactly how irresistible this man could be. He was breathtakingly gorgeous.

I pulled my face free from his grasp.

'Men love a challenge, and personally, I think you are only so interested because of how uninterested I am,' I replied.

Something curious flashed behind his eyes, but then he smirked. 'And yet, here you are sitting in *my* car,' he whispered.

I could feel my heart pound like I was running along-side the car on the motorway at seventy miles an hour. What the fuck was happening? I felt as if I was almost panting for breath.

'It was the least I could do for securing the art gallery.'

Philip hummed a little once more. 'How is that going? Tell me all about the plans.'

For the next forty minutes, I divulged everything I could about hosting Alexander's night at Kelvingrove and my ideas for promoting him as an artist in Glasgow. My heart rate eventually settled as we talked more casually about my work, his work, and his up-and-coming business trip to Berlin.

I grinned, noticing the view from the window had changed to a picturesque landscape of Edinburgh. It was only a short car journey away, but the entire backdrop was different. From the hilly cobbled streets to the jumble of medieval-looking buildings, Edinburgh seemed a million miles away from Glasgow, but every bit as beautiful. Eventually, the car pulled up onto a bustling, crowded street in the Old Town. Philip glanced out the window and let out a small puff of air, making the glass steam up a little.

'Well, it certainly looks busy!'

For the first time since knowing him, he seemed nervous.

'Of course, it does,' I reassured him, glancing out the window. 'The Cocktail Castle,' I said, reading the sign that lit up the bar in gold shiny letters. 'Nice!'

The street was lined with people hoping for a spot at the newest bar in town, and I couldn't blame them; from the outside the place was the picture of sophistication, situated in the heart of the Royal Mile with spectacular views of Edinburgh Castle.

I gulped down the last of my champagne and peeked up at him. He was still glaring out of the window, taking it all in.

'Hey,' I said, snapping him from his trance.

'Yes, sorry?'

'Will we head in?' I asked.

He was biting his lip, clearly anxious about his newest venture.

'It's going to be a great night. Look how rocking it is already!' I said, placing my hand on his shoulder. He immediately rested his hand back on mine.

'Thank you.'

Chapter Twenty-Nine

Ella

Philip held my door open, and as I slipped out, I admired the views of the castle. It seemed to light up the entire capital, sitting proudly atop the centre, packed full of history and culture. I couldn't help but feel overwhelmed taking it in. Photographers from the local press hailed my date as he entered: 'Can we get a photo, Phil? You and your good lady?' I immediately averted my eyes to the ground. *Shit*, I did not want an photo getting printed or for me to be splashed on some gossipy newspaper column. Then I felt Philip gently tug on my arm. 'Not tonight, lads,' he replied, leading me inside the bar.

'This looks amazing,' I called out to him between the chatter and trendy house music playing in the background.

He grinned, pleased now. 'The team has done a wonderful job. I have a table waiting for us.' He gently touched my lower back as he guided me through the room, leading us to a small booth in the corner where another bottle of champagne was sitting on ice, awaiting our arrival.

'Nice!' I said, darting my gaze to the bottle.

'You can have cocktails if you prefer – I'd recommend it, to be honest, as it's the speciality we're going for. The drinks are all themed around Scotland, and the spirits are sourced from Scottish-owned distilleries. But feel free to have whatever you like!' A bright smile took over his face, and I watched his shoulders finally relax as he sat down opposite me.

Now that we were seated, I glanced around the bar. Everything gleamed gold and metallic, even the huge chandeliers overhead. Cream leather booths and glass tables gave it a pristine look, while the brick walls gave it something of an urban twist. His team had managed to strike a balance of sophistication, classy, yet cool.

'We managed to get a fantastic singer up from London, too. Her name is Ronniee, and she's unreal! She starts her set around nine thirty. You'll absolutely love her. I think she sings mainly pop songs, if you're into that?'

'Yeah, that sounds great.' I instinctively wondered how close he and Ronniee were for him to be raving so highly about her music. 'How did you meet her?' I asked, trying to gain intel as casually as I could.

'I haven't met her really. I only heard her set when I was down south working and got my people to reach out. She's going to be the next big thing, mark my words!'

I nodded back. 'Amazing! And is she only coming up for the opening night?'

He nodded. 'Yes, she's recording most of the year, but we'll have live singers on every evening, just not Ronniee, of course.'

'Well, you have thought of everything. Genuinely, I'm impressed!' I called over the noise and the bustle.

'Not me, my team,' he replied modestly. 'So, when was the last time you were out like this?'

'Like this?' I questioned, not recalling ever getting brought to an opening of a fancy bar by the owner himself.

'Well, the last time you had a date?'

I glanced up from the menu I had just picked up from the table, thrown by the abrupt change of subject. 'Me? Erm . . . A few weeks ago, why?'

Philip raised a shoulder. 'I was curious. Where did he take you?'

I thought back to the serial spunker from the other week.

'It was a date my friend arranged, and it lasted all of twenty minutes.' I sighed, not willing to explain in detail what had gone wrong.

'Twenty minutes.' Philip glanced at his fancy Rolex and then back to me. 'I'm doing OK, then?'

I side-eyed his playfulness. 'When was your last date?' I returned the question, and watched him slump back.

'It wasn't so much of a date, but I suppose I did see a girl a couple of times around a month or so ago.'

I wondered if he was lying. I knew he had no reason to lie, but at the same time, I couldn't imagine him not having sex for over a month.

'And how did it end?' I asked.

'Well, you see, it didn't start. She was good to look at, but besides that, there wasn't anything of substance there.' Philip held up his hands defensively. 'She seemed more interested in what businesses I owned than me.'

I thought about how difficult it must be meeting someone genuine with his level of success. How hard he must find filtering out the girls who were more interested in a lifestyle boost, rather than him as a human being.

I reached for the champagne, but Philip placed his hand over mine.

'Allow me,' he said and began pouring. 'It's funny, I have seemed to have gone from someone obsessed with my job and overly keen on me to someone who doesn't seem keen at all.' His dark eyes flickered at me.

I lifted my glass casually. 'Perhaps you should find someone more in the middle ground then,' I retorted.

'Agh, and where would the fun be in that?'

At that moment, a young blonde woman appeared, bopping her head around the side of the booth. 'Philip! How are you?' she said excitedly. 'Great turnout! Everyone is so impressed at the renovations!'

Philip sat up straight. 'Amelia, yes! It looks great! This is Ella, my . . .'

'Friend,' I interrupted and stuck my hand out.

'Oh, Ella! It's fab to meet you! Philip's told us all about you.' She approached me, dodging my hand and going for a hug instead.

I smiled instantly at her warm, energetic personality.

'And I'm sure I included that she wasn't a hugger,' Philip said under his breath. 'This is Amelia, my PA.'

'Oh, *Amelia*! It's lovely to meet you,' I replied, immediately remembering her name, which had popped up on his phone numerous times. I examined the bright, pretty girl and wondered if the lines were ever blurred between them. She placed her hand on Philip's shoulder as they spoke closely, pointing outside at the queue forming.

'Should I run through the plan for tonight now, or . . . ?' Amelia asked Philip eagerly, hovering at the table, unsure whether to take a seat or not.

'Oh, no, no. I'm sure Ella doesn't want—'

I shook my head, sliding out of the booth. 'No, please. You guys talk shop. I'm going to nip to the bathroom.' I stood up, feeling the effects of the champagne hit me. Fucking hell, I felt drunk, I thought. But I played it down, glancing around the bar.

'Oh, it's just through the back to the right-hand side,' Amelia said. 'Or if it's too busy, there are staff facilities upstairs you're more than welcome to use.'

'Not at all. I won't be long.' I smiled back at the pair and headed to the bathroom, feeling Philip's eyes on me as I disappeared through the crowd. I wondered if they were chatting about me, or what he had told her. Probably that I'm some business associate, making sure he kept all of his options open.

The bright bathroom was busy with groups of girls with strong Edinburgh accents taking selfies and reapplying their lipsticks. I stood in line listening to them drunkenly chatting about various men leaving them on read, liking other girls' Instagram photographs or acting like complete dickheads after a few dates, and I wondered when we could expand the Dicktionary Club to other cities. This was an epidemic, and I felt like my friends and I had suddenly stumbled upon a vaccine.

After a quick pee, and reapplying some gloss to my lips, I wandered back through the lively bar, weaving and edging my way through tables of noisy partygoers. I had just spotted an empty path to squeeze by two people when one guy turned, spilling a drink down my arm.

'Oh shit. I'm so sorry!' he said.

I rubbed my arm and shook my head. 'It's OK, honestly. It's so rammed in here.'

'Ella? No way, Ella Banks! I can't believe it!'

His voice sounded familiar.

I glanced up at the stranger, and bile instantly scorched my throat.

'Joshua?' I managed back quietly, my voice swallowed by the noise of the bar.

'What the fuck are you doing here?' He put his drinks back on the bar and wrapped his arms around me, gently lifting me from the ground.

I was immediately enveloped by his familiar scent and his warmth. He was as bright and instantly attractive as I remembered. He looked older though, but even more handsome somehow, in David Beckham type way.

'I . . . I . . . came through for this bar opening,' I said as he lowered me down to the floor again. 'Wait. What are you doing here?' I was still in complete disbelief. I needed a moment to take in the fact he was really standing before me. Never in the three years since splitting up had I ever bumped into him. He had grown out his dark hair so it sat pushed back to the side. It was much more mature and sophisticated than the skinhead he'd had while we were together. He looked healthy and glowing, his arms muscular and his shoulders broad, like he'd entered his gym phase era.

'I live here now. Well, not here, more in the outskirts. It's a friend's birthday, and he told us about this place opening tonight. Fuck, you look great, Ella. So good!' Joshua rubbed my arms again, and I could feel electricity bounce between us. 'I take it you're still hammering the gym?'

As I watched his eyes skim down my body, every emotion and feeling from all those years ago came rushing back.

'Yeah, I am.' I paused, then looked up at him, just inches away from me, in reality. Was this a sign from the universe? 'I was talking about you earlier today,' I heard myself blurt out, still entirely in disbelief he was here.

'No way!' He laughed, grabbing my hands. 'Wait, let me guess: to Zola and Katy?'

I nodded back, not wanting to admit it was with Philip. 'Yeah.' I chuckled. 'Of course!' I made a guilty face, thinking of my two best friends.

'We had something really special, Ella. Jeez, I think about you constantly. Honestly, I could see something totally random and think, "Oh, Ella would love this"!' His grin was infectious, and I burst out laughing, knowing the same thing happened to me still, even after all this time.

My heart thundered in my chest. 'Oh my God! Same! I saw an advert the other day on TV and the guy was scuba diving and I immediately thought of . . .'

'Egypt! Ha!' Joshua finished my sentence and I laughed, thinking of us going on a disastrous scuba-diving trip that ended in him breaking his nose.

I didn't realise how much I'd missed this man in my life until now. He was the only one I'd ever really let in, the only man who hadn't disappointed me, the only man I ever trusted.

'My mum constantly asks about you, too. "How's Ella? Let's see her Instagram!" And I'm forced to troll photographs of the prettiest girl in Glasgow. It's a form of torture, by the way.'

I felt myself blush, and playfully pushed his shoulder, enjoying the compliment, but knowing I had to unfollow all of his family after we split to save myself from mentally destroying myself.

'Josh! We were wondering where you got to!' a voice called out.

Suddenly, Joshua turned more rigid and he took a step back, welcoming the voice, '*Errr* . . . I'm sorry. I bumped into an old friend. Ella, this is my wife, Sarah.'

I stopped, completely motionless.

Your what?

A beautiful brunette came round from behind him, and my eyes immediately fell on her large baby bump.

'Yip, a little bruiser on the way!' Joshua rubbed her stomach, and she grinned back, leaning into his shoulder.

I felt like I had been hit by a double-decker bus.

I couldn't move.

I felt my chest rise and fall with panic.

The room was spinning. I was entirely speechless.

Say something, say something.

'Con . . . con . . . gratulations,' I eventually whimpered, unable to take my eyes off this woman's rounded stomach.

'Ella!' I heard Philip's voice cut through the static around me, and suddenly he was by my side. 'I thought we would have to call a plumber out, you were taking so long in there!'

He looked at me, then at Joshua and his wife, and held out his hand.

'I'm Philip. Nice to meet you.'

'Joshua, and this is my wife, Sarah.'

I felt Philip's arm immediately wrap around my shoulder. He pulled me in tightly. 'It's great to meet you both. Are you having a nice night?'

'Yeah, man. Absolutely! It's a cool vibe!' Joshua was nodding his head, overcompensating for the agonisingly awkward situation we were both feeling.

'Glad to hear it. If you need anything, a seat perhaps for Sarah, just say to the staff and they will take care of it,' Philip added. He was holding me tightly, almost as if he was actually keeping me upright, but I was in a zoned-out daze. I'm not sure if it was the shock of seeing my ex, the shock of discovering he was married with a baby on the way or the effects of too much champagne, but I felt paralysed.

'Amazing. Yeah, we'll maybe do that. So, do you work here, mate?' Joshua added.

'I own the place,' Philip replied confidently. 'Look, we should really get back,' he continued, smiling down at me.

'Right, yeah. It was so great to see you,' Joshua said.

Philip turned my body, and I could feel it trembling in his hands. As he guided me gently through the crowds of people drinking and having fun, I kept my head low. Tears began to trickle down my face.

'Excuse me,' Philip said as he led me through the bar. 'Out of the way, please.'

I was in a trance. I was in complete disbelief.

How could Joshua be married? With a baby coming?

He looked so happy, so fresh, so handsome. But why wouldn't he? He'd managed to get everything he wanted in this world. But I couldn't understand how he could move on so quickly, while I was still stuck in the same life from when we'd ended.

Suddenly, a door shut, all noise became muffled, and I realised I was in the back room of the bar with Philip, surrounded by kegs and bottles of alcohol.

'Are you OK?' he asked in his deep masculine voice. 'There's an office upstairs, but this room was a bit nearer.'

I pushed back my tears with the heels of my hands, clearing my throat.

'Yeah, yeah. Of course. Why wouldn't I be?' I asked him.

His dark eyes looked sad, observing me.

'What? I'm fine,' I said a little too loudly, trying to convince both of us. I could feel my chin quivering from the effort of trying to smile. 'I'm honestly fine, Philip. You know I've probably just had a bit too much to drink.'

But as quiet surrounded us, and I tried to hold it all together, I let out a giant blubbering sigh.

'Fuck, I'm so sorry,' I eventually cried.

'I take it that was *the* Joshua?' Philip asked, clearly experiencing his own moment of shock.

I nodded. 'And *the* pregnant wife who I had no idea fucking existed.'

'Ouch,' Philip murmured sympathetically. 'And was that the first time you've seen him? Since?'

I attempted a snotty smile, still holding onto the pretence that I was fine. 'Yep.' I could hear my breathing hitch from all the emotions, and I held my hand to my chest, trying to regain composure. 'God, I'm so sorry. Wow. I'm never like this.'

'You never get upset?' he asked softly, resting back on a keg.

'Me? Never. I'm an adult,' I said, laughing at even the idea of it. Knowing the last time I properly cried like this was the day Joshua left.

'God, I cry all the time. Hysterically, in fact. Even an advert on the radio could set me off,' he said, and I grinned at his attempt to reassure me.

'He's just . . . you know . . . the one I always thought would . . .' I stopped myself.

'Come back?' Philip answered for me.

I held both of my hands to my face and nodded. 'I didn't want kids, and he did. Now he basically has a kid, so . . . I should be happy for him, I guess.' I could feel my bottom lip quiver again.

Philip remained silent.

'But there was always this tiny part of me that thought maybe he'd realise . . .'

Tears and snot trickled down my face again, and I sniffed loudly.

'Realise what?' Philip asked.

'Realise that I could be enough for him. Just me. Just me and him.'

I began to feel tears stream down my face again and lowered my head, absolutely humiliated and distraught over how this night had turned out.

As I cried, I felt Philip's warm body wrap around mine and hold me. I tried to push him off, but he remained there. His strong arms held me, until finally, I stopped fighting. I didn't have the energy; I felt broken. I rested my head against his tux instead, sobbing until my breathing calmed and my heart rate settled. We stood that way in silence for a few minutes.

'Better?' he eventually whispered.

I bobbed my head back, still glued to his chest.

Philip raised my chin to his face. 'You don't have to be strong always, you know.'

I nodded. 'I am usually very organised and structured, not like this. I just didn't anticipate that tonight, and it caught me off guard,' I admitted, glancing up at him.

'If you live life so organised and structured, what happens to spontaneity?'

As I fixated on Philip, my heart picked up its pace. His eyes were dark but full of kindness.

'Spontaneity?' I whispered back.

'Yes. Like this.'

Philip leaned closer, his face hovering just above mine for a few seconds. I felt his warm breath on my lips, and then he kissed me.

I paused, stepping back.

'We shouldn't,' I said immediately.

Philip stepped closer to me again, this time he placed his hand on my chin. I closed over my eyes. It felt good to be comforted. Then I felt his lips kiss me once more.

This time I wrapped my arms around him, not remembering the last time I was kissed. He opened his mouth wider, kissing me more deeply, his tongue soft and warm. His mouth began wandering down my neck, biting and grazing my skin. He turned my body around, my back now pressing against him, and I looked up over my shoulder, his dark mysterious eyes locked on me, then we began kissing more passionately this time. As his tongue wrapped around mine, his hands ran up and down my silky dress. He grunted, touching me slowly but hungrily.

I turned back around, pushing him back to take a seat on a keg, kissing him even more deeply. It felt so good giving in to him, but it also felt like taking back some control.

Every part of my body surged to be touched. I could feel blood rush between my thighs at the thought of this man between them. I tugged on his jacket, pulling it off, and Philip allowed it to fall to the floor.

'Jesus,' he panted.

But I kept going. I wanted him. I wanted to feel better.

Philip ran his hand up my leg, and I widened my legs, desperate for him to touch me. He pulled my underwear to the side and started rubbing my clit.

'Yes,' I whispered. 'Keep going.'

Philip pushed a finger deep inside of me, and I arched my back, feeling every inch of it.

'Fucking hell,' he whimpered, almost in awe. 'When was the last time you were touched, Ella?'

I opened my eyes and stared back at him.

'Not since . . .' I couldn't bear to say his name. And I was determined my ex wasn't ruining this moment for me.

I felt Philip remove his hand from me. He stood up straight. I stepped back, giving him space.

Did I do something wrong? I wondered.

He picked up his tux from the floor, dusting it off.

'Is everything . . . Have I done something?' I asked, embarrassment flushing my cheeks.

Philip shook his head. 'No, no, of course not.' He smiled, touching my face gently. 'I want to do this right with you. Not in some grubby wine cellar. I'll text Amelia and tell her we're leaving, but you are coming home with me tonight.'

I felt the hairs on the back of my neck stand up.

'Right now? But what about the opening? The singer?' I asked.

'Fuck the opening, Ella! You need this, and so do I, to be honest. I'm not waiting any longer. Come on, we're leaving.' Philip stuck out his hand, and I grabbed hold of it.

Together, we exited the bar.

Chapter Thirty

Ella

Butterflies swarmed my stomach as the taxi slowed in front of a townhouse in Edinburgh. It was only a few streets from the bar, and I didn't have nearly enough time to give myself an internal pep talk or compile a list of reasons why this was an awful idea in the first place. I felt hurt and empty, and I wanted to be comforted by Philip, even if it was just for one night. As he leaned forward and paid the cab driver, he smiled, his teeth glistening in the dark.

'Coming in?' he asked.

I replied by scooting my body towards the door and stepping out onto the street.

'Is this your house?' I asked, taking in the stunning building. It wasn't dissimilar to my flat, except it was just one large home.

'It is,' he replied, watching me take it in from the kerbside. 'What do you think?'

'It's lovely.' I smiled back at him, then added, 'Well, from the outside. Maybe you're a hoarder or something, though.'

Philip laughed. 'I suppose we'll see, eh?' He held out his hand to me, and suddenly I felt my arsehole clench. *Was I really doing this?*

He led me up the five or six stone stairs and unlocked the vast door. As soon as we stepped inside, the lights switched on, detecting our movement. The wide hallway was painted white with black furnishings. Photographs of his family hung proudly on the walls. I took a few steps, running my gaze over them. The house was pristine, clutterless, and it smelled as fresh as linen.

'Where will I sit my shoes?' I asked, slipping them off.

Philip shrugged. 'Anywhere you like.'

I blushed and placed them neatly together at the bottom of the stairs.

'I thought you lived in Glasgow,' I said, wondering if he had homes in all the major cities.

'That's probably because you never asked me,' he said, leaning against a door and watching me. 'Would you like a tour?'

I gulped, a little uncomfortable that I was even here. I never did this, and I certainly never did this with men like Philip Khan. *Was I having a breakdown after unexpectedly seeing Josh? An early-onset mid-life crisis maybe? Or was I letting the Dicktionary Club go to my head too?*

'Yeah. Sure,' I said as I approached him.

Philip opened what turned out to be the living-room door. It was a midnight blue with a large-screen television and media wall. A huge corner couch took up most of the space, and a beautiful bay window looked onto the cobbled streets of Edinburgh.

I padded over to the window in my bare feet. 'Wow,' I murmured.

I felt Philip's body behind me; he rested his hand above the window ledge, almost locking me in place.

'Stunning, isn't it?' he said softly. His fingers trailed down my arm, and I could feel my nipples harden.

'*Mmmmhm* . . . Beautiful,' I whispered back, trying my hardest to stay on topic.

'There's a rooftop garden terrace, too; it has views of the castle, Arthur's Seat and pretty much the entire city,' he said.

I turned to him, his body pressing onto mine. 'Really?'

'Mmm . . . yes.' Philip pushed a few strands of hair back from my face. 'But I don't like heights, so I don't go up there.'

I smirked curiously.

'Can I ask you something, Ella?'

I glanced up at him.

'Do you hate me a little less after tonight?'

My face broke into a smile and, almost immediately, he matched it. I put my hands on his shoulders, and he hummed, pressing me for an answer.

'I'm not too sure about that, to be fair.'

I watched his eyes turn dark as my reply seemed to excite him. He ran his hand up my thigh and began massaging between my legs with his thumb. His mouth touched mine as he whispered, 'What about now?'

I could feel my body heat rise, letting this man touch me again.

'No.' I twitched under his touch. 'I still hate you,' I replied, eyes closed.

He grinned and pushed me until my back was pressed against the window glass. I turned my head briefly to ensure no one was outside and witnessing this, but he held my chin, ensuring all of my attention was kept on him. Philip lowered himself to his knees and bundled my dress up from the floor, raising it from the ground, then he slipped my underwear off.

I watched him bite his lip as he gazed at my pussy. Then he put his face up into my dress.

His breath felt hot against my skin as I felt him position himself between my thighs. Then I felt his tongue lick teasingly up and down my labia.

'Jesus,' I yelped, my body pressing against the cold window.

I looked down at his body, working hard below me.

He began licking, sucking and teasing my clit; I had never felt pleasure like this before. It was the first time a man had pleasured me this way, and I couldn't believe how good it felt. His head bopped up and down as I felt my thighs get wetter.

I felt unsure of what to do. I felt tense, oddly anxious and aware of my strange position against the window. I hadn't had sex in such a long time it was hard to let go.

But as his tongue continued to lick, I felt shockwaves of warmth travel over my body as he groaned with his own pleasure. There was no denying it, his mouth on me felt amazing.

'Fuck, Philip, fuck!' I panted.

Finally parting my legs and allowing myself to relax into it.

I pushed his head deeper between me, feeling the coolness of the glass press exquisitely against my back. I never wanted him to stop.

And he didn't.

Philip continued circling my clit until it pulsated at his touch, bringing me to an incredible climax, and when I finally let go, he continued sucking my clit, making me flinch and shake from an almighty orgasm.

'Philip, Philip,' I moaned.

Slowly he re-emerged from under my dress, his mouth shiny from my cum. I kneeled on the floor, too shaky to stand and kissed him hard. I could taste myself off his soft lips and I'd never felt so turned on in my life. I brushed my hand over his dick bulging from his suit trousers and tugged on his belt. Philip helped and sloughed his trousers off. Next, he lowered his boxers, exposing his cock. I ran my hand up and down it, feeling every part of my body long for it. But inside, I could feel my nerves build, knowing I hadn't done it in so long. Philip continued kissing me, pushing his hands through my hair and groaning with pleasure as our tongues intertwined. Gently, he laid me back on the floor and edged on top of me, smiling down as he hovered above me.

'Do you still hate me now?'

I felt an overwhelming sense of arousal, like there was something so wrong in being with him, but it somehow also felt so right.

'I still hate you,' I replied, watching his flawless face above mine.

'Good,' he replied.

Then I felt him push inside of me.

Immediately, I whimpered, but Philip went slow to begin with, pushing back my hair and kissing down my neck as he thrust back and forth. It felt electric and mind-blowing. I wrapped my legs around his back and moved my hands up his shirt. His body was sticky with sweat, I could tell he was on the edge.

'Come inside me,' I moaned, wanting to feel every bit of this man as deep as humanly possible, and also realising with an odd jolt that my coil was still in place.

'Are you sure?' he asked, panting deeply. 'I do get tested, I promise.'

'Yes! I want to feel you cum inside me.'

And with that, he grunted and moaned, finally orgasming.

I lay on his oak floor, catching my breath, as Philip leaned forward and kissed my forehead. He pulled out and flopped down beside me.

I turned my head and watched him regain composure. His hairy chest was slick with sweat. I could tell he worked out. He looked perfect lying there.

'You have no idea how much I have dreamed of that moment,' he said, lifting my hand and gently kissing it.

I was unable to speak, still feeling tingly and euphoric.

'Was that OK for you?' he asked, leaning up to face me, perching his head on his hand.

I grinned, smugly. 'It was amazing,' I said. No matter how much I hated complimenting the guy, there was no denying his skills were exquisite.

'Well, I'm glad.' He pecked my lips again. 'You taste beautiful, Pilates.'

I blushed, not quite knowing the proper response to a fanny-taste-test compliment.

'I can show you my bedroom now?' he asked.

I leaned over and gently kissed him. 'Yes, please.'

Because right now, there was no place I'd rather be.

Chapter Thirty-One

Zola

Across Glasgow, Zola was lying in Katy's bed, working on the website. She was reading through all the additional reviews uploaded, adding extra tabs and features, ensuring it worked as smoothly as possible. She found it a great way to distract herself and keep busy as Katy entertained yet another new date in the living room. Zo was playing her favourite R&B playlist through her Beats in a bid to keep the moans and shagging sounds from next door to a minimum.

Nevertheless, she felt agitated at night, especially when Katy was dating. Despite WhatsApping Curtis a few reminders to take the bins out or to ask if he was OK, she still hadn't spoken properly with him since the fallout. The Dicktionary Club was about the only thing that kept her mind occupied and busy from the chaos she had created in her personal life.

She was accepting reviews from the gym girls, skimming over their dates and editing out any information that could be defamatory, should any legal mishaps happen. When she clicked on the next review, Zola's heart bounced in shock: *'Review of Alvaro – five stars.'*

Automatically, a large-scale photograph of her late-night finger-blasting floozie appeared on the screen.

Zola scrolled down, feeling her entire body rattle from the inside.

The date: Wow, what can I say about sweet Alvaro! He's tall, Spanish and cultured. We certainly don't have men in Glasgow like this, that's for sure. Alvaro took me to Tiffany's, where we enjoyed a steak dinner. Afterwards, we wandered through the West End and rested at the Botanical Gardens, where he recited poetry for me! Yes! Poetry! It was like a scene from a movie. After a couple of dates, we had the most passionate sex I've ever had. Let's just say that man is a giver!

'Fuck!' Zola said, pulling off her headphones and slamming the laptop shut in a panic. She immediately felt dizzy and nauseous. She didn't want Alvaro anywhere inside her mind, but the thought of him dating other women really bothered her. *Why am I jealous?* she wondered. She stood up, feeling confused, and paced Katy's bedroom floor, but she couldn't settle. She needed Katy's advice, but she wanted to ensure the coast was clear, so she pressed her ear against the bedroom door.

Silence.

Slowly, Zola opened the door and stuck her face out into the hallway.

'Katy?' she hissed.

The living room was silent, but reflected in the TV she could see flickers of light coming from some Aldi Jo Malone dupe candles.

'Katy,' Zola whispered a little louder, taking a step towards the living room.

She edged her head around the door and spotted a naked man sprawled out on the sofa, casually flicking through his phone. Just as well that sofa was scrubbed over the weekend, she thought. Then Zola's face twisted, noticing his little lifeless dick resting on his thigh. Katy must be in the bathroom. She tiptoed down the hall to find her friend.

The bathroom door was closed over but not shut all the way, so Zola quietly nudged it open. But as she stepped in, a bollock-naked Katy jumped; she was sitting on the toilet pan, looking flushed, with one hand holding her phone and the other rubbing her fanny.

'Katy McIntyre!' Zola squealed in shock.

'Agh, fucking hell!' Katy grabbed a tiny hand towel hanging off the sink and attempted to cover any modesty she had left.

'Are you . . . are you wanking yourself off?' Zola squirmed, a shiver running through her. Katy's phone was still playing, and Zola glanced at the screen. 'To *Grant Mitchell*? Fucking hell, babe!'

'Ross Kemp! And what if I was? It's my house, Zo!' Katy scowled back.

Zola's face remained twisted. 'Didn't you like *just* have sex?'

Katy's eyes rolled. 'Trust me, I wouldn't call it that. That cunt was rubbing my belly button at one point. These men should have paid better attention to female anatomy at school!'

Zola burst out laughing, and eventually, Katy did too.

'What's up? Do you need to pee?' Katy asked, finally pausing Kemp's documentary.

Zola's shoulders relaxed, and she perched herself on the bath ledge. 'No. It's just . . . One of the gym girls dated Alvaro.' She let out a sigh. 'And she gave him a five-star review, too.'

'Ohh!' Katy adjusted herself, sitting up on the pan.

'Yep, and I don't know why, but I feel weird about it. Like I'm angry at him or something,' Zola admitted.

'Awww, it's because you liked him, Zo. Of course you do, it's only natural.' Katy smiled and leaned forward to hold her friend's hand.

'No, no, wash your hands first, babe!' Zola dodged out of the way. 'I mean, I did feel a connection, but I love Curtis, don't I? Alvaro was just *so* attentive, and asked me deep questions about myself – opposed to *What's for tea, Zo?* or *Have you seen this reel of a cat in the shower?* It was just nice to feel that spark, that excitement, you know? Waiting for his name to appear on my screen. Fuck, my head is all over the place!'

'That's lust, though. It doesn't last forever. You know this, Zo!'

'But, maybe this is a sign? Maybe I shouldn't have cut all contact with Alvaro?'

Katy sighed. 'Oh God, *no!* Don't start this again.'

'What?'

'How would you have felt if Curtis was on that list? If one of them dated Curtis?'

Zola's eyes almost popped out of her head. 'Girl, you know he wouldn't be alive for a second date!'

Katy smirked. 'And there's your answer. You can connect with someone and have a moment in time with them, but ultimately, love wins. Every time. And you and Curtis love one another. Right?'

Zola's eyes welled up and she took a deep breath in. 'Right.'

'You will sort this out, Zo. Give him space or do whatever you need to do?' Katy added.

Zola nodded. 'Yeah, you're right,' she whispered back.

'Do you need me to come lie with you?' Katy asked.

Zo smiled. 'Nah, girl. It's OK, that's all I needed to hear. I'll let you return to Limp Bizkit on the sofa.'

Katy's face screwed up. 'Ew, no way! I'm going back to Ross! Shut the door on your way out, will you?'

'No probs, Mrs Kemp,' Zola sniggered, shook her head, then tiptoed back into the bedroom.

Chapter Thirty-Two

Ella

The following morning, I woke wrapped up in pristine white Egyptian cotton sheets, and immediately realised I wasn't in my own bed. *Fuck*, I thought, lifting the sheets and glimpsing down at my entirely naked body. My legs felt achy, and my vagina felt as if it had birthed a watermelon overnight. *Why didn't you go home, Ella?* I wondered.

I sat up slowly, glancing around the bedroom for my underwear and dress, seeking the best escape route. Philip was facing the opposite direction, and I could tell by his breathing that he was still in the midst of a deep sleep. I had no idea what time it was. Glimmers of sunshine peeked through the edges of the slatted wooden blinds. Carefully, I bummed my way to the side of the bed, stood up, and tiptoed around the wooden floor, picking up loose clothing that felt like mine in the darkness. Then I quietly opened the door and headed into the hallway.

I felt sticky, warm and tender from the crazy night we'd had. *What was I thinking?* But there was no denying it: the man was a freak in the sheets. I tiptoed down the staircase into the living room, then sat on his sofa and ran my fingers through my hair, taking a moment to understand what I'd done. I reached for my handbag to retrieve my phone. *No battery, great!* I had no real idea where in Edinburgh I was, though we must be near the centre, or how to satnav my way to the nearest train station. I closed my eyes for a moment to think.

No ApplePay if my phone's dead. No cash. Fuck.

There was nothing else for it; I would have to ask Philip. This was no doubt going to be awkward for both of us. I returned to the bedroom and wandered around the bed. He lay completely still, and I watched him for a moment – his long eyelashes closed over, his dark chest hair, his muscular body resting peacefully in the bed. He was certainly a handsome guy.

'Do you mean to stare like a psychopath? Or are you contemplating robbing me?' His eyes were now open, and he was looking up at me.

Shit.

'No . . . I . . . I was going to go home and leave you in peace, but my phone's died. I don't suppose you have a charger I could borrow? And I'll call a taxi or Google Map my way to Waverley?'

Philip rubbed his eyes, sitting up. 'What . . . What time is it?'

'I have no idea,' I answered.

He leaned towards his dresser and lifted his watch. 'It's only eight o'clock! Get back to bed, woman!' His hand tugged on my arm, bringing me close to the bed.

'It's just . . . I don't want to overstay and . . .'

'Ella?' His voice was deep and croaky from sleep.

'Yes?'

'I would love to stay and cuddle you, but if you want to leave, I will get dressed and take you home.'

I paused.

I didn't know what he expected. I wasn't the type of girl to lie in someone's arms all day – I had the gym to get to and meals to prep.

'You want to go home, don't you?' he asked, correctly interpreting my pause.

'Yep, yes, I do.'

Philip sighed and stretched his arms wide. 'OK,' he said, 'I'll just put some clothes on and we can head.'

I watched him stand up. Jesus! His penis was rock solid. I felt my ovaries twinge. Although, I wasn't sure they were rested enough for another round with him.

'You're staring again,' Philip commented, and I immediately raised my gaze to his face.

'You're hard again,' I retaliated.

Philip glanced down to his knob and slapped it a little, then laughed, pulling a T-shirt from his dresser. 'I'm always hard when you're around.'

I tutted slightly, wondering how many times he'd used that line. It rolled out of his mouth so easily.

'I'll let you get ready and wait downstairs,' I said.

I headed back to the living room and sat on Philip's sofa, glancing around the room without a phone for distraction. I spotted a handprint on the window and immediately thought back to him licking me out while I was pressed up against it. My body turned warm at the thought. *Jesus Christ, Ella! What the fuck were you thinking?* My eyes darted down to the floor, and I had visions of him pushing inside me for the first time. How good it felt to be whole.

'I'm ready when you are,' Philip's voice called out from the doorway, and I jumped as he startled my dirty flashbacks.

'Sure, I'm sorted.' I walked past him, slipped on my shoes and headed out the front.

Philip pressed the fob to the Bentley SUV, which lit up as we approached. He opened my door, and I slid into the passenger side. A few seconds later, he joined me.

'So, what do you have on for today?' he asked, still rubbing his eyes, trying to wake himself up.

'The gym, and I'll probably go see my friends. We're working on a project together.'

Philip nodded. 'Nice!'

'What about you?' I asked, glancing out the window, feeling uncomfortable at the formalities when the man had been riding me like the waltzers all night.

'I don't have much on. I'll swing by the bar and see how the rest of the evening went without us.'

For the rest of the drive, Philip chatted while I responded pleasantly from the passenger side, giving more attention to the scenery than the conversation. I just wanted to go home, get washed and forget about my night of sheer insanity. After forty minutes on the motorway, we glided back into Glasgow and he pulled up beside my flat. Relief swept over me.

'Well, thank so much for driving me home,' I said, unbuckling my seat belt.

'I had a really great night with you,' Philip said.

My cheeks blushed, and I smiled awkwardly. 'Yeah. Thanks.'

'I don't suppose you're free tonight?' He turned his body around, giving me his full attention.

'Awk, I'm not. I'm sorry.' I shrugged. 'I've got a thing on.' I was looking down at the floor, picking up my handbag.

'Tomorrow then?'

I hummed. 'Tomorrow, I think I'll be catching up with work. I have the exhibition next week.'

Philip let out a small laugh. 'Ever?' he interrupted.

I turned, eventually facing him properly and sighed. 'Look, Philip. Last night was fun. But it was so, *so* unlike me. I think I was just upset over Joshua, and you were really nice to me, and then one thing led to another. We don't have to do this.' I gestured my hands, pointing between us, knowing we didn't have to participate in that awkward thing people do when they pretend after a one-night stand that's it going to happen again. 'My feelings are not hurt. I will not feel sad and sit around all day, hoping you might text me. I'm not like that. It's all forgotten about.'

I watched his eyebrows raise in surprise.

'Honestly.' I managed a laugh. 'I know what this was, and I'm OK with it,' I said. 'We both had a bit too much to drink, I was emotional and you comforted me. We can leave it there.'

Philip sighed. 'All right then.'

'There is no need for any embarrassment or for us to make false promises to one another. I'm good. You're good. And it's all . . .'

'Good?' he interrupted once more.

'Exactly.' I placed my hand on the door handle, finally hoping to leave this night behind me.

'But what if I actually wanted to see you again?' Philip asked in his deep voice.

I continued looking out of the window.

'Ella?'

I felt tense. What did he want from me? I thought about Joshua and how invested I got in him, and I couldn't contemplate that level of hurt again. Not now. Not ever. 'It would end either way. Eventually,' I said quietly. 'So, we're as well ending it here, on a high, right? I honestly had fun.' I smiled. 'And thanks for the lift home.' Then I opened the car door and walked quickly up to my building without looking back.

As I entered my flat, I pressed my back against the door, feeling slightly breathless from bombing it up the stairs. After a few moments, I took out my phone and headed to my bedroom to pop it on charge. I paced my bedroom floor, replaying the entire night out in my head. From Joshua to the wine cellar, to being pressed up against the window. My insides twisted.

My phone lit up, and I dived on the floor beside the plug, immediately messaging the group chat.

Ella: *Guys ALERT!!!!*

. . .

Zola: *You OK?*

Ella: *I bumped into Joshua last night on my 'date' with Philip!*

Katy: *NOOOOOOO!!!!!*

Ella: *Yes!*

Ella: *And his pregnant wife!*

Zola: *STFU.*

Katy: *Are you OK? WTF! A wife??? WHO IS SHE?*

Zola: *Do you want us round??*

I paused, not knowing what I wanted. My body felt agitated and unnerved, like something was bothering me, but I just couldn't put my finger on it. I wondered if it was Joshua or the fact that I had stayed with Philip. I felt entirely out of sorts.

Ella: *I might pop by Katy's later. I'm not sure yet. I'm really tired x*

Zola: *Babe, we got you. We could grab lunch or dinner?*

Ella: Guys??

I felt nervous even admitting to my friends the next part of the story, but I wanted everything off my chest.

Ella: *I also may have shagged Philip Khan.*

Immediately, my phone began ringing. It was a Face-Time with Zola and Katy's faces squashed on the screen. I sat on the hardwood floor, still charging my phone while filling them in on my night of debauchery. I needed comforting, and I knew they were the only people in the world who would hear me out and help settle this horrible feeling I had lurching within me. The girls seemed shocked yet thrilled at the same time as I divulged.

'So, it was amazing sex?' Zola asked, shaking her head.

I gulped. 'It was. Genuinely the best sex I've ever had. Like, I didn't know sex could feel that good.'

'But you still told him you didn't want to see him again?' Katy asked, looking confused.

'I just don't want to complicate my life, you know. Honestly, one night with a man and I am already so agitated and completely out of my routine. I shouldn't have done it. Really, it was a huge mistake!'

Zola and Katy shared a curious look with one another.

'A wonderfully huge mistake?' Katy giggled.

'Yeah, right?' Zola turned to Katy in agreement. 'Look, don't shoot the messenger here, Ella? But I sort of think this is exciting. You've just had great sex. Come on! You're a young single woman! Embrace it!' Zola shrieked. 'You don't have to feel agitated or embarrassed. He might be just what you need in your life right now.'

'Philip is a walking headache,' I replied bluntly.

'Well, have you even considered the possibility that he could be more? A boyfriend? A fuckbuddy? Or just a fucking friend even? You two obviously have a great connection! Sex like that only happens when you're really connected with each other. Why throw it away so early on?' Zola continued to press me.

'Yeah, I don't know. Ella, we love you, but maybe Zola's right? You don't take risks or chances in relationships. Not since Josh, anyway.'

My eyes closed just hearing his name again.

'Oh God! What if Philip is the one, and you've just patched him for no reason?' Katy was panicking, getting wrapped up in one of her wildly romantic fantasies.

I watched my jaw hang open on the camera. 'Oh, I have my reasons!'

Zola hummed, unimpressed. '*Mmmmhum* . . . like what?'

My neck turned blotchy with the interrogation. 'He's a player!'

'We don't know that, Ella,' Katy shouted like she was trying to get through to a child who wasn't listening.

'Look, this is ultimately your decision, babe, and we'll support you no matter what, but we don't want you to look back on this with regret, OK? Joshua hurt you, and you survived. Look at you! But just because *he* hurt you, it doesn't mean every other man will.' Zola sounded gentler this time.

I nodded, feeling drained by the emotional intensity of it all. 'I better go, guys. Honestly, thank you, but I feel like I need to lie down.'

'Have a sleep, get a bath, and come round later, eh? We'll talk more then?' Katy smiled warmly down the phone, as if that was her way of apologising after her outburst.

'Yeah, maybe.'

'The website is looking great, by the way,' Zola said.

I smiled back. 'That's good,' I said, but I felt too distracted to care about that the Dicktionary Club. 'Look, I'll call you guys soon.'

'OK, babe,' Zola said.

'Bye, El, we love you!' Katy added, blowing kisses at me.

I hung up the call and held my head in my hands. I had done the right thing for myself by telling Philip nothing more would happen between us. I knew it, but why couldn't I shake this feeling that was rattling me so much?

*

The following morning, I seemed to feel worse. Not even an onslaught of housework was lifting the guilt. I spent the morning washing out my fridge, the oven and steeped all my appliances, but that feeling of irritability still seemed to linger.

Around two, the door buzzer rang in my flat. I popped down my glass cleaner and headed to the intercom, half expecting another one of Alexander's exhibition packages getting delivered.

'Hello?'

'So, I felt a little awkward at how we left things yesterday, and then I realised you left something in my car. I wasn't sure if I should post it or not,' Philip's husky voice said.

'How did you know what door buzzer I was?' I replied, wondering what I could have left.

'I tried them all.' He laughed a little, and I smiled. 'Do you want me to return this or not?'

I paused, my hand hovering over the button to let him in, then pressed it. I opened the flat door and paced my living room. Quickly, I dusted off my leggings, noticing little sprinkles of dust gather at my knees from cleaning, but I stopped as I heard Philip's steps getting closer. Suddenly, he was standing in my doorway.

'Great place,' he said, admiring the open-plan living room and kitchen area.

'Not a hoarder!' I tittered awkwardly. 'As you can see.'

'So, I wanted to return this,' he said, holding out one single kirby.

'A kirby grip?' I said, my face screwed up in astonishment.

'Yes, it must have fallen out of your bag or hair or something. I wasn't sure if you needed it back or . . .'

'You offered to post a kirby?'

He looked a little uncomfortable as he walked up to me. 'Yes. I suppose I did.'

I nodded. 'Well, thanks.'

'And I wanted to say one more thing, Pilates. Look, I don't know what you think of me or men in general, but what I wanted to say was . . . Friday night felt different. Special even. For me, anyway. And trust me, I don't often feel that way.'

I lowered my head to the ground. I was silent.

'Well, that's all I wanted you to know,' he said into the silence.

He turned back, heading towards the door.

'*Uggh*, it felt special for me, too, OK?' I said, finally allowing myself to look up.

He turned to face me, looking surprised. 'It did?'

'Yes! I don't do that, you know I don't!' My cheeks were heating up again as I took in his tallness, his perfect skin. 'I just feel uncomfortable with emotions and I don't like to get carried away.'

Philip held his hands up. 'Well, what the fuck are we doing?'

'What do you mean?' I asked.

He rubbed his face, looking frustrated, then his eyes locked with mine. 'Why are you pushing me away before it's even begun?'

I raised a shoulder. 'I . . . I don't know.' I could feel my face damp with streaming tears. *Jesus Christ, what the fuck was going on?* I hadn't cried in years, and all of a sudden being around this man I was Tiny fucking Tears, Glasgow Edition. 'And also, I don't know why I'm crying again. Fucking hell.'

Philip's shoulders relaxed and his face softened as he watched me. He slowly approached me and held both my hands.

'I think . . .' I blubbed, then cleared my throat and tried again. 'The problem is, if I am brutally honest, I think I do like you,' I admitted. 'But I'm so used to being alone, and this feels strange for me.' I threw my hands up, trying to comprehend my own emotions. 'I suppose I really don't want to get hurt here.'

Philip smiled. 'I understand, but I don't want to hurt you.'

I bit my lip, feeling my insecurities about him rise to the surface. 'I don't know if I can trust you. I get this feeling you're a massive player and that's the kind of guy I avoid like the plague. You have the patter, the clothes and lots of beautiful women phone you all the time, right?'

'Huh?' He cast his mind back.

'Amelia?' I confirmed.

Philip let out a laugh. 'Who you've met, she's my personal assistant and happens to be my goddaughter, too?'

Shit.

'Well, there was someone else too. When we were at Kelvingrove . . .' I held my head, trying to remember.

'Sienna?' Philip questioned. 'My sister.'

I felt my shoulders drop in defeat and embarrassment. 'Right. OK. Sorry. But even the way you act. How you said you've been tested for STIs and . . .'

'I have had sex before, but I'm not a player. I was being as honest as I could be with you, Ella.'

'Look, I'm sorry. I find it hard to trust and . . .'

He leaned forward and hugged me tightly. I could hear his heart thumping as my ear pressed hard into his chest. It felt bizarre to be genuinely comforted by someone other than my friends. My panicked mind was slowing down, allowing him to hold me. It didn't seem like he had an ulterior motive; he cared. Philip was warm and kind and, despite witnessing several of my absurd meltdowns already, he still seemed to want to be here. I felt like he was one of the very few people who knew me – the real me.

'I think I do want to try,' I whispered.

'Pardon?' Philip said; I could feel his voice resonate in his chest.

I glanced up at his face, both of us smirking a little. 'I mean, I'd be willing to give this dating thing a shot. With you, I mean.'

He gave me the widest grin.

'If you still want to?' I added.

Philip rolled his eyes back briefly as if thinking, then burst out laughing. He began kissing my face all over.

'Oh, Pilates.' He took my face in his hands. 'Of course I fucking do!'

Chapter Thirty-Three

Ella

That Monday morning, I headed to work fresh-faced, determined and excited to see my friends so I could divulge the rest of the weekend's gossip first-hand. Philip had spent the entire day at mine on Sunday, and we'd got a Chinese takeaway together that evening, before having more amazing sex and a sleepover.

I walked into the office and couldn't help smirking as I saw Zola. Katy gasped, clapping her hands as she spotted me.

'Good weekend, gurllll?' Zola asked, arching an eyebrow at me.

'*Hmmm* . . . pretty quiet!' I joked, and we all burst out laughing.

'So, how is it going? What's happening now?' Katy asked. Throughout the weekend, I had given the girls voice-note updates on Philip and me spending time together.

'It's good.' I smiled, thinking of him. 'It feels good. We spent the day and night together at mine, and . . .'

'I still can't believe you let him up to your apartment!' Zola gasped. 'And you're still alive?'

I rolled my eyes. 'Yeah, and he seems pretty tidy too. He didn't Zoflora the worktops before bed, but he does fill the dishwasher neatly.'

'Babe, no one Zofloras clean worktops before bed,' Zola said. 'That's a *you* problem!'

Katy shimmied in her seat a little uncomfortably and edged forward. 'And the sex? You had more sex, right?'

I flopped back on my chair. 'We did, and it's *pppppfft*!' I let out a raspberry, replaying visions of Philip naked and pounding on top of me in my head.

'I knew he would be good in bed. You can tell. He's such a masculine man. Like a big bear or something,' Katy said, before screwing her face up and popping her hand back down at her groin.

'Oh, are you OK there, hun? Did we keep you and your camel toe from something?' Zola said, scrutinising Katy up and down.

Katy huffed. 'Stop! It's not a camel toe.' She shuffled more in the chair and then lowered her voice. 'It's my fanny.' She pointed down. 'I'm in pure agony!'

Zola and I shared a worried glance.

'Agony?' I questioned. 'As in too-much-sex agony or something-nasty-going-on-down-there agony?'

'Or too-much-masturbating-to-Ross-Kemp agony?' Zola chipped in.

'What?' I asked. 'Ross *what*?'

'Zola, stop!' Katy warned her. 'I swear to God, it's getting worse. It feels like it's on fire and it's so itchy when I wear pants!'

'You need to get that checked, Katy. Have you had a look down there?' I asked. I was trying to stare at her face, but my eyes kept darting in between her thighs.

'No. Can you?' she asked.

'Me? God, no,' I whispered back.

'And don't look at me!' Zola tutted. 'I've seen enough of you, girl, to last a lifetime.'

'Katy, why don't you go into the bathroom and take a photo? Then you'll be able to see what's up. It could be a little inflammation.'

Katy looked nervous. Nevertheless, she nodded, lifted her phone and jigged cross-legged to the toilet.

'If that girl has crabs and I'm sleeping in her bed, she's done for!' Zola exclaimed, and I burst out laughing.

My phone began ringing from my desk, and so I switched into professional mode as I picked it up to hear a familiar Italian accent. 'Ella, how are things going with the Glasgow tour?'

I recognised Alexander's distinctive voice immediately.

'Yes, hello, Alexander.' I nudged Zola. 'Things are all organised for the weekend. We can't wait!'

'Yes, and the guest list?' he replied.

'The guest list is growing. I have a wide range of art moguls and influencers who can't wait to share your paintings on their social media.'

'Hmm . . . I must say I remain impressed you secured such a venue,' he admitted. 'And because of this, I have chosen the Glasgow exhibition to be featured in my latest documentary series. I want to capture every moment, every gesture, the whole elegant atmosphere. The production will be broadcast on the BBC next summer; they want to highlight my work to a UK audience.'

'Wow,' I gasped. 'Congratulations! And yes, absolutely. It would be such an honour! And, Alexander, thank you for choosing Glasgow.'

'But it goes without saying: no hiccups, Ella. I need everything to run smoothly.'

I gulped. 'And I can promise it will.'

'Good job! I'll send the videographers and film crew your details. They'll be in touch.'

'Great, speak soon.'

Just then, Katy returned from the bathroom, staring at her phone.

'What did he say, then?' Zola asked.

'He's choosing the Glasgow exhibition to be the venue filmed for his BBC documentary.' I clutched my hands tightly, unable to quite believe it. 'It's going to be on the telly!'

'That's beyond amazing!' Zola hugged me.

'Alexander?' Katy asked, trying to catch up. 'Saturday's event is being filmed?'

I nodded happily. 'Hell, yes. And I can't wait to tell Andrea!'

'How's the noon?' Zola grimaced, noticing Katy still looked uncomfortable.

Katy turned her phone around and flashed us her gash in the middle of the office.

'Ouch!' Zola covered her face.

A shiver ran through me. 'Babe, that's thrush!'

'Very bad thrush,' Zola confirmed. 'Looks like you're cooking up a whole loaf down there with all that yeast. It's nasty!'

'But it's not crabs,' I added, wanting everyone to see the positive.

Katy was wafting the elastic of her leggings, as if she was hoping to cause a breeze. 'Will it be better by the weekend?' she moaned.

'Get to a chemist, they'll sort you in no time.' I winked at her. 'I promise.'

Philip: *Good morning, beautiful xxx*

I smiled back at my screen, wanting to reply immediately. God, it felt good having someone message and check in on my day.

'Oh, is that big Phil?' Zola smiled at Katy, who was still completely distracted.

'It is.' I smirked.

'Is he coming to the exhibition?' Katy asked. 'I can't wait to meet him properly.'

I shook my head. 'No, luckily, he's in Berlin this weekend. He's opening another hotel over there. He's gutted he can't come.'

Zola giggled. 'Luckily?'

I sent my cheesy reply and sat my phone down on the desk. 'Yes, luckily. I don't want Andrea seeing me with him, and thinking I was sleeping with him for the venue or something. Plus, I'd have to work, you know what these things are like – I wouldn't get a minute to chat with him.'

Katy screwed her face up. 'Very true, Andrea would definitely get her tuppence in.'

'He's invited me to the hospitality awards with him next week though, so it will be our first proper outing as a couple, and I'll have to look amazing!'

'That I'll be hosting!' Katy flexed proudly; she'd managed to land Blaze Boost as their sponsors.

'Yep, and you better get us the best seats in the house,' I warned my friend.

'Noted!' Katy grinned.

'So, when are you seeing him again?' Zola asked.

'Tonight.' I was so excited at the thought of seeing his face again, knowing he'd only left me an hour before. 'We're going for a walk in the park after work, then we'll head to the gym. And on Wednesday we're going out for dinner, before he goes to Berlin on Thursday.'

'So cute.' Zola tutted, shaking her head. 'I never thought I'd see the day!'

'Trust me, you and me both!' I smiled. 'It's a big weekend, girls. Alexander's night, and the Dicktionary Club finally goes live.'

Zola nodded. 'Fuck, yeah, we've actually done it!'

'Oh, yes! We've pulled it off!' Katy laughed evilly, then held her hands to us both for a high-five, but Zola and I squirmed away.

'Hands, Katy. The scratching!' Zola bellowed. 'Get to the chemist right now, girl.'

We all burst out laughing, and I returned to my desktop, emailing Andrea the new camera crew additions for the exhibition and finalising the weekend's plans. I felt excited and motivated for what lay ahead. For the first time in years, I had a whole new lease of life.

Chapter Thirty-Four

Ella: The Exhibition

It was the evening of the exhibition, and I had nipped back home from the venue after giving the temps and assistants detailed instructions on exactly how the evening should be set up. My red silk floor-length dress hung in my wardrobe, and after a quick bath, makeup and teasing my hair into an updo, I slipped it on. The material felt cool and luxurious against my hot skin, as I examined myself in the mirror. There was a split up the left side of the dress, which showed off my gold stiletto heels. I felt amazing and took a few selfies, not knowing if it would be too much too soon to send one to Philip. *Would he think I was fishing for compliments?* I wondered. I decided not to send anything right now, but saved them in my camera roll just in case I had a champagne confidence later on.

I quickly took an Uber to the museum, keen to arrive first and ensure everything was going according to plan and the setup was precisely as I envisioned. As the driver pulled up to the venue, I felt goosebumps travel down my arm. The classically beautiful, old-style landmark was lit up in various colours from the outside, a red carpet was draped down the stone staircase, and an elegant sign outside read:

Alexander Cambi's Royal Exhibit.

Perfect.

I headed inside and watched the decorators finish clearing the rooms. A neat, circular stage had been built in the centre of the grand hall, with chairs to the left for the violinists to play. Alexander's paintings were hung all around the room, allowing plenty of space for guests to walk around and admire his work. We'd added a selfie wall with Alexander's signature spraypainted on it for the influencers to maximise their socials. A fun photo booth decorated with inflatable crowns and picture frames was also set up in the corner of the room, ensuring we hit every market, from influencers to art enthusiasts, who wanted to capture the moment. A rush of sheer pride engulfed my body; it was everything I could have wished for and more. I took out my phone and snapped a few photos capturing the setup for Philip, knowing that absolutely none of it would have been possible without him.

'Ella!' I heard a brisk voice call out. I turned to see Andrea standing with a BBC production team behind her.

I approached them with a smile and held out my hand. 'Hi, I'm Ella! Great to meet you all.'

'Glad to be here, love,' a small Cockney man replied, taking me up on the handshake. 'I'm Bill, the director for tonight's documentary. I love what you've done with the venue. It's, yeah . . .' He glanced around. 'Very regal!'

I grinned at his genuine appreciation. 'Yes, it's looking amazing. Thanks.'

Andrea nodded slowly, taking everything in. 'Hmmm . . . I must say, it is very nice.'

'So, we're good to set up then?' Bill asked. 'We want a few shots of the guests arriving.'

'Yes, of course. If you need anything, just ask one of us, and we'll do whatever we can to help.'

'Great, thanks, love.' He nodded, then summoned the cameramen and lighting technicians to follow him in getting ready to film.

'Well, well, well, you seem to have pulled this one off, Ella,' Andrea murmured once we were alone.

I inhaled a deep breath, incredibly grateful for the compliment. 'Thank you, Andrea.'

'Let's ensure it runs as *regally* as it looks, OK?' she added.

I nodded. 'Oh, it will!'

Half an hour later, the guests began arriving in the most stunning outfits. Some of them were in gowns fit for the Oscars. The servers handed them champagne flutes as they entered, and the lofty galleries echoed with the sound of their chatter as they mingled in the gorgeous venue. The all-female group of violinists had begun playing pop songs, beautifully evoking the contrasting classical and modern-day fairytale theme I'd imagined. I stood at the door, welcoming everyone and reminding them to post as many photos as they could throughout the evening with the hashtag AlexanderArtGlasgow. I beamed as the attendees streamed in, from people in the media to cool art-school students and vloggers, all equally thrilled to spend a beautiful evening in a glamorous setting, admiring stunning contemporary artwork.

Suddenly, a glossy white Hummer limo pulled up outside, blasting the Spice Girls of all things. I walked down a few stairs, wondering who the fuck was ruining my classy vibe, when Zola and Katy bounced out, waving their hands in the air. I burst out laughing, shushing them to be quiet, but they giggled like drunken teenagers arriving for a prom. Then, a group of tipsy, dressed-to-kill women followed them out. I grinned instantly, recognising them from the gym: our Dicktionary Club recruits.

'I thought these girls deserved a night of celebration after all the work they've put in for the past few weeks!' Zola yelled as she approached me on the red carpet. 'And *we* need to celebrate! Our website goes live tomorrow!'

'Ssh!' I chuckled, noticing the camera crew capturing Glasgow's finest women. I approached the gym girls, who looked gorgeous in their huge over-the-top gowns. 'I'm so glad you girls came. Thank you for everything! Without you guys, this website would never have gotten off the ground.'

They gushed their pleasure at being there, hugging me all at once.

'We loved your reviews, too, Ella! Zo gave us secret advance access today, and we have been in hysterics at some of your quotes.'

I blushed, thinking of how angry I had been at Sir Spunksalott and actually wanting to forget half of the things I'd written.

I spotted Natasha and hugged her. 'And how are you feeling now?'

She blushed, looking a little embarrassed from her gym breakdown that day. 'I'm good. Well, getting there. I have good days and bad days,' she said with a sniff. 'But I'm sure ready to guzzle some of that champagne tonight!' She pointed to the top of the stair where a server was handing out the glasses.

'Well, let's head in, and we can get stuck in together!' I laughed.

'Let's celebrate!' one of them called out loudly, followed by woo-hoos and cheers.

The girls giggled and chattered up the steps towards the exhibition, while Zola, Katy and I followed behind.

'You look unreal tonight, babe.' Zola pursed out her lips.

'Eh, so the fuck do you two! Like what?' I squeezed both of their hands.

Zola was wearing a golden halterneck maxidress, which showed off her incredible hourglass figure, while Katy had opted for a white sequined puffball minidress. Both of them looked insane.

Andrea flagged me down as we entered the exhibition, and I excused myself from my friends and headed over.

'Alexander is upstairs. He wants you to make a speech to introduce him before he appears,' she said, raising her brow as if in judgement at his dramatics.

'I can do that, sure. I'll message him to see if he's ready.'

I took my phone out of my bag while Andrea sipped her champagne. 'It's jam-packed. I didn't anticipate this turnout,' she mused. 'Especially for some garish paintings!'

I laughed, sending a message to Alexander.

Let me know when you are ready to enter, and I'll make an introduction. The crowd is huge! Ella x

'And not to mention the camera crew – this really is exceptional PR for the company,' Andrea added.

I smiled back. I didn't know if it was the expensive bubbles or the event itself, but this was the most conversation I'd had out of her since I joined Smart Reputations.

'Yeah, it's turned out better than even I expected,' I said, gazing around at it all.

'Better than anyone expected, trust me!' she scoffed. 'And to think, I had spoken to HR about a fast-track route to terminate your contract! Huh.'

My face fell as I turned to her, but she was wholly distracted by the crowds of people and hum of activity as she slurped her glass of bubbles.

'Oh, Lenny, darling! Wonderful to see you!' she suddenly gushed and darted away to schmooze over some high-up politician.

I felt my phone vibrate in my hand and glanced down.

Philip: *Red is certainly your colour! Xxxxx*

I glanced around the crowds of people. How did he know? Was he here? No, surely not. He was in Berlin. Maybe he'd seen a post on social media. Everyone did have their cameras out, and I could have easily been snapped in the background.

'And you smell just as wonderful as you look,' a deep voice whispered from behind me.

I span around in shock.

'You're . . . here!' I gasped.

'You didn't really think I'd miss your big night, did you?' he replied, leaning in for a kiss on the cheek. He was pristine in a black suit with a white shirt, smelling as masculine as ever.

'I'm sorry . . . I don't know what to say.' I tried not to simper. 'What happened to Berlin?'

His dark eyes lingered over my body. 'I cut it short.' He leaned in, kissing me again. I blushed. 'This place is looking sensational! Do you do freelance work by chance?' He grinned, buttering me up.

'I'm so happy you're here!' And the funny thing was, I felt so ecstatic to see him that I suddenly didn't care what Andrea said or did, I was just glad to be near this man.

My phone buzzed again in my hand:

Alexander: *I'm ready.*

'OK, I have to go and introduce Alexander. Zola and Katy are around somewhere, but I need to get going.' I beamed at him, leaning forward to kiss his lips. I couldn't believe this man had jumped back on a plane to be here for me.

'Yes, go! I'm quite content where I am.' He squeezed both my arms and leaned in for another kiss, then I stepped through the crowd and made my way to the stage.

As I gazed out over the crowd, the bright lights from the documentary crew caused me to squint. My eyes needed to adjust a little. I picked up the microphone just as the musicians were playing the final notes of their song.

I cleared my throat, my vision almost restored. 'Ladies and gentlemen, kings,' I darted my eyes to my two best friends who stepped closer to the stage to hear me speak, 'and queens!' Katy let out a small *woo!* 'It is an honour to have you all here tonight to celebrate the work of one of this generation's most exceptional artistic talents, Mr Alexander Cambi.' The room filled with warm applause. 'When I first pitched for this exhibition, I dreamed of showcasing Alexander's art to Scotland. And here we are, Alexander's first Scottish exhibition.' The room filled with appreciative faces. 'And with your help tonight, through sharing this unique experience on your social media platforms, I believe that together we can share the beauty of this extraordinary artist's work with the rest of the world. I'm sure you can all agree how mesmerising these paintings are.' There was a ripple of agreement from the crowd. 'Alexander, your art is exceptional, and we're all truly blessed to be witnessing your first of many, I hope, Scottish exhibitions. So, without further ado, please put your hands together for Mr Alexander Cambi.'

The entire hall turned into one immense boom of applause, and a neat, bearded man waltzed down the stairs of Kelvingrove Art Gallery like a true king himself, taking it all in. He edged through a space made by the crowd and joined me onstage, taking hold of the microphone.

'Thank you, Ella!' He nodded gratefully and turned to his guests. 'It is a pleasure being here with you tonight. I have always been a great fan of Scotland and the picturesque beauty surrounding your wonderful country,' he began in his delicate accent.

As Alexander continued his speech, telling the room about his passion for art, my eyes squinted, searching for Philip in the darkness. I found it difficult to distinguish between the men with their similar tuxedos. Eventually, my eyes fell on him, standing with his arms crossed against his chest as a slim blonde girl rested her arm on his shoulder, whispering into his ear. My eyes were straining against the bright lights. *Who was this bitch, and why was she all over my man?!* As though reading my thoughts, Philip removed her hand rather abruptly and pointed towards the stage, dismissing her. She shook her head before storming away. Shit. I couldn't see her face. *Who the hell was she?*

I glanced over to Zola and Katy, who seemed to have missed the entire interaction.

'Please have a wonderful evening, and please do enjoy the exhibition!' Alexander finished, and loud applause once again roared around us.

I tapped him on the shoulder. 'It has been a real pleasure to work on this project for you, Mr Cambi.'

Alexander kissed my hand. 'No, the pleasure is mine. This is by far the grandest part of the tour to date. I'd love to work with you again.'

'Anytime.' I smiled, genuinely glad of his appreciation and delight. *I'd actually nailed it.*

The violinists began playing their own rendition of Olivia Rodrigo's 'Traitor', while I edged towards the stage steps, following Alexander down. As we stepped back into the crowd, Alexander was quickly surrounded by press photographers keen to get a shot of him. I smiled and stepped out of the way, allowing him to enjoy his well-deserved moment of glory.

'Testing, testing!' a voice called out over the crowd.

I turned my back to see that a very drunk Natasha had climbed onto the stage and stolen the mic.

Oh shit! What the fuck was she doing?

I turned around for Zola or Katy to help intercept, but the group of photographers blocked my path, and I felt like I was getting swept further and further from the stage.

'I would like to thank Ella for inviting us here tonight and organising this whole thing. Isn't this wonderful?' Natasha screeched.

Fuck, fuck, *FUCK!* I could feel myself sweating, trying my best to barge through.

'Excuse me! Excuse me!' I called out.

'Ella and I have also been working on a new project that launches tomorrow,' Natasha announced. 'And I would love it if you ladies could all sign up, so that together we can finally get our own back on the fucking arsehole loser men of Glasgow's dating scene!' There was a shedload of venom behind her voice, causing it to echo off every inch of the cathedral-like venue.

The room turned deadly silent. Natasha had the entire audience's undivided attention.

'What is going on?' Alexander bellowed.

'So, basically, there is now a website called the Dicktionary Club,' she continued, taking the silence for encouragement, 'and it reviews all the men that use dating apps in Glasgow, so you can read up on what total dicks their previous lovers had learned they are before you date them. Genius, right?' A few drunken cheers came from some of Natasha's friends, who clearly thought this stunt was a great idea. 'But my personal favourite part of the website is the section on a celebrity – or Z-lister in this man's case!'

Oh no. No. I could feel my heart plummet out of my arsehole. I began pushing more furiously, knocking people's glasses out of their hands in my desperation to reach Natasha.

'And this week's special is Philip Khan, a local millionaire and playboy! And Ella, what a fucking hero, has actually fake dated him, to finally out him for being . . .' She glanced at her phone, reading from it: '*A cocky, arrogant, flashy, big-time show-off. Philip thinks he can buy affection with flowers and dinners. He is a complete womaniser and a full-on creep, who thinks any woman would fall for him because he has money!*'

A few amazed gasps popped off around the room as I finally got on the stage.

'Isn't that right, Ella?' Natasha nodded at me, as if we'd been plotting this entire stunt together.

The lights shone back in my face. I was dizzy and my mouth was painfully dry. The entire film crew, production cameras and assorted paparazzi faced me.

'And I should know, babe. He did the same to me!' Natasha confided drunkenly – to me, and the whole of Glasgow.

Wait. What was she talking about?

I glanced across the room at Philip, who stood frozen to the spot. People who recognised him were pointing and whispering as Natasha spoke, their eyes darting between the stage and him. Eventually, he locked eyes with me just as my head caught up.

Who was Natasha upset over that day in the gym?
Philip.

He held my gaze for one agonising moment, before he turned and stormed out.

'Wait, no, wait!' I cried, rushing down the stage steps and pushing back through the crowd to try and follow him.

What had Natasha done? Was she insane? Why would she fucking do this?

I wanted to vomit. I wanted to cry. I had to explain.

I pushed and budged my way outside just as Philip reached the bottom of the steps.

'Philip, stop!' I called out, tears flooding my face.

'Don't! Fucking don't!' he yelled back.

I continued regardless until he was close enough to touch. 'I can explain!' I puffed out. 'I promise I didn't want to hurt you.'

He turned around, his eyes glassy with tears. 'You have humiliated me, strung me along, and for what? To launch a gossip website?'

I gulped down, knowing that was exactly what I had done.

'Yes,' I yelped. 'But I didn't know you then, and now that I do—'

'Now that you do?' Philip snapped, catching his breath. 'But I don't fucking know *you*!'

I could feel myself shaking. 'I know. I know how bad this sounds, but—'

'Bad? You may have just ended my career tonight. Do you realise that? Do you realise what this looks like to the press? To my clients? I'm a fucking laughing

stock! What about my family? What will they think?'
He was clutching his head, still joining all of the puzzle
pieces together.

I paused, realising I hadn't taken any of this into con-
sideration. I was so invested in getting revenge for Katy
that I hadn't even considered how our website would
make the men feel.

'But hey, congrats! You've driven up all the publicity
you'll ever need for your new site. I hope it works out
for you,' Philip snarled bitterly, then turned and headed
through the park.

'Oh, yeah, sure. Walk away. You won't let me explain.
But do you know what, I may have done that, but how
many women have you hurt over the years, eh? Don't
pretend you're innocent when I've just heard Natasha's
speech!' I snapped back.

He held up one hand and continued into the park, not
once looking back.

When he was out of sight, I felt my body lower to
the ground. I was beaten, empty, and I felt utterly sick.
I couldn't comprehend what had just happened.

'Ella!' Andrea's voice shrieked from behind.

I stumbled back to my feet and turned to face her.

'You have ruined everything for this campaign!
Everything!'

I nodded, fully agreeing with her. 'I know,' I said
weakly.

In the distance, Katy and Zola bounced down the
steps, hurtling as fast as they could in their heels.

'Come to the office first thing in the morning. Get
your shit off your desk and HR will be ready for you!'

Andrea yelled. 'How dare you embarrass me like this!' Venom was seething through her teeth.

'No! You can't do that, Andrea,' Katy yelled back, eventually stepping past her and wrapping her arm around me. 'This wasn't Ella's fault. You saw that girl steal the mic. What could Ella do?'

'Look at the drama she's caused!' Andrea ranted. 'This is a fucking PR nightmare!'

Zola tutted, wrapping her arm around me from the other side. 'You can't fire her for this, Andrea. We set up the site, too; it's not all on Ella.'

Andrea levelled her gaze at us, her beady eyes narrowing until they were mere slits. It was the craziest I had ever seen her. 'Nine o' clock tomorrow morning, the conference room. All of you!' She turned on her heels and headed back up the steps to the gallery. 'And don't fucking dare go near Alexander. I'll deal with this shitshow!' she roared as she reached the top step.

I felt like the wind had been knocked out of me. As a gasp escaped me, my two best friends tightened their arms around me. I cried and sobbed into their shoulders.

'What the fuck was that?' Zola murmured.

'I think we might actually be getting fired this time,' Katy said, sounding as much in disbelief as I was.

'I'm so sorry. I will sort it with you guys and Andrea. I'll explain everything tomorrow and take the blame. You two don't deserve to be involved in this,' I said.

Zola shook her head. 'No. We're in this together, yeah? The Dicktionary Club was all of us, not just you. And anyway, we hate that bitch! How many times has she threatened to sack us over the years? But even she wouldn't risk losing her three top employees. Once she calms the fuck down, she'll be fine, OK?'

I gulped, trying hard to regain my composure.

'We should go, Ella,' Katy whispered, edging her head to the reporters who had followed the tempestuous scene down the steps. 'Come to mine. We all need to stay together tonight.'

My friends gazed at me, and as much as the thought of Katy's crumby, piss-stained couch revolted me, the thought of being alone after tonight felt far worse.

I couldn't speak, so I just nodded. My two friends grabbed my hands and we stumbled through the park together. Each time I felt myself sobbing, I'd feel an arm hold me tighter until, eventually, we reached Katy's.

Chapter Thirty-Five

Ella

I woke early the following morning sticky with sweat. On either side of me, I could hear the deep-sleep breathing of my two friends. Eventually, I sat up in Katy's bed, realising I was still wearing last night's dress. My face felt tender from all the tears and confusion of everything that had happened.

'Hey, you OK?' Zola murmured, stirring as I moved.

'Tell me that didn't happen last night?' I could feel my bottom lip tremble.

Zola looked weary. She nudged her head towards the door. We slipped out of the bed and headed into the living room so we could talk and leave Katy to sleep.

The sun was beginning to rise, and I wondered what time it was, although I couldn't bear to look at my phone. I wasn't ready to deal with any abusive messages from Philip or Andrea quite yet. Instead, I sat on the sofa and pulled a blanket up over my legs.

'Why did this happen?' I asked, still trying to make sense of everything.

Zola gently shook her head, looking lost for words. 'I called Natasha late last night after you fell asleep,' she eventually said.

'OK. Tell me.'

Zola took a breath. 'So, you were right, Ella. Natasha was upset that day in the gym over Philip.'

My brain flooded back to Natasha crying inconsolably in the middle of David Lloyd's changing room.

'But I didn't know it was because of Philip. She never said!'

Zola nodded. 'Yeah, I know. None of us did. So, when I gave her access to the website, she read that partial piece you wrote on him before you two properly got together.'

My eyes began streaming as I remembered boasting about how I could write Philip up without even dating him. I hadn't taken my nasty words off the website. God, I'd been so wrapped up in how good it felt to be with him that uploading to the Dicktionary Club was the last thing on my mind.

'Why didn't she just tell him? Why did she have to blurt it out over a fucking mic in front of the whole fucking city?' I asked, realising it must have been Natasha draped over Philip before she went all Kanye and stole the show up on stage.

'One of the other girls said she saw Natasha go up to him before it all kicked off last night,' Zola said, confirming my fears. 'Apparently, she made a right arse of herself, told him she missed him and asked him to leave with her and everything, but he told her to go away. He said he wasn't interested. So . . .'

I felt myself deflate utterly. They really had been a thing. 'So, she exposed everything? What the fuck type of person does that, Zola?' I asked, feeling the anger build up inside me.

'A bitter one!' Zola sighed. 'But . . . she was hurt, babe. And she's young. I'm not even sure if she knew you and him were properly together.'

I let my tired, achy body sink into Katy's grubby couch and stared into space. *What the hell must Philip think of me?* How could I even start to explain all of this?

'I'll put the kettle on,' Zola said, and she headed through to Katy's kitchen while I continued to replay everything in my head, over and over again, from Alexander's face to Andrea yelling about what a disappointment I was, to Philip striding off into the distance. That was undoubtably the worst part.

'Oh my freakin' God!' Katy burst through into the living room with half her tit dangling out of a tank top and her hair still backcombed, looking like she'd just stepped out of a cheap porno movie.

'What is it?' I sat up, turning to her.

Zola walked through, carrying two cups of tea. 'I've seen it all before, babes,' she said with a nod at Katy's boobs.

'It's all over the news!' Katy gasped, turning her phone around and making herself slightly more decent at the same time.

'What? What is?' I covered my mouth, hoping this was a weird prank and Ashton was ready to burst through Katy's door at any moment.

'The Dicktionary Club, and . . .' Katy lowered her voice, 'Philip!'

I felt dizzy and flustered, like I was going to pass out.

'Let me see,' Zola insisted, setting down the mugs haphazardly and grabbing Katy's phone. '*Millionaire Playboy Philip Khan Gets Played!*' she read aloud. The three of us exchanged worried glances.

'*Last night, Scottish businessman Philip Khan was the first to be exposed publicly on new website the Dicktionary Club, which reviews men on dating sites. PR company Smart Reputations formulated the website, allowing previous lovers to give honest feedback on men currently dating in Glasgow. The website aims to reveal how potential suitors have previously treated women, allowing users to vet their dates before taking the plunge. Khan was called out publicly at the launch of Alexander Cambi's exclusive art exhibition at Kelvingrove Art Gallery, and identified as one of the men featured on the website. We have reached out to Khan's representatives for comment.*'

Zola finished reading and glanced up. 'Well, at least it didn't name us personally, right?'

Katy let out a small cackle. 'And Andrea is getting the blame!'

'Or the credit,' I added. 'That makes us sound like the good guys. But we're fucking not.' I held my hands against my face in total panic all over again.

Zola rummaged under Katy's coffee table, pulled out her computer and let her fingers fly over the keyboard. We sat in silence, each trying to comprehend the situation.

'Holy fuck!' Zola exclaimed.

'What?' Katy moaned.

My stomach twisted; I couldn't take any more bad news right now.

'We've had over two thousand subscribers overnight!' Zola laughed in excited glee.

I sat back, unimpressed at the figures.

'It's only seven a.m.!' Katy replied. 'That's incredible.'

I was gobsmacked at how superficial my friends sounded and snapped back, 'Yeah, seven a.m., and we might have two thousand subscribers, but we a disciplinary meeting in two fucking hours and count-ing – and no boyfriends between us. Girls, we have lost everything because of this fucking website!' I stood up, pointing to the laptop, feeling myself shake with rage and fear.

'Not everything,' Zola corrected. 'We've made over ten grand in one night, Ella. The subscription is £4.99 a month! I know we've lost a lot, but at least we can make rent now.'

I held my hands up. 'Oh, yeah. Every cloud!'

'Ten grand!' Katy's face was lit up with dollar signs. 'Jesus sweet Christ!'

Zola laughed loudly.

I shook my head and picked up my bag and phone in a panic.

'Hey, where are you going?' Katy asked.

'I have to go for a walk. I'm sorry. This feels so wrong. I feel awful. I don't even want to be part of the Dicktionary Club anymore. We have just trashed Philip's entire reputation and it's like you don't care. Not to mention Alexander Cambi's first Scottish exhi-bition of his art *and* his documentary. Fuck! Do you realise how horrible that makes us?' My voice shook with emotion.

'Wait, Ella,' Katy said, standing up.

I held my hand up, not wanting to be reassured.

'No, I'm going. I'm done. I'll meet you both at work.'

'Hey!' Zola said, lifting her head from her laptop. 'We can sort it, Ella.'

I sighed under my breath, knowing some things could never be fixed. I left Katy's flat and took myself back home so I could get ready for Andrea's meeting.

As I sat alone on my sofa staring down the ticking clock, my mind began replaying the events from the previous night over and over again. From the joy of seeing Philip turn up to the sheer panic of watching Natasha ruin everything. I heard my foot tap nervously on the wooden floor, and I stood up, shaking it off before heading through to my bedroom. I slipped on a hooded jumper and leggings, and bundled my hair into a small claw clip. If today was the day I lost my job, I was doing it in complete comfort, without a fight. I knew I deserved everything that was coming down the track at me.

At ten to nine, I was sat outside the conference room, Zola and Katy at either side of me, glued to their phones, seeming much more relaxed than I'd have anticipated them to be.

'You OK?' Zola asked, lifting her head from her phone. I nodded.

'Have you heard from him, Ella?' Katy asked, and my eyes glanced at the article about the Dicktionary Club she was rereading.

I shook my head, feeling a stabbing ache in my gut.

The conference room door opened and together we shared a look with one another as no one came out to call us in.

'Well, it's not a fucking ghost, is it? Let's go.' Zola was the first to stand, looking more fired up than the rest of us, and we headed into the room where Andrea and Silvia from HR were sitting.

'Close the door behind you,' Andrea said, arms crossed and poker-faced.

Katy did as she was instructed and we all took a seat beside one another, facing the two women.

'Good morning, ladies,' Silvia began, in a friendly tone. I'd only met her a few times at Christmas parties, and she always seemed pleasant enough, but like everyone in this building, she was completely petrified of our boss. 'So, Andrea has filled me in on what happened last night, and that's why today's meeting has been called at such short notice. Now, we'd like to interview you individually on the matter, and take it from there. Who would like to go first?'

I turned to my friends, ready to offer myself up. If I went first, I could possibly save Zola and Katy's careers. Even if mine wasn't salvageable, I didn't want my friends to be collateral damage to my shitshow of a life.

'We'd like to have a group discussion, if that's OK, Silvia. Since we haven't been given adequate time to inform our unions,' Zola piped up.

I turned to my friend, darting her a confused look. *What was she doing?*

Silvia seemed a bit more anxious now unions had been mentioned, and so she focused on shuffling some

335

papers on the desk. After some heavy humming she raised her shoulders at Andrea for some sort of permission to proceed.

'Fine by me.' Andrea smirked. 'I have a busy enough day as it is.' Her beady eyes were wholly fixated on us, not flickering for a second. She was enjoying every second of this torment.

Silvia cleared her throat. 'OK, right, well. I'll get straight to it, then. Unfortunately, Ella, after the events that unfolded last night, which Andrea and I have discussed at great length, we have concluded that we have no other choice but to terminate your contract for causing severe reputational damage to the company.'

'What?' Zola blurted out bluntly.

Andrea's smirk seemed to grow wider as she sat silently observing the pain she was causing.

'No. You can't do that,' Katy pleaded. 'Ella didn't know Natasha was going up on that stage, she had no idea what was going to happen. It was out of her control!'

'*Mm* . . . I see,' was all Silvia could muster.

'Look. It's fine,' I replied, reaching for both my friends' hands to settle them. 'I deserve it. It's fine, honestly.'

'No. No, you don't.' Zola's voice was low and deep. I could almost see the blood boiling behind her eyes.

'But you two, on the other hand, we have decided to let you girls off with a formal written warning. What with creating the website and jeopardising the reputation of the company – well, you should think yourself lucky Natasha didn't call out your names on that stage and . . .'

'Lucky?' Zola interrupted her, almost cackling under her breath.

Silvia readjusted herself in her seat.

'You seriously think anyone who works here is lucky?'

I elbowed Zola to keep calm, and I watched Katy's face squirm as she knew our friend was ready to blow.

'*You* are the lucky one, Andrea. Lucky that we all put up with your bullshit for so long!' Zola hissed.

'I'd watch it if I was you.' Andrea's eyes narrowed sharply in Zola's direction.

'No, you know what, I've fucking had it with you. Look at you, sitting in that chair thinking you run some sort of marketing sweatshop here. I'm done. I'm done with *you*. I'm done with all of it! If Ella's out, I am too.'

'No, stop it!' I could feel my heart rattle against my ribcage.

'Zola!' Katy cried, panicked.

'Nah, fuck them, Katy. Look at how they are treating us, look how Andrea's always treated us. All those snide comments, threatening us with losing our jobs every other day, making us feel inadequate and insecure.' Zola scowled at our boss from across the table.

'Guys, stop it, please,' I pleaded as I rubbed my sweaty palms up and down my tired face.

'You know,' Katy said quietly, taking a slight pause, 'Zola's right.'

'Katy!' I blurted, hearing my voice screech. As much as I admired my friends' determination to back me up, I didn't want them struggling with unemployment.

'No. It's not even about you, Ella. It's not about last night. It's everything.' Katy spoke slowly, as if everything was slotting into place in her mind. 'You're nothing but a bully, Andrea. And truthfully, I've only stayed here because of these two.' She let out a small laugh of relief, finally glad to have found the courage to stand up for herself.

I turned to both of them, completely gobsmacked. I knew how much we despised Andrea, but this was their lives, their careers, their livelihood.

Zola burst out laughing too, pointing towards Andrea's face, noticing the smirk had completely vanished and she seemed anxious all of a sudden.

'Well, there you go, Silvia. I think we've made up our minds then. If you could draw up the paperwork and send it out to us, we're all more than happy to leave. Aren't we, girls?' Zola stood up from her chair, pushing it back, still giggling.

'And yeah, good luck replacing us, Andrea!' Zola added for good measure.

'WAIT!' Andrea's voice thundered through the room. 'SIT DOWN. NOW.'

Zola swung her braids back over her shoulder, raising a warning brow at our now ex-boss, then motioned her head for us to follow as she darted towards the door. Katy and I stood up and trailed behind our friend.

'Perhaps we should reassess the situation, Silvia?' I heard Andrea say. 'Maybe a termination of contract for Ella is a bit harsh. I'm sure we could come to some form of agreement to keep you all.'

Together Zola, Katy and I glanced at one another and shook our heads in sync. We'd finally had enough of her dictatorship. We'd finally had enough of Smart

Reputations, and truthfully, I had no idea what the future held, but the sense of leaving this job had already lifted an almighty weight from my shoulders.

'You know what,' I said, 'how about you reassess this?' I stuck my middle finger up, pulled the door open, yelled 'FUCK YOU, Andrea!' and walked straight out of that damn conference room.

Zola and Katy giggled like a pair of kids beside me.

'We're free!' Katy threw her head back, then wrapped her arms around both of us.

'We're unemployed,' I replied, popping her bubble in an instant, still not quite believing what we had done.

From the boardroom we could hear shouting and raging.

'Fucking hell! Did you see her face!' Zola snorted. 'Come on, let's clear out our desks before that crazy bitch calls security.' My friend nudged me towards the entrance of the offices, but I could feel myself hesitating.

'I don't want anything from here. I think I would rather just go home,' I managed to say, feeling my adrenaline crash from such a rollercoaster of high-intensity events from Alexander's exhibition to the HR meeting.

'What? Are you sure?' Katy rubbed my back, realising how awful the past twenty-four hours had been. 'Because I'm going to steal a shit ton of notepad and fill my bag with highlighters, the lot!' she added, smiling towards me.

'Nah, really, I'm all good. I'll call you guys later,' I replied, backing towards the lift, just wanting to be by myself.

'Wait, Ell, what about the rampant rabbit?' Zola called out.

I shrugged. 'Shove it up Andrea's arse. It can be her leaving gift!'

Chapter Thirty-Six

Ella

Five days passed. I remained lying in bed watching reality TV shows, keeping a low profile and staying out of everyone's way. Philip hadn't called or messaged, and I hadn't received a lawyer's letter through the post yet, which, to be honest, I was half expecting to say he was suing me for defamation of character. But nothing. Absolute silence.

Instead of work, I spent the week eating my way through Glasgow's finest cuisine, and my normally pristine home became a cluttered pit of my own depression. I couldn't face anyone, and I felt completely devastated by what I had done to Philip. My friends had tried Face-Timing me a few times each day, but I never answered, opting to text them instead. They had 'exciting' updates on the website, such as that we now had over five thousand subscribers. *The Daily Record* even offered us a story about how the Dicktionary Club was founded, but I refused to discuss it. I knew we had started with great intentions, but this project had left me with nothing but regrets. It had also left all three of us unemployed, Zola unengaged, and Katy battling her way through the worst bout of genital thrush known to womankind.

Around 4 p.m. that Thursday evening, my buzzer rang, and I dragged myself out of bed to shuffle towards it, expecting my MacTassos delivery to come through.

I cleared my throat. 'Hello?'

'Open up, biatch!' Katy's bright voice blared out.

I sighed heavily. 'Honestly, I'm not up for company, Katy. I'm sorry.'

'Hmm, I'm afraid you don't have a choice in the matter,' Zola said.

Grudgingly, I pressed to let my friends in and opened the front door before making my way back to the sofa and flopping down.

I heard the door slam shut and my friends muttering quietly as they entered my flat.

'Hey!' Zola jumped when she saw me. 'What's up, Ella?'

I knew I looked terrible. My skin felt dry with my lack of water and skincare routine and I hadn't washed my hair since the exhibition, but I didn't expect to give her an actual jump scare.

'Jesus, Ella, your house!' Katy glanced around at the clutter of takeout boxes and dirty dishes in the sink. 'This isn't like you, hun.'

'So, you're coping well, I see?' Zola asked, sitting down beside me.

I raised a brow back.

'Zo and I have been chatting,' Katy began, 'and we've decided, if you agree, we should take the website down at the end of the month.'

I sat up, surprised. 'Really?'

Zola gulped. 'Really. And I hate to say it, but you were right, Ella. It's not us, babe. We wanted to do something nice, you know, female empowerment and all that jazz. But this has brought nothing but unnecessary drama. Not only with Philip – you should see the emails we're getting from scorned women and adulterous men! We don't even know what's fact or fiction anymore.'

A wave of relief washed through me. I wanted nothing more than to put the Dicktionary Club behind me and forget it ever happened.

'But why the end of the month? We could take it down now,' I said.

'We have to fulfil the month's membership for everyone who's paid. And it means we have a bit of money behind us. Maybe we could . . .' Zola looked at Katy, who seemed like she would burst with excitement at any moment.

'We could start our own marketing company!' she exclaimed.

'The three of us?' I asked, processing the idea.

'Yes! Think about it, Ella. We only stayed at Smart fricking Reputations because of our friendship, and we are bloody good at our jobs, but no thanks to Andrea. We could totally do this together.' Zola was sitting forward, eagerness radiating off her. I could feel the excitement bouncing back and forth between them.

Right now, though, I couldn't imagine ever leaving the house again, never mind running my own company.

'We finally have the money to start this up, Ella,' Katy said, urging me for a response.

I stood up and walked over to the window. The sun was shining over the most beautiful Glasgow landscape. I took my time, thinking it over. I knew we were all hard-working and really great at our jobs, and I wondered if a few of my closest clients would jump ship if we took the plunge or if the scandal would be too much for them. Finally, I breathed.

'C'mon. What do you think, babe?' Zola asked again.

'She hates the idea,' Katy muttered dramatically.

'No.' I turned to my friends. 'I don't hate the idea at all. If we can make something good come out of the Dicktionary Club, we should.'

My friends leaped towards me, hugging me tightly for a few moments.

'We'll need to decide on a name, and we could work from someone's home until we have a premises,' Katy said, already getting carried away.

'Well, it won't be my place,' Zola mumbled.

'Still not speaking to Curtis?' I asked.

She shook her head. 'And Philip?'

I sighed. 'Not a word.'

'God, what must he be thinking?' Katy said. 'His secretary RSVPed him earlier for the awards show tonight, so at least he's going out in public.'

'Who?' I asked.

'Philip! It's the hospitality awards, remember? Blaze Boost is sponsoring it, and I set you both up on the front row. I'm still copied in on the emails.'

I felt a sting, knowing I was supposed to be his date for the evening. 'Well, I hope he has fun, I guess.'

'Oh, for fuck's sake, Ella!' Zola shouted.

'What?' I turned to her, not sure why I was getting called out.

'Go and bloody talk to him,' she said, looking massively frustrated with me.

'What? Why would I do that?' I chuckled a little. 'Jesus Christ, Zo! He knows where I live if he wanted to sort any of this out, and I don't blame him for *not* wanting to after what we did.'

Zola shook her head. 'And that's it then? Look, Ella, Philip is the first man you've had feelings for in God knows how many years, right? Why would you let him go without even attempting to fix this?'

I turned to Katy for backup, but she lowered her head, avoiding my gaze.

'I . . . I did try, Zola. Remember me in a slinky red dress and gold heels chasing a man down a set of stairs? That was trying! He didn't want to listen. He turned his back on me.' I shrugged. 'These things happen in life . . .'

Silence filled the room.

Eventually, Katy spoke up. 'I sort of think Zola's right, Ella.'

I rolled my eyes, flopping my head back.

'You don't take chances, El, you play everything so safe when it comes to your feelings. But Philip was different. In a few short weeks, he got you. You opened up to him, and you deserve a second chance if he makes you happy.'

I felt my eyes turn heavy. 'What I wrote, what he thinks I think about him, was so horrible. It was so untrue.'

'Well, go fucking tell him that then!' Zola snapped back.

'Philip deserves a full explanation. You deserve a second chance. If he hears you out and still doesn't want to go forward, then that's OK. At least you've tried, right?' Katy said.

Zola agreed. 'Imagine spending the rest of your life wondering what could have happened if you didn't at least try to apologise. Girl, come on!'

I looked at Zola's face, then my gaze went back to Katy's.

'What time is the awards show?' I asked.

'It starts at seven,' Katy replied.

'You really think I could sneak in? What if Andrea's lurking about?'

Katy laughed. 'Trust me, she won't be expecting you. Sneaking in is so not something you would do.'

I paused, wondering, as anxious butterflies swarmed my stomach.

'It would feel good to apologise properly,' I said. I bit my lip, weighing up my options. 'And I won't know if I don't try, right?'

Zola grinned. 'Too right, you fucking won't! You in?'

Eventually, I nodded back, giggling anxiously. 'Yes, I'm in. I think . . .'

Both of my friends began cheering and hollering, then ushered me into the bathroom to begin getting ready.

Outside in the hall, Katy skimmed Zola up and down. 'You know, you're great at dishing out advice, but maybe you should take it at times, too.'

Zola grinned widely. 'And what's that supposed to mean?'

'Oh, you know exactly what it means. You've been avoiding Curtis, hoping he comes to you when you were the one who was in the wrong. But you deserve a second chance just as much as Ella does. That's if you want one?'

There was a long pause.

'I don't know what I want, Katy. That's the thing. And I don't know what he wants either,' Zola said, holding her head in her hands.

'Well, you're not going to find out sitting here, are you? Go and talk it out, Zo. He deserves that. *You* deserve that.'

'I suppose,' Zola groaned.

'Don't be nervous, it's Curtis, right? Just talk it through. See where you both stand, and everything will seem much clearer after that.'

Zola headed towards the door, then turned to Katy.

'What if he's not forgiven me yet? And what if he doesn't want to talk it through?'

Katy shrugged. 'Well, then you know you've tried. But be honest with him, Zo: things were falling apart before Alvaro. You shouldn't have done what you did, but there is more than a drunken finger blast to discuss.'

Zola managed a smirk. 'Yeah, you're right. Thanks, babe.'

Chapter Thirty-Seven

Ella

It was quarter to seven, and I was in the back of a taxi dressed in a brown floor-length, halterneck dress and applying yet another layer of gloss to my lips. I'd hoped to catch Philip before he took his seat at the awards show, but Katy insisted on adding false eyelashes to my look, which also added an extra twenty minutes to the getting-ready process. My entire body shook with nerves. *What was I going to say to him? What if he told me to fuck off? Or got me thrown out?* I thought back to all the horrible things Natasha had read out from my review, and felt my stomach twinge with mortification. *Jesus, what the fuck was I doing?*

The taxi pulled up outside the Hilton and I strolled into the hotel on trembling legs. The lobby was bustling with guests who all seemed to know one another, and trays of fizz were being passed around in every direction. I guzzled a glass quickly for confidence.

'Could all remaining guests please make their way to their seats?' a man called out, and everyone began steering through the massive doors into the theatre-sized hall.

I paused at the entrance, examining the sheer number of people. *How the fuck was I supposed to find him in among this?*

'Do you have a ticket, miss? I can escort you to your seat?' a gentlemanly voice asked me, and I jumped, completely taken by surprise.

'Er. . . No, sorry, I don't.'

He approached me, reaching for my arm. 'Well, I'm afraid I will have to ask you to leave. This is a closed function and—'

'Oh God. No, I'm sorry. I don't have a ticket because I'm actually . . .' My voice shook, and I cleared my throat, taking a second to lie confidently. 'I'm the spokesperson for Blaze Boost tonight. We're sponsoring the event.' I dived into my handbag and pulled out my ID badge from Smart Reputations. 'Look.'

His bearded face instantly morphed into a friendly expression. 'Ah, excellent! Well, of course you are.' His eyes squinted at my badge. 'If you'd like to follow me, please, Ella.'

I toddled behind the gentleman as he stopped and waved at every server we passed. I could feel my chest tighten as my breathing quickened. I wondered if it was because of nerves about my lie or the anxiety of seeing Philip again – what if he'd brought a date? I was panicking.

The man led me through the back and down a corridor. Everything was dark, and I could hear growing chatter from the main space outside. *Where the fuck was he taking me?* I started to feel twitchy in case he led me to a secret sponsorship room where Andrea would ambush me.

'Ah, here's the microphone, miss. We usually look for a quick thirty-second intro on the sponsorship product, then the main hosts will begin,' the man told me, handing me a mic and pushing me towards a black curtain.

I glanced down at the mic and then back at him. 'Oh, no! I'm sorry. I didn't prepare a speech. I just came to watch.' I passed the mic back.

'Not at all,' he said graciously, passing the mic to me again. 'We couldn't put on a function like this without the backing of a great sponsor! Let the people here know about your client's product.'

I screwed up my eyes in disbelief. *Why did I have to meet the most decent man alive tonight when I was planning on sneaking in off the fucking radar?* 'You will be fine, hen. Go on, deep breaths. Off the cuff is completely acceptable!' He winked encouragingly and gave me a slight push towards the curtain's opening.

I gulped down and nodded.

The curtains opened widely, and I stood on stage facing at least five hundred people, all of whom were dressed to the nines. The lights shone brightly in my face, and the chatter of the hall suddenly died down.

Jesus, what was I doing? I couldn't do this. I had to get the fuck out of here.

I turned back and saw the kindly man give me a thumbs-up.

OK, you just have to wing it, I thought. I knew the product well enough to pull this off. Then I could figure out where Philip was sitting and approach him at the end of the ceremony.

'Good evening,' I said, startling a little as my voice filled the room. I gazed through the lights, out to the rows upon rows of guests. 'My name is Ella Banks, and I am here on behalf of tonight's sponsor, Blaze Boost, the organic energy drink which fuels your workouts.' I punched the air in an attempt to look sporty and noticed a few awkward faces and sniggers. 'Yes. Erm . . . Blaze Boost was founded in 2012.' I stepped to the edge of the stage, trying my best to locate Philip. *Front row, Katy had said, front row.* 'And it quickly became the number one go-to gym product in America because of its natural minerals and . . .'

Suddenly, someone stood up and began moving fast, excusing himself along the front. He held his head low, squeezing past guests as he headed to the aisle, trying to exit the event. I gasped as I caught sight of the side of his face: it was Philip.

Shit, shit, shit.

'Philip!' I called out in a panic, forgetting how loud my voice had become now that it was mic'd up. 'Please don't leave!'

Philip stopped mid-step. It felt like a hundred years passed as he slowly turned around to face me.

The crowd seemed confused, and a nervous chatter started up as they speculated about what was happening.

'Yes . . . Erm . . . So, Mr Philip Khan made the headlines this week, as I'm sure you all know. And the thing is . . .'

Philip looked furious and began walking once more. *Shit.*

'Well . . . it was because of me.'

351

The chatter in the hall turned to gasps as people became glued to the domestic playing out in front of them. I breathed out a shaky breath, the sound amplified by the microphone.

'Yes,' I said. 'That's right. I listed all of your supposed red flags on a stupid website I never thought would see the light of day.'

Philip slowed down. I wondered for a split second if I was getting through to him, but as soon as the thought passed, he began thundering down the aisle towards the exit again.

I couldn't let him leave, not without him getting the chance to hear me out, so I began talking much quicker.

'You heard your red flags, alleged red flags, at Kelvingrove, but please bear with me because I need the opportunity for you to listen to the green ones as well.' I cleared my throat, and now my vision was completely fixated on him. 'You are the kindest person I have ever met. You helped me, a complete stranger, with her career when you really didn't have to. You brought me dinner when you knew I wouldn't have eaten because I was working so late. You are protective and painfully honest and so, so caring. Philip, you are mysteriously handsome, playful, funny and you are so kind. Shit, I know I said that already. But the past few weeks, you have really lit me back up again.'

He stopped mid-aisle, turning slowly to face me, finally allowing himself to listen to my speech. I stepped off the stage and began walking towards him.

'You also have this warped sense of humour that is infuriating yet somehow incredibly charming.' My entire body was shaking, and my eyes began to sting with the effort of holding it all together. 'Philip,' I gulped, as I closed the distance between us, finally able to look him in the eyes. 'You make me feel safe and calm when no one else can.' Tears trickled down my face as I realised the extent to which I'd hurt him. As I realised everything I had thrown away.

I continued towards him until he was just a few feet away.

'And this past month, you have brought so much joy into my life, and I'm truly sorry that I caused you so much pain in return. I started that stupid website to get revenge on men who've hurt women on the dating scene, and I became so fixated that I thought every man out there was fucking awful and selfish and manipulative.'

A few gasps filled the posh room at my profanity.

'But then I met you. And you showed me that you're anything but. Please, please accept my apology.' My voice cracked at the last sentence as I finally came face to face with him. 'I'm sorry. I'm so sorry for everything.'

I pushed the microphone into his dumbstruck body then continued bombing it down the aisle. I had to get out. I had to breathe. The huge hall was filled with people pointing, and I could hear muffled chatter and laughter as they gossiped about me, delighted at the turn of events their stuffy evening had taken.

'Hello?' Philip's deep voice filled the room. 'I can only apologise for the disruption tonight.'

Every part of me cringed as he tried to sweeten the crowd and his reputation for the second time in a week from another fucking PR disaster I had caused.

What had I done? Why did I think that was a good idea? Finally, I reached the back of the room and lurched towards the door.

'Ella, Ella. Someone hold her at the back, please. Just for one moment.'

Two security men at either side of the door quickly stepped in front of it, arms folded, barring my exit, the hint of a smile on their bullish faces.

'Excuse me!' I pushed, but the man mountains didn't budge.

'Ella Banks, you are obnoxious.' Philip's voice boomed through the room.

I could feel the hairs on the back of my neck stand up. *Please, God, tell me this isn't happening.*

'You are untrusting, and like you said, you think that every man in the world is out to deceive you or your friends.'

I turned round to face the gasps in the room as Philip came closer, slowly approaching me with the mic.

'You are incredibly uptight, you almost certainly have OCD, you are controlling, and I think we can all agree here tonight,' he said, glancing around to interact with the guests, 'you are a tiny bit crazy.'

My jaw was on the floor. He was right. But all the while I was missing him in a deep depression this week, that cunt had clearly been concocting a list of my faults, and now I'd given him the perfect platform to air them.

I glanced around the room at the sea of shocked faces. People had their phones out, videoing the entire spectacle, and some woman at the front was stood up on her chair, keen not to miss any action up the back of the hall.

Philip eventually sighed down the microphone.

'But.'

I dared to look at him as he continued towards me with a slight smirk.

'You are intelligent beyond words. Yes, you have been hurt, so you are fiercely protective of yourself and the people you love. You're also kind, witty and undeniably beautiful. I mean, look at her, ladies and gentlemen.'

A few scattered claps filled the space, and I felt myself blushing.

What was he doing?

'You, Ella, are sensitive and loving. But above all else, you deserve to be loved.'

I felt a tear wander down my face as he finally reached me.

'Look, I could stand here all fucking day if they'd let me and list your so-called green flags to the world, but the truth is, this week has been exceptionally hard, and not because of what happened or what was printed in the press. But because you weren't with me. I am lost without you, Pilates.'

I felt a laugh fall out of my mouth, completely in shock. I plunged towards Philip, wrapping my arms around him in the biggest display of affection I could have ever managed. Philip swept me up off the ground, kissing me again and again. Around us, the room filled with applause and cheering.

A few moments later, I felt a tap on my shoulder, and my gentlemanly friend stood holding out his hand for the mic. 'I know I said off the cuff, hen, but that was seriously taking the biscuit.'

I smiled. 'I'm so sorry!'

'C'mon.' Philip held out his hand and pulled me towards the foyer. 'Fuck, I've missed you.' He kissed me once more.

'I've missed you more.' I couldn't believe the words were leaving my mouth. 'And I promise you, the Dicktionary Club is coming down. It has caused so many problems, and I'm so sorry you were dragged into it.'

He smiled, relieved. 'I'm just happy to see you, Ella.' Philip laughed. 'Is it strange that I still want to call you Pilates, though?'

I smirked. 'You know you can still call me whatever you want.'

Philip's dark eyes locked on mine, and he picked me up again, holding me close.

'Anything?' he asked.

'Well . . . maybe not obnoxious, uptight or controlling again. Yeah, that wasn't fun!' I giggled, still sweating and shaking.

'Deal!' he said, and we both burst out laughing as, and in hand, we headed back out onto the streets of Glasgow.

Chapter Thirty-Eight

Zola

Zola stood nervously at her front door, not knowing whether to knock on it or take out her key and let herself in. The sky was dark above her as she waited. *What will I say?* she wondered. *What if he has someone else in there?* It had never crossed her mind before this moment that Curtis could have moved on. But they hadn't spoken properly in weeks, and she wasn't sure what they were at this point. She needed to know.

Zola finally took a step forward and knocked on the door. She brushed down her fitted khaki knee-length dress and waited for him to answer.

The door creaked open, and Curtis stood there with his shorts and vest on. He lifted his head. 'Why are you knocking?' he asked.

Zola shrugged. 'I don't know. I wasn't sure what to do,' she admitted.

He strode away from the door, leaving it open behind him.

Zola entered their tiny apartment and looked around. She was surprised. Everything was spotless, and it didn't smell awful like she'd expected.

'You've cleaned up.' She smiled, sitting down on the sofa.

'Yeah,' Curtis replied, pausing his game on the TV and taking a seat on the chair facing Zola. 'So, what's up? Did you come to collect clothes? Or are you here to tell me how you've met other men while you've been away?'

Zola's heart dropped. *He still sounded pissed.*

'No,' she sighed.

'No, what? Which one, Zo?' Curtis questioned, crossing one leg in front of the other.

'No, I haven't seen anyone else, Curtis. I don't want to see—'

'Well, you know where your clothes are, Zo.' He nudged his head towards the bedroom and lifted his phone from the coffee table.

'Curtis.' Zola leaned forward, pulling his phone away from his face. 'I'm here to sort this out. I want . . .' She bit her lip, taking a second. 'I *need* to know what we're doing. Where we go from here.'

Curtis took a moment before answering, giving her a measured, long sigh. 'I'm not sure, you know,' he said. 'I'm not sure you want me, or this, or any of it. Your head's in the clouds, Zo. Always wanting bigger and better things.'

'Yeah? And what's wrong with that?' she snapped back. 'I want a good life, Curtis. I want to make something of myself. There is nothing wrong with wanting bigger and better things.'

'Like your Spanish guy? Eh? Was he better?'

Zola paused, seeing the hurt she'd caused all over his face.

'No, not better, of course not. But he had ambition. He didn't make me feel ridiculous or embarrassed about having dreams.'

'So, you want him then? That's what you're telling me?' There was a thunder behind his voice she had only ever heard a few times throughout their entire relationship.

'No! Wait. What?' Zola shook her head. 'For fuck's sake, Curtis, I haven't spoken to him once since that night.' She paused, regaining composure. 'Look, I'm genuinely so so sorry about Alvaro. And I felt fucking awful the moment it happened, and that's why I told you.' Zola breathed deeply, thinking about her next sentence. 'But I have been struggling with things between us recently. You know that,' she said, feeling how heavy her eyes were, and her head starting to pound with the stress of it all.

'Oh, *you've* been struggling?' His voice was still heated. 'I've been struggling too, you know. I followed you to Glasgow, and I'm sitting around here doing nothing with my life!' He sounded angry, as if he had been resenting the opportunities he had given up in London to move away and settle down with Zola in a different city. A wave of regret loomed over her, as she wondered how long he'd been feeling like this.

'I never asked you to give up on uni, Curtis,' Zola stated.

He puffed, waving his hands like he didn't want to have this conversation.

'I would support you whatever you want to do – you know that, right?' she said. 'Whatever happens between us, I'll always support you. Fuck, if you want to go back to uni

I'll help you apply right now, do whatever course you want, and we'd sort the tuition. But only you can decide what you want to do or who you want to become and recently you seemed more than happy lying around and letting me pay for everything. If you want to change so much, then do it.'

Curtis covered his face like it had all gotten too much.

'But don't we need to figure out what's happening between us too?' Zola asked, feeling her voice crumble.

He paused.

'Curtis? Do you still want me? Do you honestly think this will work?' Zola asked again.

He sighed, uncovering his face and looking at her properly. 'You know I do, innit? That's what makes this so hard. You broke me. You cheated on me, Zo. I never thought you would be capable of that.'

She gulped down, feeling ashamed. 'Neither did I.'

'But the thing is, the sad thing, yeah, is that I don't even blame you for it. I want my woman to be proud of me and like the man that I am—'

'Curtis, fucking hell, I love you,' Zola interrupted. 'That's why all of this is so hard.'

Curtis tutted under his breath. 'Look at us, man.' He rubbed his eyes and face. 'I know it's not been great between us and I do want to do better. I want a decent job, Zo. I wish I could provide for you. But I've been stuck since we arrived here. I have no mates, and nothing to do all day. I know you didn't sign up for the man I've become.'

Zola stood up and walked over to Curtis. She bent over and kissed his head. 'I signed up for you, Curtis. But only you can get up off the sofa and look for a

360

job, or go out and find some mates.' She paused briefly, defeat falling heavily over her. 'Maybe we've just grown differently. Maybe we were only supposed to have a few great years together. I love you but—'

'I will try harder, Zo,' he continued, panic rattling behind his voice.

'Curtis, what I did, it's unforgivable.' Zola almost sobbed, noticing his eyes glazed over with tears.

'But I do forgive you.'

Curtis pulled her down onto his lap and hugged her hard. They sat for a few quiet moments, Zola's head aching from the difficult conversation. She loved him, but ultimately, she wasn't sure what kind of love it was. Zola knew she needed more, but part of her still wasn't ready to give up on him.

'Why don't we download some prospectuses from the unis, have a look at what's out there? Or research some jobs that you would like?' Zola asked him.

He sniffled. 'Yeah. Yeah.'

'But I want you to be happy,' Zola said. 'We need to figure out if this relationship is really what we both want. We could start going on dates and things even? Take it slow.'

'Whatever you need to do, but I know what I want, and it's right here,' Curtis insisted, squeezing her.

Zola attempted a smile, but felt the guilt still pulse through her. She had no idea if things would work out long term, but in this moment, it felt good just to be comforted and wanted.

'I got you a present, by the way.' She turned, pulling her bag from the coffee table.

His face lit up curiously.

Zola pulled out an Xbox controller and handed it to him. 'Ta-da!'

'Ha, a spare controller! Is this a trick? You hate me playing!' He laughed.

She threw back her braids and tutted. 'Oh, this ain't for you!'

Curtis raised a brow, completely confused.

'You're going to teach me how to play, because I want to be involved in all that fun you're having!'

Curtis laughed loudly. 'You're not serious! You want in?'

Zola nodded back, realising how much she'd missed him: his easy laugh, his smile, his touch.

'Oh, it's on now, girl! I'll load it up!' He bounced up off the sofa and restarted the Xbox, setting up Zola's controller.

For the rest of the night, they laughed together, catching up in between games, making plans for the future, and telling each other just how much they were missed.

Chapter Thirty-Nine

Ella

It had been a few weeks since the exhibition, and our new PR and marketing company was finally ready to launch ahead of schedule. The night before our first official date in the office – well, my spare bedroom – we planned a night out with the boys in Wunderbar to celebrate. As Philip and I headed in, engulfed by the live music being playing loudly by the talented musician in the corner and the crowds of drunken Glaswegian girls singing their hearts out, stomping their feet off-beat, I immediately felt at home. God, I loved Glasgow.

Philip and I wove our way through the groups of partygoers and spotted Zola, Curtis and Katy chatting in a booth, waiting for our arrival.

'Hey!' I gushed as I saw our friends.

'Hey, guys!' Zola beamed. 'Oh, Philip, this is my fiancé, Curtis! Curtis, this is Philip!'

The two men shook hands and began chatting as I wedged in beside the girls.

'So, the night before we go live!' I squeezed both their hands nervously.

'Yes, and congratulations, girls! I am so pleased you took the plunge,' Philip said.

Katy giggled. 'Well, thanks to Ella, we didn't have a choice.'

'Very true,' I agreed.

'Do we have a name yet, ladies?' Curtis asked.

I looked at both my friends, and we pulled a face together. 'Lipstick and Headlines!' I announced. 'And we also have our first client.'

There was a cheer from the table at our new name.

'Already got a client too!' Philip looked shocked. 'Anyone I know?'

I nodded. 'Oh yes! You see, I contacted Alexander after the whole exhibition scandal to apologise, and he emailed back to say it was the best stunt ever to happen in his career! He said he's never had that much press or coverage before, and he'd love to work with us again.'

'I guess every cloud?' Zola squirmed, reminding herself of the horrible night.

'Exactly.' Curtis leaned in, kissing Zola on the side of her head.

'Well, let's get the drinks in and cheers to that!' Philip stood, pulling out his phone and reading a text. 'Sorry, about this, my business partner is dropping off notes for a meeting tomorrow, I hope you don't mind.'

'Not at all! Is he hot?' Katy giggled.

'Someone's fanny is feeling better,' I whispered to Zola.

'What's everyone having to drink?' Philip asked, still mid-text.

'A bottle of prosecco will do us three.' Katy pointed to us girls.

'I'll come give you a hand, mate,' Curtis said, standing and heading to the bar with Philip.

'I'm going to head to the bathroom, back in one second,' Katy said, budging past us to escape the booth.

Zola slumped back, throwing her arm around me. 'Look at our men up there – two besties in the making!' she gushed.

I watched her watch Curtis looking content about where they were heading.

I nodded back. 'Too right.'

'You know Curtis applied for university again last week? He wants to finish his business degree.'

I gasped. 'Zo, that's amazing. Good for him!'

'Yeah, I'm constantly scanning our emails to see if he's heard back, but it's only been a few days, I suppose,' Zola said, taking out her mobile and refreshing her email once more.

My eyes darted back to Philip, who was now joined by a handsome guy in a suit. He was introducing Curtis to him, waiting on our drinks arriving. *God, my man was so perfect.*

'Ella!' Zola clutched my arm, almost pinching the skin clean off it.

'Owww.' I rubbed at it. 'What? Did he get in?'

She seemed nervous, as if she had just heard some awful news and didn't know how to tell me about it.

My stomach twisted. I couldn't take any more drama.

'What? Zola! Stop it. You're scaring me!' I almost screamed.

'No. Stop. It's not bad,' she said slowly, still scanning her phone. 'Well, I'm not sure if it is or not. But . . .'

'For fuck's sake! But what?' I asked, grabbing her phone from her and reading the email she was so engrossed in.

Dear founders of the Dicktionary Club Ltd,

We came across your website on a recent news page and absolutely fell in love with the concept. It is just the missing piece to the dating app software we have created here at Flirtify. We do believe you own the entire patent on this vision, however, and as a result, we'd love to invite you to our New York headquarters to work with us in developing the Dicktionary Club stateside.

We hope this is something you are interested in and look forward to hearing from you.

Regards

Jimmy Link

CEO Flirtify app

I felt my face drop and my palms turn sticky.

'What will we do?' Zola asked.

'Oh my God, that toilet is a fucking trek!' Katy said, sliding back into the booth.

Zola remained silent. I had no idea what she was thinking.

'What's up?' Katy asked, nudging my arm.

'Katy, we have to tell you something, but not in front of the boys just yet,' I said.

'Oh, what? Fucking hell! What is it now?'

I smiled and waved to the three men as they weaved back to our table, still chatting away.

'Do I have something in my teeth?' Katy continued, using her finger and scrubbing her gnashers.

'No, babe.' Zola breathed nervously. 'We have just been invited to New York to work.'

Katy gasped. 'Shut up! What? Why?'

'*Ssh!*' I hissed, not wanting to ruin a celebratory night when we didn't know any facts. The Dicktionary Club had caused so much turmoil in our lives and to the people we cared about the most. Everything was going well now. I wasn't sure how to feel about revisiting it all again.

'Ella?' Katy whispered.

'A company wants to team up with us and bring back the Dicktionary Club,' Zola hissed under her breath.

'Nooooo!' Katy's jaw opened.

'We've got to do it, right?' Zola nudged us both.

I shook my head. 'I don't know, Zo. After the last time? I hated the person I became. I don't want to hurt anyone ever again.'

Katy agreed, nodded, then stopped. 'But I suppose we have learned from our mistakes, right?'

I turned to face her. 'Sure, but . . . really?'

'I mean, we all got second chances? Surely the Dicktionary Club deserves one too?' she continued.

Zola and I gulped down nervously.

'Here we are, ladies!' Philip arrived with the tray of drinks. 'Everything all right?' he asked, noticing my worried expression and the weird vibe at the table.

I nodded. 'Yeah, great, thanks!'

Philip smiled, then turned to his friend, 'Oh, this is my mate and business partner . . .'

'Sean?' Katy blurted, looking as freaked out as if she'd seen a ghost.

Sean tilted his head and his handsome face broke into a large grin. 'The mystery woman in the pink dress?' His gorgeous Irish accent sounded even better than Katy had described.

She nodded.

'How are you? Do you mind if I join you?' Sean asked, hovering to sit.

Katy was speechless.

'Please, take a seat, Sean. Katy would love that,' Zola confirmed, tugging Katy's arm to allow him space in the booth.

Philip began pouring out the prosecco and then raised his beer bottle in the air. 'To Lipstick and Headlines! I hope you girls make all the headlines and for all the right reasons this time.' We let out a laugh. 'I wish you every success,' he toasted us, then picked up my hand and kissed it gently.

I blushed, nodding at his sweet speech.

'And here's to Philip and Curtis for standing by us and supporting us through thick and thin,' Zola added, pursing her lips to her man.

'There's been a lot of drama in this group recently,' Katy whispered to Sean. 'I'll fill you in later.'

He chuckled, noticing a strand of Katy's hair sticking to her lipgloss and he brushed it carefully back from her face, 'Yes, please do,' he replied.

'And cheers to the end of Andrea and the Dicktionary Club! You've done it, girls! To new horizons, fresh starts and new opportunities,' Curtis said, raising his pint this time, gazing lovingly at Zola.

Together, we slammed our glasses. Zola pinched me under the table, and Katy giggled awkwardly at Curtis's speech. We avoided eye contact as we guiltily sipped on our bubbles, with absolutely no idea what trouble the Dicktionary Club was about to stir up next.

Acknowledgements

I would like to first thank my fantastic publishing company, Bonnier Books, and the Zaffre team for your support when writing this novel. Significantly, the lovely Melissa Cox has filled me with confidence and steered me on the right track throughout the process. Also, a special thank you to Georgia Marshall for all your assistance and dedication in getting this book onto the shelves! You are the best team, and I'm privileged to be a part of Zaffre and looking forward to many more books to come.

I'd also like to thank my management team, Inter Talent, for your unlimited support and guidance throughout the year. You guys go out of your way to help in every aspect of this journey and create a wonderful life for me and my family! Special thanks to Milly Bell, Jonathan Shalit and Oscar Janson-Smith. I'll always be eternally grateful for your help, and I can't wait for many more opportunities to come with you guys by my side. I couldn't ask for a better team. P.S. I'm really going to miss the aubergine group chat!

To the fabulous Rosie McCafferty for proofreading my book yet again when I was questioning and doubting the process. You are the biggest confidence boost a girl can have, and I'm so lucky to have found you! I look forward to seeing your comments and knowing that you get them no matter what. From the bottom of my heart, thank you, Rosie.

A special thanks to all the Waterstones staff, particularly the Glasgow branches, who promote the hell out of these books! I am so fortunate to have you fighting my corner. Special thanks to the fantastic staff at the Glasgow Fort branch, who have smashed the sales for my previous books! I still get goosebumps walking past and seeing my work on the window display. It is genuinely a dream come true, and I'm not naive to how much this has contributed to the success of my writing.

To my Mum and Dad for your continued support and for telling everyone and anyone about your daughter's raunchy books! Also, I thank Andy, Les, and Joyce. Thank you for helping me and my girls (including Wrinkles) while writing this book. I would never have had the time to be a mum, work in the hospital, have endless meetings and trips away, and write full-time if it weren't for you all stepping in. I never take how much you all do for me for granted, so please know how grateful I am to you all.

To my best friends, Michelle Patterson, Emma McAuley, Lisa Scott, Sarah Scott, Maggie Donnelly, Lisa Murphy and Bianca Rinaldi, thank you for supporting me and filling the group chats with the juiciest stories that help write these books! You girls are there when I need the most encouragement and fill me with unconditional love regardless of the situation. You are my soul mates, and I'm genuinely thankful to have all of you in my corner. I love every single one of you.

To Christopher for making my life so much happier, thank you for being the best, most supportive, uplifting person I could ask for. You make me laugh every day, and how kind and thoughtful you are doesn't go unnoticed. Also, special thanks to Chad for being the best and always making me smile.

And finally, to my two favourite girls on the planet, Olivia and Grace. Thank you for being the most wonderful, thoughtful, kind, and encouraging people when I have written my fifth book! I know it's stressful when I lock myself away, and we live off Just Eats when deadline day is approaching, but you take it all in your stride – with only a few moans! I genuinely don't think I'd be in this position without having both of you. You push me to be the best possible version of myself, and I'm so lucky to have you.

This one, and everything I do, is for us.

I love you to infinity and beyond, my gorgeous girls.

With love and eternal gratitude,
Sophie xx